D1118596

The Man Who Loved Dirty Books

The Man Who Loved Dirty Books

by

David Guy

NAL BOOKS

NEW AMERICAN LIBRARY

TIMES MIRROR

NEW YORK AND SCARBOROUGH, ONTARIO

Copyright © 1983 by David Guy

All rights reserved. For information address The New American Library, Inc.

Published simultaneously in Canada by The New American Library of Canada Limited

 NAL BOOKS TRADEMARK REG. U.S. PAT. OFF. AND FOREIGN COUNTRIES
REGISTERED TRADEMARK—MARCA REGISTRADA
HECHO EN CRAWFORDSVILLE, INDIANA, U.S.A.

SIGNET, SIGNET CLASSIC, MENTOR, PLUME, MERID-IAN and NAL BOOKS are published *in the United States* by The New American Library, Inc., 1633 Broadway, New York, New York, 10019, *in Canada* by The New American Library of Canada Limited, 81 Mack Avenue, Scarborough, Ontario M1L 1M8

Library of Congress Cataloging in Publication Data

Guy, David.
    The man who loved dirty books.

    I. Title.
PS3557.U89M3   1983   813'.54   83-9509
ISBN 0-453-00448-2

Designed by Sherry Brown

First Printing, September, 1983

1 2 3 4 5 6 7 8 9

PRINTED IN THE UNITED STATES OF AMERICA

For William H. Guy
mon cher maître

Acknowledgments

I would like to thank Sherry Huber for her astute suggestions concerning Part One. And Cindy Kane for her help with the whole of the manuscript. Thanks to Virginia Barber for her extraordinary patience and forbearance. And to Beth and Billy for being here. Love to all.

D.G.

Out of my great sorrows I make my little songs.
—Heine

And that reminds me of a story that's so dirty I'm
ashamed to think of it myself.
—Groucho Marx

PART ONE:
Finding Work

Chapter One

"You remember Chandler." Laurel gave a little laugh. "He's the guy we keep around to counsel people on alternate lifestyles."

Matt frowned, concentrating. "That tall skinny queer."

"You have such a nice way of putting things."

Downstairs the doorbell rang, and there was a pause, followed by a shriek of hilarity, the sound of footsteps pounding to the rear of the house. At the back door there was a terrific crack. Matt was only glad it wasn't followed by the sound of shattering glass.

Jonathan's baby-sitter had arrived.

"What does he *do* with her?" Matt said.

"They just get silly," Laurel said. "She's nice to go along with it. He adores her."

"I know. But the noise sometimes. God."

Matt was a trifle edgy. The day was still, hung low with clouds. He had just put on his shirt, and already his back felt damp; a large drop of sweat—the early leader in the race for his underpants—trickled down his spine. Laurel had said he didn't have to dress up, but he had no intention of looking like a slob compared to the rest of them. He knotted his tie. Chandler Mingins, for one, would be done up like a corpse.

Laurel was wearing a summer dress that was held up only by ruffles of strategically placed elastic. It gave the impression, in fact, of being supported mainly by her large, shapely breasts. A swift tug would have removed it in an instant. Under it she wore only a few thin inches of black bikini underpants. The dress was turquoise, shone bright against her olive skin. To say the least, it was striking.

"So who else?" Matt said.

"Stanley Killian. He used to be in pastoral care—he's an

3

ordained minister, in fact—but he's flipped out a little in recent years. His religion is still important to him. It's just a different kind of religion."

"The kind where he screws every woman in the congregation."

"He doesn't have a congregation. He just has clients now." She paused, considering. "He *does* have a lot of women clients."

"He's the guy who wears that cross."

Matt had met most of Laurel's colleagues once, at a large party nearly a year before, was trying to remember them.

"Yes," Laurel said. "Stanley's ever-present wooden cross."

"He probably regards it as a phallic symbol."

Matt had seen the type many times; he typically showed up as a chaplain around a college: the big blond beard, the fixed smile down in the center of it (especially when he was discussing some tragedy; what was it with these guys who always smiled about a tragedy?), the weird stare in his eyes. He had started off as a bookish scholar in college, then after he got a taste of therapy went completely haywire. He was going through adolescence a little late.

"He may bring his wife tonight. She's never showed up at anything before. That ought to be interesting."

"A minister's wife? Interesting?"

Laurel was standing at the mirror, brushing her hair, which was black, and long, and frizzy. It took muscle to brush that hair. She had to pause frequently to rest her arms.

"You don't have to go on and on, Matt."

"What?"

"I know you're not wild at the prospect of going out with my friends."

Not again. That endlessly repeating theme of their marriage.

"I'm glad to be going out with your friends," Matt said. "I'm delighted."

Laurel was holding a tuft of hair, idly checking the ends. Split to smithereens, no doubt.

"You don't have to make them sound like a bunch of imbeciles," Laurel said.

"Laurel." Matt gave a last tug to his tie. "I'm joking. Can't you tell when I'm joking?"

"I can tell when I don't want you to joke."

Laurel was extraordinarily sensitive on this subject. She could be as funny about her friends as anybody most of the time, but on the night of a gathering was suddenly dead serious.

4

It was as if she were afraid Matt would blurt out something in front of them. He never did.

"I'd like things to be different about this now," she said. "I really would."

"All right. They'll be different."

"It's not like when I was in school. We knew it would be just a short time. These people are my colleagues. I might be working with them for years."

"I can't like somebody I don't like."

"I'm not asking you to like them. I'm just saying give them a chance. You hardly know them. It's like the people in the program."

"I liked the people in the program. I liked them fine."

"You did a great job of hiding it."

Matt actually did have a certain affection for Laurel's friends from the counseling program, the first group of therapists she had ever been associated with. Maybe just because they weren't around anymore. But really, they weren't half bad once you got to know them. Unfortunately, by that time the program was over.

"I just want you to make an effort. Don't judge these people before you know them."

"All right. I won't. I promise I won't. Who else?"

"Ned. Did I mention Ned? Ned's going to be there."

"Of course."

"Meaning what?"

"Meaning he's your favorite counselor. Your best friend at the place. Of course he's going to be there."

Matt knew better than to say anything about him. Laurel was extremely possessive of her close friends. Her whole lecture, in fact, might have been just to protect Ned from some jibe.

"I guess I'll check on Jonathan," Matt said. "We really ought to get going."

"Okay."

He was standing at the door, holding his jacket. "Laurel. I really was just kidding."

"I know." She brushed her hair and didn't look at him. "But please don't kid so much."

Matt walked down the sagging wooden stairway to the first floor. It listed to the right, creaked at the slightest touch. One of these days he would probably take a casual step and fall straight through to the basement.

He had meant not to be that way for once. Days before, when

5

Laurel had told him she wanted to go out with some friends, he had determined to be better about it all. But he could feel now —had felt as soon as Laurel called him up short—the buzzing tension in his neck and shoulders, the little ache down his spine. It wasn't the weather that was bothering him, or getting dressed to go out for dinner. He really was nervous about going out with Laurel's friends.

It all probably did go back to the first year Laurel was in the counseling program, that first year their lives had started to change. Most of his time up to then had been spent around a certain type of person—men involved in sports, and women involved with those men—and though he wasn't crazy about such people, didn't go along with everything they did, he did feel comfortable around them. He realized to what extent he did as soon as he found himself around another type. Peasant blouses and shawls and sandals and faded jeans, potluck suppers that went heavy on the vegetables and fruit juices and sprouts (throw a little basil on everything), battered multi-colored vans pulled onto the lawn out front to park. Just the way he looked made him stand out, several inches taller than most of them, with the wide shoulders, thick chest, meaty arms and heavy hands of an athlete, his light-brown mustache carefully trimmed (he let it go bushy these days); and the fact that he was with the police department didn't help any. It wasn't that people ignored him. If anything they paid too much attention, asking about his work as if he were some kind of freak, staring at him while he talked about it as if he were describing some dreadful illness. When they weren't talking to him they were keeping up an incessant patter in a jargon he hardly understood. Therapy jokes, he called them. All through an evening with such people he felt a hollow ache in the pit of his stomach, and when he got home started a terrific argument with Laurel about nothing at all. He had to jump on somebody.

Nobody ever said anything critical about him. They wouldn't have dared. They just stood back and scrutinized. He could feel it.

Every time had been the same. Eventually he had started to relax around those people, and there were one or two he could even talk to, and by the time the program was over (because it was over?) they all seemed pretty harmless, but around every one of those social events there was a residual tension, and always, sometime, a fight with Laurel. Always afterwards he was disgusted with himself.

6

Now he had a new group to be paranoid about. His jokes about them, he knew, were just a way of being defensive (the best defense is a good offense). Someday, he hoped, he would feel sure enough of himself that he wouldn't have to act that way.

If he ever did, though, he had a feeling he would miss the jokes.

He looked all over the first floor for Jonathan and his baby-sitter, but they were nowhere to be found. He walked out into the small backyard. Behind it, at the end of an overgrown path, was the small brick garage, a battered wooden door leading into it, and Jennifer was at the door, yanking for all she was worth. She was fourteen years old, tall and bone-thin (Jonathan liked to play Popeye—a chunky older boy next door was Bluto—and she made the perfect Olive Oyl). She smiled constantly, and often broke into utterly silent laughter, as she spoke she made sudden startling gestures with her long limbs.

"Hello, Jennifer," Matt shouted, walking toward her on the path.

"Mr. Gregg. This creature has bolted himself inside the garage."

They had started playing instantly. Jonathan had probably been planning this escape all afternoon.

"Jonathan." Matt rapped on the door. "Laurel and I are leaving."

"Great." He had grown still behind the door. Before, he had been pounding on it, making monster noises.

"You take it easy on Jennifer."

"Tell her. She's the one who came after me."

Beside him Jennifer shook with laughter. One hand covered her mouth, and the other arm folded across her stomach. Had to do something with those arms. They looked as if they could wrap around her body several times.

"We bought pizza for your dinner," he said to her.

"Oh." She bit her finger. "I *love* pizza."

She said this every time, as if Matt and Laurel had been astonishingly thoughtful.

"We had them do a couple pieces with anchovies for you."

"Ah." Her eyes slowly closed, in a kind of ecstasy.

"I fed the anchovies to the cat," said the voice behind the door.

Jennifer's laughter began again. She did not do the laughing, exactly. Laughter happened to her.

7

"I left the phone number on the counter. We shouldn't be late." He hoped.

"Okay."

She looked so pretty, and funny, and happy, and alive. She could play with a seven-year-old boy for hours and never get bored. Whatever happened to adults, he often wondered, that they lost whatever it was that children had? Where did it go? She'd probably wind up, he thought bitterly, as a therapist.

There was an unnatural calm. Matt and Jennifer both turned toward the garage, to see the door slightly open, Jonathan's head poking out. She leaped—it was like a grasshopper uncoiling—but the head disappeared, door slammed shut, bolt snapped.

"It's not time for pizza yet!" Jonathan shouted.

Jennifer was laughing again, yanking on the door with all of her five-foot-seven and eighty-five pounds, or whatever it was.

About half the time they went out these days, Matt felt as if it would have been more fun to stay home with Jonathan and the baby-sitter.

Tony's face wore a haunted look. His mouth, with its heavy underlip, was slightly agape, and the little brown eyes, deep in their sockets, were glazed over. He took the news of the size of the party—"Six, please"—as if it were catastrophic, staring hard, the little knot between his eyebrows tightening.

Actually, he was just hard at work. At 318 pounds, lots of things are hard work, and walking among the tables of that little restaurant was no exception. Matt's party followed the massive rear end to the back, though they did not raise their arms and turn sideways to get between the tables: this wasn't follow the leader, and none of them weighed 318 pounds. Tony distributed the menus the way another man would have dealt a hand of cards, glanced wearily in the direction of the difficult journey back.

Thanks, Tone," Matt said.

"Anytime, kid." Tony obviously had no idea who Matt was. Life was hard enough just getting around, without also trying to remember and recognize people. He winced, gulped in some air, as he turned away. "Enjoy your meal."

The place had utterly no decor. Pale-blue walls and a nondescript brown carpet, round tables scattered at random. Kids wandered from their tables, parents yelled at them across the room, and the waitress handed you your entrée—"Take this, honey, I can't reach"—while some kid's head was butting her in the stomach. She didn't even *notice* the kid: that's how crowded it was. "I'll have yours in a minute, doll," she said to the person whose order she had forgotten. All the tables were cluttered: people added a pizza to their order the way they might ask for some rolls with their dinner.

But the place was cool, it was convenient, the food was dependable, and Matt had a strong affection for that restaurant because the quiet bar in the next room was a place where, on a hot afternoon, you could still get a short beer for fifty cents.

The fact of the matter was he liked a restaurant where the children wandered around.

"What do you recommend?" Chandler Mingins said. He wore a tight-lipped sneer, nostrils flaring, as he stared at the menu. He seemed to mean he could find nothing acceptable.

"The pasta's okay," Matt said. "The sandwiches are excellent. The salad's fresh. Other things I haven't had."

"This is the kind of place," Stanley Killian said, "where you come when Mama doesn't feel like cooking. And you all have a plate of spaghetti."

"It seems," Mingins said, "that you drop a large portion of it on the tablecloth."

"I come here for lunch sometimes," Killian said. "I love the pasta."

"You love anything fattening," Mingins said.

"The liver with bacon sounds good," Helen Killian said.

She looked like someone who would think so, Matt thought.

They had all been standing outside the restaurant when Matt and Laurel drove up, and a mighty strange sight they were. What is wrong with this picture? as it used to say in the old comic books, and the answer in this case: just about everything. Despite his prominently displayed cross, the minister looked like an Eastern guru, with his radiating blond beard, a puffy white shirt that hung over his corduroys like a smock; his wife was a pale, drab person who seemed to be standing somewhat apart from the group in a faded summer dress and large spectacles (I married a minister, she seemed to be saying by her attitude; now *what* is *this?*); the resident gay was almost a caricature, in his leisure suit and gold chain necklace, olive-green shirt and socks (Laurel told Matt he always matched that way, however outrageous the color); and the all-American boy was wearing, along with his seersucker suit, a pair of bright-blue running shoes. Yep, these people were counselors. Any money-making proposition would have thrown them out on their collective ear. Matt's first impulse was just to sail past in his car, maybe flash a polite wave out the window, but he sucked in his gut and pulled into the parking lot, fixed a smile on his face as he and Laurel made their way to the front.

"You *all* beat us here," she said with a big smile, as if that were surprising. People always beat them everywhere. They were always twenty minutes late.

She was positively radiant. She loved wildly diverse groups.

She did the introductions all around. Nearly everyone had met, and pretended to remember. Killian's wife nodded politely, a smile barely creasing her face.

Now they all sat around the table staring at the menus, afraid that if they looked up at one another they might have to talk. Didn't want to jump into anything here.

The waitress shattered this equilibrium by arriving to take their order; she poured six glasses of water like an automaton, pulled a pencil stub from behind her ear, licked a thumb and flipped madly through her pad. Her words were curt and direct. "What to drink, babe? Sure." She wrote rapidly in a huge script. "What's yours, honey?" She would be back in a moment. Service was instantaneous in that place.

"Well." Mingins took a sip of his water, held it in his mouth a moment as if it were a fine wine, then turned to Matt. "I understand we're not just celebrating Laurel's first year at the center. You're also starting a new career."

The eyes of everyone at the table turned toward Matt in unison, and he shrank. Who was the rat?

Ned Streater was glowing boyishly across the table. "Laurel told me about your new job."

Laurel was staring down at her place. She hadn't told him to broadcast it publicly.

"I hope it's not a new career," Matt said. "My career is law enforcement. But I've had trouble getting started in that here. Too many people for too few jobs. I was kind of a gym teacher for a year. Now I'm going to do some investigative work."

"How's that?" Stanley Killian wore his big beatific smile. He had produced from somewhere a corncob pipe, and was smoking a tobacco that smelled like fruit syrup.

"A man who free-lances in different things. He's got some

extra work for me to do. Mostly checking up on accident reports for lawyers, or insurance companies. He does some divorce work."

"He's a detective," Mingins said.

"How exciting." Helen Killian brightened for the first time that evening.

"Not the kind you read about in books. It's fairly dull work, really. Very routine. But it's something for me to do while I'm waiting."

"It's so nice to hear of someone with"—Helen gestured vaguely—"a manly sort of job."

Her husband beamed at her, as if he agreed. Chandler Mingins ignored this remark.

"I knew before that you'd taught," Mingins said. "I only heard recently that you were at Tabard Academy."

"You could call it teaching," Matt said. "That might be a slight exaggeration."

"You must have known Hugh Bollinger."

Immediately something at the table changed. Mingins wore the trace of a leer, as if he had just dropped a very clever witticism. Stanley Killian leaned forward, as if anticipating a punch line. Helen Killian shrank back in her seat.

"I knew him," Matt said.

"That disgusting creep," Helen said.

"I'm a little surprised you know him," Matt said.

"Chandler knows them all," Killian said, rather mysteriously.

"I did an internship in school counseling there," Mingins said. "Several years ago. I got to know a lot of the faculty."

Bollinger, in fact, had been a particular nemesis of Matt's at the school. He had been the lacrosse coach, and part of Matt's job had been to help out with the teams, but he didn't know the first thing about lacrosse, so he mostly just stood around on the field while Bollinger—a middle-aged man with a large potbelly—made jokes at his expense. Hugh was livid most of the time anyway, because he really did know the game, and would have been a good coach, but his material at Tabard was nil. His team lost game after game to inferior coaches while he stood around shouting in a redfaced rage.

He was obsessed, from the first day Matt arrived, with Matt's past occupation. "You were a cop?" he said. "A dirty copper. Ever do time on the vice squad? Ever accept any bribes?" And he found out somehow—it must have been from the headmaster—about the job Matt was leaving the school for. "You're going to be an investigator. A private eye. You'll have to buy yourself a trench coat. Brush up on the old Bogart films."

No amount of reasonable talk from Matt would stop Bollinger from this banter.

"Old Hugh," Mingins said. "He's quite a guy."

Bollinger's real problem—it hovered around him like a vapor—was booze. Matt hadn't ever thought the man had taken a nip at breakfast, though sometimes he wished he had, the way Bollinger's hands shook as he sipped at his Styrofoam cup of morning coffee. But he definitely had a couple stiff belts at lunch; he lived close enough to go home at noon, and came back from his apartment noticeably redder and more relaxed, chewing mints for his breath. His sixth-period class often complained that his lectures made no sense, though if the truth be told his morning conversation wasn't exactly a model of coherence either.

He was a boozy-looking man, with black curly hair that was thinning at the temples, so his flush after lunch extended up into his scalp. His teeth were crooked and dirty, widely gapped. His face was peppered with acne scars that clustered around his cheekbones. Despite a basically athletic build—and he carried himself gracefully, like an athlete—he had that slowly expanding belly, definitely beyond the stage of a paunch. His voice was a hoarse whisper, and he was a heavy smoker who always had a burning cigarette flattened and beat all to hell between his fingers. Worst of all, he had a boozer's wit. Dull dumb jokes that were always at your expense, so that only he laughed, with a boozy gust straight in your face.

Like remarks about being a cop, or a private detective.

"If you know Hugh Bollinger," Mingins said, "you may know about his hobby."

"I didn't know him that well." Matt preferred to keep the relationship in the past tense.

Stanley Killian, who for the most part had just been wearing his redfaced smile, removed his pipe from his mouth and spoke.

"The man has a collection of pornography," he said, "that is beyond belief."

"Books, movies, cassettes," Mingins said.

"My husband idolizes him," Helen Killian said.

"He could open his own shop on Liberty Avenue," Killian said. "Tomorrow."

"How do you know him?" Matt said to Killian.

"Through Chandler."

"My husband sniffs these people out," Helen said.

"There's nothing wrong with pornography. It's a healthy expression of a natural urge." Killian's face had taken on a deeply thoughtful look. "To see the primal scene."

"And some that aren't so primal," Helen said.

Ned Streater and Laurel, sitting together on one side of the table, were absorbing this conversation in a watchful silence.

"So you've seen this stuff of his," Matt said.

"He has these parties," Mingins said, "for little groups of friends."

"Only connoisseurs," Killian said.

"He serves drinks. Delicious hors d'oeuvres. And then, the way somebody else might bring out his slides of the Grand Canyon, he'll show some incredible movie."

"Among younger people," Helen said, "it's called a circle jerk."

"Have you been?" Matt said to her.

"That's Stanley's department," she said. "He's the family connoisseur."

"She's been," Killian said.

"It's boring," Helen said. "Primal scene or not. The first couple minutes are kind of stunning. You've heard of these things, but you've never seen them. After that it's a crashing bore."

"Are you surprised?" Mingins said. "About your former colleague."

"Not really." Too much booze, a lousy job, dirty books. It all somehow added up. "He always seemed kind of sleazy."

"Like everybody else at that school." Laurel had finally spoken. "I must say." She wore a broad smile. "I'm a little surprised at my present colleagues."

"Our secret lives." Mingins beamed at this romantic notion.

"They're all a bunch of raving perverts," Helen Killian said. "If you don't mind"—she glanced around the table—"I'd prefer to change the subject."

Fortunately, the waitress chose that moment to arrive with the food.

If you are what you eat, Chandler Mingins was a hot pastrami sandwich with a large dill pickle and an order of onion rings; Stanley Killian was a big gooey plate of ravioli and a side order of spaghetti; Ned Streater was a cheeseburger, french fries, and a malted milkshake; and Helen Killian (alas!) was a dried-up piece of liver with a hunk of bacon on top. Matt and Laurel, as they so often did, had ordered the same thing, linguini with clam sauce, a plate of cheeses and fresh summer fruits, a couple bottles of imported beer. It was as if they were trying to prove they were somehow the same.

They were actually just ordering the best things on the menu.

Once the food had arrived the counselors dropped into their counseling patter, and Matt quite easily changed the channel (Helen Killian, he noticed, was also ignoring it all, tearing viciously into the piece of catcher's mitt on her plate). As usual, he regretted his fight with Laurel, and the insecurity that had brought it on. There had been an uneasy moment when Mingins had brought up work (why, in American society, did a man always have to be defined by his vocation? I'm just being, and growing, as a counselor would say), but all in all the evening hadn't been half bad. These people were okay. What had he been so worried about?

"A toast!" Mingins said toward the end of the meal, and raised his glass of Taylor Lake Country white. Around the table were raised a glass of Gallo chianti, one of ginger ale, a chocolate malted milkshake, and two glasses of imported bottled beer. "To new beginnings. New careers." He gestured toward the Greggs.

Something of a travesty in Matt's case, but he let it pass.

Afterward, in bed, Jennifer having been taken home (somehow, earlier in the evening, she had managed to wrestle Jonathan into bed) Laurel was relaxed, content, vaguely amorous. She loved a night out with friends, loved just to talk and have a good dinner.

"It wasn't so bad," she said. "Was it?"

"It was all right." Matt was lying on his back, her head cradled on his shoulder. "It was nice."

"Next time you won't grumble about being carted off."

He probably would. He never remembered from time to time.

She was caressing his chest, moved her body so it rested against his. She liked to rub herself gently against his thigh.

"Laurel," he said. "Linguini with clam sauce. All that cheese. Two bottles of beer."

That large meal seemed to rest between him and his penis, which was located at some vague point several miles down his body.

"Just lie there. I'll do the work."

"It's always after a big meal that you get sexy. I don't understand."

"That's the only time we really get together to talk. It's such a rare thing these days."

As a matter of fact, the two of them had hardly talked to each other at all that evening. Laurel had been occupied elsewhere.

"You're the one who's always off at work at all hours," Matt said.

"I'm not placing blame. I'm just stating a fact."

Matt hated to turn his wife down. He felt an obligation, every time Laurel wanted sex, to get himself hoisted and take a stab at it, so to speak. But the hoisting would be a mammoth task that evening, or so it seemed from where he sat, and what she was suggesting—that he lie back and let her take care of things—always made him uneasy. When he relaxed and let it happen, it never happened very well.

"I'd rather not tonight," he said. "Really. Just let me touch you."

For Laurel, Matt knew, making love was the ultimate way of being close; it wasn't after conventionally romantic situations, but emotionally close ones (like a good fight) that she wanted it. Hard hugs, deep passionate breathy kisses, the man actually entering her. The first moment was the best—"Oh!" she'd say, closing her eyes—and what she liked most after that was the hard clutching, pounding hearts, Matt's loud groan at the end. "Just go through me a few times," she whispered at the moment she was ready. "Please." For Matt, sad to say (and he would not say it, did not put it into words) making love was always something of a performance. If he couldn't do it right —a large impressive erection, the requisite number of strokes (he wasn't sure how many, but he could tell you if he fell short), a spine-cracking climax—he'd rather not do it at all. He was well aware of the arguments against such an attitude, but he had it just the same.

Laurel jumped and moaned at his first touch, smiling at herself, and was already wet, which made Matt feel even worse; she was more excited than he'd thought. But he loved to touch her, the small soft motions of his fingertips that he'd learned through the years, and he loved to watch, her eyes closing, teeth biting her lower lip, a sudden wince or gasp at a thrill. Her skin as he continued took on a deeper hue, her body slowly stretching as if at a yawn, and there was a sudden catch at her throat, her back snapping into an arch: she paused for a long breathless moment, then gasped—"Ah!"—her body shuddering again and again. She had absolutely the most violent and clearly defined orgasms he had ever seen—one for her was like five for anybody else—and afterward collapsed in a heap, fell asleep, literally, in seconds.

Matt himself was slow to fall asleep, spent long minutes every night running through things in his mind, but he loved to feel Laurel draped limply across him, and to hear her softly snore.

II

She felt like a schoolgirl. It was stupid. All the times she had touched men casually, taken their arms, hugged them in greeting—she came from a demonstrative family, where a passionate hug and a kiss on the mouth were about like saying hello—and here she was hesitating, a catch at her throat, as she and Ned stood at the curb. She liked to keep contact as she walked and talked on a crowded sidewalk; a conversation felt awkward otherwise. Ned was a wiry, bouncy man anyway: you felt an urge to hold him down. There was a gap in the traffic, and he took a flying leap of a first step. That did it: she grabbed his arm and held on for dear life.

She knew why she had hesitated. A trace of guilt. That was ridiculous. Of course you should take the arm of a man you were attracted to. What would you do, only touch men you didn't like?

"You don't look like a cop's wife," he said.

"Oh. What does a cop's wife look like?"

Ned stared off in the distance, as if better to imagine such a person. "She's a big woman. Peroxide blond. She has a large Italian nose. Probably broken in a couple places. A hard face. Some scar tissue around the eyes. The kind of arm you see on a baking-soda box. I think it was a cop's wife who posed for that picture. She has big . . . " Ned paused, seeking the apt term.

"Knockers," Laurel said. "Don't be squeamish."

"Big knockers. But they're solid. Like large pectoral muscles. And she's got a leathery behind like the back of a saddle."

"You're pretty free with the stereotypes," Laurel said. "For the work you're in."

"The working day's over."

"Well. I'm not a cop's wife, at the moment." Her face was thoughtful, and she was leaning against him, keeping up. She tugged at his arm. "Let's take it easy. Where's the fire? Jesus."

She was getting a little annoyed with Ned, if the truth be known. Here she was, hoping to have a long serious talk with him, walking off to see the office where her husband would be working—after days of wondering, she couldn't stand it any longer—and Ned was treating it as a quick sprint, tossing off wisecracks as if they weren't going to talk seriously at all.

Laurel certainly did not look like Ned's version of a cop's wife, especially not that day. She wore a plain white tank top and flowered wraparound skirt, carried over her shoulder a beige cloth purse that she had sewed herself. Her frizzy hair was gathered at her neck and flopped down her back; without the barrette she would have looked like a wild woman. For someone who seemed long and thin, she had full breasts—perhaps that was the reason Ned had paused in the middle of his description—and she wore nothing under the tank top, so her bosom swayed majestically as she walked, and her large dark nipples, at the front, formed little bull's-eyes. She never wore makeup, and did not shave the hair on her body: under her arms it was dark and luxuriant.

Men stared at her anywhere she walked, and she treated them as if they weren't there. If they spoke to her suggestively, or whistled, or leered, she wasn't above telling them to fuck off.

Ned was exactly her height, but somehow seemed smaller beside her. He was a trim muscular man, like a middleweight in training, and whatever else he wore—today it was a green checked sport jacket, khaki slacks—always wore those bright-blue running shoes, ready to break into a sprint at a moment's notice. His sandy hair was long at the back, curling up at his collar. He was clean-shaven, with a fair, open, friendly face.

"You *were* a cop's wife." He spoke a little sheepishly. He could feel her annoyance.

"I was. I may be again."

"I can't imagine that. What it must have been like."

That was where her guilt lay, in talking about her marriage, not sure how much she should say. She wanted to talk—that was part of what they were taking the walk for—and Ned really was sympathetic. He was through being silly. But Laurel had the feeling, in her relationships with men, that admitting to marital problems was the last taboo. If you never brought them up, there was always that image of a solid marriage between you and someone else. Once that was shattered, nothing would be left. No telling how close you might get.

She took a deep breath. "It wasn't too hot."

"Oh?" A typical therapist's response. Curious and noncommittal.

She had managed to slow them down to a brisk stroll. They were walking on the outskirts of Shadyside, under high leafy oaks, past brick apartments that must once have been rather grand, now seemed faded and dirty and crumbling. Their trim was unpainted, tiny yards scraggly. The late afternoon was warm, and dripping with humidity, the sky a pale gray.

"I wouldn't call it anyone's fault," she said. "Partly just the place we lived, where Matt could get a job. They called it a city, though I would have said town. A little box of a house, four rooms, on the side of a hill. One box after another, all the way down. A huge expressway at the bottom."

Like such roads in most small cities, it had been lined by hamburger stands and car dealerships and lots crammed with mobile homes. All night long a roar of traffic, like the Indianapolis Speedway, and the steady glow of lights. If they had been any closer they could have read by it.

"The people were poor. That was okay. But the lives they led. The TV on all day. Radios blaring. Sometimes the TV and radio at once."

They *had* taken a break around noon. Between the game shows and the soap operas. The women went out in hair curlers to look for bargains at the K-Mart. Came home with a charcoal grill or something, because it was on sale. It sat out in the yard to rust.

"The food, God. As soon as they got married the husbands started going out to work, and the women stayed home to eat.

In three years a pretty high school girl would have three children and gain forty pounds. Like that was part of being a mother. She'd throw the kids out back to play, no grass out there, just dirt and stones, and if the kid wandered off their little patch of yard she'd beat the living shit out of him. I swear. I'd be out hanging clothes on the line, talking to some girl who seemed perfectly nice, and if a kid came up and tugged her leg she'd take a swing at him that would have felled an ox. You could see the marks of her fingers on his skin."

Laurel paled a little, remembering.

"There I was with Jonathan. Trying to stay home and be a good mother."

"They weren't exactly your peer group," Ned said.

"God."

She could feel the old things rising in her as she spoke, dread and anxiety and despair—her palms actually dampened and grew cold—but mostly, now, anger.

"Matt was on rotating shifts. The day shift was okay, though we had to get up at the crack of dawn. But the others left him beat. He never seemed to adjust. There wasn't any good time in the day. Just sitting around napping, or getting ready to go. He was good friends with the other policemen, but I never got to know their wives. I couldn't find my kind of people in that town. Somebody who didn't live for soap operas and shopping malls and Hostess Twinkies."

"How long was this?"

"Three years. In all."

"And that was when you were depressed."

"I didn't know it at the time. Didn't recognize it as depression. I was just so tired. Zero energy. I had this gnawing in my stomach. The moment I woke up. And I worried about incredible things. The energy crisis. The impending collapse of the world economy. The coming of a new ice age. I spent hours every day plotting against Jonathan's diaper rash."

"You placed the blame for that rash squarely on yourself."

"I thought I was a terrible mother. All the time."

Ned touched her hand on his arm. "I've heard this from so many mothers."

"I have too, now. But back then I thought I was the only one."

Laurel stared angrily, her muscles tense. Just the mention of this subject got her all worked up again.

"It's funny, about Matt," Ned said. "The little I've seen of him. He doesn't seem like a cop. Doesn't seem the type."

"He's not. At least I don't think so. What he'd always been was an athlete. Went to college on a baseball scholarship. Everybody thought he'd go on in that. He was a pitcher. Had a lot of people looking at him."

Laurel remembered those years with great fondness. They had promised so much. Out past left field was a pine forest, and from up on the hill behind first base, where she sat with her knitting, she could watch the tall trees swaying slowly in the wind, against wispy clouds in the pale-blue sky. The spring-times had been cool and breezy and clear. Matt had always been the big star, but baseball was no real big deal at the school, so the crowds were always small. From the grandstand behind the plate they cheered Matt loudly as he walked off the mound, and she heard the cheer as a distant echo—something about the grandstand roof muted the sound—and just before he entered the dugout he looked up at her and smiled.

"Then he hurt his shoulder the last year. Fell off a bicycle, believe it or not. It didn't leave him permanently disabled, for anything except pitching. From where I sat you couldn't tell. But the ball didn't have the old zip. The people he'd once gotten out started to hit it."

"He could have done something connected with baseball. Coached."

"Everybody said that. His major had been PE, after all. All his friends were looking for jobs in schools. But he'd never pictured himself that way. As young as he was, and still want-ing to play. It was just too hard. The other thing was, his father had just died. And his father had been a cop. Matt had grown up with that all around him. His father had wanted something else for him, encouraged him with the baseball. But when his father died, and the baseball didn't work out, I guess it just seemed the logical thing."

It had been a hard time. Matt hadn't known what he wanted to do, and it scared him; up until then, all his life, he'd always known what he wanted to do. He resisted the thought of coaching. He'd always thought high school coaches were saps. Laurel hadn't wanted him to do police work, but she didn't want to take that away from him, either. It was all he had left.

So many marriages she'd heard of since seemed to start that way, with a fundamental disagreement that never got aired.

"It was a strange emotional thing. I had very little to do with it. All of a sudden I was a cop's wife."

"And a mother."

She nodded wearily. "A mother."

"But you finally got away from that."

"After three years. A long hard time. A lot of tears, and arguments, and bitter feelings."

She thought back on those days and was ashamed. She shouldn't have been, but she couldn't help it. If she'd had half a brain, been in the least bit aware of what was going on in her, if she hadn't been trying to maintain the illusion she was a happy little mother, she would have realized in a couple of weeks what was happening to her. The sleepless nights. Terrible anxiety when she woke up in the morning. Food seemed tasteless and she lost weight. She longed to be a good mother but neglected Jonathan, stared off into space and thought about nothing. She knew she should find him some playmates he liked, knew she should get him a good sitter for a few hours and go off and do something *she* liked, but she never did. The housework piled up. She spent the whole day devising ways to make things nice for Matt when he got home, then when he did, forgot them all and started nagging and complaining. By late in the evening they were openly arguing; she had fits of hysteria and burst into tears.

The real problem was the one thing she kept avoiding. As usual. If she'd just told Matt she needed something more to do, a better place to do it, they could probably have worked that out. But she couldn't say that to him. It was inadmissible. So as an alternative she became a basket case, with a gaunt dark stare, taut nerves, fits of weeping, and let him try to figure it out for himself.

"We moved back to the town where we'd gone to college. That made all the difference to me. I had plenty of friends there, still. Matt too. I knew my way around. I found play groups for Jonathan, good sitters. I started to go out. Wandered into the counseling program. It was very big there. I got involved in therapy myself. Found out I wasn't nuts. I started to feel better, look better. All this energy was gathering in me."

"A new life. I love to hear it."

"Except the police department stank."

"Had to be something."

"It was mostly just that nothing ever happened in the town.

You broke up some loud fraternity parties, football players brawling. If there was a crime, some petty theft, you didn't just have a suspect. You actually knew who did it. There were only three or four criminals, and they kept doing the same things over and over again. And it was a very liberal community. The police had to keep a low profile. A kid called you a motherfucking pig right there on the street and you were just supposed to tip your hat and smile."

"Matt wasn't happy."

"That puts it mildly."

The tables had been turned, more or less. Not that Matt lost weight and threw hysterics, but he was grumpy all the time, frustrated. He had learned to like police work, and now they weren't letting him do it. Almost as soon as they got there he started to talk about leaving, and that hurt Laurel's feelings, because she liked the place so much. She had gotten almost superstitious about it, afraid that if she left she'd flop back into a terrible depression.

Her friends were a problem too. They claimed to be accepting of everybody, but at cops they seemed to draw the line. They tried, because he was Laurel's husband, but he felt their hostility and was never comfortable around them.

"We couldn't have stayed, really. The counseling program was so big, and everybody so happy in it, that nobody ever wanted to leave. There were more therapists around than neurotics. That's saying something, in a university town. We had to go somewhere, but I wouldn't go back to the kind of place we'd been. And Matt had to find a half-decent police force."

"Pittsburgh sounds perfect. Home, for you. And I take it the police force is okay."

"Except that your uncle had to be the chief for you to get a job. They weren't exactly bowled over by Matt's résumé, two straight jobs in small towns. Neither one lasting all that long. But I had family up here, and they heard about the job at the center. The police weren't hiring, but if Matt could ever get a job here . . . We hadn't heard of anything half as good. We just packed up and left."

So Laurel had won and Matt lost, that round, but in marriage there were no outright winners; what she gained in happiness at her job she more than made up for with guilt. She couldn't help feeling she had dragged Matt down, snatched him from a place where he had liked his job and brought him to one where he had to scrap for work, never knew if he'd be a cop again. Maybe she wasn't wild about police work, but that wasn't for her to judge: he had been happy doing it.

She knew a depressed man when she saw one, the sad defeated frightened eyes, and she understood the way he denied his depression; hadn't she done the same thing for years? Because of him she couldn't be entirely happy in her new situation. She was starting her first big job at a new place, and had to drag that old baggage around. It was unfair to him, but natural for her, to want to be rid of it.

"For a while he couldn't find anything. Took a job instructing PE at that little private school, Tabard. He'd had some courses in education. But he hated that. Spoiled kids. A weird faculty. I mean *strange*. I don't know where they drag these people up. By the end of the year he'd had enough. Now he's into this."

"I'm afraid my image of the job is all stereotypes. Shoulder holsters and slugs of rye."

"It's not like that at all. Most of it is deadly boring. Investigating someone for an insurance policy. Or to see how their credit is. They do some work for lawyers, checking on what the police give as evidence. The most exciting thing, I mean a real gas, is sitting outside a sleazy motel while some couple commits adultery. I guess you picture them doing it. Matt's just going to be part-time. But it beats working at that school. It's the closest thing to police work he's been able to find."

She was trying to make it sound good, or at least halfway normal, repeating all the things Matt had told her. The whole thing gave her the creeps, actually. Didn't even sound like a real job. A private investigator had an overload of work and would give Matt his leftovers. Free-lance, more or less. No guarantees as to how much, or for how long.

Matt had seemed pitiful, telling her, smiling excitedly as if he'd stumbled across the job of his dreams. A child scared and whistling in the dark. He was watching her reaction, seeking her approval; when she wasn't enthusiastic enough they'd had an argument about *that*. "I don't care what you do!" she had shouted finally. "Do you think I give a shit? Go off in the morning and leave me out of it."

A lie, of course. She cared deeply, or she wouldn't have gotten so mad. Here she was walking long blocks on a muggy summer afternoon just to look at the office. Hoping it wasn't too bad.

"The man he's working for has a wonderful reputation.

Some policemen friends have told Matt all about him." She could even picture that, policemen secure in their jobs talking to some poor pitiful slob who couldn't find anything, trying to encourage him. "I'm not sure where the office is. Matt gave me the address."

That was a lie too. Matt had no idea she was coming. She'd looked the address up in the phone book.

Somewhere in there they had crossed an imaginary dividing line between East Liberty and Shadyside. What Laurel had once considered a boundary—the little bridge where once upon a time the streetcar had made its turn and started the slow trek along that shady windy street into Oakland—was gone. The streetcars were long gone too, and those central blocks of East Liberty had been converted into an urban mall. It was that or implode them with dynamite. The city had blocked off the four lanes of Penn Avenue, run the traffic in a circle around it, planted cobblestones and decorative lampposts and beds of flowers. Around the circle whole blocks had been razed to put in high-rise public housing, health clinics, recreation centers, parking lots.

For Laurel it was romantic, and a little sad. Walking past all that was new—the bright-red brick of the housing projects, nondescript tan of the public buildings, flat cement wastes of the parking lots—you happened, say, through an alley, and emerged in another world, narrow and shadowed and crumbling: a dusty storefront full of Bibles and other devotional books, the high dirty side wall of a grand old movie theater, a single small door with a neon sign above it blinking BAR. It was like stumbling across the ruins of an ancient civilization, took Laurel back to the days when she and her friends had come in on the streetcar to go to a movie and do a little shopping. The renovation had been necessary—the place was rotting—but Laurel missed the days when Penn Avenue had been all bustle and traffic, dirty and various and exciting.

"I guess it's down here," Laurel said, looking to her left. "The building's on Highland."

What she finally hated to admit, what really seemed ungrateful, was that she preferred work to being at home with Matt and Jonathan. She had started out wanting to be a full-time mother and now it was as if she didn't want to be a mother at all. It was so comfortable at work, everyone helpful and friendly and full of energy, then she got home to find Matt moping around, Jonathan strung out and grumpy after a day at camp.

Ned, for instance, had been wonderful at work, helping her get settled, talking about the problems he had had getting started. He never suggested she might be having problems, just offered his anecdotes as if they were sympathy, let her get around to talking when she was ready. And she had talked, a great deal, about her own experiences in therapy, her time in the counseling program. He had almost become her therapist himself, and she even experienced a touch of transference, that closeness you inevitably feel with someone when you open yourself up. The last thing standing between them had been her relationship with Matt. Now she had smashed that to bits.

Ned was young, and she—starting a new job, a new life— felt young too. His bouncy enthusiasm stood in bright contrast to Matt's moping. He was like a new boyfriend, the kind of boy she had always liked, too, funny and fresh and full of ideas. There were times she wondered how she had ever wound up with a wet rag like Matt.

At the same time she could see things objectively. She had counseled any number of young women who, starting new careers, suddenly found themselves in love. They were giving their best time and energy to their jobs, spending more time with the men at work than they ever spent with their husbands, and of course those men shared all their interests. They were really in love not with a new man but a new situation, perhaps a new vocation, but soon they were engaged in passionate love affairs, and then arranging divorces, the division of households, the custody of children. Eventually, no doubt, the new man would become the old one, and the whole thing would start over again.

"I guess this is it." She had stopped in front of an ancient office building.

"This?" Ned said. "My God. I thought this place was long gone." He stared up at the height of it. "I went to the dentist here as a kid."

"Still a thriving center of commerce," Laurel said.

"I'll be damned," Ned said.

It seemed a small front for an eight-story office building, as if a miniature of the skyscrapers downtown. A battered rubber mat led to two elevator doors in the narrow lobby. Beside them a blind woman operated a tiny newsstand, with gum, Life Savers, candy bars, cigars. She was enormous, entirely filled the small space she sat in. Her head lolled back on her shoulders, as if, through her dark glasses, she stared at the ceiling.

The elevators, as it turned out, were open-air affairs, black iron cagework, though they were self-service; you pushed a button and rose slowly through the dead air of the shaft. Must have been all the rage in 1920. Upstairs the hallways were stone-walled, narrow, with brown wooden floors and windows of frosted glass. On the fourth floor, where they stopped, two out of three ceiling lights were burned out. Cigarette butts were scattered around on the floor. The offices were dark.

"This isn't the liveliest building I've ever been in," Laurel said.

Ned spoke carefully. "Actually, I don't think most of these places are occupied."

She could have screamed, was the truth of the matter, kicked the walls, put her fist through the frosted glass. This place had been her last hope. It was as if they were on a seesaw, Matt slowly going down while she was rising. The more success she had, the happier and more established she got, the worse things were for him. She couldn't fight a feeling that he was doing it on purpose, punishing her for being happy. She wanted to kick him, shout, "Get off your ass and *do* something! Take hold of your life!" Now, the lowest blow yet, he had taken a job here. See what you've done to me.

His depression scared her. Too close to home.

They stopped in front of the door. 414. There was nothing on it, no sign, like Acme Private Eye, a winking eyeball or a bullet speeding out of a small automatic. The glass was dark. She reached for the knob, gave it a try. Locked.

"Wonder what I would have done if it had opened," she said.

She smiled wryly at Ned. He was not smiling, did not smile back, watched her with a look of close concern.

It was normal, when you were a therapist among other therapists, to want to be whole, happy, sane—you had passed through the fire and were stronger for it—and that was why, probably, Laurel had not really talked to Ned until that day, but now the combination of things, the long story she'd told on her walk, the look of concern in his eyes, that pitiful building—all it needed was a wino stretched out on the floor— was all too much: tears welled at her eyes. He took her in his arms—that was not unusual around the center, where shows of affection were strongly approved—and at his touch the tears poured down her cheeks, and she sobbed. Her body trembled and shook against him. In the narrow hallway, two lights burned out, the doors dark, the air dead and still, they clung to each other for some time.

Chapter Two

"You get in a courtroom," Wolf said. He had taken out a handkerchief, was mopping the back of his neck. "It's all first impressions."

"Sure," Matt said.

The two men were standing up on the front lawn. All the houses along that street were on small terraces. Down below them, at the bottom of the steps, Jonathan dawdled, holding a plastic ball and bat and looking up at them.

"You got twelve people in that box, they probably never been there before. They probably never did anything in their life like that. I mean they spend their lives mopping floors or working a machine somewhere, and you expect them to sit there all day and take in evidence. They don't even listen to their husbands and wives more than a minute or two a day. Hell. They look the witness over. Decide if they like his face. They listen for maybe three minutes. Their mind's made up."

"Huh."

"You got to get those first three minutes."

He finished mopping up and put the handkerchief away. From his inside jacket pocket he took out a small pack of cigarettes, fished one out. Lucky Strikes. Matt hadn't even known they made those things anymore, much less that anyone was crazy enough to smoke them.

"This time we got a problem." Though Wolf was strictly free-lance, worked for lawyers all over the city, once he was on a case he always took it quite personally. "Our star witness gets in the box. Looks out over the crowd. Right away the jury's got a hard time to keep from laughing. He's got this silly grin. His face is round and he's pudgy all over. He looks like an overgrown twelve-year-old kid."

"I didn't know you'd seen him."

"I laid eyes on him. I'd been hoofing all day around Liberty Avenue, in and out of the scummiest places in town. Saving the one guy I knew was really a witness for last. I couldn't find anybody else who'd seen a thing. Finally I went in to see the guy we were counting on. I stood around till I heard somebody say his name. Took one look at him and walked back out."

Wolf had been holding an unlighted cigarette in his hand, now finally used his lighter, sucked in a big gust of smoke. Matt felt the pain in his own lungs.

"Anyway, we'll get this guy on the stand. Looks like he ought to be wearing short pants and holding a Tootsie Roll. The jury's already biting their tongues to keep from laughing. State your name, the foreman says, and our boy says Otto Droge. Otto Droge." Wolf winced. "Jesus Christ. He's probably got that moron grin on his face when he says it, like even he thinks it's a joke. The opposing lawyer steps up smiling. He already knows it's in the bag. 'Where are you employed, Mr. Droge?' Old Otto's probably proud of the fact. 'I manage the Bird in the Hand Adult Bookstore,' he says. Or whatever the fucking place is named. Right there we lost our case."

"Yeah." Matt couldn't help smiling, though Wolf seemed in real pain.

"It doesn't matter what he's got to say. It's all over."

Wolf was a lean spare dark man, with a nose like the beak of a hawk. He had a thin face, weary eyes with skin sagging and wrinkled under them; it was an ingratiating face, like a beagle's. Above his narrow mouth was a pencil-thin mustache, close and bristly. His body was also long and lean, straight, though it didn't seem especially sturdy. His clothes hung on him as if they'd been thrown on a hook.

"So what do you do about all this?" Matt said.

"You try to talk to Droge, first of all. That it might be better if he fixed himself up a little. Dark suit and tie, like a respectable businessman. If he tried to keep the smile off his face. You hope it doesn't come out he's got a record, which it undoubtedly will. An obscenity case from when the laws were different, but it still doesn't look good. You tell him not to make it sound like he's a close friend of the plaintiff, even though he is. Actually, he'd just been walking out of his place with the guy, who was probably still a little dizzy from jerking off in one of the booths. You try to make sure he's rock-solid, that he knows what he saw and the other side can't budge him on a thing."

Wolf took a long drag, stared off at the sky.

"Most of all, you hope you can find somebody else who saw the damn thing."

Jonathan, who had been edging closer and closer to the bottom step, now actually put a foot on it, took a step up.

"You keeping the kid," Wolf said.

"Yeah."

"Where's the wife?"

"She works on Sundays, now and then. They've got to have somebody on duty all the time." In case one of the clients went stark raving mad.

"Working Sundays. Jesus."

"You should talk."

"I work when I want. Some Sundays I go in, some weekdays I stay home. But Sunday morning's a good time. Nobody around. I can catch up on my paperwork. If I stay home the wife's always got things for me to do."

Jonathan was taking it just one step at a time, examining the ball in his hand, as if not really aware he was moving up.

Wolf looked down the steps. "Come on up, John. Johnny." He turned to Matt. "What do you call the kid?"

"Jonathan."

Wolf stared. "What the hell kind of a name is that for a kid?"

"We like it."

"It makes him sound like he wears glasses and plays with an Erector Set."

"It's no worse than Wolfgang."

"That's what I'm saying. You never heard my parents use that with me. That name never got past the birth certificate."

He looked back down. "Come on up, Johnny. It's okay."

Jonathan walked slowly up the steps, dragging his bat. He was tall for a seven-year-old, black-haired, with the striking olive skin of his mother. He was at a stage when he didn't like to look adults in the eye, or speak up when he addressed them. Now he came up the steps to where the men were, but didn't acknowledge either of them.

"You waiting to play ball with your dad."

Jonathan shrugged. "He said we were playing."

"You like playing ball."

30

"I like to hit." He tapped the bat idly on the cement. "I like to take it downtown."

Wolf grinned at the boy, who still wasn't looking at him. "You take it downtown."

"I like to drive the old man to the warning track."

Matt loved sports clichés, shouted them out when they were playing. Jonathan had a way of repeating things he heard other people say.

"You want me to get out of here," Wolf said. "So you and your dad can play ball."

"It's okay."

"You can tell me, John. You been standing down there looking at me."

For the first time, Jonathan turned and met his eyes.

"I saw you looking," Wolf said.

"I want to see your gun," Jonathan said.

"Oh." Wolf's expression didn't exactly change, but he seemed to miss a beat in the conversation. "What makes you think I got a gun?"

"He told me." Jonathan looked at his father.

"He asked if you had a gun," Matt said. "I told him I thought you carried one."

"Uh huh." Wolf squatted down, pulled his jacket back and showed Jonathan the gun in its holster. "There."

"I want to hold it," Jonathan said.

"No."

"Just *hold* it."

"That isn't safe." Wolf's face looked weary, and bored, and sad, all at once. "You know why I carry that, John."

"To take care of criminals. To blow them away."

"I never blew anybody away. I never even nicked them. I never even fired that gun."

Jonathan still had his eyes on the gun, as if memorizing its contours.

"I carry it because people expect it. The people I work for." He looked up at Matt. "It's the truth. They actually ask me, I mean people I'm doing divorce work for or something, 'Where's your gun?' Like I'm going to pick some guy off walking out of a motel." He turned back to Jonathan. "That gun's never been fired. It's never even been loaded."

"Then why can't I hold it?"

"Even so. You're never sure. You got to stay away from guns at your age. Never touch them."

He had a way of talking—his sad face gazing directly into Jonathan's—that seemed utterly convincing.

"Okay." Jonathan wasn't disappointed. He seemed to feel he'd been told something important.

Wolf stood. "It's not like the movies, John. Not like on TV. Speeding around in cars and shooting out the window. What I do all day is talk to people. Go out and find them, or call them on the phone. Look through piles of old papers. Anybody could do it."

The funny thing was, Matt thought, that it wasn't true. Those were the things Wolf did, but not just anybody could have done them. He knew how to put his hands on documents that nobody else knew existed, could turn a few dry facts from an old county courthouse into a capsule biography, and when he talked to people—maybe it was his sad clown face, that seemed so harmless—they talked back. He kept a messy dirty office that was virtually useless, drove a '66 Pontiac that didn't start half the time, and undoubtedly didn't even know how to fire that gun of his, but he was one of the best investigators in the business.

"You go across the street now, John," he said. "Me and your dad'll be through in a minute."

Jonathan went down the steps, looked both ways at the street, then flung the bat ahead of him and ran across.

"That's a good kid, Matt. A great kid."

"Thanks. He is."

"They all want to look at my gun. Christ."

Wolf and Matt had started slowly down the steps.

"This job," Wolf said. "I think you should take a crack at it tomorrow."

"Okay."

"On the one hand I'm starting you off with something impossible. I been over the ground once and couldn't find a thing. On the other hand I'm not expecting much. You'll be out on your own without any pressure. You can't do any harm."

The two men were standing at the bottom of the steps, facing each other, but Wolf was looking over Matt's shoulder, squinting into the sun.

"Don't make a big deal of who you are. Tell if somebody asks, but don't go out of your way to offer it. They'll ask, anyway. Walk around. Talk to people. Especially at that bookstore of Droge's. I didn't try there. And go over it with Droge. Let him tell you what he's got to say. Be sure it makes sense."

Matt nodded.

"It doesn't have to be perfect. The lawyer can coach him."

He had stepped to his car, opened the door. He had to reach in through the window to open it.

"The best thing would be to find somebody else. Anybody. Who saw the whole thing, can describe it in detail. Preferably a nun."

A puff of dust arose as he collapsed on the seat. He pulled the door to slam it shut, but it just banged back open. He slammed it again. Again. He leaned out to get some momentum and gave it a real yank; as the door banged into the car it sounded as if something broke off and fell into the back seat. The door stayed shut.

"Fucking car," Wolf muttered.

The engine turned over on only the third try, a huge cloud of exhaust spewing forth.

"I'll be in early tomorrow," he said. "Probably there all day."

"All right."

"Let me know how it goes. You'll be fine."

"Thanks, Wolf."

The car jerked, pulled away, sputtered and rattled up the street. Matt was enveloped in a gray cloud. Wolf was a shrewd man, an excellent investigator, a canny judge of human beings, but it was also true that the man who was putting his trust in Matt was driving around in that car. At the corner it lurched, wheels squealing, into a turn, stalled and drifted quietly down the hill.

II

Laurel loved the incongruous. Most of her colleagues found it appalling to do therapy in an office building in the center of a seedy business district—they longed for a more idyllic setting—but she loved it. She liked it that there were small businesses and government services in the building around her, that on a normal weekday she walked past room after room of petty bureaucrats, found herself suddenly—after she had entered her door—in a cozy little apartment, of plush furniture and thick rugs and soft lamps.

She loved it when, on Sunday mornings, she drove the streets on the way to work, stray winos slumped in doorways, an occasional forlorn prostitute walking home from somewhere, and she saw in the middle of the scraps of Saturday-night trash a large black family in their brightest Sunday finery, making their way to an early church service. She liked it that she was the only one for blocks around to be going to work that day, and that, to get there, she was driving through such a neighborhood.

She liked it now that, in the large quiet empty building, only—as far as she knew—her office open, she was lying on the couch where she normally did counseling, but she was not wearing her clothes, and Ned Streater, also not wearing clothes, was lying with her.

She liked stripping naked; snapping off the lamp, kicking off her sandals, then with brief quick motions removing her jersey and skirt as if abandoning convention, or her whole accumulated past. She loved being naked, itchy and scratching at once on the rough slipcover of the couch. She loved Ned's naked body against hers, the smell of his scalp as his head rested on her shoulder, the strong male smell from his armpits and groin, the soft rhythm of his breathing, like sleep. She liked his damp penis spent and resting against her leg.

All her life she had read the stories of fallen women, who finally gave in to scoundrels and afterward suffered agonies of guilt, but Ned was not a scoundrel, and it was not quite accurate to say she had given in (more like he had), and the fact of the matter was she did not feel guilty; she felt wonderful. She felt like shouting with joy and squeezing Ned hard.

She had known they would meet that day. Friday, when they had parted in East Liberty—he was going in one direction, she in the other—he had said, "I'm worried about you. Really. You seem so sad."

"It's all right. Some things are sad. It was good to cry."

"We ought to talk about it. Or you should."

"I know."

She had been looking down, speaking demurely, avoiding his eyes.

"I'm on duty Sunday," she said.

She glanced up. His face wore the eager sympathy of the born counselor.

"That's good," he said. "We can talk then. We can really talk. I'll come over."

"All right."

They were lying through their teeth. They both knew they wouldn't be getting together to talk, knew what they were really making an appointment for. Their embrace upstairs had been a gesture of comfort, but also the embrace of lovers, bright with desire. If they had had a place to slip off to they would have been lovers right then.

Their Sunday-morning meeting had been awkward at first. Ned kept her waiting an hour (she would have liked him to be there when she arrived, so she could have fallen into his arms), apparently so he wouldn't seem too anxious. When he finally did arrive, though, he looked wild, nervous and self-conscious and disheveled; he seemed not to have slept. He didn't even step over to hug her. He took the seat across from her and was actually physically trembling, avoided her eyes, kept talking about how he had burned his breakfast toast and hadn't had enough coffee in the house. Laurel had been nervous too, her heart thumping, but nothing as bad as that. As he got worse and worse—going on about his habitual difficulties at breakfast, making himself sound like a befuddled old bachelor—she gradually grew calm. She just felt strong, resolved, began quietly to smile.

"You seem a little tense," she said.

"I know." He laughed. Tensely. "I've got the jitters. I don't know what's wrong."

She stood. "Come here." He got up and slowly came to her, a little boy summoned by the teacher. "Today it's you who needs a hug." She held him around the shoulders—his own arms were like steel bands at the small of her back—and waited patiently until the shaking stopped. She didn't move, or speak. It must have taken five minutes.

Finally she pulled her head back, lightly touched his hair with her fingertips, smiled.

"Kiss me," she said.

She had forgotten what a young lover was like, so eager and ardent, his tongue fluttering wildly around in her mouth, his heart pounding against her chest until *she* could hardly stand it (what must it have been for him?) and she almost stopped him, told him to slow down. But she didn't want to sound like the sultry older woman, deadened by a steady diet of dry martinis, and anyway she was kind of enjoying herself: it was like being in high school again. Once they had stripped and were on the couch, he moved down to kiss her nipples, sucking hungrily like a baby. It actually reminded her of Jonathan.

"You have hair on your nipples," he said.

What tact. Even that didn't bother her, it was spoken so innocently.

"Yes," she said. "I do."

"I've never met a woman with hair on her nipples."

"You usually don't find out right when you meet her."

"I mean . . ."

"I know what you mean. Now you know. Some women do have hair on their nipples. You've actually met one."

He plunged into her easily—as a matter of fact, she had been fully ready for intercourse for an hour—with a groan of delight. He was light on top of her, moved quickly, like a kid doing push-ups. He seemed off in his own world. His heart was still pounding, and he was nearly breathless, gasping in little sighs. He finished with a last loud shout and a quick arch to his spine—as if she had smacked the small of his back—then collapsed all over her. Still he seemed light, the smooth clean hollow body of a boy. She reached down and cupped a hand over his bottom, held him still while he grew small.

When he finally seemed to have caught his breath, she said, "I need you to touch me."

"I know. I'm sorry I didn't go longer. I usually do better."

"You were fine. Wonderful. I always need to be touched."

He started off rapidly at that too, and at that she did stop him. "Softer," she said. "And slower. Much slower." Still she had to reach down to direct his hand, move it the way she liked, then she had to wait for everything to calm down— "Stop a minute. Just lie there. Okay. Start again"—but it was important for her to be satisfied too, not just dispensing favors to the peanut gallery, and eventually, partly because of the accumulated tension of the morning, partly because she had been thinking about Ned for two days, partly because the whole thing *was* exciting, she had a wonderful orgasm, her own back arching, the skin of her torso deeply flushed: she clutched his head against her breasts and trembled, trembled.

They lay quietly for a while. Laurel thought Ned fell

asleep—she may have drifted off herself for a minute or two—
but then she felt him stir and awaken; she could feel him
thinking.

"It's funny," he said. "I don't even feel guilty. I really don't."

If he really didn't, he wouldn't have said anything.

"Do you?" he said.

"No."

The whole thing seemed to have little to do with her
marriage.

"I would have thought I'd feel guilty," he said.

"I am still married, Ned. My marriage is very important to
me."

"I know. I didn't mean . . . "

"It's all right. Let's not talk about it."

Of course, it did have to do with her marriage. Everything
had to do with everything, finally. People were obsessed with
what they called fidelity, but there were kinds of infidelity,
and what *she* was worried about (though not at that particular
moment) was not a brief act of sex, but the whole thing of her
job and her family, the way she left the house every morning
with a spring in her stride, thought of returning in the evening
with an ache of dread. If she was really being unfaithful it
was with her job, not with Ned. But all those worries at that
moment on that Sunday morning—and this was what really
did seem wonderful—were far away, as if she had shed them
with her clothes. She *loved* being naked.

She rolled Ned on his back, reached to caress his chest.

"Why," she said, "you have hair on your nipples."

He laughed. "Yes."

"How extraordinary. How very extraordinary."

She began to kiss his left nipple, not with his kind of ardent
suckling, but more slowly, expertly, caressing with just the tip
of her tongue. She rolled his other nipple between her fore-
finger and thumb. Leaning closer, she gave a little bite. Ned
groaned.

"That hurt?" she said.

"Just right."

His cock gave a twitch and began slowly to rise. Ah, youth.
She would make love her way now, see if she could tame this
frisky colt. He seemed very young to her, younger, really, than
she had expected, and she didn't want to talk, didn't want to
confuse him with words he wouldn't understand. Laurel was

too ready with words anyway, spoke them before events had had time to settle. But if she had put her feelings into words, to that young man who, for a few moments at least, had allowed her to forget everything, she would have said—rather impetuously, but she would have meant it—I love you.

Chapter Three

The place smelled of the strong cherry-scented disinfectant used in schools, public libraries, the locker rooms at the YMCA. The front room was surprisingly large (what had this place been built as, Matt wondered, in its distant urban past?) and gray, the fluorescent lights on the high ceiling not managing to brighten it. At the front, after you had paid a quarter just to get in, was a glass showcase of what the sign outside must have meant by marital aids, mostly plastic phalluses that would have been more appropriate marital aids for a brood mare. They were battered and bent into peculiar shapes, and Matt could imagine the salesperson going into various explanations. "This guy was left-handed," or "This guy got it caught in a door as a kid." He was reminded of the old rumors that John Dillinger's twenty-seven-inch penis was supposedly on display somewhere in the Smithsonian, and could imagine customers leaving the shop with one of these items ("Sorry, we're out of the long bags"), carrying it under his arm the way men carry those loaves of bread home in French movies.

Around the walls and in long rows in that room were metal racks of extremely expensive magazines, showing on their covers only the remotest byways of sex, women chained to beds or hanging from the ceiling by their wrists, tall strong women in elaborate leather undergarments and carrying whips, a fearful redfaced woman kneeling before a man whose fat fleshy cock hung in front of her mouth like a raw sausage. A few customers stood around with their hands in their pockets, staring at the covers, but the magazines were wrapped in plastic and couldn't be thumbed through. Otherwise the racks would have been mobbed.

The real action—what passed for real action in such an establishment—took place through a doorway hung with plastic beads, like the door that a sinister Oriental woman often walked through in Terry and the Pirates.

Back there it was more like the haunted house at the Halloween fair. There were wooden floors, and booths whose doors creaked open and slammed loudly shut. All around were the sounds of men talking in deep angry voices or groaning, women shouting or shrieking or screaming in ecstasy. Feet shuffled, quarters clanked into metal boxes. No apparent echoes of pounding flesh. Matt had to pause a moment for his eyes to grow accustomed to the dark. Men stood in the shadows staring as he passed by. One nicely dressed businessman stepped up and spoke quietly: "Hi. See anything good?" Matt let this ambiguous question pass and kept walking.

At the end of that maze of corridors was a brighter spot, a high wide booth painted with a psychedelic sign, "Talk to a Live Nude Girl." A woman sat at a cash register, loudly popping gum.

"What's this?" Matt said.

"You buy tokens and talk to a nude chick." She was a heavy woman with a pasty pockmarked face. One suggestive word and she'd knock your teeth out. "Wanna try?"

Matt stared at the booth. "There's a girl in there somewhere?"

"There's a girl right here."

Matt looked back at her. She was chewing her gum aggressively, staring.

"What'd you think, I was just real good at giving out change?"

"Sorry. I misunderstood." Some chick. "Actually, I was just looking for Otto Droge."

"You don't need no tokens to talk to him."

Matt hoped he wasn't nude either. "I didn't see him out front."

"He musta went on his break. He'll be back."

Matt headed for the plastic beads.

"You come back and buy a token if he ain't around. We'll talk dirty."

She had all the earmarks of a virtuoso performer.

As soon as Matt stepped back to the outer room he had picked out Droge. There really was something boyish about him, but like the fat awkward boy who always gets picked on and always smiles about it, who laughs even when everybody is popping their knuckles on his shoulders and arms and skull, who already looks like a forty-five-year old man when he is a twelve-year-old kid. He was wearing a short-sleeved knit shirt that clung to him with moisture; his navel had sucked in a piece of cloth the size of a half dollar. His soft fleshy gut jiggled as he walked. Below it he wore khaki shorts, limp bunched white socks, black cordovans. His legs were hairy. His head was closely cropped, his face heavy, and his eyes deeply sunken, as if his forehead were thick with scar tissue. As he moved around behind the plastic penises, electric vibrators, lubricating gels, and decks of pornographic playing cards, his face—in those deep-set eyes, and at the corners of his mouth—wore a little smile.

It was worse than Wolf had said. The jury would burst into irrepressible laughter.

"Otto Droge," Matt said.

"Present." The guy even talked like a fifth-grader.

"I work for Wolf Harpe. We're investigating for your friend in that accident. I'd like to have a word with you."

At the word "accident," Droge rolled his eyes: he had the disconcerting ability—Matt had run into it a few times before —to make the irises disappear, so you saw only the bloodshot whites. The effect was vaguely nauseating, like being exposed to the innards of a live animal. "I'll talk all you want," he said. "We got to nail that bastard."

So while greasy young men in T-shirts and businessmen in trench coats and college-age men in sportshirts came through and glanced at the magazines, got a handful of quarters from Droge and drifted back to the funhouse, Droge talked, about how right turn on red was one thing but you were supposed to make sure nobody was there first, how not only was the light red for the car but the pedestrians' light to walk was on, how Liberty Avenue was a mess with what seemed hundreds of cars waiting for the light and most of the pedestrians were gone but the light to walk was definitely still flashing when Bunter Lawson took off in a dash across the street and that VW came racing around the corner the way only a VW can race, and the sound—thank God he wasn't watching—was awful, as if somebody had taken a sledgehammer to the hood, he didn't see how a human body could absorb that kind of punishment, and now Bunter had a limp for life and a neck and back that hurt all the time and they were going to nail that cocksucker, no question about it, Bunter had grocery bills and a lifetime of pain ahead of him and somebody was going to pay. All this delivered in so passionate and strident a voice that the other men in the room kept glancing back. Apparently they were having trouble concentrating on erect penises and pendulous breasts and the lips of wet vaginas spread wide.

Wolf should have talked to Droge himself. He had no idea how bad it was.

"You say the walk light was blinking." Matt got in a few words when this diatribe was over.

"It was still blinking. I saw it still blinking."

"When the light blinks it's a signal for pedestrians not to walk."

"It was on, then. It was blinking or it was on."

"It's got to be one or the other."

"If you say it was on it was on."

"I wasn't there, Otto."

"Maybe it was blinking. Maybe Bunter shouldn't have gone. Maybe he made a little mistake. That's no reason to knock him halfway across the street. It's no reason to practically kill him."

A jury would no doubt be impressed by this impeccable logic.

"You saw the car come around the corner."

"It came tearing around the fucking corner."

"But you didn't see it hit him."

"Thank God I didn't see. The sight would have killed me."

"That makes no sense, Otto. You were standing at the corner."

Droge stared straight ahead (in the direction, actually, of a bright magazine cover showing a woman take it from behind). As if better to remember the moment, he rolled his eyeballs up into his forehead. Matt turned away queasily.

"I was heading back toward the shop." He actually turned around, reenacting the scene. "I saw the car jump forward, starting, the way those little bugs do. It ran through my mind just for a second, like something you forgot to do, Bunter's crossing that street. I was reaching for the door when I heard this terrible sound."

This was their eyewitness. Who had his back squarely to the scene at the crucial moment. Who was glad to leave it up to Matt as to whether or not the walk light was on. Who even if he had been facing in the right direction would probably have had his eyeballs turned toward his eardrum, or something.

Kiss the case goodbye.

"Otto. Do you know if anyone else saw it?"

"Millions of people saw it. There were cars all over Liberty Avenue."

"I mean somebody you can point me to. Somebody who might have been with you."

"He saw it. The boss was there." He pointed to a man just approaching the turnstile. "You saw Bunter Lawson get hit."

"Matt Gregg. What! Are *you* here?"

The voice was familiar—hoarse, mocking—but for a moment Matt couldn't place it, the setting was so incongruous. He saw the flushed face first, the leering grin, then he remembered. Oh hell. Hugh Bollinger.

"Eliot's *Four Quartets*." Bollinger dropped a quarter in the slot and pushed his way through. " 'Little Gidding,' if my memory serves me. A rough rendering of Dante, fifteenth canto of the *Inferno*. It's a line that often comes back to me, as I sweep through this modern circle of hell, and run into my banker, my clergyman"—he gestured toward Matt—"an old colleague from school. What! Are *you* here?" His eyes wore an expression of mock horror. "I'm sure Otto got the full force of the allusion. Though I doubt he has either title on his shelves."

Bollinger took a hard drag on a battered cigarette. Matt felt his stomach tense. Put on your armor, folks.

"You saw Bunter Lawson get hit," Droge said. "You were out there. I remember now."

"Your poor onanistic friend. I was indeed. If the accident had taken place on his way into the shop, Liberty Avenue would have been littered with a shower of quarters."

"It's not funny, Hugh. He was hurt bad. Somebody's got to pay."

"You're entirely right. And somebody will pay. Some enormous insurance company. It's just a question of which one."

Bollinger was a man who could be elegant and seedy at the same time. His clothes were of the finest fabric, and perfectly cut, but always something was wrong: there was a spot on his tie, or his shirt was wrinkled, or—as today—his tie was knotted over one side of his button-down collar. He wore cream-colored slacks lightly checked in green, a yellow shirt, a dark-green blazer. He was deeply tanned, even up into his thinning scalp, but his eyes seemed hollow and weary, bloodshot. He had shaved that morning, but had missed a few spots. He had a touch of a patrician New England accent, and his voice was soft, but it was raspy, gruff. Too much whiskey and tobacco.

"Did you really see the accident?" Matt said.

"I was present at the scene. In the way that a man's eyes involuntarily take in what is there before them, I saw it. I'm not too sure of just what I saw. I've been trying to blot it out."

Matt considered for a moment. A drunken teacher and a dirty-bookstore owner. The teacher could be sober.

"I'd like to talk to you," Matt said.

"My initial suspicions were apparently wrong. I thought you were here to enjoy the facilities."

"We're looking into this accident for a lawyer."

"You're private-detecting? I don't see a trench coat." Bollinger's eyes were dancing. "You packing iron?"

As a matter of fact, Matt was wearing a clean work shirt and some corduroys. No reason to overdo it for Liberty Avenue.

"I'd like to talk to you if you really saw it."

"I'll talk. I'll reach far back into the subconscious, where some memory of that moment must exist, and I'll talk. But this hardly seems an ideal setting. Why don't we go have a drink?"

A drink, at eleven in the morning. Probably not Bollinger's first, either.

"All right." Matt did like the idea of getting out of that place.

"I'll be back later, Otto. I believe you have something for me."

"I got it. It's wrapped up in the back."

"I'll probably be back too," Matt said. "We'll talk some more."

The two men shook hands. Otto's hands were sticky.

Matt and Bollinger walked out, into the hot hazy morning on Liberty Avenue.

Out at the corner, where the accident had taken place, the street was four lanes wide at least, more like five or six—it was hard to tell, the crazy way people drove—lined with streetcar tracks, dotted with traffic islands, jammed with cars, crowded with people. The buildings were from an earlier time, not the towering steel-and-glass skyscrapers of the city's skyline, but four stories, or seven, stone or brick and built smack together. The street-level storefronts were operating, some remodeled—

44

Army-Navy stores, novelty shops, discount record shops, small loan companies, pawnshops—but above them, if you raised your eyes to look, you saw mostly blackened windows, or windows boarded over.

Scattered through those small businesses were the garish neon and painted signs. Adult. Lovely Young Exotics. Hot Hot. Peep Shows. Marital Aids. Massage.

"I met some people you know the other night," Matt said.

"Oh?"

"Stanley Killian and Chandler Mingins."

"Really." Bollinger's brow knit, as if this were somehow bad news. "Chandler was out at the school one year, actually. Before your time."

"He told me. They work with my wife now."

"Ah. We've all kept in touch quite a lot. We're still pretty close."

The other two hadn't mentioned that.

"Stanley's got a little shrew of a wife. Maybe you met her."

"I did."

"Fussy little bitch, at least when I'm around. A real pain in the ass."

As far as Matt was concerned she was the only sane one in the group.

"Listen," Bollinger said. "I hope you don't think I frequent places like Otto's. Walk around staring at those racks with my hand in my pocket."

"No." Hugh didn't really seem the type.

"Otto does some discreet purchasing for me. He's able to get a pretty nice discount."

"He called you boss."

"A little quirk of his. I did put some money into the place a few years ago. It's a Rock of Gibraltar financially. The private lusts of the American male."

"You're down here a lot." Bollinger didn't seem embarrassed about it.

"Not to places like that. I frequent a private club, which I think you'll like very much."

"Hugh. I've got work to do. This really is a job, however much it may be a joke to you. I've got to walk around here and look for witnesses."

"You've found a witness."

"I can't take up a lot of time with this."

"You won't take up a lot of time. There's no reason we can't mix business with pleasure, as the gigolo said. You have to let yourself relax sometimes."

It had been the same at school. Bollinger was a great one for keeping people from their work. But what the hell. Matt had found one witness. It was better than Wolf had thought he'd do.

II

They had walked several blocks up Liberty, where the buildings got shabbier and the businesses stranger. There was a Turkish bath, a retailer for artificial limbs, a window display of monster masks. Many of the stores left their doors open. Winos walked those blocks with a purpose, as if off to appointments. There was a glass door, painted black, marked Private; they pushed their way through to a stairway with a rubber matting all the way up, a single light bulb at the top. The stairway smelled strongly of stale urine. At the top was a wooden door marked Members Only.

"You're my guest," Bollinger said. "Step in."

The inside was dim, a background of air-conditioned silence broken by a recording of an electric guitar, wearily whining. Down one side was an elegant mirrored bar. The furniture in the room was all the same, black plush chairs like scooped-out cubes, so they had high armrests and a soft back to lean on. They all faced in the same direction. Small round white tables were scattered around. At the front of the room a light shimmered where, on a small stage, a girl was dancing. The notes from the guitar were drawn-out, wailing. The dancer wore an intense stare on her face, fixed at a point on the back wall of the room, and moved as if seeking, swimming, through the light. It almost seemed that she was in motion, making some progress toward a distant goal.

If she was, indeed, swimming through the light, she was skinny-dipping.

"What are we drinking?" Bollinger said.

"I don't know." The voice had broken Matt's concentration. "Beer, I guess."

"Heineken's okay? I hope to God you're not an Iron City man."

"Anything's fine."

"I'll get it. Have a seat."

The woman had small tight breasts that were mostly nipple. They hardly moved as she danced. Her face was narrow and intense, cheekbones high, eyes staring. Her hair was dirty-blond and short; between her legs it was dark and scanty. Her mouth and fingernails were painted scarlet. She was slender and hard: when she turned she had the most muscular back Matt had ever seen on a woman, a taut white bottom that didn't so much as jiggle.

With her back to the audience, legs spread wide, hips swaying, she bent slowly over and began to move her hands up the insides of her thighs.

"Lovely girl, eh?" Bollinger was back with Matt's beer, and what looked like a vodka martini for himself.

"She's something."

"Drama major at the university. Dance student. She'll sit right down with a ginger ale and tell you about it if you want. Naked as a jaybird, and about that worried about it. If somebody touches her she swings with her fist. I saw her bloody a man's mouth in here one night. But she's a monomaniac about her work. Loves to talk about it. By the time she's finished, of course, she's sweating like a horse."

"So's everybody else in the place."

Her scarlet fingernails had reached the cleft of her buttocks, and she gripped herself, making imprints in the skin.

"She's an ardent lesbian. Told me herself. As far as she's concerned she's dancing in front of a bunch of stiffs."

"Stiff is the word."

"It used to be the strippers downtown were these whory-looking women with big floppy tits. Walked around and took things off with obscene expressions on their faces. You could get blown backstage for a couple bucks."

"Wonderful."

"Now they get these university dance students. Marvelous bodies."

She had turned again to face her audience, stared down at her undulating body. She cupped the small breasts, squeezed them, her face in an expression of stark agony. Slowly one hand began to move down the center of her body. She watched it in wonder.

"Question," Bollinger said. Already he had nearly drained his drink. "Why is the average place on Liberty Avenue maintained like a cesspool? I mean sperm on the floor. Piss. Syphilitic perverts standing around in the corners and drooling. You could keep it clean. You can keep anyplace clean. And the undesirables out."

"Sure," Matt said.

She had watched her hand, one finger in the lead, reach its target. She shuddered as it touched, began slowly to move her hips. The hand moved a couple inches further: the finger curled under and disappeared.

"I'll tell you why. Men, when they go there, want that kind of atmosphere. They think it's what they deserve. They don't like what they're doing. Don't like themselves when they're doing it."

"Huh." If the truth be told, Matt wasn't paying much attention.

"They want to wallow in their own shit. Poor chaps."

She seemed actually to be stimulating herself, caressing her breasts, rolling her hips. Her head was thrown back. The guitar solo, too, was moving up and down the scales in spasms, nervously.

"She gets a friend to make the tapes," Bollinger said. "She creates the dance, and *he* accompanies *her*." He drained his glass. "Beer okay?"

"Oh. Sure." Matt took a long swallow.

Her torso had begun to shudder, contract, in spasms; the muscles of her thighs were trembling. The veins at her neck stood out as if etched. The guitar purred like a jungle cat.

"The members here have a healthy attitude," Bollinger said. "None of this dirty-bookstore shit." He hardly seemed to be looking at the show. "Though I must say I found the stairway a little rank."

The guitar progressed to a single piercing note. The dancer's body froze, her face fixed in a scream. She stood that way a long moment, then shuddered terribly once. Her body grew limp. The lights snapped off.

"Bravo!" Bollinger shouted. He was the only one in the place who was clapping. "Bravo!" The solo handclaps echoed in the dark room. "Movie time," he said to Matt, rose slowly from his chair. "Need anything from the bar?"

"I'm fine," Matt said.

Bollinger shuffled away.

Just behind where the girl had been dancing—Matt hadn't noticed, but now he could see that the swirling lights had been projected—was a screen. Except for a low gleam from the bar, the room was in total darkness, and onto the screen, suddenly and blurrily, leaped a movie. It started with a raucous blaring soundtrack, like back in grade school when the teacher hadn't known how to run the projector. *Industry on Parade,* Matt was half expecting. The men in the room, though, were better-behaved than the kids back at school; they didn't shout in agony and hold their ears. For some reason—this too had sometimes happened back at school—the title came out backward. *Cream Rinse,* Matt managed to spell out.

The music from the soundtrack suddenly ceased, and with loud clattering footsteps—finally the projectionist figured things out, and turned it down—a young couple walked into a sparsely furnished living room. The walls were a sickly green. The furniture seemed to have been borrowed from a cut-rate motel. The couple was staring very pointedly at the ceiling light fixture. The woman, in particular, seemed to see in it all the vast mysteries of the universe.

"I don't know what happened," she said. "It suddenly went out."

"It's probably just the bulb," he said. "I brought one over." He held a bare light bulb in one hand.

He was a man of medium height, with a lot of wavy brown hair. His face was dark, scored with pockmarks, but seemed friendly, wearing all the time a small amused smile, as if he knew something no one else did. One of his front teeth was chipped.

"Do you have any tools?" the woman said.

He grinned lazily. "I got all I need."

"It's so high." The girl wrinkled her brow in concern. "And all I have is this funny ladder."

It *was* a peculiar ladder. It was built along the lines of a small stepladder, but was higher than that—roughly chest height—and wider, and its steps were padded.

"Why do you have that?" the man said.

"Oh, I use it for . . . things." She blushed slightly, lowering her face, then glanced up at him coyly.

She was rather more noticeable than the man. She wore high white boots, and tiny red shorts that in their day had been known as hot pants, and a blue shirt whose shirttails were knotted just under her breasts, exposing her belly. Her breasts seemed substantial, and swayed dangerously in her blouse as she moved, though she was a tall trim woman. Her large bottom filled the little shorts to the bursting point. She had long shimmering blond hair, obviously dyed, and her face wore a look of hurt sincerity, as if people were always kidding her about something. Her mouth was somewhat oversized, and moist, and pouting.

Bollinger came back with another drink, plopped into his seat. "Little Annie Fanny," he said.

"Oh! Don't hurt yourself!" the girl said, as the man started up the ladder.

He did seem to be taking it the hard way, backing up step by step. He also seemed to be having trouble getting the next line out, biting his lip, seeming to glance at somebody offstage. Finally he broke into a grin and spoke it.

"I hope my bulb fits into your socket," he said.

The girl was deadly serious. "We'll find a way to squeeze it in," she said.

The camera's view switched artistically to the top of the ladder. Down below, the girl's face showed deep concern, as if the man were scaling Mount Everest. The closest thing to mountains in that room, however, were her breasts, whose creamy white tops—like the snow-capped peaks of a mountain—showed clearly from that height. The camera switched to the man's face, which stared down hungrily. He bit his lip in confusion.

"Maybe you'd better steady me up here," he said.

"I will," she said.

She stepped up the ladder and gripped his buttocks, pressed her breasts to his thighs.

"Uh," the man said.

"He's got a bit of a wobbly foundation," Bollinger said.

Matt stared at the screen, the pulse at his throat throbbing.

The woman was pressing and rubbing her breasts against the man. They were bulging and squirting around like oversized water balloons. If he was able to change a light bulb under these conditions he was a mechanical genius.

"Is this all right?" the girl said.

"Perfect," the man said.

She laid her head against his fly, as if to listen. "There seems to be something moving around in here."

"Yes."

"Some small creature stirring to life."

She reached a hand to his zipper.

"Careful," Bollinger muttered.

Slowly, gingerly, she unzipped his fly. As she reached the bottom something enormous fell out.

"Oh my God," she said.

Now the audience knew why this man had been selected for his role, despite the pockmarked face and chipped tooth. Now they knew the reason for his small amused smile, his air of easy confidence.

"Oh my *God*," the girl said.

"Magnificent," Bollinger said.

Matt glanced at him out of the corner of his eye and, a little uneasily, moved away.

"You *did* bring everything you need," the girl said.

"Yeah." He was wearing a big dumb grin.

"But I'm not sure your bulb will fit into my socket." She spoke with a certain awe.

The man delivered his punch line with a perfect aplomb. "We'll find a way to squeeze it in."

Tentatively, as if sampling an exotic hors d'oeuvre, she took a little taste. "Mmm." She tried a little more.

"I guess you're supposed to imagine it's yours," Bollinger said. "My abilities to fantasize do have some limits."

Matt was made uncomfortable by Hugh's obvious fascination with this outsized penis.

"I sometimes wonder," Bollinger said, "if there's as much cocksucking going on as we're led to believe."

"I hadn't given it much thought," Matt said. What a time for Hugh to strike up a conversation.

"I mean the sexual revolution and all. Supposedly practices have changed. But you've got to wonder. Do women really enjoy that kind of thing?"

The woman on the screen certainly seemed to be enjoying herself, moaning and cooing, slurping noisily, her head bobbing up and down like a small float on a choppy sea. She looked like a child on a hot day who is worried that her popsicle will melt.

"I don't think they do," Bollinger said. "Or it wouldn't be the feature attraction in so many of these movies. Men wouldn't want to see it so much. I think about such things a lot."

Apparently so.

"For gay men, of course, it's the central act."

51

"I wouldn't know," Matt said, loudly and pointedly.

In the seat in front of them, a man turned angrily around. "Would you two please shut up?"

"What's the matter?" Bollinger said. "Can't concentrate?"

"Shut up or get out of here," the man said.

"Why don't you just move?" Matt said. "There are plenty of seats."

"He can't get up," Bollinger said.

"I came here to watch a movie," the man said, "not listen to your stupid conversation."

"Take your raincoat out of your lap and move," Bollinger said. He laughed, in what was meant to be a falsetto giggle, but it came out more like a coughing fit.

"You son of a bitch." The man began to rise.

"Watch out, Matt. He seems to have some sort of blunt heavy object on his person."

Matt had leaned forward, but the man was only changing his seat, muttering to himself. He was, indeed, holding a raincoat carefully in front of himself.

"These guys need silence," Bollinger said. "Can't let the real world intrude. By the end of this movie there won't be a dry fly in the house."

Things on the screen had progressed rapidly. The girl had removed what little she had on—hadn't taken a minute— and had also, miraculously, lost her fear of the ladder; she sat on a high rung while the man got down and also stripped. She leaned back and smiled, and he buried his face between her legs. A closeup ensued, which reminded Matt of a trip he had once taken through the Luray Caverns. There was even a small pink stalactite.

"Gynecologists never come to these movies," Bollinger said. "Too much like the office."

The ladder was a useful prop. The girl's fears proved to be unfounded—apparently it was bolted to the floor—and anyway she must have been lying about them, because she proceeded to clamber athletically all over it. The whole thing was more like a gymnastics exhibition than a sexual act. The girl continued her squealing, moaning, cooing—now and then she let out a blood-curdling scream—while the man was mostly silent, gritting his teeth in some excruciating position while she pummeled away at him. His penis, rather than becoming more involved, was becoming less so, swaying around at something below half staff. It kept folding up like an accordion when he inserted it, then flopping lifelessly out. The girl looked down worriedly.

"He's losing it, poor fellow," Bollinger said.

"I can't really blame him. It's taking a terrific beating."

"This isn't a joking matter. The man's livelihood's at stake."

Suddenly there was a cut to a new scene, the girl pounding away at the penis with her hand, roughly at eye level. Her face shone with anticipation. It was like in cartoons where the rifle doesn't go off so the guy picks it up to look down the barrel. Sure enough, the gun picks that moment to go off.

There was a terrific gushing.

"That I don't get," Matt said. "Is that supposed to turn somebody on?"

"We hate them and we love them," Bollinger said. "We're never sure which."

The girl, of course, was purring warmly, smiling at the camera, licking her chops. The whole thing had made quite a mess. She gave a little wink.

The film snapped off. Again Bollinger was the only one to applaud. A couple men down front had turned to look at him.

"What happens now?" Matt said.

"A brief interlude." The guitar music had started again. "Then some more dancing. She has an act with a snake. You wouldn't believe where that thing crawls."

"So we have some time to talk."

"All the time in the world. I'm going to freshen this drink." Hugh shoved himself out of his seat. Freshen was hardly the word. The glass was empty. "How's your beer?"

"I'm fine." He had forgotten all about it.

"I'll be right with you."

Bollinger stumbled toward the bar. Some of the men in the room had scattered, flushed like a covey of quail, when the lights came on; others were gathered in groups and talking, as if they were just settling down to a poker game. A few had walked to the bar.

Surprising himself, Matt was rather taken with the place. His experience with nude dancers and the dirty movie—that distinguished art form—was rather limited. At college he and his friends had gone to see strippers a few times, middle-aged women who came out mostly nude and shook things around for

53

a while; the highlight of the performance was when one particularly daring exotic briefly lifted her g-string at the end. She might as well have showed the crowd her armpit. The dirty movie was primitive in those days, either documentaries of nudist camps, where all the women seemed to have acquired enormous bottoms along with their liberal attitudes, or pornographic adventures in which the girls never showed more than their breasts and in which couples simulated intercourse, moaning and thrashing around while wearing their underpants. Talk about a dry fuck.

He had seen the more striking recent innovations—couples who really got laid, and who performed a wide variety of other acts—only a few times. They were all around, of course, but he no longer had the guys from the dorm to go with. You never felt quite right going by yourself.

Something in pornography, Matt had to admit, struck a responsive chord in him. Not dirty pictures, unless they suggested some drama, and not dirty books: they were too badly written to be convincing. But some of the old movies, if they had a little plot, even a fair number of contemporary commercial novels. If they included one characteristic scene.

In his erotic daydreams—that continuous erotic daydream that had started far back in his childhood—Matt never pictured himself as a suave sophisticated talker who easily seduced women. He had been an awkward, gawky boy; such a dream was too far from reality. What he imagined instead was that a woman noticed him—some elegantly beautiful friend of the family, or a cheerleader from high school, or a luscious stranger on the street—and understood, saw that he was not a big blustering oaf but a gentle boy who wanted desperately to approach her but couldn't: she saw what he wanted, and she took the initiative, she did the talking he couldn't do.

Whether it was just coincidence, or whether many men felt as he did, that scene was repeated endlessly in pornography. Not of aggressive women, exactly, but women who were extremely available. Actively compliant. He had just seen a rough version of it again.

It was true that pornography got boring after a while—how many times did you want to see a penis plunge into a vagina? or anywhere else, for that matter—but for a few minutes it was astounding, a beautiful woman who did it all, enjoyed it all, who never said a man was doing it wrong, or doing something she didn't like, or doing something perverted. There were no clumsy men, such movies said, only frigid women. Such a message did not get boring right away.

They weren't sexual acts that men were watching. They were dreams. Myths. The woman who saw what you wanted, did the talking you couldn't do. The beautiful woman who did it all.

From the bar, Matt suddenly noticed, Hugh was gesturing to him—he might have been gesturing for some time—and he walked over. The bartender stepped away to serve another customer.

"There's a place next door that has some girls," Bollinger said. "My friend at the bar tells me one of my great favorites is working today. I'd like you to meet her."

"Hugh. This is the time we were supposed to talk."

"We've got all day to talk."

"But there's an intermission now. It's quiet in here. A perfect time."

"There are lots of perfect times." Hugh had taken Matt's arm, was steering him away.

They were walking toward the door they had come in, but instead of going out pushed their way through a door beside it, into a room that was also cool and dark and—after the door had shut behind them—silent. The walls were black, with a few psychedelic posters hanging around. The heavy shag carpet was scarlet. At first Matt thought they were alone in the room, then he noticed, on the low couch beside them, a woman sitting. She stood.

"Professor Bollinger," she said.

"Good day," he said.

"Woman" may have been a slight exaggeration. She was quite short, on the chunky side, and as she stepped closer Matt saw that she had the plain face of a girl, brown hair hanging down in bangs over the blackheads on her forehead. She had a large fleshy nose, still had a pimple or two, and seemed a little nervous, like a wallflower who has finally been asked to dance. She was wearing a transparent black negligee—the color co-ordination in this place was a trifle monotonous—under which her heavy breasts, and brown nipples, were plainly apparent.

"Is Angel here?" Bollinger said.

"She's with a customer."

"How long?"

"Maybe another ten minutes."

"That's not bad. You can take my friend back."

"Look, Hugh . . . "

"Matt. You've got to meet Angel. All my friends do, sooner or later. It's an experience you don't want to miss. The party's on me."

"You'll come with Celeste, won't you?" The woman had taken his arm, and blatantly brushed it with one breast. Matt could feel the large nipple.

"Heavenly music, Matt."

Matt swayed. The nipple brushing him had sent a little tingle up his arm, and he had never, anyway, been able to refuse the wallflower for a lady's choice. There was something slightly desperate in the damp hands that grasped him.

"I guess I can spare a few minutes," he said.

After all, the woman had approached him. He didn't have to talk. She seemed to know what she was doing.

III

Lying on the massage table—it had a mattress, was more like a hefty double bed—Matt stared at the ceiling of the little room and shivered. He definitely thought the air conditioning was on too high. "Take off your clothes and lie on the table," the girl had said, and that was easy for her to say; she didn't have to lie around in the cold for ten minutes waiting for something to happen. The place smelled of baby powder, baby oil. It reminded him vaguely of the old days with Jonathan. All it needed was the smell of a dirty diaper. It reminded him also of long waits on the doctor's cold examining table while the doctor was probably off someplace grabbing his nurse's ass. You wondered what kind of torturous examination he had up his sleeve that day.

He wished he hadn't come. It had all happened quickly, of course—from his meeting with Droge to his trip to Bollinger's club and now to the little room that smelled like a baby's nursery—but with a few minutes to think about it he wished he had resisted somewhere along the line. He wasn't supposed to be lying around with his clothes off. He was supposed to be out pounding the pavements, doing his work, looking for witnesses to Bunter Lawson's accident.

He stared at himself in the long mirror beside him, his pale naked body covered with goosebumps, his face tense, and rather sad.

The door of the room quickly opened and closed; a woman was standing inside. In Matt's first glimpse of her—he could still see the face for a while afterward, as when a light has gone out and you can still see the glow—she wore a deeply serious expression, as if pondering some problem. With one swift motion she peeled off the short nightie she was wearing: she was naked, and smiling.

"I'm Angel," she said.

Matt had expected something like the girl who had brought him in, the kind of sullen girl with droopy tits whom everyone had taken out in high school because she let you feel her up. She let you, but she didn't like it, frowned and grimaced the whole time. This was no high school girl, no girl at all; she was a woman, and she was spectacular. Her breasts were full underneath and had the little upturn he had only seen in men's magazines; she had pale-pink nipples. Her tummy was smooth and slender, with a shallow round navel. Her hips widened in a classic curve; her bottom was large and round, but taut. Her hair was long, hung straight over her shoulders; between her legs it was a shade darker, a dark gold. Her smile was not in the least bit lewd, but bright, and friendly, and frank. She might have been stepping to the table for a firm brisk handshake, but in that case would have brushed Matt's penis, which, at the sight of her, had given a little jump.

"Hello," Matt said.

She traced a line down his chest with her index finger. "You're . . . "

"Matt."

"Ah. Matt. Been here before?"

"No."

She was caressing his chest with her fingertips, staring at it as if it had an interesting configuration.

"I think I'll have you turn over first. I like to start on the other side."

Matt flopped over reluctantly. He could no longer see her as well, though her slender flawless back and shapely bottom showed clearly in the mirror.

"Mmm," she said. "You have a nice body to work on."

You're not so bad yourself, babe.

The only rubdown Matt had seen was of fighters in the movies, where they were covered with some kind of grease and trainers dug their fingers into the flesh as if it were wet clay, slapped it loudly, gave a series of rapid karate chops along the spine, like Ricky Ricardo playing a conga drum. He had also once read an article about what was known as legitimate massage, a deep probing in which a muscular masseur rearranged your spine, put several internal organs back into place, and in general handled your body like a piece of wet spaghetti. At the end of this massage you were tied to one end of a shower room and blown away with a fire hose.

Angel's hands were warm, and soft. From the moment she stepped to the table a hand had rested on him somewhere, his chest, his arm, his back. Now she climbed up beside him, her legs gathered under her, a warm flank pressed against him. She sprinkled his body with powder. Her hands began to move, softly, smoothly, going over his whole body to rub the powder in. She started on his back, working the big muscles, down one side and up the other, rubbing just firmly at first, then gradually starting to probe, dig in. Matt felt himself relax. Her thumbs dug slowly up his spinal cord, inch by inch, soothing the nerves. She worked the big muscles again, gripping them hard. She placed her palms on the small of his back, leaned until there was a little crack. She massaged his shoulders, the heavy muscles of his arms, the soft muscles at the side of his neck, the column of the neck itself. His whole torso was growing limp. Her fingers dug into his scalp, probed the soft places at the base of his skull. Her fingertips began to drift, barely touching, tracing light designs on the muscles she had handled roughly. Matt could barely feel them. One hand strayed, drifted away from his back in the direction of his thighs.

"You're a friend of Hugh's," she said.

"Yes."

"The professor, we call him here."

"Oh?" Matt laughed.

"He's very learned. Don't you think?"

"I don't know." Bollinger had certainly put it over on these women.

"A lifelong student of Eros. He says."

"That much I believe." Who wasn't?

"And he's a teacher. A professor."

"I guess you could call him that."

"We do. Professor Bollinger, we all call him."

She had moved down slightly on the table. Her hands on his legs were doing about what they had done on his back, rubbing at first just firmly, then beginning to dig, the backs of his calves, his thighs, his bottom. Especially sensitive were the insides of his thighs, up toward the top. As if by accident, but they never missed, her hands kept brushing between his legs. Now one began to touch more deliberately, gentle fingernails that tickled down as far as they could go (Matt lifted himself off the mattress slightly, helping) then traveled back up. A finger probed the cleft. Matt groaned.

"That's good?" she said. "Or not?"

"Good," he said.

She started again.

"Hugh's a very generous man," she said.

"Oh?"

"Brings his friends in here. Treats them."

"So I'm not the first."

"No. Not by a long shot."

Her hand between his legs had continued. He had raised himself with his knees, so she could caress his balls, warmly grip them, clutch his cock. Her body had come to rest alongside his, press up against it. He felt one breast touching his back, the warmth of her loins against his thigh.

"I think you're ready to turn," she said.

Matt struggled around toward her. She had let go of him and moved away, but only a little, now pressed up against him and clutched again. Her mouth was inches from his. He leaned to kiss it. She turned away.

"I don't kiss," she said.

"Why not?"

"I just don't. Don't kiss. Don't ask for the one thing you can't have, when there's so much you can."

"Like what?"

She brushed one of her nipples. "Kiss here."

He buried his face between her breasts, inhaled the scent of her body. He took one soft nipple into his mouth, sucked it gently. It was sweet. Angel was caressing his own nipples, roughly, digging in with a fingernail. He touched a hand between her thighs. She clutched his head, ran her fingers through his hair. After a while he looked up.

"You don't get excited," he said.

"You wouldn't want me to get excited."

"I would."

"I wouldn't do as good a job. Besides. If I got excited with every customer, they'd carry me out of here at the end of the day."

"But what a day."

She laughed, pushed him onto his back. "I think you're about ready to finish."

"What do we do?"

"It's not what we do. It's what I do. You just lie there."

She had moved around on the bed until she was lying in the opposite direction, her feet up toward his head. She leaned on one elbow, which was resting between his legs. She reached across the bed for a bottle of oil. Her breast, as she did, brushed his cock.

"You don't do anything else?" he said.

"Such as." She had poured oil into one hand, eyed him coyly.

"Screw."

"Heavens. That would make me a prostitute." She was smiling. "You don't take me for a prostitute?"

"I didn't mean it that way."

She had anointed both hands with the oil, began gently to rub it onto his cock.

"I think screwing is overrated," she said.

"Really?" Matt groaned at a quick stroke of her hand.

"Men are obsessed with it. As if it's the only thing worth doing. But lots of things are sexual. Far more than we ever think. There's no one sexual act."

"No."

"Your whole body, at the moment, is a sexual object. I could touch you anywhere."

"Yes."

"Of course, the place I'm touching is the most convenient."

Since she had begun touching his cock, she had been staring at it with rapt attention, a little smile. Only occasionally did she look up at him. She was stroking, but at an agonizing rate, her hand inching up and nearly moving off, then slowly descending again. His cock gave rapid little throbs at every stroke. She seemed to smile at this. Now and then she reached up and flicked the tip with her thumb. Her left hand was tickling between his legs with her fingernails.

"Men are so intent on performing a task," she said. "That they forget to feel. They need to learn to relax. Concentrate." The word was a gentle command.

Matt's chest was full, his whole body flushed. There was a hollow in his throat that almost tickled. He felt pinned to the bed, as if his cock were a stake she was slowly driving in. He had never before had such an erection. It felt a foot long, as big around as a bologna sausage.

"You're ready," she said.

"Not yet."

"Don't fight it. It's time."

She looked into his eyes, and suddenly abandoned the slow strokes, began a deliberate heavy pounding. The feeling intensified. The rhythm seemed menacing, inevitable.

"It's wonderful," he said.

"'Feel it," she said.

"I don't want it to end."

"That's the best part."

"Not yet."

"Yes."

With her left hand she dug a fingernail just beneath his balls. He shouted, felt his legs jackknife. Blood rushed from his head as if he would swoon. There was a hoarse gasping at his chest. A spurt of hot semen shot onto his belly. He convulsed on the table like a man in pain.

Angel's hand had gripped him tightly, now gradually relaxed. He felt his legs slowly descending. "Relax," she said. "Feel it relax." She had cupped his balls as if to comfort them. She continued stroking even as his penis softened. His eyes were closed. He felt himself sinking into the mattress. He had almost dozed off when he noticed she wasn't there.

He opened his eyes. She was standing beside the bed, rubbing her hands with a towel. "Still with us?" she said.

"Just barely."

"You'll recover eventually. They always do." She finished with the towel. "There's a shower down the hall, when you're ready."

She pulled the black nightie back on.

"You're not going?" he said.

"I have to. Wish I didn't."

"Stay and talk a while."

"Maybe another time. Today I've got to run."

"It was wonderful. Magnificent."

"I want to see you in here again real soon." She smiled. "Lover."

She tossed him a clean towel, gave a little wave. The room gave a shudder, as it had before, when the door opened and closed. As quickly as she had come in—say, fifteen minutes before—she was gone.

IV

Finally, late in the afternoon, it had rained, long and hard, washed the low gray clouds out of the sky. The dining room, where Matt liked to sit in the evening with a beer, was a dark room anyway, and as he looked out the window to their little backyard, the foliage was heavy, dripping with water; the evening seemed dim, and green, and cool. From the kitchen—it was Laurel's night to cook—came the sound of pork chops frying; he could hear her banging around to wash the potatoes. From the living room, behind him, came the blare of the television; Jonathan was finishing up his allotted television time, watching a show about a typical American family who had somehow become stranded on another planet, where they kept running into western heroes, famous buccaneers, man-eating plants, and gory monsters. Matt sat with his beer—he had bought the kind of heavy rounded glass that was used in the best old-time bars—and puffed on his pipe, staring out at the yard.

After a while he walked out to their little kitchen, where the floor sagged with his steps, the wall above the stove was grimy from years of frying. The phone was out there, on the opposite wall.

"I think I'll try Wolf again," he said.

Peeling apples at the stove, Laurel nodded.

Matt felt an odd mix of emotions. On the one hand, there was nothing like a spine-snapping orgasm to lift his spirits; it had left him feeling cheerful all afternoon. What incredible luck! to wander into such a situation and encounter, almost literally, the woman of his dreams. On the other hand, he had lost track of Bollinger completely, came out of that little room to find only Celeste sitting there, no help whatsoever; she didn't know whether Hugh had stayed or gone. He had looked

Hugh up in the phone book, spent the afternoon trying to call him, even drove by his house to see if he was there, but had no luck. He felt sheepish calling Wolf with nothing definite to report, but thought he'd better.

"Yo." Wolf had answered the phone.

"Wolf. Where you been all afternoon? I tried to call."

"I spent the afternoon in the parking lot of the Howard Johnson's Motor Lodge. Divorce case. The most exciting thing I saw was when they came out for an ice cream cone. But I am now a witness to a suspicious circumstance. A couple spent four hours of an afternoon in a closed motel room. And when they finally came out they exchanged a lingering kiss. That's the word I'm using. Lingering."

"Good word."

"How'd it go with you?"

"I talked with Droge. I don't think he'll be much help."

"Goofy-looking guy."

"He also didn't see much. I mean he says he saw it all. But when you get right down to it he's shaky on the details."

"Wonderful."

"But I found another guy. Who I used to know a little. Hugh Bollinger."

"And he saw it."

"I think he did."

There was a prolonged silence on the other end of the line. "You forgot to ask?"

"He saw the accident. We didn't get down to details. But I'm getting back in touch with him. And he'll look a lot better on the witness stand. Downright respectable. If we can keep him sober."

"Jesus Christ."

"He's the best I can do so far. That's not the easiest place to look for a witness."

"I know, I know. Anything's better than Droge. But you got to get on it. Talk to this guy as soon as you can. If we got nobody, we got to know that."

"Okay."

"Give me a call when you have something."

Matt hung up, heaved a long sigh. It could have gone worse.

There had been the problem, earlier, of what to tell Laurel about his day. He didn't want to make it sound as if he hadn't done anything; on the other hand, he didn't think he'd better go into absolutely everything he had done, or that had been done to him. He knew she'd be fascinated by some of it. He tried to make the part with Bollinger sound a little less sleazy: they had traveled to an exclusive men's club where, for the delectation of the members, certain highly erotic acts were featured. She had been interested in all he had told her about the dancer, somewhat less interested by the details of the movie ("I don't want to hear about your obsession with the size of a man's penis." "I'm not obsessed with it. I'm telling you what happened in the movie." "All men are obsessed with it. There's nothing stupider"), and utterly disgusted by what happened at the end of the movie. "No woman should put up with that. No matter how much she's being paid." Matt had left out any account of the end of the morning. He made it sound as if Bollinger had had to leave suddenly and they'd parted ways.

She was slicing up apples to cook with the pork chops when he hung up the phone.

"Does he think this sounds promising?"

"Maybe. Anyway, he wants to hear what Bollinger has to say."

"I'm not sure he'll be so reliable a witness as you make him sound."

Ever since he had come home that day—in fact, whenever in the past month he had brought up the subject of his work—she had taken the same attitude: a certain weariness came into her voice, and her face tensed, almost winced, as she looked at him. She watched him as he talked as if he were marginally insane, kept her mouth clamped tight as if biting off the words she would like to say. He couldn't tell her the simplest details of his day without facing this attitude.

Suddenly—perhaps because he was at a point where he was least sure about his job, was going through incredible contortions to put a good face on it—he had had enough.

"Laurel." He sat down at the little table where they kept the toaster and where, most mornings, they ate breakfast. "I don't appreciate your attitude toward my work."

"Oh." She turned an utterly blank face toward him. "What is my attitude?"

"You act like it's something an idiot would do."

Her whole body, as she stood at the stove with the paring knife, was taut. She looked as if she wanted to launch into a passionate speech, say all the things she had never said, wave the knife around, perhaps use it to carve up his face a little and then plunge it into his midsection. She seemed to be holding all those possibilities back. She spoke carefully, her face only twitching slightly.

"You're sure you're not projecting that," she said.

"I *knew* you'd say that." He slammed his fist on the kitchen table. "You always say that. You're always trying to put it back on me."

"Arguing again!" Jonathan shouted from the living room. He did not like it when his parents argued, especially when one of his favorite shows was on, and when they did he shouted at them louder than they were shouting at each other.

He had made a point, though. They were only starting once again an argument they had had many times before.

"You always put it back on me!" Matt shouted.

Laurel was facing away from Matt, seeing him just from the corner of her eye, her mouth tight and trembling, as if she were selecting the proper plan of attack.

"All right," she said. "Let's say I am the way you're saying. That is the way I feel. Should that matter to you?"

"Of course it should. My own wife."

"Would you rather I'd pretend to feel another way?"

"I'd rather my wife would support me in what I'm trying to do."

Those words, which so simply expressed a reasonable request, which in fact expressed what—in her own way—she was trying to do, touched Laurel. She put the knife down, turned her body to face him.

"Matt. I do support you." (The unfortunate double entendre made Matt flinch.) "I support you in what you're trying to do. To find some work that will be important for you. I can't always agree with you about what that is."

"You haven't approved of a thing I've done since we left school."

"That's not true."

"It is true. It is. First it was you and your counselor friends, sitting around looking like you were going to die every time I mentioned something I'd done. As if I spent all my time practicing police brutality."

"Don't put it off on my friends."

"But that's where it started. Where you started off on this

stuff. As if I should spend the whole day sitting around eating yogurt and talking about my sex life, like all of you did."

"Now you're attacking my work. This isn't necessary."

"Then we moved here because you found a job, that was just ducky for you, and when I scraped around and finally found a way to make a few bucks you didn't like that either, couldn't stop talking about how crummy the school was, how stupid all the teachers were."

The things he was saying were true enough, but he made it sound as if she were tearing him down, when really she was just trying to keep him from sinking into something that wasn't right for him.

"I felt terrible, Matt. I felt this horrible guilt. That I had found just the job I wanted, and you were having to work at that scummy place."

"Don't feel sorry for me. Don't pity me. That's the worst thing there is. The most condescending thing."

"I know, I know. I'm sorry."

"I took the job. I did what I could with it. I didn't complain. But now when I finally get away from it, I get something close to what I really want, you don't like that either."

Couldn't Matt see the long downward arc, from a police job in a college community to a third-rate private school to a sleazy private detective agency run by one man? Anyone could see he was accepting scraps, reaching for less and less.

"Matt. I have no objection to police work."

"You do. You always have. You can't go back on that now."

"It isn't necessarily what I'd choose for my husband to do. But if that's what he wants—I just don't like to see you putting up with things. Settling for less than what you are."

"I have to live in the world. I have to settle for what there is."

Laurel's face had quietly calmed, as if she had come to a decision.

"I saw that office, Matt."

Matt reddened. "What." He spoke the word dumbly, not like a question.

"I went down to the Highland Building and saw that office. Where Wolf has his detective agency."

Matt looked away, annoyed and embarrassed. "What'd you do that for?"

"It's pitiful, Matt. It's pitiful. The building's falling down all around it. There are two years of cigarette butts in the hallway. Dust and dirt all around. They don't bother to change the bulbs in the light fixtures."

"Wolf just keeps that office as a convenience. He doesn't really use it. He's hardly ever in there. And he's that kind of man. Uses makeshift things." Matt had to smile, thinking of that incredible car.

"Now you're on this supposed case. With a man you actually know, from that other creepy place. Chasing through dirty-book stores after a worn-out alcoholic."

"Laurel. This case isn't what I'm doing. God. This case is not what I'm doing."

"A man is doing what he's doing, Matt."

"It's just a crazy thing that happened to come up. We've just got to get it out of the way. We probably have it out of the way."

"I can see it being one thing like this after another. Checking up on somebody's husband. Looking for a homeless kid. Any poor lost soul who can scrape up a few bucks can ask you to do anything he wants."

"Things won't always be like this. You've got to believe me. Wolf looks like a funny old guy, but he's one of the sharpest men in the business. In the city, anywhere."

Laurel didn't believe him. He could tell to look at her that she didn't believe him.

"I wish you were doing something else," she said.

"God!" He jumped from his chair, slammed the heel of his fist against the wall. "I wish I were doing something else. I wish I were doing it somewhere else. Anywhere but here."

"You'll crack the plaster!" Jonathan shouted from the living room.

Laurel sat limply, her hands in her lap, her eyes sad and defeated.

"I wanted to be a ballplayer!" Matt shouted. He was storming around the little kitchen, in the small space between the stove, table, refrigerator, and pantry. He was a big man, who looked as if he could wreck the place with a few quick swipes. "I was a ballplayer. A damn good one. My fastball could break a brick wall. My arm went dead."

"You could go on in baseball somehow. Coach."

"I just did coach. At that dumb fucking little school. How'd you like it when I did that?"

"I don't mean coach at the worst hole in the city."

"You have to work at the places that are there."

"There are other places."

"I didn't want to coach. I wanted to play. So I went into police work. Because my old man was a cop. I grew up with that all around me. I was proud of him. I loved him."

"It was a good thing." There were tears in Laurel's eyes, tears of frustration. They had been over it so many times, this litany of failed hopes. "It was a good thing to do."

"Then we had to move. I agreed we had to move. I wanted you to find a good job. But I couldn't be a cop here."

"You can be a cop here. The jobs have to open up eventually. If you can just wait."

"I have to live in the meantime."

"We have my salary. My parents can help us out."

"I mean I have to live." As hard as he had pounded the table, he hit his own chest, with his fist. "I have to live with me. As a man."

Laurel stared through her tears at this passionate angry man who was making almost no sense.

"I have to have something to do!" Matt shouted.

Jonathan ran into the kitchen, his face rapt with fury. "I can't hear my show."

"Take your fucking show and shove it up your ass."

It wasn't really his show he was worried about, but his parents; he burst into tears and ran out of the room.

"There are things I'd like to do," Matt shouted. "There are things I'd like to do. I can't do them." He was staring into the dark abyss—Laurel knew it well—of nothing worthwhile in his life to do. "I have to take what I can get. I have to do what there is."

He bolted out of the house, slamming the back door behind him.

Laurel hurried to the living room to see about Jonathan.

Matt was wearing his cloth bedroom slippers, and the grass in the backyard was long, and very wet (he kept meaning to mow; somehow he got less done when he was around the house a lot than when he had worked full-time). His slippers immediately got soaked. He walked around the perimeter of the yard a couple of times as if he were taking laps. Little flecks of drizzle had started falling out of the sky, prelude to another shower. In his anger he grabbed a branch of the cherry tree and started to shake it; cherries started plopping all around him. and so did a shower of rain from the leaves, wetting his hair and soaking his shirt. He noticed the elderly woman next door watching him through the venetian blind of her kitchen window. It was all he could do to keep from giving her the finger. He started his laps of the yard again, soaking wet. He felt like an utter fool and didn't care. After a while, in the evening breeze, he actually started to feel a chill. He walked around the side of the house and in the front door.

Jonathan and his mother were sitting together in one of the chairs, Jonathan still sniffing a little.

"Is it raining again?" Laurel said.

"Only on me," Matt said.

Her eyes were weary. "You look terrible," she said.

"I'm sorry, Jonathan," Matt said. "I was just mad."

"It's wasn't a nice thing to say."

"I know. I'm sorry."

"It makes no sense, anyway."

"I know." Matt started upstairs to change his clothes.

Jonathan spoke to his father's back. "I missed the end of my show."

Laurel had gone to some trouble with the dinner, pork chops lightly fried and then steamed, stewed apples, mashed potatoes, and green beans, but for Matt the food had almost no taste: he chewed it listlessly, running everything together. His glass of light white wine might as well have been Kool-Aid. Afterward he played a game of checkers with Jonathan, saw that he got a bath, read to him from a comic book.

"I'm glad you're a detective," Jonathan said while he soaped himself in the tub. "That's what I want you to be."

Matt leaned down and ruffled his hair.

Downstairs he and Laurel read for a while, Matt leafing aimlessly through one magazine after another. He couldn't find anything he liked; the rattling of the pages got to be almost continuous. Finally Laurel got up, came over and sat on the arm of his chair. "I'm sorry," she said. "The whole thing really isn't any of my business." He was too tired to answer, didn't want to get into all that again, but if he had he would have said she had been right, he had spent his adult life going from one pitiful job to another and was ashamed of all of them. (They should have changed sides and argued those positions for a while.) They walked upstairs to make love, but their hearts weren't in it; their bodies, as they lay together, felt strange in one another's arms. Matt's orgasm was mild, and came, he felt, too soon. Laurel's seemed to take forever, so that his hand almost cramped up as he touched her; when she finally finished she gave one loud shout as if in anger. Afterward they lay awake, not talking, both staring at the ceiling. Laurel was thinking, if the truth be known, of her young hungry ardent lover, who adored her spirit and fed on her body as if it nourished him. Matt, on the other hand, was thinking of that mysterious woman who gave exquisite pleasure, who asked nothing more of him than to give him pleasure and who disappeared as quickly as she had arrived.

Chapter Four

The door didn't close right, was the problem—you couldn't lock it—so you never knew if somebody was home or not. The place was dim, not a light on, but she liked to do without lights; she was a little nutty about it in fact. "Laurel?" She might be upstairs, in the front room, where she liked to sew. "Laurel?" Matt didn't hear anything, no sounds from the old floorboards. That settled it. You couldn't even shift your weight in that place without setting off a series of cracks that sounded like an exchange of gunfire.

He walked through the dark musty rooms back to the kitchen, took a bottle of beer from the refrigerator and collapsed into a chair. After a couple long swallows from the beer he got up and opened the back door, so at least a little breeze came in, and some sunlight. The yellow tulips in the backyard had been rejuvenated by the rain the day before, stood tall and bright in the afternoon sun.

It had been one of those days when he ran around for hours and got next to nothing done, like Christmas shopping for a seven-year-old, or searching through a government building for the proper tax form. He had a vague feeling—he was trying at the moment to suppress it—that every day was like that for a private investigator.

The morning had started with the exquisitely painful ordeal of getting Jonathan off to day camp (the boy spent ten minutes deciding on things for his knapsack, then had to go back to get a book for quiet time; two blocks from the house he realized he had forgotten his bathing suit, and when they finally pulled up to camp he informed Matt he needed eighty-five cents. Exact change, please). From camp Matt went straight to Bollinger's house, but either Hugh was out making some pornographic purchase or he was too hung over to get to the door. Matt headed for Liberty Avenue to do the work he should have done the day before. Otto Droge was off (thank God), but he did talk to the nude chick (that was the only way she'd consent to an interview, if he bought the tokens and went whole hog, so he had to stand there watching her scratch—crabs, probably—long enough to find out she hadn't seen a thing; at the end of the time she'd said, "Ain't you gonna show me what you got?"). He talked to clerks, shopkeepers, bartenders, parking-lot attendants, ticket sellers at movie theaters, the manager of a massage parlor. Between conversations he kept trying Bollinger from a pay phone. Nearly everyone he spoke to reacted the same way; they brightened, grew immediately serious, said of course they had seen the accident and they wanted to talk about it, but what they had really seen was the aftermath, the blood and broken glass and the dent in the hood ("Them bugs are made outta tin"). Almost no one had been outside when the accident actually happened, and no one who had could accurately describe it.

At one forty-five, footsore, sweating, Matt was standing in a battered phone booth whose door had been torn off. Bollinger answered on the first ring.

"Matt. I've been trying to call you."

"No kidding." One of life's little ironies.

"How was your session with Angel?"

"Fine." Where he stood, in fact, was just half a block from Hugh's club, and he could see the blackened second-story window behind which Angel worked.

"Only fine?" Matt could hear the leer in his voice.

"It was great. Super." I'm deeply grateful for all you've done for me, you pervert. "Listen, Hugh. We've got to get together about this accident."

"That's why I was calling. What about tonight?"

"Great."

"I've got a few friends coming over."

Not so great.

"No, Hugh. I don't want to do this around other people. We really need to talk."

"That's what I meant. You could come early. We'd have some time alone."

"I don't want it to be mixed up with a party. I don't want to have a time limit."

"I'm showing a special movie. Something along the lines of

what we saw yesterday. But far far better. A world premier."

Maybe the stars would be there. "Even so, Hugh."

"And Angel's coming."

"Angel?" Matt felt a little catch in his throat.

"She's really rather taken with you. I was hoping she'd come anyway. But she was delighted to hear you'd be there."

Matt felt an odd ache in his throat, a reluctant yearning. He was like the guy who walks the wrong way out of his diet club and catches the scent of a sausage pizza, the reformed alcoholic who with the first taste realizes he has mistakenly taken the punch with gin.

"I'd like to see her," he said. "It isn't that I don't want to see her. I'd just rather not get it mixed up with this other thing."

"You make life so complicated." Hugh should talk. He never did one thing but that he brought three others with it. "Come at eight. We'll have plenty of time. I'll give you a vivid description of the accident, then you can watch the movie, chat with Angel, anything you want."

"We've got to do the work first."

"We'll do the work. I swear to God we'll do the work." He spoke with the deep sincerity of the lifelong alcoholic. They had that way of insisting. "I'll see you at eight."

The phone crashed down. He was already late for an appointment with a bottle of vodka.

Matt had, however, taken that opportunity to leave Liberty Avenue. He had run like a thief. There didn't seem to be any reason to hang around. His interview with Bollinger sounded more promising than anything he was finding there.

Now he sat and stared out at the tulips, took a long pull at the beer. He felt a little funny around the stomach. Maybe a sandwich would help. He knew food wasn't really what he needed, that what he was feeling was actually just nerves after a hard day, but he rummaged around in the refrigerator anyway, came out with some chipped ham, mayonnaise, fresh garden tomatoes, pickles; while he was in there he grabbed a few things from the crisper drawer. He stepped to the table to get some bread—Laurel always kept a fresh loaf in the bread box there, homemade whole wheat—and found a box of Triscuits, stuffed a couple into his mouth. God. He was starved.

It wasn't pure lust that drew him to Angel (though in the absence of another word that would do pretty well) but something more like a yearning for excitement, a desire to lose himself, a need to escape the little worries that plagued him day by day. He wanted something that would snatch him up for a wild ride, and all his life he had found that in the lure of the forbidden. The keyhole to the bathroom where his sister was in the tub, her big breasts soapy and bobbing at water level; the dark recesses of the garage where a neighborhood girl let him kiss her and touch down into her pants; the excitement he still got, always, when he lowered his head into the musky warmth between a woman's legs. The pounding heart, hollow throat, jittery stomach: you are not supposed to be here. That was why men really liked the shops on Liberty Avenue, why the movies had to keep getting more and more extreme, why even the seediness was an attraction (Hugh was all wrong about that) and why there was something fundamentally wrong about a clean, well-appointed adult club. It wasn't an improvement to make the place respectable. That missed the whole point.

My God, he was getting as bad as Bollinger. Our foremost theoretician of the dirty book. He'd better concentrate on his sandwich.

The proof of the pudding was in his excitement; you could measure it, so to speak, in inches. In those few minutes with Angel he had had an incredible erection, that stood on his loins like a disembodied object; she took it coyly in her hand and he stared at it in amazement. If he had put it inside a woman he would have gone off like a grenade and blown her to pieces; he was surprised that the orgasm he did have, with Angel pumping it like some primitive weapon, hadn't knocked down the wall behind him.

With Laurel the last few times he had felt just the opposite; he looked down before slipping it in (anybody got a magnifying glass?) and wondered if he shouldn't build a few splints around it. His orgasm wasn't like a primitive force that jolted from his pelvis and sent a wave shuddering through his whole body; it was more like a little accident he'd had (I'm sorry. I couldn't help it). Nothing about Laurel, exactly: she was actually better-looking than Angel—*nobody* had a nicer body than Laurel—but these days, with his job situation up in the air, day after day going by with nothing much to do, he didn't feel like a man around her, more like a beaten sheepish dog. His tail between his legs, indeed.

He was only about halfway through his sandwich when she

got back with some groceries, and even that was embarrassing. A stack of chipped ham on thick slabs of whole wheat, slices of juicy ripe tomato, lettuce, cucumber, green pepper, paper-thin slices of Bermuda onion (was this a sandwich or a salad?), a side order of Triscuits, a good start on a second beer, with the first can still sitting there: so *this* is what you do with all your time now that you have a new job.

"Having a little snack?"

"I missed lunch. I was starved." (It was a lie. He'd had an enormous lunch. He didn't know what was wrong with him these days.)

"You'll spoil your dinner."

"I could eat a good dinner right now."

"You are eating a good dinner right now."

"It'll be all right, really. I'll be hungry again in an hour." He took a quick chomp out of his sandwich, about half a garden of produce falling down on his plate, and got up to help with the groceries.

She didn't look her best. Her hair was dirty, which didn't help any, but she also hadn't slept the night before (a feeble orgasm was worse than none at all), so she looked pale, and dry, and wrinkled, and grumpy. It didn't look like the best time to bring up a touchy subject, but if he didn't say it right away he wasn't sure he'd be able to. He thought he'd try a positive note.

"I think Wolf and I are almost finished with this case."

"Great." She tossed him the word like a medicine ball. Do something with it.

"But I've got to do one more thing. Tonight."

"Ah."

"I'm afraid it'll take most of the evening."

She was putting the groceries into the cupboard, ramming them home with incredible speed.

"I tried to get it all done today. I walked the streets all morning." You gotta believe me, honey.

"There's no need to apologize," Laurel said.

"I wasn't apologizing."

"It's all right." She stopped with the groceries, set the bag on the table. "Matt." Deliberately she turned to him, leaned back with her hands resting on the table's edge. "I had no business saying what I did last night."

She brushed away some hair that had fallen over her forehead, made herself look at him. Her eyes seemed terribly tired.

"I got all wrapped up in one thing, like worrying about your work, and forgot another that's just as important. That it's entirely your business what you do."

Matt could not look into those vulnerable eyes. "I know you've been worried."

"It's been an obsession. For weeks and weeks. But it's really just like an old lady who's looking for something to gossip about. A way of not thinking about herself."

Matt did look up at that—it was quite an admission—but Laurel was looking away, out the door.

"I had this realization last night. Late. Like a feeling, a sudden insight. I almost woke you up. That we could be together and still apart. That we could each have the things we do and let them be just that, not worry all the time about what the other does. That we could support the other person in his work, even if we don't entirely like it, that we could support it, just because it's his."

She knew what she was saying was very nearly banal, knew also that it sounded suspiciously like a family television series from the fifties. But she meant something else. She didn't mean that the wife would suppress her real feelings about her husband and blindly support him (in the meantime nagging him about lots of little things that were her way of getting back at him); she meant she would know her real feelings about it, encompass all the ambiguities, and still stand behind him.

"Maybe it's just a mirage. It's so far from what we've been doing. From what I've ever known anybody to do. But it seemed possible. Last night."

It was a sweet thing she was saying, the confession of a dream, or a kind of plea, and normally it might have been an occasion for closeness, maybe a long hug. But they were bruised, numb, in that prickly mood when they just didn't want to touch each other—the previous night, before the bruises had formed, it might have been different—so they just had to stand there, with the words between them.

Matt felt suddenly guilty. "Maybe I don't have to do this thing tonight."

"Matt." Laurel closed her eyes. "Please. That's the whole point. That you should do it."

"There's got to be a better time."

"It's a perfectly good time. What else do you have to do?"

"I'd rather stay home with you and Jonathan. I don't want

to be gone all evening. I keep letting Bollinger call the shots."
Matt shook his head.

"You're impossible!" Laurel threw her hands in the air,
stared at the ceiling. "Matt! The whole point of what I'm
saying is that you should feel free to do it. You shouldn't even
consider me. That you should feel as free about this as if I
didn't even exist."

"I do, I do."

Didn't she understand that other profound truth, that once
he really felt free to do it he didn't want to anymore?

"If you don't do it now I'll feel like some terrible shrewy
bitch. You *have* to do it."

He couldn't believe it. They had switched sides again.

"All right. But it'll just be tonight." He was actually making
this promise to himself. "Just one more night."

"I don't care if it's a hundred nights. The next ten years."

"Oh God. Don't say that."

"I don't care if you spend every night of your life talking to
Hugh Bollinger."

What a thought. It already seemed a lifetime, and it had
just been one day.

"Right now"—Laurel's wild eyes had caught sight of the
clock—"somebody's got to pick up Jonathan."

"I'll go." He had to make up for his guilt at getting what he
wanted. "I can take my sandwich." Though he would have to
cradle it with both hands. "You want that beer?"

"It'll be here when you get back." She wasn't especially
interested in a beer in the middle of the afternoon.

"Okay." He hurried out. If she needed to find him, she could
follow the trail of lettuce bits.

Laurel sincerely believed all she was saying. It had come to
her in a sudden illumination, that in nagging Matt about his
work she was just entering a long line of women through
history who had decided what their husbands should have and
then driven them mercilessly until they achieved it. Politi-
cians' wives, for instance. Like Lady Macbeth. In contrast to
that the night before she had had a sudden beatific vision of
an ideal couple, both of whom felt secure in their careers,
returned to the house at night and discussed perhaps their
work or perhaps just other things, both of whom were interested in what the other did but never so personally involved
that they had to attack it. She couldn't put faces on this couple,

it was true (certainly not hers and Matt's) but she felt a definite conviction at least of their potential existence.

Her vision of careers was part of a larger vision, of two people who lived together and had a family but whose lives were also entirely their own. She hated it when Matt seemed, in however indirect a fashion, to be asking her permission to do something, hated also the thought that her freedom might in any way be circumscribed by him. So many women she knew and counseled seemed to need a man to run their lives (you take it; I can't do a thing with it) so they handed themselves from father to boyfriend to fiancé to husband, and if they ran into a new man at that point they had to give themselves over entirely to him, or go back and ask their husbands what to do, or some combination of the two. Laurel didn't like the thought, with her thirties breathing down her neck, that she had by her marriage cut herself off from any kind of experience, but she also wasn't interested in a complete break. Just stretching the seams a little.

She was not quite aware that her suggestion to Matt about their careers—that they be entirely separate and self-sustaining, not judged and not necessarily even known about by the other—was also a veiled suggestion about the rest of their lives. She was not entirely aware of the extent to which these grand theories on the dynamics of marriage related to a particular situation in her own life.

She was aware, smiling as she put away the rest of the groceries, that she was not entirely sorry Matt planned to be out of the house that night.

II

The face already had a glow, a grinning contentment, that beamed right up into the thinning temples. If a boozer could stop right there, Matt thought, if he could drink just the amount that would hold that constant buzz, he'd be fine. But he couldn't. Bollinger would keep slopping it down, throwing back bourbon and water as if it were beer, and pretty soon that gentle glow would become a fiery red, his head starting to droop.

"I always wanted to be a writer," Bollinger said.

He was sitting on the little couch he had, leaning forward with his arms on his knees, as if he were constantly about to get up, but he never did. His belly hung over his belt. His drink was within easy reach on the coffee table in front of him. He reached for it frequently.

"I'm sure that's a typical English teacher's lament. Pour four ounces of bourbon into any English teacher in the country and you'd hear the same thing. But I did want to be a writer. I always thought I would be. When I was a kid I used to take a train into the city and walk the streets, see the houses and dirty tenements and people in the diners and bus stations and think that someday with the novelist's art I would penetrate their lives and tell their story. It was something of an obsession with me. I'd sit in the train station, on one of the wooden benches that lined the marble floors there, and I'd see the people around me, poverty-stricken families, and psychotics, and lonely old women, and I'd think, I will know you. Someday I'll know you, and I'll tell your story, the story you cannot tell, and you'll thank me for it. You'll see your story and be glad I have told it. The thought gave me a kind of glow."

That very same glow, ladies and gentlemen, is available to you now, in middle age, for the price of a fifth of bourbon.

"The dreams of youth," Bollinger said.

"With me it was baseball," Matt said.

"You were going to be Joe DiMaggio."

"Don Drysdale." Bollinger was a little before Matt's time.

"Ah. We were a pitcher. A fastball that blazed like a comet and a curve that dropped off a table."

I came closer than you, you filthy old cocksucker.

"The thing of it was," Bollinger said, "I had talent. I won all the English prizes at school, and I edited the literary magazine, and when I got out of Bowdoin the old man was ready to set me up in an apartment, five years, ten years, whatever it took, he said. But none of that for me. I got a job back at the old boarding school, bright young English master, and I told lots of people what I wanted to do. My old teachers were still there, and I was a champion around the place. Every night, after the boys were in bed, you could hear up in my third-floor apartment the typewriter blazing away. Cigarette after cigarette, and black coffee by the pot, and bang bang bang on the old typewriter. I had incredible energy in those days." Must have been before the booze. "Four hours of that at night and I was still able the next day to lecture on 'The Rime of the Ancient

79

Mariner' and coach third-form lacrosse. My old senior master would come over on Friday evenings and go over what I'd done with red pencil. A marvelously decorated manuscript. I've still got the damn thing."

With that Bollinger did finally launch himself off the couch, padded over to a desk in the corner that was scattered with papers. Probably ungraded themes from last spring. Matt wasn't sure just what he was to do. For all he knew Hugh was planning to pace around the room and give a brief reading in his hoarse earthy baritone. But when Bollinger reached down into the bottom drawer and said, "Yes. Here," Matt took it as a summons and walked over beside him.

The manuscript was typed, for some reason, on lined yellow sheets, which seemed remarkably well preserved considering their age. The type was somewhat faded but still legible, and in the margins you could see the comments in red, "Transition drags a bit here," or "Marvelous touch!" Matt wasn't sure whether he should reach for the thing or read it over Hugh's shoulder or what. Bollinger, as a matter of fact, seemed to have begun reading it himself, his brow tightening and face settling into a frown of concentration.

"There's brilliance here," he said. "God. There's brilliance here."

"It was called *Brookline Mass*?" Matt had caught a glimpse of the words on the front.

"A working title. I might have stuck with it. There was a play on the word. Like mass for the dead. The novel had religious implications. There was also the obvious meaning. That all the people in this world were dead in a sense."

"Was it published?" The answer seemed apparent, but Matt felt he had to say something. Show he took the whole thing seriously.

"It was never finished. Two hundred twenty-six pages, that whole long winter and well into the next summer, and I swear I was barely started. Just the tip of the iceberg of Brookline Mass. I suppose I should have made an outline before, or at least a rough plan, or maybe started on something a little smaller. But the books that were around in those days, the first novels especially, were all monstrous. Styron. Mailer. James Jones. I wanted to enter their company. The novel was king in those days. A wonderful time."

Nowadays the dirty book was king.

"I petered out. I think I might have been all right if I had taken the offer from the old man. Been living on my own. I'd have had nothing bolstering my ego, no other kind of work to fall back on, and I'd have been forced into a confrontation with my manuscript. But that prep-school world sucks you in. Committee meetings, extracurricular assignments, all that piddly shit that drains your best energies and lulls you into thinking you're doing something. I needed some quiet time to think. The courage maybe to scrap the whole thing and start in a new direction. But pretty soon I was busy busy busy. And tired tired tired. And boozy boozy boozy."

He leaned over and dropped the manuscript with a thump into the drawer.

"You were right to get out of the teaching game." A glint had come into Bollinger's eye at the thought of his favorite subject, Matt's prospective career. "It drains a man."

"You've never done any more writing?"

"I've often thought I should go back to my manuscript and try to salvage something. A novella from part of it, or a book of stories. So far, sad to say, I have not done that. Time may be running out."

Matt had apparently said the wrong thing. Bollinger had reddened, was looking away from him.

"The loss to world literature is no doubt enormous. I should feel perfectly terrible about it. Just now, if you'll excuse me, all I feel is an overwhelming need to piss."

The need to urinate had never come at a more propitious moment as far as Matt was concerned.

The evening so far had been strange, not anything like what Matt had expected. He had pictured Hugh running around, getting things ready, people starting to arrive or already there, and imagined he would have to pin the man down, extract details from him question by question. But Hugh had been perfectly ready as soon as he arrived, hors d'oeuvres and nuts and chips sitting around in plates on the tables, booze and soda set out in the kitchen. He had even been, for Hugh, reasonably sober. He had sat Matt down on the couch, sat in a chair himself, leaned back and paused, closing his eyes, and proceeded to recite a detailed description of the accident. Perfect. It could have gone into a courtroom transcript immediately.

Hugh had been approaching from the Point, on the same side of the street as Lawson, and had seen him and Otto talking. The walk light was blinking, it was true, but it had just started to blink, and the street was perfectly clear, so the car had an ample view. Bunter Lawson had taken something of a leap from the curb, but after that had slowed down, striding purposefully, and was well clear of the curb before the car started. The driver, in Hugh's opinion, must not even have looked. He had not slowed down as he approached Lawson, who unfortunately froze at the sight of the car. Hugh had a distinct recollection, in fact, that at least for a moment he saw the back of the driver's head from where he was standing, which meant the man was looking in the opposite direction from where the car was going. Maybe making faces at the cars he was turning in front of.

No matter how many questions Matt asked, how many details he picked up on, Hugh spoke with confidence. He had the ability, he said, to see things in his memory as if they were happening that very moment. He was the perfect witness.

Wolf would be delighted. The whole matter had been disposed of in twenty minutes. There had been nothing to do since but sit around telling maudlin stories from the past.

The place surprised Matt a little. He knew that the father who had been all set to support the young novelist Hugh Bollinger had since that time died, and left him, if not quite a fortune, at least plenty to live on. The place hardly showed that. It was a simple duplex apartment, a living room, a small kitchen, a couple bedrooms. The furniture was very ordinary, and old, and not especially plentiful; one soft battered easy chair actually had a quilt thrown over it in place of a slipcover. There was just one photograph on the wall, of a much younger Hugh Bollinger with a championship lacrosse team he had coached; he had had thick curly hair, and no paunch, and a big healthy grin on his face. Other than that the wall just bore some posters, those big color travel posters that say Paris, or Rome; and a large muddy violent poster of the blocking for a pass play in the NFL; and a few small framed Japanese erotic engravings. (At least the Japanese thought they were erotic. Matt's first reaction was always, What the hell are those people doing? and then he had the long process of deciding whose leg was whose, and in what way that helping of goulash down there resembled commingled human genitals.) The television was a portable, stuck off in a corner, and the combination stereo and tape deck wasn't even a component system. Loads of books were around, arranged neatly on bookshelves and in little piles on tables around the room, but not the massive collection of leather-bound erotica he was expecting. That must be elsewhere. There were an enormous number of murder mysteries, arranged neatly by author despite the fact that most of them were cheap paperbacks. They seemed to be the prize of the collection.

At one end of the room, conspicuously set on a bookcase, was a movie projector. It looked to Matt like a new and first-class piece of machinery, and didn't seem to belong in the apartment. It faced a bare patch of wall with the shades pulled down around it. Neither he nor Hugh had mentioned the projector, though it was the first thing you noticed when you walked into the room.

Matt walked back to the table and took a small sip from his beer, just one more in the long line of beers that stretched back to his late-afternoon snack. They had left him feeling bloated and dopey, and he didn't really want another, but Hugh had made a special trip for a six-pack of Heineken and Matt didn't see how he could refuse. The man was an immensely courteous host, even if he was a trifle disorganized.

Matt was feeling okay. There was something relaxing about being around Bollinger alone, with his gruff quiet voice, friendly manner, rumpled exterior. It was only in a crowd that he got loud and obnoxious, tried to entertain. Matt wished the party didn't have to begin.

"I hope I didn't bore you with my sad sad story of the past." Hugh had rearranged himself in the bathroom, straightening his tie, tucking in his shirt. He had not, however, managed to get his zipper all the way back up after he peed. Matt wondered if he should say something, or if maybe Hugh just liked to wear it that way, for effect.

"No," Matt said. "I like it. Hearing about somebody's real interests."

"A long history of compromises and renunciations. That's what anybody's life is."

"I guess."

"So we look for escape. In good whiskey." He had brought the bottle back with him, was livening up his drink. "In mystery novels." He glanced toward the projector. "In erotica. There are no failures there."

"At least we don't see any."

"True. We don't know what lies on the cutting-room floor.

But a pornographic narrative is a fairy tale. A man wants something and it falls into his lap." His lap is right. "They're stories of utopia. Of paradise."

If John Milton were alive today he'd be grinding them out in a porn shop.

"Real life isn't like that." Bollinger capped the whiskey. "You don't get what you want just for wishing it."

"That's for sure."

Bollinger had walked the bourbon bottle back to the bar, seemed, as he did, to be taking stock of the place.

"It's a second-rate world, the prep-school world. At least for teachers. I never realized until it was too late. When I was a boy I idolized those people. A lot of my masters. I thought they were brilliant, wise, charming. They defined a kind of charm and then fulfilled it. Formed a whole little world with its customs and values."

If there was ever a man who must have had the prep-school world by the balls, it was Hugh Bollinger.

"What I think now, I never saw it at the time, but what I think now is that I was afraid of the other world. Where my father wanted to set me up in an apartment. I wanted to go back to that smaller world, that special world, where I had been a prize-winning English student, an all-league lacrosse player, where my masters still marked my papers and called them brilliant, where I was perpetually the young man bright with promise. Not the mature man who does something, but the bright man who is about to. Who's always about to. You know, I still feel that way sometimes. Incredible as it may seem when you look at me. Spare tire, rotten teeth. I still walk around half the time feeling like a young man who will some-day write a brilliant novel."

Such feelings were not all that foreign to Matt. He still sometimes got the feeling that his shoulder problems were temporary (he was on the twenty-day disabled list), that some-day he would take up his baseball career again and move directly into the majors. It was ridiculous. If he had been in the majors right then he would have been almost over the hill. Though there were exceptions. If he could just develop a knuckleball. . . .

"The prep-school master," Bollinger said, "is the perpetual adolescent."

"You're being too hard on yourself, Hugh." Matt didn't mind

lying. "You've been a good teacher. A great coach. You've done a lot for your students."

"I don't deny I've enjoyed it all. I genuinely liked lacrosse, and I at least used to like literature, and I always felt at home in the atmosphere of a school. Some of my greatest friendships, the most valued friendships in my life, have been with the boys I've taught and coached. A wonderful intimate bond. But they're so young. It's not quite a real relationship. I'm drinking bourbon, and they're drinking Coke. I have to think of subjects they're interested in, or tone down what I'm saying to their level. And they all go on. They get married, and have children, and move into the world of business or the professions. I can't tell you how many times I've had a friend come back and have been animatedly talking to him and have suddenly realized he doesn't give a damn about how the lacrosse team is doing or what the fourth-form curriculum is like. He's looking at me as if I'm a bit demented, which I probably am. And in the old days at boarding school, when the new boys would come in, I'd see some nervous frightened fourteen-year-old dressed in a new blazer and trying to haul his trunk up the stairs, and I'd think, *That*, Hugh Bollinger, is your true spiritual brother."

Matt felt rather helpless to answer this long lament. "It's hard to be starting over," he said. "Year after year."

"Prep school is the pornography of life. You don't get to do any real things. Just pretend."

In that case, old boy, you should love it.

"But I'm getting morbid. Sloppy and sentimental. We should be talking about something interesting. Like my party."

Bollinger was probably past the point of no return. His pleasant glow had taken on a deeper hue, and he had started to swallow hard, his chin on his chest, and to slur his words just slightly. His smile had a sort of mushy quality. From what Matt had seen in the past, his condition wouldn't change much from there, though he would continue to pour the bourbon down.

"What's the story on that?" Matt said. "I don't get a real clear picture."

"Tonight is a very special night." Bollinger once again swallowed a belch that had been trying to fight its way out for at least five minutes. "When we move beyond fantasy to reality. Abandon our illusions."

"Oh." That helps me a lot.

"Like my little confession to you. Maybe this will be the night, finally, when I quit thinking of myself as the young novelist bright with promise."

That was okay for Bollinger. Matt still thought he had a shot at developing a knuckler.

"We're going to see a movie," Matt said. "Some special movie you've got."

"But not a pornographic movie."

"I thought it was."

"No. Pornography is fantasy. This is a movie about sexual reality."

"I see." This movie must be unbelievable. "Who's coming?"

"A select group. A very special audience. I wouldn't want just anyone to see this."

Matt felt a tickle of nervousness in his throat. It was like in high school, when you tried to make it seem like a casual question, but it was really the reason you had brought the whole subject up.

"And Angel is coming."

"Angel is definitely coming. She's looking forward to seeing you."

"Does she know the others?"

"I discovered a long time ago, Matt, there's no telling who Angel may be acquainted with."

They heard from downstairs the door open and close, then a slow progress up the stairs. "Ah," Bollinger said. "My first guest." But he did not move to let the guest in, and as it turned out did not have to; when the footsteps paused at the top a key slid into the door, and it opened. A young man entered, wearing a pale-yellow turtleneck, a light-blue sport jacket, faded jeans, loafers without socks. His hair was damp, as if he'd just had a shower. He looked, in fact, as if he had just gotten up, his eyes blinking back sleep, his face wrinkled. He squinted at the smoke from a cigarette in his mouth. He was apparently carrying, in a large square container, the film. "Hi, Hugh," he said. And, "Oh. Mr. Gregg."

"I think you can call him Matt." Hugh turned to Matt. "Won't that be okay?"

"Sure."

"It takes a moment of getting used to. But we're all friends here."

"Yes."

It galled him to say the word. Matt had been expecting somebody from school—had thought through his old colleagues, choosing likely candidates—but he had not expected this. A student, an old friend of Hugh's, last year's lacrosse captain in fact, but not somebody Matt had ever cared for. A snotty arrogant bastard, who treated teachers more or less like servants. For a moment he was so surprised he couldn't remember the kid's name—apparently he had blotted such things out —but then it came back to him. At least he wouldn't have to ask. Todd Hunter.

III

What Jonathan really liked, Laurel often thought, was just the chance to sit for a long time with his mother. He didn't really care that they were reading. She would put an arm around him, and he would lean against her breast, making little clicking noises with his mouth, tapping his fingernails against his teeth, all the time breathing softly, like the soft sweet breathing of a baby. Sometimes, whispering, he would echo some of the phrases she said, as if fascinated at the sound. The whole thing very nearly put Laurel to sleep—her shoulders would go limp, eyelids grow heavy—and she was surprised he stayed awake, but he always did, and always complained when she wanted to stop. "It's early. You've hardly read anything." With a long wide yawn, she would protest, it was not early, it was getting very late, and they had actually read a great deal, look—ruffling the pages—at all they had read. It was time to go to sleep. "Just a couple more pages," he always said.

She had learned to suggest they stop two pages before she actually wanted to stop.

They were sitting on the bed in his small bedroom, a recliner pillow behind them, just that one bedside lamp on in the whole upstairs. All the windows and doors were open, letting in, as if from far off, the sounds of the city—buses on the avenue a couple blocks away, cars on the street just outside, kids playing basketball on the lighted playground behind the school—but not letting in much breeze, just now and then a gentle ripple of air. The most noticeable sound, from the little window beside the bed, was the crickets chirping in the backyard.

They were reading a comic book that had been translated from the Dutch, a series of adventures about a boy and girl who had the same bone-thin body as Jonathan. Laurel found the books, with the improbable incidents and childish plays on words, rather insipid, but the children often put things over on adults, and they faced moments of danger with courage and skill, and Jonathan loved them. He wanted to read the books over and over, night after night.

They were reading the last two pages for that evening when there was a knock at the front screen door.

Jonathan paled. "Who's that?"

"I don't know. Let's go see."

They walked down the steps just far enough to see the door, and a man standing at it. "Come in," Laurel said.

A rather nervous-looking young man walked in and smiled—or gave a fairly good imitation of a smile—up at Jonathan. "Hi!"

"You remember Ned," Laurel said. "My friend from work."

"No." Jonathan looked relieved—he was always a little anxious on evenings when his father was gone—but also disgusted.

"You've met him a couple times. When you and Matt came to pick me up."

"I don't remember." Jonathan had turned and headed back up the stairs.

Actually, Jonathan had a fantastic memory. He remembered everything.

"Can you at least say hello?" Laurel said.

"Hello." The voice was flat. Jonathan was already almost out of sight up the stairs.

Laurel shook her head at Ned. "Make yourself comfortable. I'll be down in a few minutes."

"No hurry," he said.

Jonathan was walking rather stiffly back to his room. His face had clouded over, and he flung himself hard into bed. "What's *he* doing here?"

"He came to visit. Is there anything wrong with that?"

"No."

He was sitting very still against the recliner pillow, not looking at his mother.

Laurel finished the last two pages while Jonathan sulked. He hardly looked at the pictures, and would not lean against her. "Read a couple more pages," he said when she finished.

"I just read a couple more pages."

"Read a couple *more* pages."

"No."

"You never read anything extra. Every night the same thing."

"I read extra pages every night."

"It's always the same extra pages."

She hadn't been fooling him after all.

"You're just mad because I have company," she said.

"I don't care if you have company. Have company all you want. Have company every night." Jonathan had made his face totally impassive. He would not look at his mother. "At least lie down with me for a little while."

That was his favorite thing, for his mother to lie for a while in bed with him. He had probably thought that with Matt gone she might stay—as she rarely did—until he went to sleep.

"Jonathan. I have company."

"Just for a little while."

"What will my company think?"

"A few minutes!"

"All right. A couple minutes."

Laurel actually enjoyed lying with Jonathan. He would curl up against her hard, as if he were still in the womb, and after a while would half forget she was there, say things to himself, sing little tunes. He might take notice of her now and then, ask a question, then whisper the answer softly a couple times, as if registering it with his other self. He had a mind that was incessantly active. Usually he lay awake for quite some time.

As she lay there with him, she often reflected that the little things he wanted—to sit against his mother while she read, lie against her while he went to sleep—were the kinds of things we all want, and rarely get. She often felt guilty when she got up to leave. But that was the way of the world, the one thing we all had to learn. You never get all you want.

Just then, she thought with a smile as she lay there, she was trying to satisfy too many men.

When she got up—she had actually stayed nearly ten minutes—Jonathan said, "Goodnight, Mom."

"Goodnight, Jonathan. Tomorrow night I'll stay longer."

"You better!"

God. Another demanding man. At the age of seven they were already impossible.

She stopped in the hallway a few moments to collect herself before going downstairs.

Laurel had never felt more clearheaded about anything in her whole life. Her theories about marriage had taken on a mystical purity, a self-evidence: she *knew* they were right. She had read many times about the difficulties of adultery, how the first occasion was accompanied by stabs of guilt, subsequent occasions led to a descent into alcoholism and sexual perversion; how from then on a wave of shame passed over a woman at even the mention of her husband, or at the helpless cry of her innocent child.

Laurel thought it was all bullshit. As a matter of pure fact, she did not believe in the concept of adultery, which viewed sex in marriage as one thing and out of marriage as quite another; she believed in a world in which one had relationships of varying intensity with a variety of people, some of the relationships involving sex. She had actually very much enjoyed her first experience of (what other people called) adultery, on that Sunday morning at the counseling center. The sex wasn't great, but it was novel; she liked the new tastes, the new smells, the new body on top of her with its different breadth and density, the new idiosyncratic penis. She had not felt terrible pangs of guilt the next time she saw Matt. She actually liked him more. It was easier to love a man when he was not supposed to be your whole life.

As she started downstairs she felt the flow of adrenaline, her pounding heart, and stopped a moment to enjoy it. Excitement was a nice thing.

Ned was in the big easy chair in the living room, reading a magazine. As Laurel came down—barefoot, in cutoff shorts and a peasant blouse with nothing underneath, so her nipples showed against the white cloth—he rose to meet her.

"Getting impatient?"

"No. I was just looking at *Time*."

Was that not in itself a sign of fierce impatience?

She stepped to give him a hug, held him a long time. She was always surprised, hugging him, at how small a man he was. Embracing Matt was like jumping into your father's arms when you were a little girl: you hoped he had a good grip, because you sure weren't doing much. But she could really get her arms around Ned, whose body in a way seemed slighter than hers. She liked the clean smell of his neck, and the way his hair curled up at the back of it; she always reached up to play with the curls. She could feel his body trembling slightly, and his heart pounding: she held him hard to calm him down. She leaned back to kiss him, but felt him shrink a little from the kiss: his mouth didn't open to hers.

"This is all right?" he said. His eyes looked small, and very serious. "You're sure this is all right?"

She hoped this wasn't the beginning of a debate on ethics. "Meaning what?"

"I was just thinking, Jonathan. I thought he might come down."

"He doesn't come down."

"I wasn't sure."

"He might call, but he doesn't come down."

"If he found us like this. That would be awful." His eyes stared, as if he were a small boy himself seeing the primal scene.

"I'm used to being careful about Jonathan. It's a way of life when you're married."

"New to me."

"Sure."

She tried another kiss. If anything it was a little worse. He was closing up like a clam.

"Maybe you'd like to relax a while," she said. "Some wine? Or tea?"

"I'll take a cup of tea."

"Let's go out to the kitchen."

"I can get it. Shouldn't you be here? In shouting distance?"

"Ned. He's seven years old. We don't sit around all night listening for him."

"I didn't know."

"If he needs anything he'll scream his head off. They'll hear him three blocks away."

She would have to calm down, that was all there was to it. Usually she was at the other end of this: Matt had worked himself up with some fantasy and was starting down the home stretch before she was even off the starting line. This time it was she who was ahead of Ned. She would have to slow down and give him a chance to catch up.

It was frustrating all the same. A golden opportunity. She hated to spend the time drinking tea.

The lights were off on the way back, and she left them off. Out in the kitchen the only light was the flame she ignited on the stove. She fixed his tea quickly—it only took a little water —soaking the tea bag in a large white coffee mug. For herself she took an identical mug and, without a word, filled it two-thirds full of the burgundy they kept in a gallon jug on the kitchen table. She wished it could have been whiskey, or brandy. She would have liked to feel the fire going down.

While Ned carefully sipped his tea, she leaned back against the stove and took a big slug of the wine.

"I guess I'm a little nervous," Ned said.

"It's all right."

"I was kind of surprised when you called."

"Pleased, I hope."

"Oh, of course. Pleased. I mean, usually I just watch TV at night." They laughed. "Then to get your call."

"Yeah." She should get such calls.

"I guess it also makes me nervous"—he paused, fiddled with his cup—"coming into another man's house."

Laurel looked into her wine. "It isn't just his house."

"I know."

"More mine than his, actually. If you start counting up."

"I wasn't talking about finances."

"I don't like it when you make it sound like property. A couple alley cats staking out the neighborhood."

"It's not my more enlightened side. But there's an element of the alley cat in it for me."

They ought to have him fixed.

"I'm just trying to be honest about how I feel," Ned said. "It's better for me to tell you. I like Matt."

"Good. I like him too."

"It bothers me a little to be doing this to him."

Laurel bit her mug. She had to keep cool. There was a logical discussion here that was perfectly reasonable if she took it step by step. If she skipped any steps she'd find herself shouting.

"I don't really see that you're doing anything to him," she said. "I was kind of hoping you'd be doing something to me."

Ned frowned. "Of course."

"It isn't like you'll be incapacitating me. I can be used again."

"You know what I mean."

"I do not know what you mean."

"I come into a man's house and screw his wife. With his child in bed upstairs."

"This is not *his* house. That is not *his* child. I am not *his* wife."

"I'm not saying that's all you are. But it's a part of it. For me."

"I'm tired of being someone else's property. That's the whole point. You have to check me out before you can use me."

"Laurel."

"We could make up an invoice for Matt to sign. Copies to all concerned." Jonathan could initial it.

"Please."

She was being unfair to Matt, she knew. Less than any other husband did he treat his wife like property. It was only in her own mind, carefully shaped through years of indoctrination, that she had seen herself as belonging to someone. It had taken her months of work to rid herself of this notion, and now she was running into it in Ned.

"I don't think of you as property," he said. "Mine or his."

"What have we just been talking about?"

"I'm not talking about things I think. I'm talking about feelings. Vague notions. From God knows where."

"Let them stay there. Feel other things."

"I am. But something, from somewhere, is making me nervous."

"So be nervous."

"I am."

"All right."

Back where they started. Both of them bruised, though, and exhausted. How about another lap?

They both took long ruminative drinks from their mugs, as if savoring the beverages.

"Sure you don't want some wine?" Laurel said. "Tea will just make you jumpier."

"I'm not much of a man for wine. Got any vodka?"

"I'm sorry. No."

She knew so little about him, when you came right down to it. She knew his ideas ad nauseum, his outlook on the world. They had spent many an hour in serious discussion at the counseling center. She knew his experiences in therapy, his preferred methods of counseling. But she didn't know the small things. The little habits that add up to a life. Vodka. Good heavens. That hardly seemed the drink for Ned Streater.

Really to know a person you had to spend hours with him. Casual hours, when not much was happening. You probably had to live with him. Oh God.

"What would you be doing?" she said. "If you had your way."

"Doing?"

"If you were out with a woman, say, and trying to seduce her. Or just with a good friend and you knew you were going to bed."

Ned grinned. Laurel mouthed her cup impishly.

"How would you spend the evening?" she said.

"I guess I'd go to a restaurant. A nice place, with a band for dancing. Have some drinks, a good meal. Wine with dinner. I do like wine with dinner. Afterwards listen to the band. Dance some. Talk. At the end of the evening go home and make love."

"Far into the night."

He smiled. "Yes."

"Then what you get is an old dark house and a cup of weak tea."

Ned laughed. "It's not like I'm doing the other thing all the time."

"Dreams are so nice. The real world so grim."

Laurel's eyes were sad. The wine seemed to be making her maudlin.

"I guess I just always expect the other person to feel the same way I do," she said. "Evenings out on the town, dancing. That all seems so far away to me. All I saw was that some time was free. Matt would be gone, Jonathan tucked in, you could come over. We'd spend some time downstairs, maybe drink some wine, kiss a lot. When Jonathan was asleep we could go upstairs, take all our clothes off, lie on soft sheets. Not all night or anything, but a good long time. We wouldn't be so frantic as the first time, could do things right. Rub each other's backs, and you could kiss my breasts a long time. I love that. Afterwards we'd have time for a little snooze. It's not nearly as elaborate as what you're saying. I guess that's what happens when you're married awhile. Your fantasies narrow."

"I wouldn't say they narrow. Maybe just refine. Yours sounds pretty wonderful to me."

Laurel did not know—any more than she knew what Ned liked to drink—how exactly right it was, what she had said. Ned was turned on by words, not sexual words exactly, but ordinary words, and the images they evoked. Soft sheets. All our clothes off. Breasts. He stepped to kiss her, really kiss her this time, and she was ready: their mouths fell open in unison. His was warm from the tea, and sweet. Their tongues fluttered lightly together. His hands clutched first at the small of her back, kneading, then moved to the juncture of her legs, the slight declivity at the top of each thigh; he squeezed. Her knees buckled; she pressed up against him and felt his swelling penis, felt herself starting to open and grow moist. His tongue probed deep into her mouth. It must have been some motherly instinct, or the fruit of many years' experience, that made her hear the quiet crack of the floorboards: she broke away, pushed Ned in the chest, like a punch with the flat of her hand; his tongue slipped across her cheek and left a wet spot there.

They were panting, breathless, as if parting from some terrific struggle.

It was the thin form of Jonathan that appeared in the doorway, his voice finally friendly, as if he were ready for a long chat. "Who turned out the lights?" he said.

IV

"So it's Matt, is it?"

"Yeah."

"For Matthew?"

"Yep."

"Funny. I never knew your name. Usually I know a teacher's name. I don't know why I didn't know yours. Didn't occur to me to wonder, I guess."

Matt nodded. He was supposed to reply to this idiocy?

"We never got to know each other much," Hunter said.

Too bad we couldn't have left it that way.

Matt wore a smile, of course. An old habit from his years of teaching. You ran into a kid who under other circumstances you wouldn't have spent two minutes with, and you had to tolerate him, pretend to consider what he said, actually act as if you valued it. Teaching was the most shit-eating of all professions. He didn't know how he had gotten involved in it.

He did know about Todd Hunter, though. Met him in college a number of times. The bluff hearty manner, deeply fatigued eyes, rakish good looks, the trembling hands of the early alcoholic. A vodka tonic, he had said, when Hugh asked him what he wanted to drink. At his age Matt hadn't even known what a vodka tonic was. Hunter took from his pocket a battered pack of Camels—unfiltered—and removed a wilted cigarette, lit up. He carefully allowed a small cloud of smoke to escape before, inhaling, he sucked it back in. Thank you, Humphrey Bogart.

He was standing at the projector with the cigarette in a corner of his mouth, threading the film.

"You're interested in movies?" Matt said.

"Everybody's interested in this kind of movie."

Matt reddened. "I mean, you brought the movie up. You seem to be operating the equipment."

"Anybody can operate the equipment. Except old Hugh. He's a trifle nonmechanical. But yes, as a matter of fact. I am interested in photography. And film, or getting to be. It's a lot harder. More subtle. It's a hobby of mine."

"Not something you plan to go on with."

"Go on?"

"As work."

"I haven't given much thought to work. I have to sow my wild oats."

He looked as if he'd already reaped the harvest.

"I can't remember where you're off to next year."

"University of Vaginia."

Matt ignored this show of wit. "Good school."

"My fourth choice, but I figured all along that's where I'd go. The others were unrealistic. I had a little bad spot in my junior year. Like practically the whole thing. I actually wanted to go to Dartmouth." He squinted at Matt through a haze of smoke. "The most distinguished drinking school in the country."

A laudable ambition. "Virginia's not bad."

"Definitely in the top five."

Matt didn't think he cared to hear a rundown. But this explained why Hunter had majored in alcohol in prep school.

"Will you play lacrosse at Virginia?"

"God no. I don't have the lungs anymore. Or the liver."

Broken in body at the age of eighteen.

"You know," Matt said, "I was always a little surprised you were at Tabard. It never seemed quite right for you."

"I wasn't second-rate enough?"

Matt smiled. The little bastard.

"No reflection on the faculty, of course. But I came to Tabard rather abruptly. Got kicked out of Greenfield."

"Not for academics?"

"No. A drug-related thing. There was a bunch of us. For a while I was afraid I'd screwed myself for life, but the college admissions people say they understand that kind of thing these days."

If they didn't, there wouldn't be anybody to admit.

Bollinger came in from the kitchen with the drink. "I hope I got this right." He glanced at Matt. "The gentleman is very particular about his drinks."

Hunter sipped. "Ah." He nodded. "Not quite, but it'll do." He took a long swallow. "There's nothing like the first drink of the day."

"The first? You've been abstaining."

"I just got up."

Bollinger rolled his eyes at Matt. "The gentleman keeps odd hours."

"Put on some music, Hugh," Hunter said.

There was an air in the room of everything centering on Hunter, everything being done for him. Matt was made uneasy by this feeling, but Bollinger was thriving. He had grown considerably more energetic since Hunter had arrived.

"Todd has me playing some crazy music lately. Not exactly to my taste."

"Better than that Rudy Vallee crap of yours."

"Frank Sinatra and Tony Bennett. A far cry from Rudy Vallee."

"Not to me. Anyway, my music will be a good background to the movie."

Bollinger plugged a tape into his machine and an assortment of electric guitars started screaming. A male voice groaned unintelligibly. Bollinger winced apologetically at Matt.

"How are things with your girlfriend?" he said to Hunter, heading back toward the chairs.

"She's not my girlfriend. Just some crazy kid."

"I've heard you talk about her." Bollinger was starting to slur his words a bit. He reminded Matt of a drunken old woman who was trying vicariously to recapture the romance of her youth. "I think you really care for her quite deeply."

Hunter ignored this embarrassing drunk and turned to Matt, as if confiding. "I'm in the process of being seduced by an incredible fourteen-year-old girl."

There was a tromping up the stairs. With the music on and turned way up, Bollinger staggering around arranging things, Hunter apparently confiding in Matt, it was growing hard to concentrate. The door shoved open to a loud noise of voices. A large woman was making her way in, her mouth hung wide to blare a greeting, and behind her, in a blue leisure suit at least a size too small, was Otto Droge.

Hunter ignored their arrival. "She's the cousin of a friend of mine. A very good friend, who I know from Greenfield. Farrell Haynes. She's been staying at his house while her parents get divorced. One of those sticky sordid situations. The odd thing is, she looks exactly like Farrell. Just a longer head of hair on exactly the same face. Fortunately he's good-looking. She's a beautiful little girl. A trifle young, I have to admit."

The hubbub at the door was considerable. The woman, who Matt assumed to be Mrs. Droge, was kissing Bollinger's mouth, and Otto was holding his arm and shouting at him. She wore a light sleeveless summer dress that hung straight down on her chunky body. On her face was a purplish splotch of lipstick that looked as if someone had thrown it at her mouth from five feet away: an excellent shot, but not perfect. Her bare arms were muscular. She looked like a pulling guard in drag.

"I want to hear this!" Bollinger was shouting hoarsely and drunkenly over at Hunter. "Don't you go on with that story." He seemed trapped in the amorphous clutch of the Droges.

To say the least, they seemed a peculiar pair for Hugh to be intimate with.

"Right from the start she was all over me," Hunter said. "We'd be sitting on the couch in this little den they have, and I'd look to either side and see the same face, just one with longer hair. It was uncanny. But on that long-haired side all kinds of things were going on, her whole leg pressed up against mine and her hot little hand constantly touching me and her head sometimes leaning over on my shoulder. She wears the most wonderful perfume. I'm over at Farrell's house practically every day. This was getting hard to take.

"One day Farrell was out, coming back in about ten minutes, and the two of us were in the den alone. 'You're never nice to me,' she said, with this stupid little pout on her face, and I said, 'What are you talking about?' 'You never seem happy to see me,' she said. 'My friends at home all kiss when we meet.' So I leaned down and put a little kiss on her cheek and she said, 'Not like that. That makes me feel like your little sister.'

What the hell. I decided I'd give her a kiss on the mouth, but when I leaned down she threw her arms around my neck and gave me an amazing kiss, a positively virtuoso performance. I honestly think it was the best kiss I've ever had, and here in my arms was the body of this child."

By this time Bollinger and Droge had joined them. Mrs. Droge had gone out to the kitchen to mix drinks. She didn't need to be shown the way.

There was an elaborate hors d'oeuvre, a fancy cheese spread on crackers with an olive slice in the middle. Droge had two of them in his mouth before he even started to chew. "This is the child porn star?" he said around the food. He seemed to take no notice of Matt whatsoever.

"Shut up," Bollinger said. "Let him go on."

"So I asked Farrell." Hunter still seemed to be talking only to Matt. "I mean this *was* his cousin and all, more or less under his supervision, or so it seemed. He said it was all right with him. I took her out. There were absolutely no preliminaries with this girl. I drove her to the Oval on a dark warm evening and before the car had even really come to a stop she was all over me, kissing and clutching me tight and guiding my hands all kinds of places. I didn't have to do a thing. In fact I couldn't do a thing. I was given no initiative. Finally she had me out of my pants and was working away with her hot little hand. I once visited a rather expensive prostitute in Boston and I swear her hands were in no way more talented than Madeline's. She even produced a handkerchief out of nowhere to keep me from making a mess. Got me cleaned up and back in my pants without spilling a drop."

Speaking of orgasms, Droge looked as if he were about to have one any second. He was still chewing nonstop, popping hors d'oeuvres into his mouth as if they were peanuts. "So last night you finally took her home." It seemed he was in on the story up to that point.

"Last night the parents were out. I drove straight over to my house, parked the car in the garage. Took her up to my room. Not even the pretense of a date." He allowed himself a wry smile. "You can imagine what I was expecting. Some kind of wild scene. An orgy out of the Marquis de Sade. But it wasn't like that at all. Believe it or not. She didn't want to go up to my room in the first place. Then she didn't want to take off her clothes. Didn't want to get into bed. I couldn't understand what was wrong, kept asking her what it was and she wouldn't say anything. But I am rather persuasive in such situations. Besides, I'm stronger than I look."

A nervous giggle from Droge. Oh boy. Force.

"She did have a beautiful body. Very soft flesh, small delicate breasts, light-brown hair between her legs. But she didn't want to kiss, didn't want to touch, wouldn't respond to anything. She wouldn't even wrestle with me, just kept covering everything up. Her hands were cold as ice. For some reason, I can't really explain it, the whole thing was a terrific turn-on to me. I had an erection that just would not quit, it stood there solid as an oak. I'm not normally a cave man. But finally I just pried her legs apart, got myself between them, my cock right up to the spot, and she suddenly went limp, very still and deadly white, looking up at the ceiling, waiting. You would have thought she were facing a firing squad. I pressed up against her, waited, leaned back and pressed again. Again. Nothing. I reached down and felt around with my hand. I was amazed. She was absolutely dry as a bone, and you talk about tight. I might as well have been trying to fuck her kneecap.

"By this time I was practically out of my mind. I put it back and gave a real shove, everything I had, I might have gotten in about a millimeter, and all of a sudden she started to throw some kind of fit. Her breath was coming in little pants, and her face got all red, and her body started writhing and trembling all over. 'I can't! I can't! I've tried and I can't!' and she burst into tears, real hysterics now, screaming and throwing herself around in the bed. Bring on the men in the little white coats. I didn't know what the hell to do. First I tried to hold her down, and that just made it worse. I guess she thought I was trying to fuck her again. Then I just lay back and let her scream, fortunately our walls are pretty solid, and that seemed to do the trick. She went on and on, but eventually wore herself out, finally just lay there shaking and sniffing. It was like a kid who's thrown a temper tantrum.

" 'I'm sorry,' she started to say. 'I'm really sorry.' She started in on this long story about how she had been trying, for two years she had been trying, to have intercourse, and every time she tried it was always like that, she found out she couldn't and then she started hyperventilating. Other times, like that night in the car, she got so excited she could hardly stand it, but when it was a matter of intercourse she couldn't get wet at all. She had apparently started these experiments in screwing when she was twelve years old, for God's sake. She kept lying there sniffing. 'You must be mad. You must be awful mad.' I wasn't really, just kind of relieved she had finally stopped crying. I did still have a terrific erection. Eventually she noticed this, rolled over without a word and gave me one of those virtuoso hand jobs. I could feel her getting wet where her cunt was over my leg, but I didn't want to say anything. I'd had enough for one night."

Droge was giggling again. He hadn't had enough. He'd like to hear the whole story again.

"Honest to God." Hunter shook his head. "That is the most depraved little girl I've ever met."

Nothing compared to the little boys all around him. Matt didn't know about the other two—they had seemed to enjoy the story, and hurried over to hear it with their tongues hanging out—but that was a kind of pornography he didn't particularly care for. More like what Bollinger had called sexual reality. Matt liked it when it was just pretend.

What they were, Matt thought, was the horny boys sitting around the dorm listening to the kid who almost got laid. The dorm stud. As usual he was taking advantage of some confused helpless girl.

It was a good thing Laurel wasn't there. She would have kicked Todd Hunter halfway across the room.

"Though I must say," Hunter said, finishing his story, "she gives the best hand job I've ever come across." He glanced toward a noise at the door. "With one possible exception."

A huge burst of laughter from Bollinger and Droge. Standing at the door in a rakish beret, blanching slightly at the sound of the laughter, was Chandler Mingins.

"Come in, Chandler," Bollinger shouted. "We've just been talking about you."

This was too much. First it was last year's lacrosse captain, then the manager of a dirty bookstore, and now one of Laurel's colleagues from work. Any minute a priest would walk in and begin celebrating Mass.

Matt felt a sudden need to go to the bathroom. He wasn't drunk exactly, but in that bloated state when beer went directly to his bladder. He might as well have poured the bottle straight into the toilet. Eliminate the middle man. He felt himself weave a little as he walked out, on his way passed Mrs. Droge carrying two frothy sweet-looking drinks. "Hiya," she said. In the bathroom was a small shelf of books—Rabelais, Henry Miller, Frank Harris, *My Secret Life*—and a large poster of an enormously muscular man screwing a woman from behind. She had a marvelous sleek body, and wore on her face an expression of violent ecstasy, but he seemed more interested in the spectacle of his own pectoral muscles. At the bottom of the poster were the words "Bodybuilders Pump Harder."

When he came out of the bathroom he was met by Bollinger. "Matt. Angel's downstairs."

"Downstairs?"

"In the other apartment. I own that too, keep it furnished. I thought you knew."

"I had no idea."

"Most of the time I rent it out. But not at the moment. I thought you'd rather see her alone."

"Sure." He'd rather be anywhere than upstairs with those creeps.

"There's a stairway straight into the apartment from the back hall. Out the kitchen the other way. Grab a beer before you go."

"Okay."

Out in the kitchen, Chandler Mingins was mixing a martini.

"Well." Matt tried to summon up a friendly grin. "I hardly expected to see you here."

"I knew you were coming. Hugh told me when he called." Chandler wore a tight, serious expression, almost angry. He must have been offended by the laughter at his entrance. "I didn't think you knew him that well."

"I don't. Or didn't. We just ran into each other again."

"I guess you know the boy too."

"The boy? Oh. A little. I helped coach that team."

"Bollinger's on a long-term campaign to seduce him."

Matt just stared. Mingins was gazing back with his gray-green eyes, his mouth tight, almost fierce. Talk about projection. Laurel should have been around for that statement.

"Really, Chandler." Matt gave a little laugh. "I don't think he's the type."

"If you don't mind my saying so." Chandler sniffed, looked away. "I think I know more about the type than you do."

"I don't mean he wouldn't be"—Matt shrugged—"inclined that way." After all, it was an old prep-school tradition. Cold showers, hard bunks, and a quick blow job from your roommate. "I don't think he's interested in seducing anyone anymore. I think he wants to talk. And drink. And watch dirty movies."

"He wants to do all those things. He especially wants to do them with Todd Hunter. But his motivations aren't quite so benign as you'd make them out. It's a world you don't understand."

"Maybe so." Matt hated the arrogance of some of Laurel's gay friends. You just don't know, little man. "What's the difference?"

"I hate to see a beautiful boy like Todd corrupted by an old fart like that."

No doubt Chandler had someone better in mind.

"It sounds to me like Todd's been doing some corrupting himself lately," Matt said.

"He's a good boy. He's basically a good boy. I've known him for a couple years. He can't help it if some little whore's been leading him on."

So Chandler had also heard the story of Todd's young friend. The interrelationships of these people were fascinating.

"It's Hugh Bollinger who's a menace." Chandler was rummaging around in the refrigerator. "He has no place around young people. I've been saying that for years."

Matt quietly slipped out. He thought he would forgo that bottle of beer. The people at this party were too weird to be believed. They deserved each other. He found the back hall Bollinger had been talking about, and a dark stairway down to a door at the bottom. It was dark where he was, though he could see back through a doorway to the lights of the living room. Everyone was gathered around the chairs where he and Hunter had been sitting. As he started down the stairs he glimpsed the broad beaming face, wrapped in a halo of beard, of Stanley Killian.

V

"Now do you believe he's asleep?" Laurel said.

"He might be faking," Ned said.

They were standing in the upstairs hallway outside Jonathan's room. Laurel had never known anyone who slept quite like Jonathan, flat on his back, his legs spread wide, knees up in the air. He snored—on a somewhat muted scale—like a sailor. He could have a coughing fit in that position, talk in complete sentences, even sometimes answer someone who came in to cover him or give him a dose of medicine, without even waking up. He was hard to awaken from his natural deep sleep. It took several minutes of expert attention.

It was pleasant to be standing like that for a moment, in the dark quiet house, a mild breeze drifting through, as they listened to his miniature snores.

"He's gone for the night," Laurel said.

"You're sure."

"We could make love right beside him on the bed. He'd never know. We'd be assailed by a swarm of probing feet, elbows, and knees. But he'd never wake up."

"You're the one who said he'd never come downstairs."

She shook her head. "I can't understand that. You must look sinister. He figured out you were trying to get into his mother's pants."

It had been strange behavior for Jonathan. He had given up his jealous routine completely, come downstairs and been utterly charming, told Ned about day camp, about school during the regular year, about a movie he had seen a couple of days before on television. He had showed Ned his action figures and his electronic game. Most stunningly of all (Laurel had been sure all this friendliness was just a stall for time) he went cheerfully up to bed at her first suggestion that he do so and fell immediately into a deep sleep, from which he wouldn't awaken, she was sure, until morning. A model child.

In the meantime, of course, she had been aching to go to bed with Ned. Jonathan's very cheerfulness had prevented her from sending him up earlier. Maybe he had known what he was doing after all.

"Come on," she said. They stepped across the hallway into the bedroom.

It was an old house, in an old style: that was its charm. The front bedroom was her favorite. To the right was an alcove just right for a double bed and a couple bedside tables; there was a window beside it. The room widened in the center, and across from the door was a window seat to the gable of three windows that jutted out at the front of the house. There were cushions on the seat, and that was her favorite place to knit or sew, looking down on the street. To the left was an old gas heater, the kind that lit up a small section of the wall in little flames; they dressed in front of it in the winter. They hadn't put much in the room, just a worn throw rug, a couple dressers and an old rocker. On summer nights they opened wide all the windows—four in all—and the door, opened the windows and doors of the rooms across the hall, so the evening breeze traveled gently through the house. In the morning a mocking-bird sat in the tree beside the bedside window and awakened them with a loud elaborate concert. It was as if they occupied the tree with him.

That night, of course, she and Ned had the bedroom door closed.

"It won't bother you to be using the master bedroom," Ned said. "The marriage bed."

Laurel had already stepped to the window seat, where she always threw her clothes when she undressed. Her blouse was off, and the pale moonlight shone down on her breasts. "Stop talking and take off your clothes." The longer this went on the stupider he got. She dropped her shorts and stepped out of her underpants: she was naked. "We've wasted enough time already."

It was usually on a day like this, when she hadn't actually been doing things but just thinking about them—as on days after she had had an erotic dream, or when she and Matt had just fooled around a little in the morning—that she got to a point where she didn't care about foreplay, didn't want a man to be delicate and understanding, didn't want him to be expert (above all she didn't want that): she just wanted to do it. Her thighs felt heavy and thick, and ached on the inside; often there was a dull ache in her lower back; between her legs she was wet and warm. She didn't even want to give herself an orgasm; that would have helped some, but only for a little while. She wanted to get it in. "No fooling around, no fooling around," she would whisper at Matt, while she kneaded his back, breathed into his ear, tickled between his thighs, wrapped him in her legs. She knew the things that cranked him up.

Now she stepped naked to where Ned was—he had taken off his pants but still wore his shirt; his thin penis was just starting to rise—and he laughed a trifle self-consciously, tossing down his pants: she gripped it in her warm hand and gently squeezed. He gasped, reached out and touched her arm. She touched the tip between her legs, brushed it there, looking down. She put him between her thighs, closed them and squeezed, wrapped her arms around his shoulders and gave him a long kiss. She felt his knees tremble, heart pound; her hands slipped down and gripped his narrow butt. She gave a hard squeeze and he groaned in pain.

"Sorry," she said.

"It's okay."

"I don't know my own strength."

They had not stopped kissing to talk; their mouths still gently touched, tongues caressed.

"I'm just about out of my mind," she said.

"I know."

"I don't want to wait any longer."

"Okay."

She could feel him trembling and straining between her legs.

"I'm going to walk over and put myself on that bed, and I want you to get on top of me and put it in." She squeezed him with her thighs. "No fooling around."

"Right."

"We can kiss and touch and talk about it later."

Thus Laurel's dream of a different kind of lovemaking, where they would lie around at first just rubbing each other's backs, where he would spend long minutes gently kissing her breasts, went up, so to speak, in smoke. She did not pull the bedspread down (no soft sheets) and did not even give him a chance to take his shirt off, though she did raise it so his bare chest would touch her breasts. His first stroke plunged in all the way. "Oh!" she shouted, as if to say, At last! She lifted her legs to get him farther in. She rocked on her bottom, meeting his thrusts, gripped his butt and pulled him into her stroke by stroke. The insides of her thighs were soaked. His head lay hard on her shoulder, his mouth open at her neck, and she heard him groan. He did not seem to come violently, but went on a long long time. When he tried to roll off she held him on top of her. She liked to feel a man grow small inside her.

Finally he did roll off, and lay staring at the ceiling. "That was wonderful," he said.

"Wonderful." It was very wet where she was lying. She would have to change the bedspread.

"Did you have an orgasm?"

"Not yet. I've got it in my plans. But I want to rest a minute. Let's get under the covers."

She wouldn't have believed it five minutes before, but she was actually slightly chilly, a breeze drifting in the window, her body damp with her sweat and probably also with Ned's.

They pulled down the spread and got in. The sheets felt soft and clean. She lay on her back for a while enjoying them.

"Okay," she said after a couple minutes. "I want you to touch me."

"Do you want it another way? I could kiss you."

"No. Touch me."

"I don't mind. I really like to."

"It's all right. I just want to be touched."

"No trouble. Really."

"Touch me."

She knew in theory that there was an elaborate sexual adjustment for them to make, though she had preferred to ignore that fact in her fantasies of this moment. At times she thought a long checklist should be provided to potential couples all over the world, with a variety of questions and four possible answers: Yes, No, Sometimes, and What the hell is that? Each partner should have to agree to the other's list before they started an affair. It wasn't just specific acts, of course, there were more subtle things, such as the fact that Ned at the moment was touching her about twenty times too fast. (When she was in one of these incredibly sexy moods, she seemed to have to go back and start over completely to have her orgasm. There was fucking and there was touching, and sometimes they seemed completely different.) When she mentioned this fact, of course, he would be terribly hurt—she was criticizing his skill as a lover!—unless she did it exactly the right way. *Fragile* was stamped indelibly on the male ego. She touched his hand with her own. "Slower, darling." She started him at roughly the right rhythm. Maybe he could take some lessons from Matt. There was a man who knew how to touch. Through years of expert instruction, of course.

She let Ned go on his own way, sometimes a little too fast and sometimes a little too slowly. She didn't try to teach him subtleties. All it really took was some rubbing. Just generate a little friction. She did have an orgasm, and a pretty nice one, but her body was so heavy and numbed—this really had been a frustrating day, right up until about five minutes ago—that all this first orgasm did was get her back to normal. *Now*, she would have said (she didn't think she'd better say it at the moment) she was ready for some sex.

They lay on their backs and let the breeze blow over them. Only their fingertips were touching. For some reason Laurel didn't feel—as she always did with Matt—that she wanted to cuddle up with Ned. His body seemed slightly strange now that she had had an orgasm. Where, for instance, did he get such a skinny butt?

After a while Ned spoke. "I'm sorry I was so fast again."

They always needed to know how they had done.

"That was just the way I wanted it," Laurel said.

"I never seem to go on long enough to satisfy you."

"You did satisfy me. I'm satisfied." Not that she couldn't go for a little more.

"I mean when we were doing it."

"That's the way I always have an orgasm. That's the way I like it."

"Really? You never do it just by screwing?"

"Only if I'm touched at the same time. That's fun now and then. But I find it kind of . . . distracting. I usually like to have my orgasm afterwards."

There was a long silence. Ned seemed to be absorbing this information.

"You know," he said finally, "you can work on that."

"Work on it?"

"There are kinds of therapy that work on your sex life. Make it more satisfying."

Wait a minute. She was under the impression she had been reassuring him.

"There is no such thing as a sex life more satisfying than mine."

"That's what everybody thinks. Then they're surprised when they go through this therapy and find out how much better it can be."

The little twit. "What the hell do you know about my sex life?"

"I know what you just told me. And I've experienced a little of it."

"So that qualifies you to be my sex therapist."

"I didn't say that."

"It sounds wonderfully convenient. Will you accept a check?"

"I never said anything about being your therapist myself. You're the one who's bringing that up. But I would think that you of all people would be open to the idea of therapy."

"I am open to the *idea*."

"It doesn't sound that way to me."

This was really too much. Now she was such a closed-up

frigid bitch she didn't even want to be changed. She knew she shouldn't have tried an affair with a younger man.

"Ned." She'd have to straighten this child out. "You don't understand."

"I do understand. This kind of therapy has done a lot for me."

Ah. A convert in our midst. Nothing more boring than that. But it did explain a lot. It explained, for instance, why he was so concerned about his performance.

"I mean you don't understand about me," Laurel said. "I've been through all this. Worrying about how I am. Wondering if it's okay. I've read books. Talked with other women. I've spoken with men and women therapists. I finally just decided it was all stupid. I love my sex life. I love the way it is. I adore having intercourse, and in the right hands"—make that hand; oh, forget it—"I have wonderful orgasms. Incredible orgasms. All the orgasms I want. I do think I know a little more about being a woman than you do. And I'm not interested in being changed. Not in bed."

"You never know when a relationship may bring about a change."

"I'm not interested in a man who's setting out to change me."

All this did, of course, raise the question of why she was interested in anyone other than Matt, with whom she had worked all these things out, with whom, in fact, she had largely become what she was. They had been through it all, and parts of it had been a hell of a struggle. No, she didn't much care for oral sex (there wasn't anything terribly painful about it; there was just this large warm rather odd object in your mouth, that you had to be careful not to scrape with your teeth, and that might suddenly lurch in your mouth and make you gag; the whole thing could be done, but there was nothing particularly enjoyable about it); and no, she didn't care even one time to try anal sex (sometimes she wanted to state a simple opinion, which seemed to her actually a physiological fact, that there was an opening for ingestion and one for elimination and still another one ideally suited for reproduction); and she didn't want to try it upside down in a rocking chair or strung from the ceiling in leather and chains. Sometimes she thought the sexual revolution missed the whole point, which was that people should do what they liked to do, what naturally came to their minds. What Laurel really liked, what she actually liked best in the whole sexual repertoire, was to lie on her back and get—pardon the expression—laid.

She didn't want to go back and relive the struggles of early married life. She just wanted to have a little fun. See what somebody else was like. Maybe she should have chosen a partner who was a little more fully formed.

Ned as he lay there seemed rather chagrined. He hadn't apparently expected to provoke an argument.

"I'm sorry," he said.

"Okay."

"I guess in a way I'm actually just worried about me."

Brilliant deduction. "You shouldn't be."

"I can't help it. It's something I always wonder about."

"Was someone complaining?"

"Women don't always complain."

"I do. I scream my head off. But you're just what I want, if you'll be what you are. Young, and vital, and ardent."

"It's all been so hectic. So hurried and frantic. I've hardly even gotten to know you."

"It's true. We need more time."

"I don't even know the things you like to do. And you don't know about me."

The checklist was an idea whose time had come.

"We'll learn eventually," Laurel said. "We can find time to experiment. It can be fun that way. Or you can just tell me."

Ned laughed. "I don't like to just tell you. Like I'm making a demand."

"It's not a demand. You're expressing a wish. It's the easiest way to get things across. Say them."

"Yes."

Laurel bit her lip, glanced at him. "There's something you're thinking about right now."

"No there isn't."

"There is. There is." She turned toward him on her side, smiled. "I can tell by the look on your face."

He reddened. "There's always one thing. The thing you can think of right offhand."

"That sounds like a good place to start."

He shifted uneasily on the bed. "It always sounds so blatant. Like an X-rated movie."

"We're not in a movie. It all depends on the context."

"I guess."

"The best way to say something is just to say it."

He rolled over on his side and faced her. "It might make you mad."

"So I'll get mad."

"For all I know you think it's perverted."

"It undoubtedly is."

They were both grinning broadly now, waiting—as the joke went on—for the punch line.

"It's something I really love."

"Let's have it."

"It's the thing in the whole world I like more than anything else. From a woman."

"Great."

"There's something about it that just seems sweet to me. Incredibly tender. Touching."

"Say it."

He cupped her hand in the two of his and looked into her eyes. "I want you to blow me," he said.

VI

The door as it opened dragged on something, and the light inside was dim. It took Matt's eyes a moment to adjust. The room he entered was larger than the living room upstairs. The walls were a uniform off-white, the ceiling lowered, and the carpet was an extremely thick shag, the color of burgundy; that was what the door had been dragging on. Everything down there seemed low, and dim, as if the apartment were occupied by vision-impaired dwarfs. To his left was a long low black vinyl couch with wide armrests, to his right a couple of easy chairs of the same design. Across the room—at first he could barely make it out—was what seemed to be a low double bed. The light above it intensified, brightened that far side of the room, and he saw, sitting in the middle of the bed, Angel.

"Close it tight," she said. "It locks."

Matt scraped the door back shut, found the latch and clicked it.

The single contour sheet on the bed matched the wine color of the carpet. Against it Angel wore a white cotton dress, gathered with a thin belt at the waist; it was cut low at the front, and her arms were bare. Her blond hair hung straight and soft around her shoulders. Her feet were bare; white sandals rested on the carpet beside the bed. She seemed paler than Matt remembered. Her face looked thinner, and in the bright light above her seemed rather drawn, though she smiled. She wore small wire-framed spectacles. Her legs were gathered beside her, and she leaned on her hand. The mattress, as she shifted, bounced oddly; it was a waterbed.

"How's Matt tonight?" she said.

"Pretty good." He had been startled by the sudden light. "How's Angel?"

"All right. I hope you're not just going to stand there."

"No." He took a couple steps, gazing around. It took a few moments to take the place in. "What the hell *is* this?"

"Surprised?"

"I don't believe my eyes."

The place looked like the set for a cheap dirty movie. It was an auto mechanic's dream of a classy bachelor pad.

"This is Hugh's other apartment," Angel said. "Hugh Bollinger's famous downstairs apartment."

Matt could hardly walk on the carpet, it was so thick. Somebody should really get in there with a power mower. The place was cool, like a cellar for vintage wines, though the upstairs had been stuffy. At the far side of the room the wall jutted back. Across from the bed it was all mirror.

"What the hell?" Matt said.

"Some people like to watch themselves."

"Not Hugh."

Angel laughed. "Hugh's nothing to look at." She lay down and rested her head in her hand. "Why don't you come over here with me?"

That much closer, she still looked different. It might just have been that she had been wearing makeup the other day, or been up and moving around, but it seemed more than that. The smile she wore now was not quite convincing. There was a tension around her eyes, which seemed drawn and hollow. The little glasses made her face look narrow. She seemed more serious, more—he would have said, without really knowing—herself. In a way, to him, she was more attractive.

He walked over and sat down beside her on the bed, creating a mild turbulence.

"I didn't know about any of this," he said.

"Not too many people do. Only Hugh's special friends."

"He rents this place?"

"I don't think anymore. He used to. But not"—she gestured vaguely with a hand—"like this."

"You've been here before."

"I've been here."

"For one of Hugh's parties."

"Not what you'd really call a party. Maybe . . ." She smiled. "A very private party."

From the upstairs apartment they could hear faintly the sound of the music, mostly the dull throb of the bass. Occasionally they heard the clatter of shoes on the hardwood floor.

"All the action's upstairs," Matt said.

"So far." She reached a hand to his chest, slipped her fingers inside his shirt.

Her lips were slender, delicately shaped. The light scent she wore was musky. He leaned slowly to kiss her—a moderate ripple washed over the bed—but she turned away, so his lips brushed her cheek.

"I think I told you before," she said. "I don't kiss."

"I love to kiss. I always kiss."

"You don't always kiss me." Her lips were pursed in a little smile, but her eyes were hard. "Kissing is intimate. My kisses are . . . reserved."

"You have a husband."

She raised her eyebrows, as if amused.

"A lover?"

"It's none of your business."

"I don't mean to pry. But I'm really interested. I'd like to know about you."

"Lots of people would. Nobody does."

"This is all so strange."

"That makes it interesting."

"What are you doing here? What am I doing here? And this place. It's weird."

"I don't know." There were only two buttons on her dress, above the belt, and with a short glance down, as if she had just gotten the idea, she started to unbutton them. "Hugh keeps this apartment to use. What all for you're not sure, even I'm not too sure, but here it is." Slowly she drew an arm out of her dress; one breast appeared. "I'm a woman who makes a living going with men. Massaging them. whatever. He's paying me some money to be here tonight. Very good money. More money than I can really refuse." She had pulled the other arm out, carefully arranged the dress under her breasts so it didn't wrinkle. "He said you'd be down. I remembered you from before. It sounded fine."

Her breasts were taut and soft at the same time, marvelously round, the nipples pink.

"Hugh's a fat old man." She was looking down at one breast, ran a finger along the top of it, smiled. "Not as old as he thinks he is. But he doesn't do much anymore. He thinks about it a lot. Talks about it. He likes to know it's going on, even if he doesn't exactly want to do it. It's sad in a way. Kind of pitiful. Also kind of stupid. But that's how he is."

"Yeah."

"He likes to do it by proxy. In absentia. He likes to be upstairs, and know there's something going on downstairs."

She reached out a hand and started, at the top, to unbutton his shirt.

"You've done this for him before," Matt said.

"It's most of what I have done for him."

"With other men."

"Not other women."

"Like who?"

"What's that matter? You're down here at the moment."

She had his shirt unbuttoned, tugged out of his pants, baring his chest. She reached out with her hand spread like a fan, lightly caressed him, brushing his nipples.

"The man fascinates me," Matt said. "I'd like to know about him."

"Apparently so." She did not raise her eyes to him, still looked at his chest.

"What a man like that does downtown. Places like yours."

"You might be disappointed."

"I don't care what it is. I'm just interested."

She shrugged. "He talks."

Matt could have guessed that much.

"On and on. Forever. He pays for our longest session sometimes, seventy dollars, then he just lies there and talks it away. I rub him, or I don't. Sometimes I just lie there and hold myself against him. It doesn't really matter. He does it with the other girls too. But mostly me."

"That's all?"

"He gets me to tell him things. What other people have come in and asked for. The first time I ever went with a man. The kinkiest thing I've ever done. He just likes to hear the words. I make a lot of it up. Sometimes, once in a great long while, he gets excited, and I get him off. Nothing I haven't done to you."

It all sounded pretty tame, and a little pathetic. Matt could have guessed at most of it.

"He has me entertain his friends. That's the thing he really likes." She reached down and, with one finger, traced the line of his fly. "It's a lot easier if they take their clothes off."

"That's understandable." He had jumped slightly at her touch.

She had found what she was looking for, cupped it, squeezed. "I always do the job I'm paid for."

Matt had never taken his things off on a waterbed before, and it proved far more difficult than he had imagined. The turbulence was terrific, a rowboat braving a typhoon, and the sound was also disturbing, as if a rhinoceros had taken in too much fluid and was flopping around on his back in discomfort. It was worse when Angel was thrashing around too, but she finished quickly, lay there and watched him struggle.

"What's the point of these things?" Matt said.

"They're supposed to be very sexy."

If he'd known they'd be using a waterbed he'd have taken a Dramamine.

When he finished undressing he just lay still for a moment and enjoyed the calm. Angel gingerly rolled his way and touched a hand to his chest. "Why don't you just stay still and let me work for a while?"

That sounded like the safest idea under the circumstances.

At first she just touched with her fingertips, tracing delicate patterns. She played with the hair at the top of his chest. She touched with her whole fingers, rubbed slightly harder, massaged the soft muscles between his shoulders and neck. Her fingernails tickled lightly in the hair under his arms. His eyelids had fallen shut; he felt on the verge of dozing off. She rolled his nipples between her finger and thumb, gently tugged. Her head moved over to rest on his chest, her hand slid down his belly. She gripped one leg where it joined the other; the sensation shot up his spine. A fingernail tickled for a while between his legs. Her hand moved up and cupped his balls, rolled them gently. With her fingernails she caressed around and beneath them. Her hand moved slowly to encircle his cock; she gripped it at the base, squeezed.

She raised her head from his chest; her hair fell down and caressed him. She lowered her mouth to his nipples, kissed with just the tip of her tongue. She sucked them softly, then harder and harder; she gave little bites with her teeth. She traveled slowly in a roundabout route down his torso with her tongue, dry and fluttering; she paused a moment at his navel to probe, continued down. Her mouth arrived at his balls, breathed warmly, caressed with the tongue; she held them in her hand and took little bites. Her fingernail started tickling again between his legs. She held his cock by the tip against his belly, traveled slowly up its length with her tongue, licking back and forth; she traveled down again, up again. He could barely feel the caresses, as if they were just out of reach. She raised his cock in the air, encircled it with her lips, lowered her head and took it far into her mouth. She sucked hard, fluttering with her tongue. Her fingernail still tickled between his legs. She slowly moved her mouth up and let him slip out.

She paused and looked up at him. "I can do it this way. Or if you want you can put it in."

Her face as she looked at him was matter-of-fact, as if she were taking his order at a lunch counter.

"I thought you didn't do that," he said.

"We're not downtown now. And I know who you are."

She held his cock almost impatiently, looking up at him.

"I guess I'd like to put it in," he said.

She nodded. "All right." She slid up beside him on the bed.

Suddenly everything seemed serious in a way it hadn't before. Angel's face, which had been so coy when they were together before, was almost solemn. This is the real thing, Matt thought. The real thing.

He got on top of her carefully, trying to keep the waterbed still. She glanced up and smiled, as if trying to be pleasant. "Let me take it." She reached down and found his cock, placed it at the right spot. There was moisture at the opening, but farther on she seemed all closed up. "Go in slowly," she said. "Take it easy." He proceeded carefully, with gentle motions from his hips. It was very tight and harsh going in, and he was very hard; it felt wonderful. Angel's eyes were closed, her face frowning. She kept whispering, "Easy. Easy." His cock was throbbing from the tight grip she had on it; he stopped a moment to let it calm down.

"Sorry it's so rough," she said.

"It's all right. I like it."

She smiled weakly. "You're almost there."

He started again. She seemed more relaxed now, her eyes

still closed. For a moment her face looked young, almost innocent; it didn't seem to go with the voluptuous body she had.
It was a human face, somehow touching for being human,
blank as the face of a sleeping child. He gave a slightly harder
thrust, felt himself nearly all the way in: he leaned to the
softly parted lips (were they parted in pain?) and kissed them.

"No!" With a single shove, a swift motion of her whole body,
she pushed him off and out of her. "No!" Her voice was shouting. "I told you I don't kiss!"

Matt found himself on his back, the waterbed kicking up a
storm. Talk about coitus interruptus. He tried to turn toward
Angel, who was struggling, in all the turbulence, to sit up.

"I don't kiss. I told you I don't kiss! I don't *kiss!*"

She swung with her whole arm, hit him on the face with the
flat of her hand.

On his back again. God. His nose was buzzing. His eyes saw
stars. He reached up with his hand and came back with a
splotch of blood.

"I've had it with this!" she was shouting. "I've had it with
this!"

Matt started again to try to sit up. "Listen . . ."

"Get out of this bed!" She had fallen to her side and was
pushing against him with her hands and knees, his back
pressed against the hard wooden frame. Matt leaned against
her, fought off her hands, but his heart wasn't in it. "Get out
of this bed!" Her hands dug into his chest; his back scraped
across the frame. "Get out of this *bed!*"

She gave a last hard shove and he fell, with a plop, the three
feet to the floor.

"Do you like this? Do you like this?" It was as if she were
shouting at the whole room. "Does it turn you on?"

He saw them for a moment in the mirror, she sitting up
again, her fists clenched, muscles trembling, he collapsed in a
heap on the floor. There was a splotch of blood above his
mouth.

"Angel." He turned to her. "I'm sorry."

"It was the one thing I asked you not to do. The one thing I
said you couldn't do. So you did it."

"I forgot. I was so excited."

"Oh so was I. So was I. Couldn't you tell?"

He rolled to his knees in the soft carpet. "I'll remember now.
Really."

"You're damn right you will."

"I really won't try to kiss you again."

"Fucking right."

He had started to stand, put his knee on the bed. "Okay?"

"Get back in this bed and I'll tear your balls off."

She looked as if she would, too, her fists still tight, muscles quivering with rage. He remembered from just moments before the strong hands that had held him, sharp fingernails that caressed.

"I'm so sick of all this," she said.

Matt stood at the bedside with his hands on his hips, his penis still standing dumbly, straight and hard. All dressed up and nowhere to go.

"You want to know things," she said. "You're so interested in the truth. Look." She pointed at the mirror, and he stared, under the harsh glare from the light on the wall, at their reflection: the slumped man bewildered in his excitement, the furious woman trembling in her rage. Was that some kind of truth?

"That mirror's two-way," she said.

At first he thought she was just using an expression—that works both ways—but then it struck him, the special meaning of her words.

"What do you mean?"

"You've heard of that. They can see out, but you can't see in."

He stared again. His rather ridiculous image stared back at him.

"You're just saying that."

"I'm not. I'm not. Hugh Bollinger's probably back there with his soft dick in his hand right now. Getting off on this scene. At least in his mind."

He looked hard at the mirror. It actually was set in a narrow frame of wall that ran all around it, not, as he would have thought, cemented on the wall.

"You like watching dirty movies so much," Angel said. "Now you're in one."

He stared around the edges of the mirror. "How do you get in there?"

"You don't, from here. There's a little stairway from upstairs. But you can't get in from here. Unless you break the mirror. Maybe you could knock it down with your gigantic prick."

Actually, as Angel had started telling him of the mirror, his erection had started rapidly to diminish.

"I don't believe this," Matt said.

"I'm sure you don't. You want to get the truth, and then when you get it you don't believe it."

Matt looked for his clothes, which were scattered around on the floor. He started gathering them up.

"Don't you like being watched?" Angel said. "Being part of a peep show. You ought to try being a woman. The whole world's a peep show."

He had found his underpants and was putting them on, was pulling on his pants. He found himself moving rather rapidly.

"You get used to it, of course. To the point that you hardly even notice." She had fallen back on the bed, raised up her knees, spread them wide. "This is the way Hugh likes it. Give us a good shot, Angel." She mimicked his hoarse drunken voice. "Be sure to give us a good shot."

"I'm sure he does."

"He pays. It's more than most men do. He pays for what he wants. He's really very generous. He just has certain weaknesses. For watching people. Listening in on things. And for playing pranks. He loves a good practical joke."

"I can see that."

Matt had his shirt on now, was all tucked in, had sat on the floor to put on his shoes and socks.

"Like the one about that accident he supposedly saw."

Matt looked at her. She had been lying on her back, staring at the ceiling, now turned to face him.

"What do you know about that?" he said.

"I know everything about it. I know it all."

She rested her head in her hand, gazing at him, a trace of amusement in her eyes.

"That was the first thing he said to me, that day you were downtown. 'Angel, I'm about to become the witness to an accident.'"

"He was at the scene of the accident. Somebody saw him there."

"He's at the scene of a lot of things. That doesn't mean he knows what's going on. He's off in a drunken stupor. Or running a dirty movie in his mind."

"But he saw this accident. He described it to me in detail."

"He made that up. Came to me that first day and told me he

was going to. He went to his friend, the one who saw it, and got a few details. Worked it all out. He knew what you'd want to hear. He's good at making things up."

Matt was astonished. The rest of it was bad enough, weird and kinky and sick, but it went with Bollinger somehow, with his odd sad life. This, perhaps because it was close to Matt, seemed worse. The man had invented testimony about an accident.

"Would he have gone on the witness stand?"

"Never. He doesn't get himself in trouble."

"When would he have come out with the truth?"

"At the perfect moment. He has a way of picking that. Maybe at that party he's having upstairs. With a lot of people around. Or maybe the day of the trial. In front of your boss. His specialty is humiliation."

That was what Matt was feeling at the moment, a large measure, a gnawing at his gut like hunger.

"I don't understand it."

"Anything for a laugh. But he also needed to keep you around. Keep you interested. He needs somebody like you. A man who can get his cock hard."

"He could have found another way. This was my work."

"He had to think of something in a hurry that first day. He had seen an opportunity. Another vicarious thrill." She glanced toward the mirror. "There was one of those in that room too."

As she spoke, he could see the little room, the full-length mirror alongside the massage table. He felt his humiliation welling into anger.

"It's a nice way you make a living."

"I don't expect to do this forever. I couldn't do it at all if it wasn't for guys like you. And it's just for the money. I always get paid. I'll get paid for tonight, you can bet on that."

Matt felt a churning like nausea in his stomach. He actually thought he might be sick. All he had done the past few days, the story he had been pursuing so assiduously, so seriously, had finally just been a joke, one more thing for Hugh Bollinger to practice his hoarse giggle on. Matt had been trying, pitifully enough, to do his job, and the whole thing had been made a mockery.

"Who all knows about this?" he said.

"His story? Just me and him, that I know of. Maybe his fat friend from the bookstore."

"And all"—Matt gestured toward the room around him—"this?"

"I don't know. But I imagine they're all upstairs right now. Or crowded behind that mirror. Why don't you go ask them?"

"I can do without that."

The thought of facing those people was more than he could stand. Their weird faces, as he gazed absently toward the mirror, loomed up in his memory one after another. He should have known when they first met not to get mixed up with them. He should have known just by looking at them. The one thing he hoped was that he would never see them again.

VII

Laurel walked over from the stairway and flopped in a chair, slouching; wearily, she closed her eyes. Ned had followed her down the stairs and just stood at the bottom watching her, didn't say anything for a few moments.

"I guess I might as well be going," he said finally.

"I guess."

Laurel did not open her eyes or move in the chair. Ned took a couple steps toward her.

"I don't want you to think I didn't have a nice time," he said.

"God." She shook her head. "It was a fiasco."

"I really don't feel that way. I think it was nice. At least for a while there."

She frowned, opened her eyes. "I wish you wouldn't go quite yet."

"I was just thinking." He shrugged. "Matt might be getting back."

"He won't be home for hours. He made a point of saying he'd be late. And we won't be doing anything incriminating. I just want to talk. I hate to leave things . . . like this."

She had, in fact, removed all the evidence. She had changed the sheets, changed the bedspread, working with the kind of fierce energy that stemmed from anger or frustration. "That's all right. I'll handle it," she said when Ned tried to help. She had gotten her clothes on, straightened the room back up perfectly. She would have been very good at an affair, at the practicalities of it, if only the other part would work out. Whatever that was. The affection. The compatibility.

Ned went over and sat on the far end of the couch, on the other side of the room. He couldn't have found a place that was farther away from her. If he could have, he would have. He looked like a mild peaceful person who was there to settle a quarrel between two warring factions. But there was only one other person in the room.

"You must feel like a whipped dog," Laurel said.

"I feel fine. Really. I had a nice time."

"In this whole situation you've been the victim. The innocent bystander."

Ned smiled, shrugged. "Not so innocent."

"I can look back on this whole thing and see how it happened. I mean going back for months."

She was lying more than sitting in the chair, her hands folded at her waist, eyes staring up at the ceiling. She paused, reflecting.

"I've really been feeling strong lately," she said. "Especially at work. I feel I'm ready to start. My life's work is beginning."

"I know. You've been a different person. It's been good to see."

"There was that long bad period. Living in that dumb little town, staying home with Jonathan. God almighty, what a nightmare. When I finally got away from that, back to school and then to work, I felt I'd been let out of prison, or cured of some dread disease. I looked around and saw the sun could still shine, flowers still bloom. It was as if they'd let me out by mistake. I'd stepped out when somebody's back was turned. I wanted to run like a thief."

"That was perfectly natural. A natural feeling at the time."

If he made one more remark like a counselor she was going to pick up a lamp and cave in his head.

"Matt was so unhappy. Moping around, all wrapped up in himself. Everything was driving me away. I was glad when I had to work extra hours, glad when I had to work weekends. And I was getting to know you. You were so full of energy, so unencumbered and free. We had all kinds of things in common, and however far apart we were in everyday life, me with my husband and child, at work we were about the same. Kindred spirits. I thought we could have a nice affair, keep it separate from my other life. It would be another thing, like going off to work in the morning. Both things could go on at once."

"I do think that's possible. I still think it's possible."

"It was a dream. A fantasy. There was a real person there. Who had a daily life of his own, wouldn't be available at my beck and call. For whom the whole thing, coming into my house and being my lover while my child was asleep and my husband gone, that whole thing meant something different than it did to me. Who had a variety of things he liked to do in bed, that weren't necessarily my things at all."

"I didn't mean it that seriously, Laurel. I didn't mean we had to do it. It's something we can work out."

"I didn't know you, is the point. I had this whole elaborate thing worked out, but it didn't actually include you. It involved some other you, who only existed in my mind." She shook her head. "I feel like a schoolgirl, with a stupid schoolgirl crush. Then she finds out her teacher already *has* a wife."

"You're always putting yourself down. Making yourself sound small."

"I don't want to be this person."

That was an exceedingly strange thing to say. We're quite sorry, old girl, but right at the moment there's no other person available for you to be.

This whole grand philosophical argument, this reexamination of hopes, dreams, plans for the future, all stemmed from a simple request for a blow job. That's what was so humiliating. It burst her bubble but good, plugged her right back into the days when she and Matt had been trying to work things out sexually, had gotten into fight after fight about it. Sweaty bodies on the bed, hurt looks in sad eyes. If it could have been like a tasting party at a smorgasbord (you want some of the pickled herring? I don't think so. Doesn't appeal to me. Maybe a little section from the artichoke hearts) it would have been fine. But it never was. It was all so personal. Behind the disputes over specific things were the words that were never quite spoken. I hate to say this, Matt, but all these things you like to do, I don't have any idea where you found them, probably in a cheap paperback somewhere, but don't you think they're a little, I mean, don't you think you're a little on the perverted side? Frankly no, Laurel. I don't think so at all. What I think is that you're not in touch with your true feelings. The deepest sources of your sexuality. You can read about this in all those psychology books you like so much. Look it up in the index.

Look under "frigid." They had worked things out, of course, with much pain, but there was still a lingering feeling, in each of them, that things weren't exactly perfect, that prevalent suspicion of the modern marriage that your partner isn't quite right. Which conceals the fear that you aren't quite right.

The person Laurel wanted to be was the fearless woman of her fantasies, for whom everything worked out because she was so adaptable. The person she did not want to be was this one who cut everything off, stemmed the whole flow of a relationship, just to hold a line she had drawn eight years ago.

So what she was really thinking about as she spoke to Ned was not what she was talking about. She was thinking about giving him a blow job.

She stood from her chair. "I want to do it."

Ned grinned, puzzled. "What's that?"

"I've changed my mind." She took a couple of steps in his direction. "I've decided I want to blow you."

Ned reddened. This was not the kind of thing somebody said to you every day.

"No, Laurel. It's all right."

"I really do. I'm tired of all this. Of saying I want to change and then keeping everything just the same. I want to try something new."

"You said you didn't like it."

"I don't like it. I don't dislike it. It's entirely neutral to me." The Maybe category on her checklist. Perhaps that wording should be changed to: I don't mind.

She had walked over to the couch, sat beside him.

"I don't know if I want to do this," Ned said.

"That doesn't matter anymore. Now I want to do it."

"I don't know if I can do it."

"I'm sure you can. I'll be very helpful." She gripped his thigh. "Do you want to stand up? Or do you like to take it on your back?"

"I don't know." Ned wore an expression of utter bewilderment. "I guess on my back."

"Great. Lie down."

Laurel was determined, as single-minded as, earlier in the evening, she had been about getting him to bed. She wasn't at that point thinking of Ned as a person, just a human being with a penis. She had something she wanted to do here. She unbuckled his belt, unbuttoned and carefully unzipped his pants, unsnapped his underpants."Lift up." She pulled everything down to his thighs. His cock was slender, an advantage to her, she supposed, and already stiffening; her words, as the expression goes, had not been lost on him. She stroked with her thumb, tickled with her fingertips. She leaned down and, affectionately, gave it a little kiss.

A major problem with blow jobs, as far as she was concerned, was that all the positions were uncomfortable, but she was determined to do it right this time, straddled him with her legs and leaned down with her head. She picked up his cock in her hand, put it in her mouth, and tentatively, just to test her gag reflex, saw how far she could take it in. "Oh!" Ned groaned. "That's good." Remarkably far, really. His cock was quite hot; she wondered if it stayed that way all the time, or if her words had heated him up, or if it just seemed hot because she wasn't used to having it in her mouth. She pulled her head up slowly, went down again, went up and down carefully again. She wouldn't have said she didn't know how to do this—that would have been a perfectly silly thing to say—but in a way she actually didn't; she had never done it for very long, and didn't know if there were any variations she was supposed to perform. She did, however, have a good knowledge of the vagaries of the penis, and thought she could improvise from there. She continued up and down, concentrated on the sensitive area beneath the tip. Apparently she was doing okay, because Ned was squirming all over the couch, groaning and sighing.

At that point she was starting to remember the main feature of the discomfort of all this, basically the same as on a trip to the dentist; you had to keep your mouth stretched wide for so long. At least the dentist let you catch your breath and spit now and then. But she was also thinking that if the whole thing turned a man on so much, to the point that he was flopping around and shouting (it must have been the *idea* that turned him on; for sheer skill in stroking she was sure she could have done better with her hand) she might as well go ahead and do it; she could relax her neck and jaw later. "Oh God! God!" Ned kept saying. She had been stupid to avoid this act for so long; it was spite that made her resist. She did hope that Ned wasn't going to take much longer—this was no time, she should have reminded him, to practice his delaying techniques—and she was noticing that just a slight grazing from her lower teeth had a profound effect, when she heard, as if from another life, three steps bounding up the porch. She almost didn't recognize the sound, it was so little expected, and she went on for a moment before she let Ned slip out of her mouth and gripped him with her hand. Matt was staring at them through the screen door. He was staring very hard, frowning, as if it took terrific concentration for him to under-stand what it was he saw. For a moment she and Matt just looked at each other—neither said a word or made a gesture—then he turned and disappeared back down the steps. She wanted to shout at him, jump up and run after him, but she didn't know what to say. Ned hadn't even heard, he was so preoccupied. Her hand, out of long practice, had continued to squeeze; she felt Ned's hips jump, and semen spurted onto his belly.

VIII

He only knew he wanted to drive, to move, to get away; he didn't know where. He found himself at the far end of the street (the way you might, on a sleepy morning, find yourself at the breakfast table with a cup of coffee and no recollection of having brewed it) where it was narrower, the houses more run down and closer together, cars parked tightly on both sides. A large dark empty truck, flashers blinking, was blocking the road. Not a soul was around. He had to stop, back up through the narrow one lane for traffic, make the turn that he should have made in the first place, then cut over one street and out onto the four lanes of Linden. He couldn't take those short narrow streets. He needed room to think.

A senseless phrase had popped into his mind and kept re-peating itself. You want a dirty movie, you get a dirty movie.

He had had it all planned out. At first on the way home he had been feeling a desperate anxiety, full of dark dark thoughts, but after a while, as will happen when a man reaches the end of the line, a resolve developed. At first it was just something he had decided to tell Laurel, a way to dismiss the evening he had spent, but as he thought it out it came to seem a decision for his life, that would solve all his problems. He would give up detective work, abandon his wait for a job on the police department; he would quit doing dumb things like watching kids on a field with a whistle around his neck. He would find some real work, he didn't care what, pumping gas, fixing motors, tending gardens, anything as long as he could get his hands on it, see it begin and see it end. He hadn't been himself lately; he'd been distracted, never quite there when he was around Jonathan and Laurel; he'd been sensitive, jumpy, short of temper. The problem was really that he'd been waiting, he'd had nothing to occupy his energy, his attention was unfocused and spinning off in all kinds of crazy directions. He couldn't face what he was doing because facing it was painful; he didn't admit he was waiting because he knew the wait was futile. At last he was able to see that the past year, the past three or four years, had been desperate and fruitless. He was ready for a new beginning.

By the time he got home he was bounding up the steps. He knew Laurel would be glad at the news.

For a moment after he arrived it was as if he were at the wrong house, the wrong block, the wrong city: he couldn't be seeing that. It was like some final ironic comment on the past few days: you didn't have to run all over the city looking for this. It was right here in your own house all the time. The scene he saw had a vividness it had never had in any movie, or even in his imagination. The plain living room, with its musty odor, yellowish light, deep-green flowered wallpaper as a backdrop; the long couch with its worn and faded arms, stuffing showing at the cushions; the man with his mouth wide and groaning, eyes shut tight, pants torn down to his thighs; the woman crouched compactly above him. It looked to Matt in the moment he saw as if she were really *working*: cramped into an awkward position, her head laboring up and down, mouth stuffed to the point of gagging; when she turned his way a long string of saliva hung from her mouth briefly, then broke away. Her look as she saw him was not one of horror, exactly, or even astonishment, more like sudden sorrow, or deep concern. Whether for herself, or for him, he didn't know.

In your whole life, no matter how long you lived, you never knew the person you were living with. Never.

Matt wouldn't have been surprised to know Laurel was attracted to another man. He wouldn't have been surprised (it would have pained him deeply, but he wouldn't have been surprised) to know she was having an affair. For years, as a kind of playful banter in bed, they had talked of people they were drawn to, imagined erotic situations (what would you do if you really had the chance? If I were out of town, say, and somebody

127

came over?), toyed with the forbidden to show it was harmless. These attractions existed, they were a fact of life, and Matt knew that, given enough time and the vagaries of life, anything could happen. He was a little surprised at Laurel's choice of men: Ned Streater seemed too fresh, enthusiastic, a little too much off the front of a cornflakes box for Laurel. But she loved her work, loved the people at work, and though he was younger Ned had helped her get settled there, was something of a mentor for her. Matt knew such bonds were strong.

It wasn't who she was with that stunned him. That hadn't been the real shock.

There had been a time, not too many years ago, when Matt had thought of sex as a series of acts. That was the way his friends talked about it, the way it was pictured in drama and song, the way it was treated in books on the subject. You learned how to do these things (*technique*: get the moves down and put them to work), learned an approximate order in which they occurred—there could be some variation in that—then you were ready for anybody, could plug in anywhere. Sex partners were interchangeable, like spare parts.

Often enough in his early marriage it had been like that. Laurel laboring at some task she felt obliged to perform, Matt fantasizing a person who really cared for it, neither of them particularly present, involved. There had been accusation and bitterness, sometimes actually spoken, in what they did. But in time, as if abandoning a dilemma, they had given that up, settled into things that avoided occasions for pain, and sex for them had come to be something else. It was not acts, it was people, joining each other in ways that were personal, private, unpredictable. They gave what they could, took what was available, tried to leave the other satisfied. That kind of sex could no more have been taught in a book than friendship, or virtue. The sex of acts—however much it was codified in books approved by the American Medical Association and the Fellowship of Christian Athletes—was a fabrication. It was the sex of popular literature, magazine advertisements, dirty books, situation comedies, massage parlors, soap operas, movies, strip shows, women's magazines, whorehouses. There was nothing wrong with it. It was pleasant enough in its own way. It just wasn't the real thing.

Laurel giving a blow job was Laurel performing a sex act. Matt didn't think she did that kind of thing.

There would have been better days for him to find out.

That world of sexual acts had its attraction also for him, of course. He had proved as much in the past few days. But such behavior for him was furtive, frantic, peripheral, neurotic. It was what he did when he was running scared. It had nothing to do with the core of his existence. Matt knew Laurel cared for Ned, he knew Ned was close to her center of things, and knew now, from what he had seen, that her relationship with Ned was vastly different from anything she had with Matt. It was as if Matt had caught a glimpse not of his wife being unfaithful, but of a whole other world, an incomprehensible world, where Laurel went down on men, sucked them off. It was a world he had never imagined to exist. And his wife, at least some of the time, lived in it.

His whole life suddenly seemed ridiculous. The earthshaking decision about his work that he had made only a few minutes before was fundamentally phony. The fact of the matter was that he had no work in his life. The pragmatic careers he had been planning were for Laurel, for Jonathan, but at the moment they seemed to have no part in his life. He would have said he was not so petty as to leave his wife for a single infidelity, but he also couldn't imagine seeing her again. He didn't want to hear an explanation of what he had seen. He didn't want to know what it was about her relationship with Ned that made that kind of sex different, what it was about himself that made her seek out Ned. Of course she would prefer a man like Ned, with his settled career, his interests similar to hers, to a man who couldn't find a job he liked and hardly knew what she was talking about half the time. Already Matt's mind had raced forward to a future where Laurel and Jonathan lived with Ned, he lived off by himself somewhere—such a future perfectly reflected his present feelings—and the sorrow of that vision ached in his heart. He didn't at the moment mind the thought of living apart from Laurel (as far as he was concerned she could go fuck herself) but he couldn't bear the thought of a daily life without Jonathan.

A man empty of work, without a family: the future stood before him like a dark void. He didn't even know where he was driving so frantically.

And then he did. A part of him had all along: he had taken the left onto Murray—was passing now the closed shops, the few lighted theaters and eating places, occasional nighttime strollers—and was heading straight for Bollinger's house. He had wanted before to slink away, forget Bollinger and his friends and the fact that he had ever known them, but now there was nowhere to slink to. Bollinger seemed in some way responsible. Matt no longer cared how stupid he felt. He wanted to confront the man, take his stupid joke and shove it down his throat.

The street when Matt got there was quiet, dark, lined as it was with high leafy trees; the houses sat well back from the sidewalk. They were dark, or dimly lighted. It was a neighborhood of older couples, shopkeepers, clerks, salespeople, most of whom retired early. The only house brightly lit was Bollinger's, and that only on the second floor. The first floor was dark, and the door was locked when Matt got there and tried it. The windows upstairs were open, but Matt could hear no music or conversation. The door to the stairway was also closed, but opened when he gave it a shove.

Upstairs the door was ajar, and the living room very much as he had left it, except that no one was there. Half-filled drinks were on the tables, ashes and cigarette butts filled the ashtrays, bits of food were scattered around. The plate of hors d'oeuvres was empty. The air was stale, smoky, and boozy. The film projector was still there, and still facing the direction of the wall, but no film was on it, only an empty take-up reel.

Matt took a slow tour of the apartment. The light was still on in the kitchen, bottles of liquor and club soda open on the counter, ice trays out and melting, bags of pretzels and cans of peanuts open. There was even a steady prolonged drip from the faucet, which Matt shut off. The lights were off in the back rooms—a guest room and Bollinger's small bedroom—and there was no sign anyone had been there, but at the bottom of the back stairway the door was open slightly, and a dim light shone.

Matt stood at the top a moment in silence, carefully listening. Not a sound. He tested the first step for a creak, then the second; very slowly, he walked down.

The light as he pushed open the door was extremely low, the way it had been when he first walked in, before Angel turned it up. The only sound was the quiet hum of the air conditioning. At first Matt thought he was there alone, but then he saw, straining his eyes, a figure stretched out on his back on the waterbed. Hugh Bollinger, asleep. Apparently he did use the room occasionally for something more than a peep show. Maybe he just liked to lie there and let his fantasies surround him. Matt stepped closer, saw that the man's legs were draped across the wooden frame, more as if he were passed out than asleep. He wondered at the scene that might have preceded that. Bollinger and Angel, she touching him and talking or maybe just talking, maybe describing Matt's performance that night. Bollinger and—if Chandler Mingins was to be believed—Todd Hunter, reliving some passionate boyhood attachment from Bollinger's past. Perhaps some combination of the three of them, Bollinger watching while the two of them enacted some dream. Or maybe Hugh had brought Mrs. Droge down for a quick bang. Nothing on that night would much have surprised Matt.

He hadn't intended to disturb Bollinger—it wouldn't have done much good, if the man was so boozed up as to have passed out, and anyway, Matt could never feel much anger at someone who was unconscious. Then he saw, as he got closer, how awkward the man's position was, his arm bent behind his back, his head twisted sharply to one side; and he saw, when he was closer still, the dark wet stain on the sheet of the bed. It wasn't until he turned up the light—the control was beside the bed—that he saw the stiff clot of blood in the hair at Bollinger's temple, the wound that looked as if the whole side of his head was crushed, the stark stricken expression in the open staring eyes. Matt reached under his collar for a pulse, but already knew what he would find.

The man whom his friends had liked to call the world's oldest living adolescent was no longer living.

PART TWO:
Working

Chapter Five

The room was one of three upstairs from the street, the farthest one back along the small hallway. It was narrow, with a cot along one wall and a sink with a cold-water spigot on the other. Above the cot was a cavernous diagonal crack in the plaster, patched over in the middle with a piece of masking tape. Beside the sink was a straight hard wooden chair. The light was a dusty bulb hung from the ceiling. The only window, a small one, was eight feet up on the wall, as if to prevent even the slightest breeze from reaching the occupant. The first night Matt had gone to the trouble of dragging the chair over to open it, so bugs had flown in, moths, batting around the dim bulb. Through the window he saw a small patch of black sky. Three stars.

For two nights and most of two other days he had occupied the room, sitting on the cot, reading newspapers, smoking burley tobacco in a cheap pipe he had bought at the all-night drugstore.

The occupants of the other room were also not permanent. They didn't stay even a whole night, or more than about twenty minutes of one. There would be quiet footsteps in the hallway, the sound of water running—Matt winced, thinking how cold it must be—the rhythmic squeaking of the cot springs, the sound of water again. Voices occasionally murmured, no chatter, no laughter. Only one man so much as audibly groaned. Occasionally the woman spoke a sharp word. The couples walked quietly and wordlessly out.

For long stretches of time there was no one else in the upstairs rooms.

When he had left Bollinger's that first night, it had been all he could do not to burst wildly through the downstairs door. He had actually seen a murder victim only once in his police experience, when the body was wrapped in a stretcher and other policemen were around; he had not been alone in a dim room with a man he had known, blood still damp on the sheet beside the body and the eyes open wide in frightened astonishment. Matt walked quietly upstairs and out of the apartment, all the time thinking, Notice things, notice things, while blood pounded in his head and his eyes swam dizzily. The only thing he particularly noticed was the reel of film lying in the open case beside the projector, part of it dangling down to the floor. As if that were the one loose end in all he saw, he tucked the film in, closed the case, and—later, he would wonder why—picked it up and took it with him.

By the time he had dropped the case into the back of his car, he knew what he had to do. There weren't too many alternatives. He had to find Wolf.

He knew it was a long shot, despite Wolf's penchant for odd hours, that he would be in his office, but he hadn't counted on the building's being locked. He wasn't thinking too clearly. In the pale light of the lobby the rubber matting was rolled up, and a mop stood against the wall in a bucket of gray water. Around him the street was deserted, only a couple of storefronts lighted. Down on Penn, the lights were brighter, and he saw a solitary streetwalker, a gang of kids scuffling, two men on the street corner sharing a bottle from a paper bag. Through the heavy air of the summer night echoed the bass throb of radios from the housing projects. Matt pounded on the metal doorframes, shook the doors to make them rattle, shouted through the crack between the doors. Nobody came.

Back around the corner, halfway up the block, was a phone booth, and beside it, up three small steps in front of a doorway of yellowish light, a woman sat in a folding chair. She wore a pink faded housecoat, had one hand in a cloth purse in her lap. Her hair was gray and scraggly, her face pinched. As Matt stepped into the phone booth she picked up a can of beer and drank from it, watching him.

He let the phone ring eight times, though he knew the office was small enough that anyone who was there could have stopped it after two.

As he stepped out of the booth he was cursing their stupidity at being so casual about things, Wolf saying day after day he would have a key made for Matt and never doing it, Matt writing Wolf's unlisted home number in a matchbook and dropping it into the top drawer of his dresser.

"You looking for a room?" the woman said.

"I was just trying to call a guy."

Matt was not looking straight at the woman, but watching her out of the corner of his eye. She, too, did not look at him, but gazed down the dark street, as if something were happening there.

"Because I got a room," she said. "If you're looking for one."

Her face was pale and worn. Her mouth curved to one side, as if it were shaped that way. She even drank from that side, holding the beer there to pour it down.

"You can have it for the one night." She smiled, like a sneer. "But I got to have my money in advance."

A perfectly reasonable request under the circumstances.

His days were uneventful. The first morning he had gone to Wolf's office early, waiting for him to arrive, but he began to get jittery as people in the surrounding offices noticed him— a platinum-blond secretary from the loan office down the hall kept finding excuses to clatter out and stare at him—so eventually he left. Regularly, every half hour for two days, he had called from the pay phone outside, but there had been no answer. He had taken his meals at a café down the street— four stools at a low counter and three booths—where there were just a couple choices on the menu every day, but where the food was surprisingly good, pot roast with mashed potatoes, pork tenderloin and candied yams, a delicious peach cobbler. The first morning, after moving his car into one of the huge lots by the housing projects, where nobody would notice it, he bought a toothbrush and shaving things at an all-night drugstore; around noon the second day he bought a spare shirt and some underwear at a discount clothing place. He bought and read some magazines. He smoked his pipe. Each evening before he went out to dinner he paid for another night in his room. On the second day, the woman gave him new sheets for the bed.

"Once a week," she said, "whether they need them or not."

Much of his time he spent sitting on his bed mediating over the thought that if there was one person who was a logical murder suspect, in motive, in opportunity, in the strength required to deliver the blow, it was him.

He read all the newspaper accounts. The first morning

there had been no mention of Bollinger at all. The early evening edition had a small article at the bottom of the front page—Man Found Dead—that included little more than vital statistics. It said the police were investigating. The paper the next morning had a much fuller article, including a picture that seemed roughly the right vintage but showed a man in beaming good health. It gave a brief account of his career, mentioned his degree at Bowdoin and jobs at three different boarding schools before he moved to Tabard. He had led lacrosse teams to New England prep-school championships in 1958 and '59. He was survived by a sister who lived in California. The police had pronounced the death a homicide, and were continuing their investigation.

The article in the evening edition was substantially the same, but mentioned that there had been a gathering of people at Bollinger's house on the night of his death.

Late the second afternoon there was a knock at Matt's door.

Matt was sitting on the cot, his back against the wall, reading a magazine. For a moment he froze and stared at the door. It was locked, but flimsy; a healthy twelve-year-old could have put his shoulder through it. Jack a chair under the knob, prop the bed against it: the whole thing would come tumbling down in a heap. There was the window, of course, but even if he could hoist himself up there was a two-story drop outside to a row of garbage cans.

"Who is it?" Matt said quietly, not sure he wanted to be heard.

No answer.

He put the magazine down, sat forward on the cot. A slight squeak. He took two silent steps, stood by the door, put a hand on the latch. "Who is it?" Nothing. There had been only three quiet knocks, as if they might have been struck on another door, or might not have happened at all. He slowly moved the latch, quietly turned the knob, and—bracing his foot a couple inches behind it—opened the door.

The sweet scent of stale tobacco, a long lean silent figure, the sad terribly weary eyes. Wolf.

"Jesus Christ," Matt said.

"In the flesh," Wolf said. "Open up."

Matt let out a long gust of air. He hadn't realized he'd been holding it in.

"You could have said something. You could have answered when I spoke."

"I might have disturbed the other guests. And I wanted to be a surprise." He tried the door. "Your foot's still there."

Matt stepped back and let him in.

He wore an ancient seersucker jacket that hung on him limply, a dark-blue shirt that belonged on a plumber, a narrow black tie. Pushed back on his head was a dark straw hat with a plaid hatband. His collar was unbuttoned and the tie pulled down. He gazed around the room impassively; for a long moment he stared at the window.

"Nice," he said. "You decorate yourself?"

"Pull up a chair," Matt said.

"You give me a lot of choice."

Wolf dragged the chair into the middle of the room, swung a leg over and sat on it like a saddle, his arms resting on the chair back. Matt sat on the cot. Wolf took out a cigarette and examined it deliberately. He tapped it on the seat back, lit it with his lighter, took a deep drag.

"Jesus, Matt." He spoke huskily through the smoke. "What a mess."

"I've been trying to call you."

"I spent a couple days at the precinct station. The police got an idea I'm harboring somebody."

"I wasn't sure they'd make the connection."

"Bollinger had one of my cards."

"I gave it to him that first day."

"He left it on his dresser, unfortunately. And a couple people they're questioning said you were there that night."

"You're sure nobody followed you here."

Wolf slowly closed his eyes. "Please, Matt. Give me a little credit. They think I'm halfway to Penn Hills."

"I can't believe you found me here."

"Janis saw you first. That big girl at the candy stand."

There was something wrong with what Wolf had said, but for a moment Matt couldn't remember what it was. Then he did.

"She's blind, Wolf."

"She just wears those glasses. You try to snitch something from her stand, you want to see how blind she is. You'll also see how broken your hand is. She's got a dumbbell bar back there."

Jesus. "It's illegal to pretend you're blind."

"You're a fine one to talk about illegal. Anyway, she never

said she was blind. Just sits there with those glasses on. It gets her sympathy."

Matt shook his head. The people Wolf knew. "So she saw me."

"She keeps an eye on that lobby for me. After that I just wandered around. You were lucky to find Velma here. There aren't many rooms on this block. And I was glad to hear you're eating right. That's home-cooked food down the street."

The man was uncanny. "If you can find me the police can find me."

"These people tell cops nothing. And they can smell one a mile away."

"They didn't smell me."

"You're not a cop anymore. You're a guy on the run. They can smell that too."

"That old woman just sits on the stoop, Wolf. Taking in money."

"She's got her hand on a thirty-eight in that purse. Shoots right out of the bottom of it. Three jigs tried to rob her one night last year. Pardon me. Black persons. She killed two."

"God." Matt shuddered.

"You're in good hands." Wolf dropped the cigarette on the floor. "As long as you stay in the building." He squashed the butt with his foot. "That's enough from me. I want to hear you talk for a while."

Matt started at the beginning, at his meeting with Droge and Bollinger. Wolf was interested to hear of Bollinger's club—"I thought it was just sleazy places down there"—but not overly interested in what happened. "Spare me the details," he said, when Matt mentioned his first meeting with Angel. But he didn't think Matt was wrong to go to Bollinger's house, and he thought Bollinger's story sounded straight enough. "I would've never known it was fake." Matt told it all, going downstairs to find Angel, leaving in anger, coming back to discover the corpse. He did not say he had gone home in the meantime. He made it sound as if he had driven around awhile, thinking things over, then returned.

"You should have called the police," Wolf said when he finished. "You should have called them from Bollinger's place."

"I know. But I was shocked. And scared. And guilty. I'd been ready to knock Bollinger in the head myself."

He didn't tell Wolf the real reason he hadn't called the police, that it had at least as much to do with discovering

Laurel as discovering the corpse. He hadn't wanted to see anybody. Hadn't wanted to face it all. He'd wanted to run.

"What did the police say?" Matt asked. "Did they tell you much?"

"They weren't snotty about it. They told me plenty. You're not the only one they can't find. This Hunter kid's off somewhere, some kind of trip. It *could* have been without knowing anything. But it's suspicious. And they can't find Killian either. They scared somebody from the scene when they found the body. They're almost sure it was him."

"That must have been after I was there."

"Sounds like it. Of course, they don't know that. And I don't think they know about this girl. This Angel."

"Huh."

"They didn't mention her. They mentioned everybody else. But they're mostly looking for people they can't find."

Like him. Matt picked up his pipe, frowning, tamped the tobacco.

"I've been giving this a lot of thought the past few days."

"I should hope so."

"If there was one thing I would have tried to do . . . I mean, I didn't know you'd show up. But if I'd decided to leave this place. If I'd decided to do something. I would have gone looking for Angel."

Wolf gazed toward the floor, his chin hung over his arm on the chair back, considering.

"She seemed to know a lot. Much more than she told me that night. There was something going on that I didn't know about. And she really knew Bollinger."

Wolf nodded.

"If the police haven't found her, all the better. But I don't think we should go to her at work."

"God no."

"You'd have to get her address. But I think I should be the one to see her."

Wolf looked up at Matt, arched an eyebrow. "Oh?"

"She knows me. She knows I'm in as much trouble as she is."

"You like this girl."

"Come off it, Wolf. I'm trying to save my skin."

"I know that. I want to make sure you know it."

"She's got to be scared. Especially if nobody's come to her. She won't want to talk to a stranger."

"Maybe not."

"She'll know I'm okay."

Wolf shrugged. "I guess it's no hair off my ass." He slowly stood from the chair, stretched, all but tore the seams off his jacket. "It's worth a try." He set the chair back by the sink. "But if this doesn't pan out, if it doesn't lead to anything"— he turned to Matt, looked at him—"I think we should go to the police."

Matt took a deep breath. "God."

"I know it looks bad. But it's only going to get worse."

"I guess."

"It's a lot better you going to them than the other way around."

At the door Wolf turned again to look back at Matt. "I don't need to ask this, after being here for a while. But I wouldn't mind hearing you say it. You didn't kill this Bollinger."

"No, Wolf. Hell no. Jesus."

"Don't look at me like I'm crazy. Somebody did. Probably with less cause."

It suddenly occurred to Matt how strange Wolf's position was. How little Wolf really knew about the man he was working with.

It was good to have him around, though, good to have him on the job. Matt began to realize how hard it had been just sitting around and waiting. He did feel a little nervous an hour later when he went out, but his dinner was uneventful, and the landlady seemed no different when she took his money for the third night. He spent the evening reading. He was surprised, around nine-thirty, to hear the quiet knock at the door again—he hadn't expected Wolf until the next day— but he wasn't unhappy to hear it. Things had finally started. He would be doing something. He stepped to the door and opened it.

It was Laurel, carrying a sleeping bag. "Wolf said I'd need my own bedding," she said.

II

They were sitting on the floor, cross-legged, their knees almost touching. Laurel had unrolled her sleeping bag, and

Matt had hauled down the narrow mattress off the cot. The bulb cast a pale light, leaving parts of their faces in shadow. Their own shadows were monstrous and pale on the yellow wall.

"You were one of those anonymous faceless men who have appeared at the various stages of my life," Laurel said. "The classic progression. My father, and the innocent boy who was my first love, and the handsome knowing man who seduced me, and you. Who came along, as I knew you would, when my adult life was beginning. You were what I did when I graduated."

"You should have gone to law school," Matt said.

This was not the way Laurel had wanted things to go. She had wanted it to be quick, and clean, but Matt seemed to want to drag it out, and now they had started one of those endless arguments that never seemed to go anywhere. Already it felt as if they had been talking for hours, though it couldn't have been more than ten minutes. Soon they would be exhausted and babbling incoherently. What worried Laurel was that they weren't touching. She wanted contact, even if it was slaps and punches, but Matt sat back warily, eyeing his antagonist.

"I don't mean it wasn't you. In another way it very much was you. Big, and quiet, and gentle, an athlete who didn't seem an athlete. Scowling and confident on the field, and shy off of it. And from a different background, somehow. Your father a policeman. You weren't one thing or the other. You opened your mouth and the wrong thing came out. I liked all that. I was tired of the predictable people I ran around with. I liked you."

In spite of himself, Matt swelled a little. It was always gratifying to hear himself praised.

"In another way it was just me," Laurel said. "Drifting along, waiting for things to happen. For my life to pick me up and mold me. I was so trusting. So passive. So young."

Laurel hated that younger self, who had gotten her into this fix. Matt, of course, had loved that girl.

"Everybody needs something to do when they graduate. You were mine."

"Wonderful."

Just what Matt had always wanted to be.

"The turning point was having Jonathan. Woke me up like a slap in the face. Was *this* my life, I thought, the smell of sour milk and baby piss and dirty zwiebach crumbs? I didn't *have* a life, my life existed only to make things better in other people's lives. That was what came from drifting, and letting my life shape me, and turning myself over to men. If I was going to have a life of my own I'd have to do it, pick it up and shape it, and not wait too long about it either."

Matt had heard that part of the story before—it never varied—and always hated it, Jonathan spoken of as a liability, a dispenser of dirty diapers (Jonathan! the human being Matt loved most in all the world!). He was not just that to Laurel, any more than Matt was just something to do after college, but that part of the experience seemed to overshadow everything else in her memory. The whole thing was spoken of as if it were Matt's fault, as if he had forced it on her, when as far as he could remember it was she who had wanted to have the baby, and stay home to raise it.

"It could have been something else," she said. "Probably it could have been a lot of things. But once I got started with counseling it seemed the one thing, the thing I'd always wanted to do. It filled my life, and I couldn't imagine myself without it."

If it could have been something else Matt wished it had been construction foreman or librarian or plumber, anything. Jobs in counseling were so scarce. That was the beginning of their problems.

"It was natural to fall in love with someone who felt the same way."

Matt looked up. Laurel had flushed; the pulse in her neck—he could see it—was throbbing; her breath was coming fast. There was a tenderness in her eyes, almost tearful, because she knew what she said would hurt him. But she had to say it.

"You fell in love with him," Matt said.

"I fell in love."

There were all kinds of things Matt wanted to ask, and to ask them all at once, like: What had that twerp ever done for her? Had he held her hand during a long night of labor, watching their son be born? Had he given up a job and picked up everything and moved to a new city so she could have the job she wanted? Had he rearranged his life so he could stay at home more and share the burden of child care? Had he taken even a tiny fraction of the accumulated shit of eight years of marriage? Love, as far as Matt was concerned, was the terribly intimate closeness that comes from passing together through the repeating crises of life, and now she was feeling love for someone who hadn't even passed through the crises himself yet, much less passed through them with Laurel.

His chest was boiling. His muscles tensed until they jumped. He felt ready to scream.

"A man," he started, then stopped, confused. "Other men. Not me. Because I've always tried to be understanding and sensitive." He had meant to speak sarcastically, somehow came out sounding sincere and pompous. "But other men. They don't want their wives to leave the house. They don't want their wives to work, they especially don't want them to work with other men, but not because they're trying to persecute women and stifle them politically. It's not some grand conspiracy on the part of the male sex. They're afraid the women will get out of the house and like what they see. They'll like what they see, and they'll want to leave. And these insensitive repressive men, who don't in the least understand women, who have no respect for the rights of women, who are straight out of the dark ages, and a disgrace to the modern world, are right. It happens. Every goddam time. The woman gets out of the house, and she likes what she sees. And she wants to leave. And she leaves."

Laurel nodded sadly. These women were her clients. "It happens."

"You ought to chain your woman to the stove and throw the key away. If you want to keep her."

There wasn't much Laurel could say under the circumstances. She could only speak of how she felt.

"It was as if I'd missed a part of my life. All these friends of mine, colleagues, were starting their life's work like me, but everything was open to them. They could work till all hours, or they could go out after work and have a drink, or they could have a cheap affair, or fall terribly in love, and there I was with my stodgy old life having to go home every night and get dinner for my husband and son."

"*I* got the dinner."

"I don't mean literally. I had to go home."

"Stay out and have a drink. Stay out and drink all night." Two beers put her away anyhow.

"I couldn't bear the thought that because of one mistake, one momentary whim, because I'd unthinkingly turned my life over once again to a man, that I'd given up all the freedom everybody else seemed to have. That because of one moment my life was fixed, while everyone else had these wonderful possibilities."

Matt could plainly see the next stage of Laurel's life. After a childhood under the thumb of a businessman father, then a brief bohemian period at college, she had fallen in love with Matt because he seemed a pleasant change from her intellectual and political and dope-smoking friends (Laurel had always been one to do the unexpected) and even from her cozy suburban childhood. She settled down and had a child. Next she had taken up a career and fallen in love with a new man because he was immersed in that, because he was a refreshing change from the drab domestic life she had been leading. Now she would run off with him, she would blossom in her new career, she would no doubt have another child (these things happened) and in oh, about nine years, she would probably decide she didn't like being involved at home and at work with the same man. She would find herself being drawn to a new man. Probably a cop.

"So what's it like?" Matt said.

"What?"

"The life of a swinging single. You seem to have had a taste of it."

"It wasn't quite all I had dreamed of." Laurel looked down, reddened. "As a matter of fact, it reminded me a little of marriage."

Matt sincerely hoped it wasn't that bad.

"It wasn't even quite as good as marriage, actually. More like the worst parts of marriage. Or being forced to relive all the awkward and unhappy parts of your marriage at once. Maybe that's what hell will be like. I mean it was the first time, so you were awkward and embarrassed. Then, you already had a kid, so you had to worry about him barging in too. The moral questions came up, which was like being a sophomore in college again. And I was aware that the sexual adjustment would probably take a minimum of three years. Meanwhile the other person didn't know any of that. He didn't know that for me it was all like a bad memory. For him it was all a new and marvelous discovery."

Even as she spoke, Laurel hated herself for talking that way, making it sound worse than it was because that was the kind of thing Matt wanted to hear. It hadn't been perfect, and it had been awkward, but it had also been terribly exciting. There was nothing to match that scary excitement of the first time.

Matt didn't seem amused, which made Laurel try all the harder.

"It was like going back to relive your youth, knowing what you know now, and seeing how stupid and embarrassing it all was."

"It didn't look that bad when I saw you," Matt said.

That was what stuck, the one thing that would never be any different. It wasn't what Laurel had done, or what Matt knew she had done; it was what he had seen, and what she had been seen in. Another form of discovery would have been completely different. That moment—Matt staring, Laurel turning to see him—would remain a part of their lives forever.

"That wasn't what it seemed," she said.

"It most certainly was."

"I mean it wasn't the way it looked. That we were together doing something we both enjoyed. It was me trying to prove something, to prove it to myself, that I really did want to be someone new, make a clean break. All it really proved was that I was the same old person, with the same old likes and dislikes. But I do feel ashamed about it. Or at least embarrassed. Or maybe just sorry. I know why I did it, and I don't blame myself, but I'm sorry you had to see it. I wish I'd never done that to you."

"I wish it too."

They were both staring down, not wanting to see each other, but finally Laurel looked up, and for the first time, really, she touched him. She touched a hand to his face.

"I don't want it to be like this, Matt. Sitting here talking as if neither of us had the least thing to do with this. I'd rather you'd beat me, or pick me up and throw me out. We've got to make contact. It's what I came for."

He looked up at her, out of deeply shadowed eyes. He disliked the feeling of her hand on his face, wanted to swat it away like a fly. But he didn't want to hurt her. He didn't care enough.

"What do you want?" she said.

Meaning far more than she knew, or even than he knew, Matt spoke without a thought.

"I want things to be the way they were."

With sudden quiet tears, he wept. Laurel pulled his head to hold it against her shoulder.

"I want that too," she said.

He had asked for the one thing that could never be.

His head on her shoulder, Matt sobbed for a while. It was oddly silent, inward weeping, though his body shook until it ached. Laurel was glad for at least that show of feeling.

As she held him, felt him sob, she spoke.

"I wish things could be settled," she said. "That I'd do something and it would be over, finished, I'd go on from that and do the next thing. People talk about their lives as if they are that way. But not me. Nothing's ever finished, it always runs over into the next thing, and anyway I keep doing the same thing over and over again. I've gotten out of the house and I've found a career and I've fallen in love and I've been with another man, and I still have to have my career, it's a part of me now, but most of all I'd just like to be back with you and Jonathan. I wish I could say it, could shout it to the whole world, I'll come back to you and love you and be with you forever, but I can't. Because as soon as I said it the whole thing would be wrong. Maybe even because I said it. I don't know that I'll never want another man, I don't know that I'll never want Ned again. I don't know that I won't want to chuck the whole thing and go off by myself. I don't even know I won't do it. But right now I want to be with you. I want it terribly. I'd like to tell lies, the lies everybody tells to be sentimental and stay together, but I can't. I want to stay, but I might want to leave. I love you and Jonathan but someday I might love somebody else. I want my life at home but I have to have my life outside too. I can't make the big promises. They don't exist for me. If we get back together, that will have to be enough."

It was not, of course, enough. It was, however, all there was.

Tired, eventually, from their awkward position, they slumped over and lay down. Laurel still felt a craving for contact, for the clutch and penetration of sex, but she was afraid to say anything because she didn't know how Matt felt. He had not said a word since he started crying.

If anyone had asked him earlier in the day, he would have said he was doing fine. Actually, he was suffering from an exhaustion so extreme he was numb to it. He was like the high-powered executive who works at a fever pitch for days at a time, then feels something snap. In a matter of moments after he had lain down with Laurel, he was asleep.

III

The room was hot, and dead still. It was the kind of stifling sticky heat that only an old room in the middle of a city seems to have. The window was open, but no breeze stirred. It was dark; after they had lain together awhile, Laurel had taken Matt's clothes off (he had hardly budged) and snapped off the light. Laurel wore only a shirt herself. Normally in such heat she slept naked, but in those surroundings she didn't feel entirely free.

The building was busy that night. Footsteps passed the door, and Laurel heard the murmur of voices, the running of water, the squeaking of springs. ("It's kind of a . . . " Wolf had been flustered. "Sort of a . . . " "Whorehouse," Laurel said. "Not exactly that," Wolf said. "More like a short-term parking lot.") Matt lay on his side, snoring lightly—he slept as if to blot out the world—and Laurel was on her side also, snuggled up near him with her back. Their bodies were covered by a film of sweat. Where they actually touched they grew damp. Laurel was not in the least bit sleepy. She lay with her eyes open, staring off at the darkness, occasionally blinking.

Matt was having a dream. Later he would think of it not as a dream in which anything happened, but simply as a scene which conveyed a mood. It may have been the end of a longer dream, but this last scene was all he remembered. From a low grassy sandy hill—a dune, it seemed, on a tropical island—he looked down on the ocean. In the tropical climate, the air was stiflingly hot, and still. One after another, gentle waves broke on the shore. Around him on the dune, and on the beach below, and throughout the water, every couple of feet, were growths of what seemed a brown seaweed. They stood out of the water about a foot, columns curved like rams' horns, as far as the eye could see. There was a consciousness observing it all, lying on the dune; the languorous stifling still day, latent with a kind of power; the endlessly breaking gentle waves; and, all around, the endless vista of identical seaweed columns.

In the midst of that scene, still observing it clearly, Matt began slowly to awaken.

As he did, he became aware that he had an enormous erection.

He never knew, later, how much his memory of the dream included subsequent thoughts about the dream and how much actually came to him then. Thoughts did, however, occur to him at the time—he was distanced enough from the dream to be thinking—and he became aware as he awoke that he was not actually in the dream, but that the consciousness observing the scene was his, and that all around, as far as the eye could see, those small tight columns of seaweed were actually erect penises.

His own erection did not seem the kind that a man *has* (as when a man says, "I have a hard-on," or "I hope I get a hard-on"); it just seemed to exist, independent of him, like the columns of seaweed on the dune, on the beach, and in the sea. It was as if the columns of seaweed were the erections of a lifetime, and something in the languorous power of the dream seemed to say, You don't have them. You don't get them. They simply are.

He became aware that, like the warm moist heat that hung above the bather on the island, a woman's body was resting against his. He reached down and touched her bottom. It was shapely, firm, soft.

Laurel was wide awake. She was aware of Matt's restless sleep, the kind of sleeping one does in the summer. Occasionally he gave off a quiet groan, and he was generating enormous body heat. In places he was wet to the touch. When he touched her bottom she was not surprised, because that was something he often did in his sleep, though usually she was also asleep. "Did I feel you up last night?" he would say, some mornings, and she would say, "I think so," as if remembering something from a dream. "I must have," he would say, smiling. Midnight feels, he called them.

A man was not responsible for what he did in his sleep.

Matt at that moment had no idea it was Laurel he was touching. If he had he would not have touched her in that particular way, because she did not like being touched from behind—it felt "sneaky," she said—and she especially did not like it when he touched what she bluntly referred to (all euphemisms aside) as her asshole. He was forbidden, in fact, to do so, on pain of a hard fist to the ribs. But Matt was only partly conscious, just knew there was a woman beside him who had a terrific ass—he was running his hand up and down it, his finger grazing her asshole—and he had the strong feeling that if he played his cards right, he stood a good chance of getting laid.

Laurel didn't know what the hell was going on. She didn't know whether Matt was asleep and giving her a midnight feel, in which case she didn't want to wake him up, or whether he was awake and purposely feeling her in a way he was not supposed to, to test her, or make her mad. She didn't much care. She was in a sexy mood herself—she had been sure they would make love as soon as they saw each other—and she also felt so bad about the way she had treated him that she didn't care what he did. He could squeeze her ass, touch her asshole; he could crawl down there and kiss it if he wanted.

"Matt?" she said quietly.

There was no answer.

The man in question didn't recognize the name.

Matt was giving this woman a terrific feel. He was running his finger along the cleft of her ass, stopping now and then to probe her asshole, then squeezing her ass, which was soft but firm to his touch. Now he ran his finger past her asshole and touched the lips of her cunt, which were hot, and wet (like the warm moist air above a tropical island); he kept his finger moving and slid it inside her. "Ah!" she said. (Laurel was partly gasping in relief that he had gotten away from her asshole.) She was soaking wet, and hot as a pistol. She reached back to his cock, and gave it an expert squeeze. This woman was ready to be fucked, no question about it. Matt himself, of course, had a hard-on that felt as if he could fuck from now until doomsday. He pushed her over on her belly, lay on top of her, so that for a moment his cock was wedged in her ass. The scent of her hair—his face was buried in her hair—was faintly familiar, and brought him further awake. He had taken hold of her wrists, which lay above her head, so she was face down, her limbs spread, totally helpless.

"I'm going to fuck you," he said.

Laurel did not reply.

She did not much like to be fucked from behind. It made her feel helpless, and she did not like quite *that* helpless a feeling (though she did like being fucked on her back by an overwhelmingly passionate man). She did not like the impersonal feeling of taking it from behind; she liked to see the man who was screwing her, to hold him, to squeeze him hard. But more than anything else she liked passion in a man, a man with only one thing on his mind, who wanted to hold her down hard and fuck her brains out, and it was exciting to feel Matt doing things with such certitude. It was wonderful to feel him so excited, and it had even felt good when he put his finger in: there was nothing like that first penetration. Now he was sliding down between her legs, and she spread them for him. With a single slow stroke, he was in her.

Matt had just realized it was Laurel he was fucking (this is no whore! this is my wife!). Until then she had been just a faceless woman (though that ass, come to think of it, had been mighty familiar, and he should have known that cunt anywhere), but with that first stroke he had come fully awake, and finally recognized the scent of her hair. He couldn't believe what he had been doing to her. Now he was holding her wrists like a rapist, and riding her ass as it curved up to meet him, and fucking with a stiff prick way up inside her, and by God she was groaning and sighing and moving around as if she loved it. He wanted to explain the things he had done— Listen, Laurel, it was all a dream, I didn't mean a thing—but this hardly seemed an appropriate time. Right at the moment she was occupied.

He had moved his face to rest his cheek on hers—"Laurel," he said—and she reached up with a hand and touched his face.

"Matt," she said. "I want you to love me."

"I do love you. I adore you."

"I don't mean now. I don't mean when we're"—she chose her favorite expression—"doing it. I mean the rest of the time. When you were sitting around before I got here. Or three days ago, before you saw what you saw. It's been so long since we've really felt together. I want to know that you love me."

"Of course."

"I want you to tell me."

Matt's cock felt enormous inside her. Their bodies were soaked, lay sweating together like two wrestlers slickly grappling, and he felt relaxed, and strong, was breathing freely— no narrow band around his chest—for the first time with Laurel since he could remember. It was his dream self that was fucking her, that part of him that lolled under a tropical sun serene in the power of sex, and it seemed to him that Laurel was calling to his other self, who did not feel her from behind and touch her asshole, who did not mount her like a hairy sweaty animal, that part of him that tried to be a good husband and do what she wanted in bed, who was reasonable at all times and searching humbly for a worthwhile job and for weeks now, possibly years, had been utterly miserable. He was humping and humping her, every stroke felt wonderful, and he had a sudden conviction that if he betrayed his dream self, if he went back to the man she wanted him to be—who sat around supposedly loving her all the time—he would lose it all.

"I hate you," he said.

"Oh!" Her cry was of pain, as if he had thrust too deep, but it was pain at his words, the very words she had not wanted (or secretly wanted) to hear.

"I love you and I hate you. Part of me loves and part of me hates. I'm going to fuck you with the part that hates."

"Please." She was pushing herself up with one arm, trying to turn, as though—if she could get over on her back, if she could face him—she could get to his other side. "Fuck me with the part that loves."

"No." He pushed her back onto the mattress. "For once I'm fucking with the part that hates. For once I'm admitting it."

"Oh." She collapsed onto the mattress, as if knocked there by a blow, started quietly to weep.

"I'm glad to see you cry. I want to see you cry."

"No." She shook her head as she sobbed. "No."

"I want you to hear this."

He grabbed her by the shoulders, squeezed her hard, making her sob all the more.

"I hate you for trying to make me somebody I'm not. Who sits around like a stupid prick always loving his wife. While she's down on her knees for another man."

"I want to be loved." Laurel dug her fingers into the mattress, weeping bitterly. "I deserve to be loved."

"I hate you for never letting me do what I want. Suck your tits hard. And lick your armpits. And fuck you with my tongue. And tickle your asshole."

"I should like what I don't like. You expect me to want what I don't like."

It was just as well Matt did have Laurel in a helpless position, the way she was kneading the mattress, clawing with her fingernails.

"I want you to *hear* me while I'm telling you this. Can't you for once keep your fucking mouth shut?"

"I don't have to listen to this." She pounded the mattress. "I do not have to listen to this."

She was wrong. She did have to listen.

"I hate you for hating me," Matt said. "For trying to get away from me and Jonathan. For going off every day and liking the place you go more than you like me. For loving those people and thinking they're more interesting than me."

"I don't like it more. I do not like it more."

"You goddam cunt of a liar. I know you like it more."

Laurel was not lying to Matt, however. She was lying to herself. She had not admitted to herself that she liked it more.

"Most of all I hate you for sucking the cock of that skinny little creep. That fucking little worm. I hope he came in your mouth. I hope you choked on it."

"I'm sorry for that, Matt. I am sorry for that. I wish I hadn't done that to you."

"Can't you shut up? Can't you for once shut the fuck up?"

"Just hear that one thing."

"Shut your mouth or I'll pound it shut."

"All *right!*" Laurel was sobbing uncontrollably.

Matt knew, even at that moment, that he would not do such a thing. He would never hit her.

Laurel was not sure.

"That little faggot was probably pretending it was a man. That's what he really likes. He had to ignore your tits."

Matt had gripped her armpits, which were soaked (he adored the smell of Laurel's sweaty armpits, a fact which totally grossed her out), held her there while he continued fucking.

"I hate you for fucking him, if that's what you did. It undoubtedly is. I hate you for bringing him into my house. I hate you for letting my child see him. If my child saw him. I hate you for all the times you've hugged him, and all those other faggots down there. Probably wanting to fuck every one of them. Probably doing it too." Matt didn't seem to notice the odd paradox of what he was saying. "I hate you for liking those people. For liking all those people. But especially that little bastard in the jogging shoes with his one-inch cock."

As a matter of pure fact, like many small slight men, Ned had a rather long cock. Noticeably longer, anyway, than Matt's.

Weeks later, Laurel would laugh at all the things Matt had said in the long and incredibly obscene speech he was starting just then. One afternoon, in fact, she sat on the window seat in the front room and laughed so hard and so long that she actually thought she was going to throw up, or possibly asphyxiate herself. Everything he said had at least a grain of truth, and might have cut to the quick if he had said it another way, but his hatreds were couched in such peculiar terms—she had never heard such an outpouring of filth—and ran together in such absurd juxtapositions, that they were finally just funny. "I hate you for dragging me to this goddam city. For all the godforsaken fucking places I've had to work. I hate you for neglecting our darling son. And for sucking the cock of that little cunt." (Laurel's all-time favorite.) "I hate you for never sucking mine. For all the perfectly normal things you've never let me do. . . . "

His argument went around and around.

Laurel had continued weeping for a while, but eventually she stopped. You can only cry for so long, after all, and she was actually glad Matt was getting his hostilities out, and she didn't want to lie there and cry while she was getting probably the best fuck of her life. These were things that it was natural for Matt to hate, but he had never said them before. Eventually he slowed down, perhaps getting winded, or concentrating on what his body was doing, popping out an occasional non sequitur. "I hate the way you always talk first thing at the breakfast table. Blabbing away with your mouth full of cereal." (That, in Laurel's opinion, was a dirty lie.) He was not thrusting faster or harder, exactly, but somehow with more conviction, wrapping his arms around her, cupping her breasts, lightly gnawing on her shoulders. Finally, toward the end, he spoke in the hoarse rough voice of the primitive he was pretending to be. "Reach down between your legs and tickle my balls."

Laurel had never had what was known in the heyday of Freudian psychology as a vaginal orgasm: she had never come just from the motions of intercourse. She had come during intercourse—when she and Matt had found a position in which he could comfortably touch her—but not often; as far as she was concerned, having that big thing in her vagina was just a distraction from a really satisfactory orgasm. Matt would eventually decide that it was only on this night, when all their emotions were out in the open, that Laurel had an orgasm from intercourse. She never disabused him of this notion. The fact of the matter was, though, that lying flat on her belly like that, with Matt banging her in that endless act of intercourse, her clitoris was constantly rubbing against the mattress, and she found herself—she could hardly believe it—on the precipitous edge of an enormous orgasm. She kept not quite going over. But now, as she reached between her legs to gently claw his balls (a caress which, at the height of intercourse, made him literally scream), her wrist pressed directly on the spot, and, with that slightly increased pressure, she came, her hips bucking as if to throw him out, her cunt shuddering in rapid little spasms, and Matt, also at her touch, locked his hips with his cock in her to the hilt and spilled an incredibly long and copious orgasm, his mouth gasping over her ear, his body bouncing around over her own convulsions.

It was the famous simultaneous orgasm, celebrated in marriage manuals since time immemorial.

For a long time they lay without moving, catching their breath, while his cock gradually grew small inside her.

In many ways the funniest thing Matt had said was the last one—just after he had rolled off her and they had cuddled together, ready for sleep—but she never laughed at it.

Matt, himself, had not been exactly sure what he meant, but the words to his ear had a ring of truth.

"I hate you because I love you," he said.

Chapter Six

What Matt had expected was to walk up the street and be descended on from all sides, men dashing out of doorways, out of alleys, cars swooping out of sidestreets and down from Penn, lights flashing, sirens whooping. He hadn't realized to what extent he had been hiding in his little box of a room, the narrow hallway down to the toilet, the few steps to the outdoor phone booth and the half block to his diner. He was like the man afraid of open spaces, whose head spins dizzily when he exits his room for a barren courtyard. But no one noticed. Nothing happened. He walked up the block, out of the building's shadow and toward the commercial section, and the world went on quite as if he weren't there.

The morning sun blazed through a yellowish haze. Across from Matt a streetcleaner moved like a burrowing insect, brushes spinning, water spraying. Up on Penn a section of street was being torn up, jackhammers jumping and pounding; chunks of cement lay sprawling, and gray dust filled the air. Men in business suits stood on corners and in doorways, as if waiting for appointments. Women with shopping bags sat collapsed on benches, already beat. Vagrants sat sweating with their shirts open, eyes red and bleary, avoiding the sun. East Liberty was constantly renovating, never seemed any different. It had to move at a trot just to stay still.

Matt had awakened that morning to fingertips drumming on the doorframe. Laurel, who always slept deeply (except at calls from Jonathan) snored softly through it. The room was a mess, the mattress askew on the floor, sleeping bag shoved to one side, clothes strewn everywhere. Matt rummaged around for his underpants and pulled them on, opened the door a crack to make sure it was Wolf, stepped out quickly and closed the door behind him.

It was cooler in the hallway, an early breeze drifting through the front windows.

"Sleeping in," Wolf said. "Must be nice."

"We got to bed late," Matt said.

He stared at Wolf as if awaiting an indiscreet remark. He was in no mood for indiscreet remarks.

"Everybody did." Wolf hadn't so much as smiled. "I got that address you wanted."

He handed Matt a slip of paper with an address on it, a street in Point Breeze near Westinghouse Park.

"You think this is a house?" Matt said.

"One of those old apartments. I drove by. It's on a street of houses, though. Nice little street."

He spoke as if the fact surprised him.

"This Angel doesn't get along too great with the other girls. I got the impression, which you get around women practically every time you bring up another woman, that they're jealous of her. They admit she does a lot of business. They got their suspicions why. They even admit she's good-looking, although they can all name one or two other things wrong with her. But they don't like her. She isn't like them. She's not nasty, but she doesn't have much to say. I think that's why they gave me the address. 'She in some kind of trouble?' one of them said, like she hoped it was true. I told her it was an insurance thing."

That was what Wolf always said. He could have rattled off a long story if he'd had to.

"She's off today," he said. "Usually she works days, but she's off today."

"I'll go down this morning."

Wolf had his hands in his pockets, was staring lazily at Matt.

"You're sure you want to do this alone."

"If something sounds interesting you can go after me. Or the two of us can go. But first it should be just me."

Wolf nodded. Utter deadpan.

"I'll call you," Matt said.

"I'll come by tonight. Maybe late this afternoon." Wolf glanced at the door. "I'll knock first."

"Okay. And thanks, Wolf. For telling where I was. I'm not sure I would've said to."

"It's hard to say no to that woman."

Wolf wasn't giving Matt any news.

Wolf had been walking toward the door, now glanced at Matt, nodded toward the paper in his hand.

"I hope you appreciate that. I had to buy a hand job to get that information."

Poor brave Wolf. Sacrificing his body in the line of duty.

"How was it?" Matt couldn't help smiling.

"I could've done better myself."

Matt and Laurel ate a late breakfast in the diner, facing each other at the booth farthest back: eggs over easy, sausage, home fries, a stack of buttered toast, two steaming pots of coffee. Laurel had the look of a woman deeply rested. She ate ravenously, piece after piece of toast with gobs of preserves, so that Matt, somewhat to his embarrassment, had to order more after the first stack. Once he had gotten food into her (at that point she looked ready to go back to bed) he said, "I need to talk to you, Laurel. There's trouble," but even that hadn't fazed her.

"The worst trouble's over now," she said. "After last night. Anything else I can handle."

Matt hoped she was right.

To Laurel he told a slightly different story from what he had told Wolf. He had gone to Bollinger's knowing there would be a party, but he had gone early, to talk to Hugh. He had waited around while the guests arrived. One was Todd Hunter, an old student of his from Tabard; another was the man he had gone to question downtown. Somewhat to his surprise, Killian and Mingins were also there. They had all come to see a movie, just as Helen Killian had said.

"Weren't you intrigued?" Laurel said. "Didn't you want to stay?"

A little, Matt said, but the place felt sleazy, and the company was boring, and the movie didn't seem to be starting for a while. He had gone home—Laurel lowered her eyes at the mention of that—then driven around awhile, aimlessly. On a whim he had returned to the party. He found everyone gone, Bollinger dead.

"I knew something was wrong when you didn't come home, but I thought it was just"—she gestured vaguely—"the other thing." Her eyes were clear as she spoke, and she gazed at him directly. "I kept calling Wolf's office but no one was there. Then yesterday the big article was in the paper, and in the afternoon Chandler Mingins called me. He'd spent hours with the police. He wanted to talk to you. After that the police came to the house. They wouldn't believe I didn't know where you were. We'd had an argument, I said. I was sure that was why you were gone. They weren't too impressed. They even asked Jonathan some questions. *He* may have convinced them." Jonathan was the most emphatic member of the family. "Yesterday I finally got hold of Wolf."

"I've decided to emerge from my hole," Matt said. "I want to see what I can find."

"Matt." Laurel reached across the table and took his hands. "I know you want to do the right thing." She was afraid that after all Matt had been through, he would try to vindicate himself with some heroic deed. "I think you should go to the police."

"That's impossible now. It's too suspicious."

"It's only suspicious that you haven't gone. I'm sure you can explain that. And it's Stanley Killian they really suspect. Helen's called me a couple times, frantic. Something happened at the party. Chandler wouldn't say what. He can't believe Stanley would kill a man. But he's worried sick."

Matt would have to find a way to talk to Mingins.

"Laurel." He wasn't sure he could explain. He had to tread rather lightly. "Something weird was going on at that party. Something I've got to understand. There was a woman there. I talked to her awhile. She seemed to know what it was." Perhaps more than any one thing in that whole case, Matt wanted to know what Angel had to do with it all. "If I go to the police I won't get to talk to her. Or it won't be the same." He would have to tell them about Angel, and they would immediately bring her in. "But if this doesn't work out I will go to them. I already promised Wolf."

"This isn't cops and robbers anymore. This is real."

"That's what I've been saying all along. What I do is real."

"But this isn't what you do, anymore. This isn't your job. Nobody's going to pay you. It's a job for the police."

"The first thing I ever did. The first job I ever had. Things got all screwed up. A man got killed."

"That wasn't your fault."

"But I can't just walk away from it. I'm doing some piddly little thing, checking out an insurance claim, then a man gets killed and I don't even look into it. I could never respect myself if I did a thing like that."

Laurel took his hand, stared rather helplessly. So much of

Matt's recent floundering had just been an effort to respect himself.

"You decide to respect yourself, Matt. Nothing happens to let you do it. You make that decision. For yourself."

"I have made it. That's why I can't walk away from this."

Laurel shook her head. If he had really made it, it seemed to her, he could walk away from it.

"You have to do what you have to do," she said. "I want you to do what you have to do. I guess." She stared at his hand, in hers. "I just wish you didn't have to make it so hard on yourself."

The lot where Matt had left the car was out around the perimeter of East Liberty, where once there had been a neighborhood of narrow streets and small houses; now there were just the massive brick housing projects, vast stretches of concrete. A phone booth was beside the parking lot, and on an impulse Matt stopped and dialed home. That had been the first thing he had asked the night before, when Laurel showed up. "Where's Jonathan?"

"I got Mrs. Delgatti to spend the night," she had said. "I told her it was an emergency. He was delighted he wouldn't have to go to camp. But he's a little tense. I haven't given him much in the way of explanations."

Tense was hardly the word. Jonathan answered the phone, and as soon as Matt spoke his name the boy exploded. "Where have you *been*? Where did you *go*? I've been alone here for two days." He meant he had been without another man in the house. "I want you home right now."

"I'm not far away. Everything's all right. But I can't come home."

"The police were here, and the phone keeps ringing, and Mom won't tell me anything, and now I'm here with Mrs. Spaghetti." Matt and Jonathan had worked a number of variations on the woman's name.

"What did you tell the police? Laurel thought you'd convinced them."

"I said if you'd been here I would certainly have known about it." He probably had convinced them. "I want you here this minute."

"Laurel's on her way."

"I want *you* to be here."

It was anger in Jonathan's voice, but behind it, Matt knew, there was fear. He hated to make his son afraid.

"I can't come home right now. I'm on a case."

"You don't have real cases. You just ride around in a car."

"This case is real. For once it is real. A man's been killed."

There was a pause on the phone and, when Jonathan spoke again, a change in his tone. From a world he didn't understand—his father gone, his mother not answering questions, Mrs. Delgatti out in the kitchen creating a pizza (he thought only restaurants did that)—he had been transported to one that he very much did understand, and that, oddly, frightened him less. His voice was no longer shrill. It was lower, conspiratorial.

"Are they after you?"

He meant the killers, but the irony of his question was not lost on Matt.

"I'm after them. They don't know where I am. The police will just get in the way. That's why I can't come home."

A logical explanation as far as Jonathan was concerned.

"Do you have a gun?"

The old obsession. Matt smiled. "No."

"You ought to have a gun."

"It isn't that kind of thing. I've got to talk to people. Figure things out."

"Oh God." The voice sagged with disappointment.

"Maybe you're right, though. Maybe I should get a gun."

"If you do, I get to see it."

"You get to see it."

"I get to hold it."

"Sure."

"I get to shoot it if I want." He had gone too far. "Just in the air."

"Jonathan."

"I'm staying here with Mrs. Spaghetti! This place smells like Beto's Pizza!"

"All right, all right. We'll see. Listen, Jonathan. I'd like to be there with you. It isn't that I don't want to. I miss you."

"Okay." Jonathan was not much of one for sentiment. "Be sure to get the gun."

As it turned out, the boy wasn't giving bad advice.

It was not true, as Wolf seemed to suspect, that Matt was going to Angel because he was attracted to her. Not that

Angel's attractions hadn't crossed Matt's mind, and now and then he imagined a scene (how could he *do* that, he wondered, when so much was involved that was important to him, and when he had just had sex with his wife, whom he loved?) where he went to question Angel and they wound up finishing what they had started. That was not, however, the reason he was going. It was also not quite true what he had told Laurel, that he was going to see Angel because of what she knew (though it did seem possible she knew a lot, and that it would be an advantage to talk to her before she went to the police). He was going to see Angel for much vaguer reasons, that woman who had stepped into a room with him and so casually stripped; who knew every inch of a man's body, at least of his; who had done such wonderfully erotic things with him, then thrown him out of bed for a kiss he might have given a fourteen-year-old schoolgirl. She was the mystery, as far as he was concerned, and he had the vague feeling that if he solved what he saw as a mystery, everything else would fall into place.

It was a side street one block up from the park, and seemed to have been around awhile; the houses were of the beige brick or dark rough red brick you find in older places. The building had a glassed-in vestibule, four doors inside. Already in the vestibule you caught a scent of mildew. From the position of her doorway Matt figured Angel had an upstairs apartment. It was the kind of place that had another locked door at the top, the tenant buzzed the guest and checked him out from there; but after Matt rang the bell the footsteps came down the stairs. She wasn't taking any chances.

Later, just as he would always remember her sudden appearance in the massage room, he would always remember the way she came to the apartment door. Her hair was gathered in the back, hung straight down. Her face seemed pale and thin in her wire-framed glasses. She wore a man's shirt that hung outside her pants. Her feet were bare. Her jeans, rolled up at her shins, were torn. Everything on her looked baggy.

This was what a prostitute looked like after hours?

When she saw Matt she bit her lip, perplexed, then reddened slightly.

"Angel?" He spoke quietly, as if he weren't sure.

"That's not really my name." Her face hardened, as if resigned. "Just my disposition. The name's Sandra. Sandra Kendley." She stepped back and opened the door, revealing a long dark stairway. "Come in."

He had actually expected a little argument. He hadn't thought he'd be taken in so readily.

The stairway was dark, and dank, and all the way up—Matt taking the lead, the woman behind him—the steps creaked. Once they got upstairs, though, the place was bright, with three high windows down the side, two at the front and back; it gave you the feeling of being part of the trees around it, the heavy summer greenery. With the windows wide it wasn't stuffy. Birds sang a few feet away. The ceilings were high and airy. The plastered walls were freshly painted. The floor was solid, stained a dark brown.

Matt wasn't sure just what he had expected. The only places where he had seen this woman before had had dim lights, scarlet shag carpets, wall-high mirrors. He had once read an article about Park Avenue prostitutes, and it turned out that instead of being seedy dope addicts or children of the slums, they were sleek elegant women—models, mostly—who happened to have extremely expensive tastes and needed to make a lot of money. They had enormous wardrobes, pedigreed poodles, fashionable apartments. They wore furs in the winter and vacationed on the Riviera. You couldn't have told one from a corporate lawyer's wife.

This hardly looked like the fashionable apartment of an expensive prostitute. More like a place where one of Laurel's friends might have lived. A counseling type.

The sensibility that had furnished this place was far from domestic. The inside foyer where you stepped after climbing the stairs was jammed with three bicycles, a rusted wagon, two sleds, boxes of tools. The long high room of the apartment was divided unimaginatively into sections, living in front, dining in back. The living room was cluttered with a hodgepodge of furniture, three ancient overstuffed chairs, a high wicker throne, a table fashioned out of a door. A small portable television rested on a peach crate. Books and magazines lay on the floor, sweaters were thrown over chairs, and on the dining-room table—it would have taken ten minutes to clear it—were papers, a typescript, stacks of books, a small portable typewriter.

"We usually eat in front of the TV," Sandra said, with a wry glance at the table.

With the spectacles down on her nose she looked thoughtful, even scholarly. Her feet padded along the bare floor. The shirt effectively hid her breasts.

"I knew somebody would come," she said. "I hadn't figured it would be you."

"It probably isn't," Matt said. "I'm strictly on my own."

"I wish it were somebody else. Nothing personal. But I like to keep my lives separate. Even Hugh, as much as I told him"—her face had grown serious—"was never actually here."

Matt nodded.

She offered him tea, and he said she shouldn't bother, but she said this would be a break from her work and she liked tea at her breaks. She was in the kitchen only long enough for the water to boil, came out with a teapot and two white mugs. "That should steep a minute," she said, setting things down.

"Nice table," Matt said. It was the one he had noticed before.

"A remnant of my marriage," Sandra said. "The bedroom door."

She seemed perfectly serious. Matt wondered if it had been torn off during a playful spat.

"Are you surprised?" she said.

"What?"

"At all"—she gestured around—"this."

"I'm just getting used to it. I guess I am surprised."

"You had expected . . . "

Matt hesitated. "Another person, I think."

Sandra nodded. "This isn't exactly the image I project at work."

"I started to see a little of this that night at Hugh's. I saw a little part of the real you."

"I am glad you came, in that way. Even if it wasn't for . . . this other thing. I feel terrible about what happened that night. Between us. I'd like to try to explain."

"It wasn't just your fault."

"In a way I'll be explaining"—she gazed around—"all this. How I got from here to there."

That wasn't all Matt wanted to hear. It was definitely a step in the right direction.

She poured the tea, set a cup across the table for Matt. She gathered her legs under her, held the white mug in two hands. Steam drifted up toward her face. She did not look at Matt, but toward the windows at the back, where sunlight poured in through the green leaves.

"I've never been squeamish about bodies," she said. "Lots of people say it, but with me it's really true. Long bodies and short bodies. Fat and thin. Bellies, and chests, and armpits, and asses. Cocks. It's bare skin. Good to the touch. To me there's no morality about it. Morality has to do with hurting somebody, or taking advantage, or holding power. But not with touching. Or touching a particular place. To most people the way I make a living is the most sordid thing in the world. Going into a room naked with a naked man and touching him. Letting him touch me. To me it has nothing to do with morality. It's making bodies feel good. Touching, tickling, probing, caressing. Skin to bare skin. I don't go out of my way to argue about it. It's just the way I feel."

Matt himself applauded this attitude. He thought it entirely wonderful.

Sandra sipped carefully at her tea.

"When my marriage split up—this was about a year ago, a friendly split—I knew I had to do something. I was months from finishing my dissertation." She glanced wistfully at the table with all her papers on it. "Still am, for that matter. I didn't want to be wealthy or anything, but I'm not a part-time hippy. I have children. I didn't want to be one of those graduate students on the brink of poverty. Tutoring somewhere, or typing papers. I talked to the kids about it . . . "

"You talked to the kids."

"It's important that children know what their parents are doing."

"What did you tell them?"

"That I'd be rubbing men's bodies. Doing massage. It was all right with them."

Matt could imagine such a conversation between Jonathan and Laurel. Jonathan wanted no man's body rubbed but his own.

Apparently Sandra was one of those mothers who discussed everything with her children.

"I took the job. As long as I only worked days. I wanted to be with my children at night, even if I was busy all the time. It's worked out well. I've made lots of money. Saved some. In a few months I'll be able to quit. Do this full-time."

There was a note of anxiety in her voice. She sounded as if she would rather do massage full-time.

"What's your field?"

"Early childhood ed."

Matt could imagine her job application. Previous employment . . .

"Where does that lead?"

"God only knows. Listen. Ask me about my sex life. The number of hand jobs I give in a day. The number of men I blow in a year. But please don't ask about my graduate work. It's too embarrassing."

Matt understood. He had known graduate students before.

"It was at work that I got to know Hugh Bollinger. A stranger man never stepped into the place. But he was so nice. And generous. Money meant nothing to him. He paid for the most expensive session, and always left an enormous tip, and between the two did almost nothing. With his body. But his mouth. Lord. A sixty-minute session with Hugh Bollinger was like ten rounds in the ring with a heavyweight. He was at you the whole time. What did I do with other men there, and what had I already done that day, and what was my sex life like elsewhere, and how had it been when I lost my virginity. Did it hurt a lot. Was it very bloody. At first I tried to put him off, I wasn't wild about having my privacy invaded, but after a while I gave in and made it all up. The path of least resistance. He was so involved with the periphery of sex, seeing it, thinking about it, talking. I honestly think if I could have gotten him to take a good look at me and use his hands a little he'd have gotten excited like anyone else. But he was never quite there. He was always outside the door, looking through the keyhole."

With a drink in one hand and the other in his pants.

"From there it went on to other things. He knew the owner and got special favors. Paying to watch me through a two-way mirror. Arranging things ahead of time and watching me with somebody he knew. A friend he brought in. Paying me to do special things with the friend. Finally coming to his place and doing things there."

Sandra sipped from the tea.

"That's where I should have drawn the line."

"You did that often?"

"Only once before you. When I first took the job I was only going to work with my hands. But the guy he asked me to be with had been to the parlor lots of times, first with Hugh and later by himself. He was so soft, so obviously clean, and terribly appreciative of me. I knew he wouldn't be any trouble. Hugh offered a lot of money."

"Stanley Killian."

Matt had considered the possibilities; "obviously clean" left Otto out.

Sandra nodded.

"He was upstairs the night I was with you," Matt said.

"He was almost Hugh's opposite. Very eager about doing it, perpetually excited, but never feeling good about it and excusing himself all the time. He loved his wife but she wouldn't do this, and he'd never had a chance to do that, and if just for a second I'd touch him there—all these perfectly normal straight things—then afterwards he was so grateful and apologetic, pulling on his clothes as if he couldn't wait to get away from me. The whole time Hugh was behind his mirror, getting himself off or whatever he did, but there didn't seem anything wrong with that. Old Stanley was having the time of his life."

Matt could imagine Killian, who even as he defended absolute sexual freedom blushed fiercely and wore an embarrassed smile. No matter how much he took off, he never stripped himself of his conscience.

"Then there was you," Sandra said.

Finally they looked at each other, he staring, her face as impassive as it had been all along. He wondered how she would have described him if she had been talking to someone else.

"I should have stopped before that. Probably long before that. By the time you walked into that room I knew I didn't want to be there. There was lots you didn't understand. Stanley was one thing. It was ninety percent playacting. The wicked forbidden whore of his dreams. But with you it was different. Much closer to real. It was closer to having sex with a stranger."

That may have been true for her. Only Matt knew the extent to which, for him, she was a woman he had known forever.

"I didn't want that," Sandra said. "I didn't want it to be real." She shrugged. "I didn't want to kiss."

"I got that impression."

"I honestly think I would have stopped it all after that. Never gone back to that room, or gotten mixed up with Hugh again. Of course, we'll never know."

She was looking out the window again, her legs folded in front of her, arms clasped around them.

"I should have gone to somebody right away. As soon as I knew Hugh was dead. But I didn't know until a whole day later, when I saw the evening paper. Then I kept expecting somebody to come to me. And the longer I waited the less I wanted to go. Who would go to the police, with the story I had to tell?"

Matt knew the feeling. He also knew the anger Sandra had shown that night, the opportunity she might have had. Did she have the strength to deliver a blow that would cave in a man's head like that? She looked as if she did.

"Who knew you were there?" he said.

"I'm not exactly sure. Hugh, of course. You. Other than that I only saw that young friend of Hugh's. That grossly depraved boy."

"Todd Hunter."

"And those overweight wife swappers. God, what a crowd."

Wife swappers?

"The Droges?"

"That was after everything was over. The party had broken up when they got down to me. But if there's one thing I'd want to know about that night, one thing I think might tell the whole story, it's what was in that movie Hugh showed."

"Oh?" Matt felt a little light go on in his head. Bing!

"They kept talking about that, joking about it. Something had happened when they were showing it."

"Funny you should mention that." In all that time, all the hours he'd spent pondering things, he hadn't given the movie a thought. "I think I've got it down in my car."

II

The park was actually not far from where Matt lived, though he hardly got over there anymore. When they had first moved to the city, he and Jonathan had come often, that summer when Laurel immediately started to work and he hadn't found a job for a while. While other kids raced from one thing to another, Jonathan settled into something until he really got a feel for it, his face in a kind of dull rapture while he mesmerized himself with a single activity. Once he had stayed on a swing, in the same long steady motion, for forty-eight minutes.

Now Matt watched the children who crowded the park on a weekday summer afternoon, swinging on the swings, clambering over the jungle gym, sliding, spinning themselves dizzy on the merry-go-round. It was a huge crowd of kids. He thought he even recognized a few.

"You think you'll get much done?" he had said to Sandra. He hadn't really wanted to leave.

"An hour's an hour. Besides. I want to be alone when I explain this to my kids. They'll be getting home from camp."

"You're going to explain it to them."

"I'll say something. I've got to give them some reason for sitting around watching a movie they can't watch."

At first he had been stumped. It was one thing to have the movie sitting down in his car, quite another to figure out a way to see it. He knew there was a projector at the school. but he couldn't think of a safe way to get at it. For a few silly minutes he was intrigued by the thought that there was still probably a projector at Bollinger's. Sandra had access to equipment at the university, but couldn't picture showing such a movie in a seminar room. He racked his brains trying to think of somebody who had one. He called Wolf a couple times but got no answer. Finally, in desperation, he called Laurel.

"I can't think of anybody who owns one," she said. "You can check them out of the public library. Just like a book."

"Anytime?" Matt said.

"I'll call."

She called back and said that they did have one projector available, that you needed to own a library card and make a deposit and fill out a questionnaire to get it.

Matt hesitated. "Could you do that?"

"Really, Matt. I don't think they have a stakeout on the A-V room of the public library. Waiting for you to come in."

"It makes me nervous. Going down there and signing things."

"Jonathan will be furious. Mrs. Delgatti might as well move in here."

"This is the last thing. I promise."

"As long as it's important."

"I think it's important. I hope it's important."

He tried Wolf again and this time he got him. Immediately he thought of saving Laurel a trip.

"No I don't got a projector. And no I don't got a library card. And no I don't got time to watch movies this afternoon. I'm busy."

"This is the movie Bollinger showed the night he was killed. Sandra, Angel here, she thinks it might have something to do with who killed him."

"Even dirty movies, Matt. I'm on a job."

"It's not an ordinary dirty movie. That's what I thought before. This is a movie Bollinger made himself."

"I'm sure it's a work of art."

"It's a movie of the people who were coming to the party."

There was a long pause on the phone. "Jesus Christ."

"At least I think that's the movie I've got. I picked it up that night at Bollinger's. After I saw the body."

"Why the hell'd you do that?"

"I don't know. It was just there. Anyway, I got it. I think it's the right movie."

"How'd he get them to be in it?"

"They didn't know, most of them. He took it from behind those mirrors of his. It was a little joke, this showing at the party."

"Somebody didn't think it was funny."

"Laurel's getting a projector. She should have it here by four."

"I'll try to get there. But I got to see this guy. It probably won't be till after that. Maybe you can show it again."

"Yeah. You can catch the late show."

He hoped Wolf got there. He wanted him to see it. He wanted as much help figuring this out as he could get.

For a while he had been killing time until Laurel arrived, strolling through the park near Sandra's house, smoking his pipe, watching the kids on the swings, their long lazy arcs, the little puffs of dust as their feet scraped the ground. Now he walked on a slow diagonal across the park, that long stretch of green, back toward Sandra's.

She had heard about the movie long before, when Bollinger first had the idea. He had been planning it for weeks. She didn't know too specifically what was in it, and didn't know what everyone's reaction had been when it was shown. The night of the party, she said, she stayed down in the basement after Matt left; she hadn't wanted to go upstairs and see those people. By the time it got down to her only half the

party was left. Bollinger and the Droges were laughing up-
roariously, Todd Hunter rather less. He seemed troubled, and
truculent, possibly a little drunk. From what she gathered,
Mingins had left in the middle of the movie, deeply offended.
Killian had pretended to take it a little better, but left in
obvious embarrassment immediately afterwards. It was his exit
that especially provoked the mirth of Bollinger and the Droges;
Hugh kept mimicking his stuttered goodbye, his shit-eating
grin. It seemed the idea at that point was to get something
started among those who were left, at least that was what
Bollinger wanted, and the Droges—"They're ready anytime"—
but Sandra was having none of it, collected her money and
got out, and she had the idea Hunter wasn't too wild about
it either. She couldn't blame him. The group that was left
was hardly choice.

"Do you think Bollinger had a thing for Hunter?" Matt said.
"Mingins thought he did."

"Mingins himself did. At least that's what Hugh said."

"That doesn't mean Bollinger didn't."

"I used to wonder about Hugh a little, that way. Sometimes
he showed me the magazines and stuff he bought, and it was
never gay, at least not what he showed me. But when he talked
about it, I don't think he was conscious of this, but when he
talked about those straight scenes, he always seemed more
interested in the men."

Sandra stared thoughtfully.

"The other thing is, he had a glow around that boy. It was
a little sad, because the kid was such a creep. It was the glow a
man has, or more often a woman, around someone he loves.
It was also the glow of a teacher around a prize pupil. I
thought maybe he just loved the way he played lacrosse."

Even that, as Matt well knew, was an essentially erotic
relationship.

When he got back to the apartment he just walked in;
Sandra had said she would leave the door open for him. As
soon as he did he heard the bass blare of the television. Just
like his place. He made plenty of noise going up the stairs—
he didn't want to walk in unannounced—and when he got to
the top found Sandra picking up papers from the dining-room
table, with the harried anxious look of a disorganized person
who had decided finally (such a person makes this decision
every few days) to get organized. She had also draped, across
the end windows, old sheets, as makeshift curtains; the side

windows were shaded by trees and didn't let in much light. The room was quite dim.

"I thought I could clear at least a patch of this table," she said. "We could move it into the center of the room, project on the wall."

Matt was staring at her children. He had expected kids around Jonathan's age, perhaps slightly younger, but the boy in front of the television, sprawled all over a chair as only a young person can be, was at least fourteen—he had a squat thickening body, a huge head of curly blond hair—and the girl, long and leggy with her brown hair cut short, seemed not much younger.

"*These* are your kids?"

Sandra spoke in annoyance. "Could you at least pry yourselves away from that thing long enough to say hello to Mr. Gregg?"

They turned and greeted him, the boy standing to speak— he stood in a slight crouch, as if poised to pivot and take the ball to the hoop—the girl just nodding. They both wore a becoming shyness. Their eyes drifted back to the television.

"How old are they?" Matt said.

"Ken's fifteen. Terry's twelve."

"And you were a child bride."

"Too young. Far too young. I had one kid, then another, before I ever had a chance to go to college. I was working to get their father through." She spoke as if explaining the mess on the dining-room table. "Then he did the same for me. But that's why I'm in this fix now. Too old to be in school." She stared helplessly at the papers.

She had spoken of her children before, but it was one thing to hear the words, quite another to see flesh-and-blood people. You never thought, when a woman stepped into a room with you and casually stripped, probed you with her knowing fingers, that she might be somebody's mother. He thought of the kiss he had tried to give her, the shy thick-muscled boy in front of the television. My kisses are reserved, she had said.

"I wouldn't trade them for anything," she said. "I just wish they'd come along a little later."

She was busy—she had the look of a woman who has suddenly realized another woman is coming to her apartment, and that the place is a mess—but she wouldn't let Matt touch anything, so he decided to go outside and wait for Laurel. It wasn't until he got outside, sat on the front steps and lit his pipe, that he really began to grow apprehensive. From his earliest years a man dreams of the compliant woman with a marvelous body who comes to him out of nowhere and does whatever he wants; now he had found this woman, and, out of all the things in the world he could do with her, he had worked himself into a situation where he was going to introduce her to his wife. What would he say when he did that? Who would he say Sandra was? In the background of this imagined meeting hovered all the things he had not told Laurel about the past few days.

But before he could work out a strategy the car drove up, their second car, an ancient VW bug that ran some of the time, and before it had even really stopped the door flew open and Jonathan was running at him full-speed. He felt tears spring to his eyes—he hadn't admitted to himself until then how much he had missed the boy—and Jonathan was obviously delighted to see him too, so it only flashed through his mind for a moment that something was wrong. Wait a minute. What's he doing here?) when the boy had reached him and leaped into his arms. He couldn't remember when he had had such a greeting from his son.

"Where is it?" Jonathan said.

"Where's what?"

"I know I can't shoot it right now. I just want to see it."

"Jonathan. We only talked a couple hours ago. I haven't had time to get anything."

"Dad!" Jonathan dropped out of his father's arms, shouting in disgust.

"What do you think I am, a miracle man?"

"That's the only reason I came!"

Laurel was stooped into the back seat of the VW, tugging at the projector.

"Matt," she shouted. "Come and get this. I think it's the first projector Edison made. Or Eastman, or whoever. It weighs a ton."

Already Jonathan had slumped in anger, twenty seconds into their reunion. Matt walked to the car.

"I thought you were getting Mrs. Delgatti."

"The woman needs some time to herself. Besides. As soon as I said I was seeing you Jonathan had to come. I thought it was nice."

"He can't watch this movie."

"I gathered as much. He can play out here. Or I'll take him to the park. We'll figure out something."

Matt picked up the dusty black case by its leather handle—it really was incredibly heavy—and walked toward the apartment. Things were not going at all well. He was walking upstairs with his wife and son, to the apartment of a whore of his acquaintance (funny to think of her that way, but it was true; by their deeds shall ye know them) where her kids were waiting. His mission was to screen a dirty movie. He couldn't picture this scene. The women, like two women anywhere, would be checking each other out (would Laurel know immediately? Would Sandra think, "Sure. I can see why he'd want a little on the side"?). Sandra's kids would probably go back on what they had promised and want to stay; from the sound of it, she wouldn't be above letting her adolescents sample such a movie. Even if they did go out, did you really want your son playing with the children of a whore? What would they play? Maybe he'd catch something. Matt wasn't even sure, come to think of it, that he knew how to operate a projector. Now Jonathan was slumping—"Let's go home, Mom"—and Laurel was annoyed and angry, and Sandra was no doubt running around desperately trying to clean.

The three of them trooped up the stairs to find that Sandra had moved the table into the middle of the room. Somehow, miraculously, the papers had been gathered up, neatly arranged at the sides of a center space.

She smiled at Laurel. "I'm Sandra Kendley."

Laurel smiled carefully. "Laurel Gregg." Matt could see the wheels turning.

"My son came." Matt was abashed to say it. "Jonathan."

"Great. The kids can be together. Ken, Terry. Why don't you take Jonathan outside?"

The boy immediately leaped up and turned off the television. Matt had never—and he had his teaching experience to fall back on—seen an adolescent react so quickly. "Bring the Frisbee," Ken said to his sister.

"These two will teach you how to throw a Frisbee," Sandra said.

"I know how to throw a Frisbee." Jonathan clattered after them in disgust.

To Matt's almost certain knowledge, Jonathan had never touched a Frisbee in his life.

Matt heaved the projector up, carefully placed it on the table. "I'm not sure I know how to run this thing."

"I can run them all," Sandra said. "I had a course in it."

"You must be in education," Laurel said.

They were off.

Matt should have known: get a couple of academics together and you never had to worry about those awkward silences. Their fields were close enough, at least had psychology in common, and soon they were gabbing about courses, comparing textbooks, working on the projector together, Sandra giving Laurel little things to do. Whatever sizing up of each other they had to do seemed to have been done. Matt got some chairs and arranged them around the table. The women didn't seem particularly to know he was there.

Men went about their first meetings so much differently, jabbing and parrying, circling warily, their guards up at all times to protect their egos. It was odd to observe the women: Laurel seemed much the more sensuous one, dark, bosomy, with her wild hair and low voice; Sandra in her presence had become a pale bespectacled schoolteacher. Men thought they could tell about women by looking, but they were wrong. Matt defied any man to step into that room and say which woman went down.

"We're ready," Sandra said, turning to him.

"You'll run it?"

"I'll run it."

He spoke to his wife. "This is the movie Bollinger showed his guests the night he was killed."

"You told me."

"Sandra hasn't seen it, but she's heard about it some. It's like a *Candid Camera* show. The people didn't know they were being filmed."

"Some of them," Sandra said.

"It shows them having sex. People you know."

"Yikes." Laurel spoke softly, reddened.

"You might not want to watch," Matt said.

"I guess I'll be embarrassed. It sounds fascinating."

"We'll all be embarrassed," Sandra said. "But somebody who saw this movie commited the murder."

Unless you did it, Matt thought.

"So we watch this thing and decide who it was," Laurel said.

"Exactly," Matt said.

Sandra flipped the switch. After all this it would probably turn out Matt had picked up a Bugs Bunny cartoon by mistake.

For a moment Matt didn't recognize the setting, because he was seeing it from a new angle, actually just a corner of it. Then he did: it was Hugh Bollinger's downstairs apartment. The camera was behind the mirror, that long two-way mirror on the wall, and the bed was just a couple of steps away. Sitting on it in profile, naked and alone, his butt on the wooden frame and his shoulders hunched slightly forward, was Stanley Killian.

"Oh God." Laurel covered her mouth. "I'm not sure I can take this."

"Now's the time to leave," Matt said. "If you think you want to." He found himself wishing she would.

"It takes a minute to get used to," Laurel said.

Killian was flushed, smiling, staring, leaning back on his hands. His body looked big and soft: a shallow puddle of flab lay around his gut. Though there was no woman around, he already had an erection, or at least a healthy start on one. He started to stand, then didn't, as if he had been told not to. A naked woman stepped into the picture.

"That looks like . . . " Laurel spoke in perfect innocence. "That's you."

Sandra snapped off the projector. "You didn't tell your wife who I am."

"We didn't get time to talk."

"I thought you'd tell her outside."

"Jonathan was there."

An air of tension had snapped over the room like a trap. Laurel was blushing furiously. Sandra was pale with anger. Matt moved around in his seat, his chest boiling. No one looked at anyone else.

"I work as a masseuse," Sandra said. "It's how I'm putting myself through school. I did some extra work for Hugh Bollinger. Stanley and I have sex in this scene."

"I was just surprised." Laurel seemed on the verge of tears. "I won't interrupt again."

"I should have told you," Matt said.

Sandra snapped the projector back on. Things were off to a wonderful start.

As soon as Sandra stepped close enough on the screen, Killian embraced her; they tumbled onto the waterbed and bounced, riding the waves. For a while they were just a tangle of bodies. Killian's face was buried at her shoulder, then moved toward her breasts. Sandra's own face strained above his head, as if holding herself out of water where she would drown.

"He's a terribly ardent man," Sandra said. "Hungry, hungry." Her voice had wavered at first, then steadied. She seemed to be speaking to clear the air. "He's soft, and gentle, but like he's holding himself back. As if he'd eat you alive if he ever let go."

He was stooped above her somewhat on all fours, feeding on her body like an animal at a trough.

"He gets a little sloppy." He had moved away from one nipple, left it damp with spittle.

Soon the big disheveled head moved down between her legs. Sandra was moving her hips, rolling them languorously, but her face stared down as if annoyed, or worried. When he looked up, though, she smiled at him, mussed his hair, pushed his head back down.

"God," she muttered, beside the projector.

Laurel was staring intently, astounded to be watching such a thing.

"Stanley's a shy man," she said. "Despite the way he talks. Trying all the time to be suggestive." She spoke slowly, deliberately. "A couple of women at the center have gotten annoyed and called his bluff. He backs right down."

"He's the kind of man who likes the exchange of money," Sandra said. "That makes it all easier. He's not confessing a need. Just making a payment."

"I think he'd die watching this," Laurel said.

Matt knew Laurel must be put off, watching that scene. She didn't like a man's face there. He also knew she was critically assessing Sandra's body as she watched. She wanted no one's to be nicer than hers.

The camera never moved, of course, and much of the action was obscured, not like professionally made porn, where a dedicated photographer would wedge his head up somebody's ass to get a good shot. For a while Sandra had Stanley on his back, caressing him, then using her mouth. She tried to mount him that way, but he argued her onto her back and clambered on top himself. The final scene mostly featured his sizable rear end and heavy testicles, everything jiggling while he pounded away. Matt was reminded of livestock he had seen at the county fair. Aesthetically speaking, the climax was too long delayed. Killian suddenly humped away furiously for a few seconds, then collapsed in a heap.

"One down," Sandra said.

The screen had gone blank for a moment. The projector made a clicking sound.

"The poor man," Laurel said.

Sandra glanced at her curiously.

"I just mean . . . " Laurel reddened. "Having to watch that."

"Ah."

Images reappeared. The setting was the same, but the participants different. They were already together in bed, slightly out of focus. One was caressing the other's chest. When Matt made a quick check—who's who here?—something was indefinably wrong. Then it came to him. Both were men.

Sandra fooled with the projector. The focus improved. The one doing the caressing, leaning rather dotingly over his partner, was Chandler Mingins.

"Well," Laurel said. "If there was ever any doubt in my mind . . . "

A general air of relief settled over the room at the realization that no one present was a participant in this scene.

"Who made these movies?" Matt said. "Who did the filming?" The second guy on the screen was Todd Hunter.

"Hunter set things up," Sandra said. "He was the one who knew photography. But he showed things to Hugh. It was really just a matter of pushing a button."

"This is the kid I told you about," Matt said to Laurel. "The lacrosse player."

Mingins' body was long and thin, tight and stringy, like a face that had been lifted. He wore a thin gold chain around his neck, a copper bracelet on his wrist. Even naked in bed, he seemed immaculate. His cock was tiny, perched above his balls like a little bull's-eye. Hunter, on the other hand, had a fat lazy cock that lay on his belly like a challenge. He had the sharply defined muscles of an athlete, no spare flesh anywhere. With an arrogant grin he grabbed Mingins' hand and guided it between his legs.

"Chandler doesn't try to hide anything," Laurel said. "I mean he doesn't go around talking about it. But I don't think this would . . . surprise anyone."

179

"No," Matt said. "Everybody knows."

Hunter was urging Mingins' head toward his cock. Matt had the feeling, watching, that it was not so much a sexual gesture as an attempt to rid himself of the man's attention. They seemed to argue a moment. It was also obvious, as Matt watched, that Hunter knew where the camera was. He had arranged Mingins on his far side, was rotating slightly to keep everything in view. Mingins was kissing down his body, drawing little patterns with his tongue. As he reached his belly he lay his cheek there a moment, away from Hunter's view. His face wore an expression of rapt adoration.

Hunter, at the same time, was mugging for the camera, making broad faces of horror and disgust.

"I only met that boy a couple times," Sandra said. "I didn't like him."

"Me either," Matt said.

"For me he was the most repulsive of Hugh's friends. And that's saying something."

Matt had to put Otto right up there.

The scene continued that way, Mingins in earnest and attempting a virtuoso performance, Hunter discreetly mocking it. Matt himself was uncomfortable watching; he had never seen two men make love before. Laurel, on the other hand, was delighted. "You can watch either one," she said. Mingins sucked Hunter until he was hard, then moved up beside him and lay on his back. They seemed to argue some more. Mingins caressed him, tried to take the boy in his arms. Finally Hunter grabbed him and rolled him over on his belly. The older man faced away from the camera. Hunter looked down at him, musing, then turned toward the camera and held his nose.

"Nice," Sandra said.

In the limited amount of pornography Matt had seen in his life, he had never seen the act that followed, at least not between two men. If anything, Mingins' bottom seemed smaller and softer and more vulnerable than a woman's. Hunter arranged things for maximum visibility. Mingins did seem genuinely to enjoy himself, squirming around underneath and moving in rhythm. At one point he reached back and took Hunter's hand, placed it under him, apparently on his cock. There was no particular finish. The film must have run out in the middle of the act.

"I swear," Laurel said. She was curled up in her chair. "This movie is an education."

"If Mingins killed anyone," Sandra said, "he should have killed Hunter."

Two new figures flashed on the screen, smiling, laughing, waving at the camera. It was a full frontal shot. They were both nude.

"Time for some comic relief," Sandra said.

It was the Droges.

In many ways the two of them had the same body, heavy blocky chunky torsos. Her breasts were small—hardly larger, in fact, than his—and his genitals were inconsequential down there in the hairy rolls of fat. It was a little like the Japanese engravings at Hugh's. Maybe the Droges had posed for them. Otto leaned over and bit one of his wife's breasts; she laughed and gave him a hefty slap. A large white German shepherd stepped into view.

"Hugh told me they raised dogs," Sandra said. "I hope this isn't what I think it is."

Outside, the Kendley children were putting on a Frisbee exhibition. They had obviously spent many hours practicing. Terry was a slender pretty girl whose quiet smile suggested shyness, though she found it easy now to talk to Jonathan. He had chosen to stand near her. Ken looked like a wild man, with his huge head of kinky blond hair. He was built like a miniature adult, or like an ape, low to the ground, heavily muscled, with long arms that curved slightly as they hung. Terry could do a few tricks, and explained them to Jonathan as she did, but mostly she threw the hard spins for Ken, who did what seemed to Jonathan an incredible array of stunts. He never just caught the Frisbee, but let it spin awhile, on his fingertips, on his knuckles. He caught it behind his back, between his legs, batted it repeatedly in the air, kicked it with his feet, bounced it off his head, all the time keeping the Frisbee alive, maintaining the spin. He could throw forehand or backhand, throw a bounce pass, throw behind his back, even fling it with his foot. Jonathan, who was a receptive audience for any trick, shouted exclamations of appreciation and admiration. "How do you *do* that?" he kept saying.

Jonathan, that summer, had picked up a casual habit of

profanity. It was a mannerism, more like a wordless grunt than an expression with meaning. It could seem a complaint ("Aw, God") or a shout of breathless wonder ("Ah! God!"), but Jonathan spoke it with almost no inflection, more one word than two. "Ah God."

At every trick Ken did, every subtle twist he put on an old trick, Jonathan shouted, "Ah God!"

Ken and Terry didn't leave Jonathan out; they showed him how to throw and catch, and Ken taught him to catch the whirling Frisbee on one finger. Ken could throw a spinner almost straight in the air, to himself, so he kept giving Jonathan short easy throws, letting him practice. Jonathan stood amazed, watching the Frisbee whiz around on his finger.

He worshiped older, more talented kids, loved it when they paid attention to him.

After about ten minutes, Ken said, "Want to find out what our parents are doing?"

"They're watching a movie," Jonathan said. "Not a good movie. Just some dumb thing my dad found."

"We don't know what kind of movie," Ken said.

"I'm not supposed to go back into the apartment," Jonathan said.

"I didn't say anything about going back into the apartment." Ken pointed to a high maple tree that grew up along the side windows.

"Ah God," Jonathan said.

Ken ran to the tree. Jonathan loved to climb, but only small things where he could easily be careful and where there wasn't much risk. He had never seen anyone climb a tree that size. Ken, however, had obviously climbed it many times. He made an easy leap for a low branch and climbed up his usual footholds as if he were walking up stairs. Jonathan drifted toward the tree, staring up in amazement. "Don't get too close." Terry touched his shoulder. "He has been known to fall." Ken easily reached the branch nearest the window, straddled it like a bike and slid his way out. He had to lean slightly to his right to see in the window, reached for a branch to steady himself. As Jonathan stared up into the green branches, sunlight pouring through, he saw Ken lean, squint, go pale—his mouth dropping open—and fall.

"Ah God!" Jonathan shouted.

Ken was one of those instinctual climbers who are as at ease sitting twenty feet up in a tree as most people are in an easy chair in front of the television. He had been stunned, thrown off balance, by what he had seen, but had not really fallen, just moved one branch to the right the way someone else might sprawl across an armrest. He hung by that branch for a few moments, staring in the window, then shinnied in toward the trunk, glanced down, and dropped to the ground.

He was brushing himself off when the others ran over to him.

"Go get the Frisbee, Jonathan," he said. "Go get the Frisbee and we'll play catch."

"What was the movie like?" Jonathan said.

"I couldn't see. That was the problem. I leaned too far when I couldn't see."

Jonathan raced after the Frisbee.

"You're not going to believe this," Ken said. "That movie." He avoided his sister's eyes, still looked pale. "It was a woman being fucked by a dog."

"Come on." Terry brightened; her smile widened. "A woman can't be fucked by a dog."

"I swear to God. You climb that tree."

"I'm asking Mother."

"Don't you ask her. Don't tell her I climbed that tree."

"I'll tell her I looked."

"She knows you can't climb that tree."

Terry and her brother often talked about sex, especially about things their friends were rumored to do. Though he knew much more, and had taught her much of what she knew, he was oddly uncomfortable around the subject, more intense and serious than she. She liked his embarrassment.

"Did she kiss him?" she said. "Did they hug and French-kiss like lovers?"

"She was getting it from behind," Ken said. "Just like dogs do. The dog was jumping up and pounding away like crazy, and the woman was kneeling in front of him and laughing."

"I don't believe she was laughing," Terry said. "She'll probably get fleas."

The Frisbee came sailing through the air and hit Ken above the eye.

"Ah God!" Jonathan shouted. "I'm sorry."

"She'll probably have puppies," Ken said.

* * *

"Now I can die," Laurel said. "Now I've seen everything."

"I'm not convinced this is really happening," Sandra said.

The Droges had put on an incredible exhibition. It wasn't so much what they did as how they did it, leering at the camera, posing for it, putting everything on display. They could have made holding hands obscene. They kissed with their tongues outside their mouths, darting them like lizards. Otto didn't suck his wife's nipples but bit them, twisted them with his fingers. She held her vagina open so the camera could see into it a couple inches; he raked his tongue across her clitoris, thrust it inside her. She offered her ass and he bit it all over, tongued her anus. She chewed his balls and sucked his rubbery cock. The whole thing wasn't having much effect on him. It was interesting—Matt had noticed the fact before—that men experienced in porn films rarely seemed to get it up from what the woman was doing. It was as if they were jaded from too much experience. You noticed a splice in the film, and suddenly the man had a hard-on, as if he had done something special offstage. You had to wonder what. But there was no splice in this film. Dotty pulled and stroked and tickled while Otto lay on his back, lifeless; after a while she gave up and straddled as if to mount him (nothing to mount) then bent over while the dog jumped on her, thrusting away frantically and clutching with his paws. Obviously the animal was marvelously trained, and it was apparent from the way Mrs. Droge was squirming around that she was enjoying something about the experience, but it was not entirely certain— the viewer could comfort himself with this—that she was being penetrated in intercourse. Her husband mauled her breasts while she squirmed. The scene ended vaguely, as she collapsed on the bed near Otto and the dog jumped up beside them.

"The Droges and Hugh had a wonderful relationship," Sandra said. "They did things and he watched. Supplied the money when they needed it. Often they hired a prostitute of one sex or another to join them. I believe the dog was their own. But they did everything. Wife-swapped. Made movies. Staged orgies. Droge has bounced around from one job to another, but lately he was working in that porn shop, looking out for special items for Hugh. It was all very cozy."

The film was still flickering, and another scene came on, in a different setting. It was a smaller room, just a few feet across, with a wide table like a bed in it. A man lay stretched out on the table. Once again, because of the new perspective, Matt didn't recognize the room. The man faced away from the camera.

Sandra snapped off the film. "I didn't know that was on here."

"Turn it back on," Laurel said.

"That wasn't one of these people from the party."

"Turn it on," Laurel said.

Sandra flipped the switch. It suddenly dawned on Matt what the room was. The man shifted on the table, turned toward the camera, a face troubled, weary, anxious. It was Matt.

"I don't think we should watch this," Sandra said.

"I'm going to watch," Laurel said.

"If you two want to watch I'm going out with the children," Sandra said.

She walked behind the projector and quickly out the door.

Like other segments of the movie, this one had been spliced in places, shortened. Also as in other parts, the view of the camera was obscured. But it did show Sandra's—Angel's— sudden entrance, as she threw off her nightie; it showed Matt's expression soften and change; it showed parts of the massage, as her fingertips drifted over his body, strayed between his legs; it showed him hungrily sucking her breasts while she stared down blankly; it showed him writhing in his orgasm, Sandra digging between his legs to produce a violent spasm. When the scene was over the movie ended, started flapping; Matt got up and turned it off. Both he and Laurel had watched without a word. Finally he turned to look at his wife.

She was not looking at him.

"I guess this makes us even," she said.

"I guess."

She was staring down at her hands, as if studying them.

"I would never have gone myself," he said. "Bollinger took me."

"I didn't see anyone holding you down."

"No." He made a dry sound, like a little laugh.

Laurel looked up, but still didn't look at him.

"You looked so happy," she said.

"It felt good. It felt wonderful. I didn't have to do anything, just lie there. She touched me some ways you don't touch."

"So I'll touch you those ways. If it's so terribly important. I'll touch you . . . " Her lips trembled.

"It's not important."

He knew, anyway, that she wouldn't enjoy doing it.

"You never seem so . . . " Tears had appeared at her eyes. "You *never* look that happy with me."

"I didn't look too happy at first." It frightened him, actually, the miserable face he had turned to the camera. "But it was like she came out of nowhere. She looked great. Smelled great. She was mine for the taking."

"The thing I don't understand." She wiped at the tears with her fingers. "The thing I will never understand. I know I'm really no better. What I did was probably just as bad. But I've known Ned for a year. We saw each other day after day. We worked together, had long talks after work. I loved him. I know that didn't mean I could fuck him. But there you are with this woman you don't even know, who walks in this dirty little room and takes off her clothes, and just because she has a nice body, she lets you suck her tits and tickles your asshole, you're in a state of ecstasy. Honest to God. You don't even know her, and it might as well have been me in there."

It was true. In some ways it was just because the woman was a stranger, because he had no responsibility for her and no future with her, that he enjoyed himself so much.

What he couldn't understand was how Laurel could love somebody else. He could never have done that.

"I want to be loved for me," she said. "For my person. Not because I have two tits and a cunt. I want you to love *me*. And you don't."

He did, actually. But he knew what she meant.

Laurel got up and walked out the door. Matt followed. They walked down the dark stairway.

Outside, Sandra was playing with the children. She was something of a Frisbee wizard herself, but just now was making easy tosses to Jonathan. He caught and threw them back like a veteran. When Laurel came out Sandra walked over to her, pale and solemn and resolute.

"I'm sorry," she said. "I didn't know that was on there."

"All right." Laurel stared blankly at the woman.

"It was nothing personal. I didn't know him then."

"I guess you don't know any of them." Laurel was rolling the word whore around in her mouth, dying to spit it at her.

"It helps me sometimes . . . " Sandra bit her lip, swallowed. "It helps me to remember men are babies."

The last thing Laurel wanted to hear at this point was a prostitute's philosophy of life. "You don't treat them that way."

"You know, I really do." She brushed back a couple strands of hair that had drifted into her eyes. "I rub them with baby powder, and I rub them with baby oil, and I cradle their heads and rock them a little and let them suck my breasts. Sometimes it's all I can do not to diaper them. That's where it all starts, after all, when we're babies and want to be stroked and held and to have our mouth full. We never get enough. That's the way men are when they come to me. They think they're big and tough, they think they want to screw me, then I put them on their backs and stroke them a few minutes and they turn to jelly. Moan and gurgle and coo."

"And wet themselves." At that moment Laurel found the whole process revolting.

"Exactly. When they're men we think it's dirty and awful, that they'd go downtown and pay for that, but when they're babies we just think it's cute. We stroke them, and hold them, and play with them. It's interesting when you think of it. Babies don't know who it is, or care. It's all right for babies, why not for men?"

A car screeched around the corner. Even before the cloud of exhaust appeared, Matt—who had been standing back from the women, pretending to watch the children—knew who it was, from the engine knock that was already unmistakable half a block away. The car clattered to a halt and Wolf emerged, slamming the door with an awful metallic crunch. He wore his most winning smile, the gold cap to a tooth gleaming in front.

"Hope I didn't miss the matinee," he said.

"Christ." Laurel turned on him, started to move. "This whole thing is his fault."

"Laurel," Matt said.

Sandra stared in puzzlement, no idea who the man was.

"Whatever it is, lady"—Wolf held up his hand, like stopping traffic—"I didn't do it."

"You're the one who dragged my husband into this mess." She was marching straight at him. "Took him out of a perfectly good job and sent him downtown on your filthy errands. You're the one who knows these scummy people and has that stinking office and spends his days sniffing around motel rooms. Who wants my husband to spend his life wallowing in this crap. Just because you like it. If it weren't for you none of this would have happened."

It wouldn't have done any good to reason with Laurel. It wouldn't have helped to mention that Matt had met most of the people involved in this matter at his previous job or because of her present one, that Wolf had never asked Matt to work for him, that he probably didn't need him and certainly didn't want him for the rest of his life, that he had sent Matt downtown on an insurance matter and hadn't even known Hugh Bollinger existed. It wouldn't have done any good to mention that Wolf hated divorce work. Laurel was looking for an object for her anger, for the pent-up frustrations of weeks and months, and with Wolf's arrival she had found it.

Wolf's brow was knit in bewilderment. He still held up a hand like a traffic cop, still wore his grin, watched her as she walked across the grass and stopped in front of him.

Out of nowhere she swung a roundhouse right. It caught him flatfooted, landed square in the middle of his face. He stumbled off the curb, and bumped back against his car. Blood spattered out of his nose.

In all the confusion, Matt was never sure what happened. He saw Wolf holding up his hand and smiling, then staggering back with blood on his face, saw Laurel lunge at his face with her nails clawing, Wolf catch her wrists instinctively. By that time Matt had grabbed her. He'd had no idea how strong his wife was, how hard she would be to hold when she was angry to the point of hysteria. She was screaming and struggling and swinging blindly, Jonathan shrieking, Wolf shouting in bewilderment, so Matt hardly noticed when a new car screeched up, then another, three men rushed out and separated him from Laurel, two on his arms and one on her (they should have worked it the other way); he still didn't really understand even when Laurel was standing limply, staring in horror, while his arms were snatched behind his back and handcuffs snapped on his wrists.

"She's my wife," Matt said, as if that explained everything.

"You can lose one guy, Wolf," the man with the handcuffs was saying. "You can lose two." Matt felt a sudden cramping between his shoulder blades. "You got to be awful good to lose three."

"You got careless," the second man said. "Jesus. Alls we wanted to do was ask the guy some questions."

Wolf was back against the car, splattered with blood, a look of utter incredulity on his face.

"Yeah," the third guy said. "Although I gotta admit. This whole thing looks mighty peculiar to me."

Chapter Seven

Matt walked out of the police station the next afternoon with a feeling of utter freedom. It was ridiculous. The last thing Dennis O'Rourke said—the detective who had been questioning him, a big meaty guy whose jowls sagged, hair was starting to go on top, whose upper lip had the distinct nick of an old scar in it, like a swipe from a razor—was, "Don't leave town. Make sure people know where you are all the time. Wolf. Your wife. And how about staying off the case now, huh? Leave it to the big guys. We get paid." Matt grinned, blushed, smiled sheepishly.

He had no intention of staying off the case.

The desk sergeant who handed over his stuff said, "Want to make a call? You're allowed all you want, now."

"That's okay," Matt said.

"You got to at least get a ride."

"I'll catch a bus."

He stepped out into the summer afternoon. A light haze hung over the city, but there weren't actually any clouds in the sky. The streets were bright and hot. He didn't know quite where he was, but he had a vague feeling, and could judge from the length of the streets, that he was well up from the Point. He would walk around until he got his bearings, then find a bus stop.

He felt like a schoolboy on a day off from school. Nowhere to be, nothing to do. No one even knew where he was. He couldn't remember when—as a husband, a father, a bread-winner—he had had such a feeling.

It was odd the way things had worked out. The detectives who picked him up had been coming to get him, so they had no interest in his surroundings. They did bring Laurel and Wolf along—Laurel brought Jonathan—but released them when it had been established that that bizarre scene was mostly a domestic squabble. They had ignored altogether the woman and two children who had been standing on the lawn playing Frisbee. When they finally got around to asking who she was— and that was only after they had been over everything else, from Matt's entrance into Bollinger's house on—Matt just said she was a friend of his and Laurel's, that they had chosen her apartment as a place to meet because they didn't want to be discovered. She was an old friend of the family.

By that time he had settled on a policy of shielding Sandra. He didn't quite know why. Probably it was something as simple as that she hadn't been questioned yet, he knew it would be difficult for her—what with the various jobs she had done for Bollinger—so he did what he could to see that she wouldn't have to. One lie led to another. He said he had been with a woman the night of the party, that Bollinger had fixed him up downstairs with a woman, but that he knew her only as Angel. The police had heard that much from the Droges. Matt admitted to having first talked to Bollinger the previous afternoon, but mentioned nothing about their stop in the massage parlor. He said he knew a movie had been shown the night of the party but he didn't know anything about it, he hadn't seen the reel when he returned to the house and didn't know where it was now. On other things he played it straight. He even admitted—as he hadn't to anyone else—that a major reason he had been so shaken up that night and hadn't been able to call the police was that he had found his wife with another man. O'Rourke had raised an eyebrow at that. Some swinging couple. Both fooling around on the same night. But even though O'Rourke had given him only about four hours' sleep, had alternated with a couple other guys and questioned him constantly, Matt had no problem keeping his stories straight. He knew what he wanted to tell.

A peculiar thing happened during those hours of questioning. He would have said even as he walked into the station that he was sympathetic to the police. He had been a cop, after all; his father had been a cop; he had been around policemen all his life. But something about withholding information, about the act of lying to them, sitting there knowing he could sneak off later and talk to Sandra, take a look at the movie, made him hostile to the police, or at least competitive with them. He didn't want them to get that information and solve the case. He didn't want them to solve the case. He wanted to have the information, and solve the case, and come back later and drop it in their laps. He wanted to win.

The problem, of course, would be trying to persuade Wolf.

He found his way to Fifth and took a bus to the east end, enjoyed the tour of those back streets that he seldom saw. He got off near Sandra's and walked over to pick up the VW where Laurel had left it when they were taken to the station. After a while he got it started, and drove into East Liberty. On his way up to the office he noticed the woman at the candy counter, stopped and looked at her awhile, but she just stared past him blankly, at a point halfway up the wall.

He still wasn't sure he believed it.

Wolf was sitting at his desk going through some papers. The room was blue with cigarette smoke.

"O'Rourke called," he said. "I told him I was surprised he'd let guys like you out to walk the streets."

"It's no trouble finding me," Matt said. "All they got to do is follow you."

"I want to tell you." Wolf threw down his pencil. "That's bullshit about three guys. I could lose thirty guys if I had to. I didn't see the third guy."

Wolf's frown looked comical, perhaps because of the bandage on his nose.

"Broken?" Matt said.

"Clean. Seventeen years I'm in this business and I never broke a thing until now. My partner's wife. With the back of her fist." He pounded his desk. "I hope you got a tough beak."

"I keep my guard up."

Wolf smiled weakly. He lit a cigarette. He could have just inhaled the air.

"So they didn't book you."

"Why'd they take me in at all, is what I don't get. They still think Killian did it. They're sure of it. That night they found the body—one of the neighbors thought he saw a prowler over there, gave the police a call—they found Killian's car out front, took the license number because it was parked a funny way, like a sudden stop. Then when they were inside they heard it start and pull away. He's burst in on people a couple times since. Wild and irrational. Looking for that movie. They think he'd kill for it. They think he has killed for it. They're worried and want to stop him."

"You can't blame them."

"I tried to explain that was after I'd seen the body. That

Bollinger must have been dead when Killian got there. But they think maybe he came back, looking for the movie. Or that he was hiding somewhere when I was around."

"There's a nice thought."

It had occurred to Matt that the apartment had a perfect hiding place, one where Killian could have seen anybody who came downstairs.

"So what'd they want with you?" Wolf said.

"They thought I might know where the movie is."

"They must have thought they were pretty clever."

"I told them I hadn't seen it."

Wolf covered his eyes with his hand. "Jesus Christ."

"They're going to catch up with Killian, the way he's running around. But the whole thing doesn't make sense to me. The guy's a wimp. I can see him wanting this movie. I can see any of them wanting the movie. But I can't see him getting violent about it. I can't see him killing for it."

"Wimps have killed people. But that's not the point. They asked you a question. You told them a lie."

"They're paying no attention to anyone else. Mingins makes a complete fool out of himself in the movie. He's a very proud man. And there's something wrong with this Hunter kid. He drinks like a middle-aged alcoholic, fools around with little girls. The police haven't been able to find him. They say even his mother doesn't know where he is. But I've got to wonder how hard they've been looking. There's all the guys from school that can be questioned. And a kid he mentioned to me the other night. This good friend of his. You could look into it."

"While you hang around East Liberty in your luxury apartment."

"I talk to Droge. It's the Droges and this Hunter kid who were there after everybody else left. If you find Hunter that's one more thing the cops don't have."

Matt knew he was asking the man a favor. He thought Wolf might be intrigued by the situation; it was far more interesting than most of what he did. But it didn't pay a cent. Wolf was a businessman.

"We don't have to do this, Matt. You come clean with the police and we'll be out of it."

"I was with the man the night he died. I was probably with whoever killed him. I'm at least a peripheral suspect. Of course I want to do it."

Wolf leaned back in his chair, closed his eyes.

"I can see how you wouldn't," Matt said. "The whole thing's nothing to you. I'll do it myself if you want. If you'll give me a few days off."

Wolf's brow tightened. Like experts in many fields, he hated the thought of someone else doing a job he knew he could do better. Even if he didn't want to do it.

"You work for me less than a week," he said, "and already you're asking for a vacation."

"You could give me some help," Matt said. "Some suggestions on how to go about it."

There were no suggestions in that business. You had to feel your way.

Slowly Wolf opened his eyes, leaned forward in his chair. He took out his notebook, picked up a pen. He wore the vague sleepy expression that he always wore when there was work to be done.

"Give me what you got," he said.

II

"I think the real problem"—Dotty Droge was moving toward him, carrying a can of salted cashews and a bag of tiny crackers shaped like fish—"is that we don't feel right about what we are. If we did, we wouldn't be so uptight about letting other people express themselves." As she leaned down to put the containers on the table, Matt got a perfect view down her shift to her small bare breasts. It didn't really matter. You could easily see them through the material. "The key to everything is accepting yourself. I'm okay"—she touched herself lightly with her fingertips, gestured toward Matt—"you're okay."

I'm okay, Matt thought, taking a handful of cashews. You're a dogfucker.

He had called before he came, and Mrs. Droge ("Oh, call me Dotty," she had said. "Everybody does." He believed it) sounded absolutely delighted to hear from him, as if he were an old dear friend. She would love to see him. They could have a drink together. Otto, unfortunately, had to work late at the store that night (dishing out quarters to perverts), but the two of them could talk. At first Matt had balked, then decided it was a good idea. Otto's halting conversation and leering white eyeballs probably wouldn't add much to the discussion anyway.

The Droges lived in a little box of a house on the slope of a hill, out in O'Hara township. It reminded Matt of the place where he and Laurel had lived after they got married. A white frame house on a small patch of grass, no trees, no shrubs. Down the hill a hazy vista of more houses on more bare yards. Inside, the Droges' furniture seemed straight out of a catalog. Early American mobile home. There was nothing on the walls, not even any bookcases, though there were some magazines under a table in the corner. *U.S. News and World Report*, Matt made out, and *Wrestling World*. Against one wall, in a dark-stained cabinet, was a huge color television, the one substantial piece in the room.

Out back, as he came in, Matt had noticed the fenced-in pen from which two white German shepherds eyed him eagerly. Probably thought he was there for an orgy. One of them was the most versatile talent since Rin Tin Tin.

"It was years ago," Dotty said, "that Otto and I made the decision to fully express our sexual selves. Far ahead of our time. Though for longer than you might think there's been a small group of like-minded people in this country. Freethinkers, free-lovers. What more recently have been called wife swappers or swingers. Maybe you'd like to see our newsletter."

She handed him a magazine from under the table, went out to the kitchen to get their drinks. *Club Amour*, the publication was called. It reminded Matt of a yearbook, or the album of mug shots down at the police station. It was the Sears catalog of the sex world. There was page after page of photographs, first by geographical area, then by sexual preference. All the pictures were black-and-white snapshots; some were nudes, though not exactly posed, just straight shots like those a doctor might have. "Psoriasis," one could be labeled, or "The Last Stages of Syphilis."

All fanatics are alike, Matt thought; it was what he had been thinking ever since he had entered the house. They have peculiar bodies, and they have that weird cast to their glance, and they live in houses like this one, their lives stripped of everything but that single obsession. He might have been looking through the yearbook of the John Birch Society, or of an odd religious sect.

He wondered if the Droges had listed their dog.

"It's as organized a group as the Rotarians," Dotty said,

drifting in with their drinks. "Or Kiwanis or somebody. We've belonged for years. Wonderful relationships."

She had insisted on making him a mixed drink, one she had read about in a magazine a few weeks before. Matt hoped it wasn't this magazine. Otto didn't have any beer in the house. Matt wasn't sure he trusted a man with no beer in the house.

In the interval between Matt's phone call and his arrival, Dotty had apparently fixed herself up. Her brown hair was short and combed with a part. The featured color of the day was purple: her fingernails were purple; her toenails—she was barefoot—were purple; her eyelids had a hint of the color; and her mouth was painted a garish purple that reminded Matt of the bubble gum Jonathan sometimes chewed. Matt wondered if the lipstick, also, was grape-flavored. Her garment was like nothing else Matt had ever seen, except possibly a contour bedsheet. It was plain white, fastened under her arms with elastic, then went straight down from there. When she passed a window Matt could clearly see she had nothing on underneath.

She sat near him on the couch and gestured with her drink. They sipped. To Matt it tasted like spiked Kool-Aid.

"Very good," he said.

"I think I've got it just about perfect." Her tongue lightly licked her lips.

"So it was through this club"—Matt gestured toward the magazine—"that you met Hugh."

"Possibly." Dotty stared off vaguely. "It's been so many years. I think we just had some mutual friends. But Hugh . . ." She touched Matt's arm, confiding. "I loved the man. But in a way he's an example of what I'm talking about."

Matt wasn't sure. Hugh was no blushing violet where sex was concerned.

"You were aware"—she glanced down modestly—"of his potency problems."

"Not firsthand." What was the woman implying?

"He hadn't had it up for years, was the impression I got. He wasn't too free in discussing it."

It wasn't usually the first thing you brought up over cocktails.

"I think Hugh was a man who, if he'd been born thirty years later, might have had a wonderful time. Nobody, after all, has a better sex life than gay men nowadays. He might have felt better about himself, might have been able to live more freely. He might have written about it, and released the creative potential he certainly had in him. But he never did any of that. He was a repressed queer of a generation ago, who pretended to be straight. Lived in boarding schools, and coached sports, and had boys up to his rooms and took them on little outings, and fell in love with them. He never acted out his sexuality, or felt it freely. Instead he formed these romantic attachments, which he insisted on calling friendships."

"So you think he was definitely gay."

"I don't know if he was gay. Certainly bisexual, as we all are. But he was frozen in that early adolescent stage when boys have crushes on each other, they get together and look at dirty pictures of girls, and talk about them, and masturbate to them. Everything Hugh did was like that. Taking friends downtown. Showing them things, like a funny uncle. Paying a woman to take care of them. Even these schoolboy jokes of his. Hugh's elaborate practical jokes. You've heard about this movie he made."

"I saw it."

Immediately Matt wished he hadn't said that. Probably he was just trying to say something to her—I know about you and the dog, toots—but she didn't react to that. She reacted to something else.

"You saw it."

"I saw it."

"You know where it is."

"I don't know exactly where it is. I could probably put my hands on it."

"The police have been looking for it."

Something had changed. Dotty, who up to then had been giving a rather controlled performance—a fat woman impersonating a vamp—was suddenly agitated, her brow furrowed, lips tight. She seemed to want to ask a dozen questions at once, to grab Matt by the shoulders and shake him.

"I shouldn't have told you this," Matt said. He tried to smile. "I wasn't thinking. I know the police are looking for it. I didn't tell them I'd seen it."

"Ah." She bit her lip.

"I thought it might hold a clue to what happened. I didn't want them to have it. I wanted to have it."

"I do think it holds a clue. I think it holds many clues."

Matt shrugged, gave a little laugh. "You have my secret."

"My lips are sealed."

They were also moist. And pouting. (And purple.)

"How did you get it?" she said.

"I found it that night. I had come back after I left the first time. The police do know that."

"I wondered what had happened. I thought the boy must have taken it."

"No. Nobody had taken it."

That suddenly seemed to Matt an exceedingly strange fact.

"Do the police know what was in it?" he said.

"Of course. That's just what I've been saying. We have nothing to hide. We told them all about it. Our scene was more or less a joke anyway. We knew what was already in the movie. The major acts were covered. We wanted to find something off the beaten path."

They had succeeded.

"It was more or less a simulation. A lot of bumping around. Though I don't mind admitting I found it exciting. Talk about animal passion."

Dotty was blushing slightly, but also smiling again. She was back in her role.

"It was a riot to watch. Some other people weren't so amused by their appearances."

Matt wondered at what she said. It was easy for her, talking to him, to pretend everything was fine, but it must be at least slightly uncomfortable to know the police were on the track of a movie in which you got it on with a dog. However fine the pedigree. Matt wondered if the act was even legal in a farm state like Pennsylvania. After all, sheep were one thing . . .

"Incidentally." Dotty moistened her lips. "I enjoyed your performance very much."

"It was no performance." Matt felt himself redden. "I had no idea the camera was there."

"All the better. But you didn't seem to have any of Hugh's problems." Her eyes flashed. "At least not from where I sat."

"So people were upset." Change the subject. "But one was more upset than the others."

"Apparently. The police suspect Stanley Killian. He was here, you know."

"Here?"

"The night after the crime. Going on like a madman. He swore he hadn't killed Hugh. But he had seen the body. He had come back again later. Like"—she smiled pleasantly—"you."

"The police told me."

"He was crazy to get his hands on that movie. Convinced it would ruin him if he didn't. He'd decided we must have it. But we thought the Hunter boy did. At that point."

"You didn't notice if Hunter had it when he left."

"We left before he did."

Bingo.

"The whole thing got rather awful after the others left. Hugh wanted to get something started between Hunter and that prostitute. He would just watch, as usual. But she was having none of it, got her money and left, and the Hunter boy was in a strange mood. Peevish, angry about something. Hugh was getting maudlin, he was very drunk by this time, saying it didn't matter how mad Mingins was, that Mingins had never cared for Hunter in the way that he had."

"He was making a pass at him."

"Possibly. It all seemed very private. And personal. Rather awful, as far as I was concerned. It shouldn't have been this grand melodramatic moment. We left."

"You told all this to the police."

"Many times. But I think these wild appearances by Killian have gotten their attention. He showed up at Chandler's place too. I think they see him as a threat. He might do somebody harm."

"What do you think?"

"I'm waiting to see. But I think the real culprit in this crime . . . If it really was a crime. And not a mistake. Or an accident. I think the real culprit is our failure to be honest. About who we are. What we are. What we want. If we'd just allow ourselves to be ourselves"—her eyes held the hard bright certainty of the fanatic—"there wouldn't be any crime."

III

Matt lay on his back, his pillow propped against the headboard, his hands behind his head. All the lights in the house were off, but the streetlamp just outside was bright, so there was plenty of light in the room; he could see the dressers, with all the clutter on top of his, the gleam of metal around the gas burner, his clothes piled on a chair in the corner. The old wood of the house emitted occasional creaks and groans. A breeze drifted through the windows. In the next room Jonathan snorted, flopped around on his bed. Beside Matt, lying on her belly and facing away, Laurel snored lightly.

He loved to lie awake for a while and listen to the nighttime sounds of the house.

All afternoon he had dreaded his return to the house. After talking to Dotty Droge he had gone to a bar for a beer, then wound up, like a coward, ordering dinner there, spending a long time over it. When he finally got home, Jonathan was already in bed. Laurel had hugged him for a long time, her body collapsed against him, but there was something of a dead weight about it: their bodies did not quite meet. At the police station she had seemed almost relieved that he'd been taken in; at least he wouldn't be hiding anymore. Now at home it seemed there wasn't much to talk about. He told her the police detectives' speculations about the case, and she listened with interest. She didn't ask if he was going to continue to look into it, and he didn't say he was. She seemed to know that he was. Neither of them spoke of the whole idea of doing detective work at all, though that had been a subject of some interest in the past. He didn't mention Sandra, or what he had told the police about her, and Laurel didn't ask. Their conversation, in fact, was such a minefield of things they didn't want to bring up that it was quite boring. Laurel looked beat anyway, and said she was going up to bed. Matt followed. In bed she just rolled over to go to sleep, didn't cuddle up as she usually did. She only rolled over immediately like that when she was very angry or very tired. She did say, after lying there for a moment, "Jonathan told me about thinking you need a gun. How he's going to get to hold it, and shoot it. I think you should show him your old one. The whole thing's turning into an obsession."

"I know."

"I think you should do it tomorrow."

"Sure."

"I guess this is an occupational hazard."

She didn't go into the lecture about how furious that made her.

As Matt lay in the dark, listening to the crickets in the yard, the distant sounds of city traffic, he was aware that his marriage was in pretty desperate shape, but somehow it didn't follow that he was worried about it. They had hit rock bottom, but at least the ground was solid down there. Always in the past he had wanted not to hurt Laurel, and now he had hurt her terribly, as she had hurt him, but it no longer seemed to matter as much. They were both still alive, staggered, but standing. Maybe it was a good thing to be willing to hurt your wife.

All through their marriage they had been pretending things to save one another; now there was no more pretending. She had seen him with the whore of his dreams, and he had seen her with the man she loved. Suddenly it all seemed rather silly. Not that it wasn't real—she had really loved the man, and he had really wanted the whore—but in some essential way it wasn't important. Matt didn't know how Laurel felt (maybe she had been sitting there all evening trying to tell him she was going to leave him for the man she really loved) but he felt beyond it all, as if he had been through the experience that drives couples apart and still wanted to stay. He also felt—this seemed the most unusual thing of all—that if Laurel wanted to leave that was all right too. It was her decision, and he would survive. He was no longer desperate about holding her.

It seemed to him that finally they were two unattached people, who if they chose to stay together would be doing so not out of habit, or convention, but because they really wanted to.

He also had the bizarre conviction—it made no particular sense—that everything would work itself out if he could just find out who killed Hugh Bollinger.

Chapter Eight

By some coincidence (or perhaps not; Matt had laid out a number of paperbacks and Jonathan had made the choice) the book they were reading before bed that week concerned a notorious gunfighter who had entered the lives of a homesteader family. From the moment you laid eyes on the man you knew he was a killer, but for a time he tried to start a new life, become an ordinary ranch hand. The only echo of his former life came at odd little moments, like the time he found the boy of the family playing gunfighter and tried to give him a few pointers; suddenly a twisted look of agony came over his face and the play gun dropped from his lifeless fingers. Aside from such minor lapses he was fine, but of course there was trouble in the valley (it had been growing like a cancer for months) and you-know-who felt compelled to do something about it. In that evening's reading they had entered the long scene of a major gunfight. Already the gunfighter had picked off a hired mercenary in a straight draw and a local thug who had tried to ambush him from the balcony. An ominous scarlet stain was starting to spread at his lower right shirtfront; still, he seemed to have the situation well in hand.

It took some time for Matt to persuade Jonathan they had reached a good stopping place. He never tried to interpret his son's reading for him, he didn't believe in such things, but at the moment he was sensitive about the subject—it was the day he had shown Jonathan his gun—and he felt a need to say something.

"You know, Jonathan, it's perfectly all right to play with toy guns."

"I'm not going to play with your gun, Dad."

"I know you're not. I'm not talking about that. It's okay to play with toy guns. To shoot the bad guys and get rid of them. And it's okay to read books where some of the guys are good and some of the guys are bad, and the good guys come along with guns and kill the bad guys. And everything's good again."

"Thanks for giving away the ending."

"I'm not talking about this book. I mean books in general. I don't know what happens in this book."

Actually, he did. He had seen the movie years before.

"I just don't want you to think that's the way it happens in real life."

"I know. In a real gunfight the guy on the balcony would have blown him away."

"I mean that in real life there aren't some guys that are good and some that are bad. There are two sides to everything. And using a gun doesn't get rid of what's bad. It only adds to it. There's always a better way to solve things."

"You have a gun."

"I had to use it for my job before. When I was a policeman. I thought I might need it if I got that job again."

It seemed months since he had had any real hope of getting such a job.

"And now you're going to use it on this case you're on."

"No." He had to quit humoring the boy. "I don't need it on this case. I'll solve this case by talking to people. Thinking. Being reasonable."

Jonathan looked disappointed, but took the news bravely. "Anyway. Tomorrow I get to see you shoot it. And I get to pull the trigger once."

"If I have time."

"You better have time." Jonathan squinted in mock anger, shook his fist at his father's chin. "Or I'll kill you."

Sometimes Matt wondered why he bothered.

"Who's the guy downstairs?" Jonathan said.

"Chandler Mingins. A friend of your mother's from work."

"She's not here."

"He might know something about this case. He knows some of the people involved. I'm going to talk to him."

"I'd like to listen."

"You've got to get to sleep."

"I just want to sit there. I'm not even tired. I won't say a word."

"I have to do this alone, Jonathan. This is work."

"Aw!" He slammed his head on the pillow, pulled up the sheet. "Now I'll just lie here awake. All night."

Anytime Jonathan lay awake for twenty minutes or so—he really felt this way; he wasn't exaggerating—he thought he had been awake all night.

"You'll be all right. Just close your eyes."

"I'll close *your* eyes."

Matt turned out the light, pulled the door to.

It hadn't gone too badly. That morning Matt had taken Jonathan up the dark stairs to the third floor and showed him where he kept the gun, took the case out of the old trunk and opened the case. Jonathan could be a wiseass about almost anything, but he knew when a moment was serious, and seemed to appreciate his father's trust in him. He stared solemnly while his father took the gun out of the case. Matt took it apart, showed him how you saw whether or not it was loaded, told him always to treat a gun as if it were loaded. He showed him how it worked, let him pull the trigger. He let him examine the bullets. That day he was waiting for an important call, Matt said, but the next day, if he had time, he would take Jonathan with him to the firing range.

He wasn't at all sure he would have time. Things had been moving more rapidly than he had expected. Wolf had spent the evening before snooping for information about Todd Hunter. The father wasn't around, and the mother was utterly ineffectual, the kind of woman who never knew where her son was and always seemed befuddled about it. It didn't help any that she was plastered. Wolf had gone to several of Hunter's friends, tried others on the phone—names Matt had given him of kids from school—but didn't get anywhere. Most of them hadn't seen Hunter since school let out, said he didn't hang around much with kids from school. But he did have some luck with the name Hunter had dropped at the party, Farrell Haynes (though Mrs. Hunter didn't even recognize the name when Wolf mentioned it); the father's name was the same, listed in the phone book, and though neither the boy nor the parents were home when Matt went over, a young female cousin was. Matt didn't bother to fill Wolf in on her erotic peculiarities. It turned out it was Haynes that Hunter had gone on the fishing trip with, to an old hunting lodge northeast of the city. The girl had precise directions to the place. She was a sweet kid, Wolf said (again Matt was tempted) and very helpful. God knows what story Wolf had told her about why he wanted to see Hunter.

"How'd you do with Droge?" Wolf had said that morning, when he called.

"I didn't see him. But I talked to his wife. She's the mouth-piece of the family."

"And?"

"She wasn't a whole lot of help. She seems to think it was Killian too. But she did tell me a few interesting things about Hunter. I'd like to ask him some questions."

Wolf had left immediately after the phone call; he had to be the one to go, because Matt wasn't supposed to leave town. He said he would call as soon as he could. It was after three o'clock when he finally did.

"I'm bringing the Hunter kid back. He's packing his stuff up now. This whole thing was news to him. He's pretty shaken up."

Matt considered that a moment. If Hunter really hadn't known, he must have had a terrific shock.

"You think he's on the level?"

"Hard to say. The other kid looked surprised too. These guys haven't seen any papers if they haven't wanted to. I'm calling from a market eight miles away, and it's the closest thing. The lodge doesn't have plumbing or anything. It seemed to hit him hard when I told him. But he wasn't in real good shape before I started to talk either. He's a nervous kid. And they got enough booze up here for six months. Anyway, he wants to come back."

"I'd like to talk to him."

"He wants to talk to you. He said he did, as soon as I told him we were partners."

"You'll have to bring him to the house, though. Laurel's out tonight."

"Jesus, Matt. You the baby-sitter every night?"

"Just bring him to the house. It's as good as anyplace."

Matt was in no mood to discuss the arrangements of his marriage.

As soon as he hung up, he got the idea of having Chandler Mingins over too. He thought it would be interesting to hear their stories together.

Things had not gone any better with Laurel that morning. She woke up looking as tired as when she had gone to sleep, did not lie in Matt's arms and snooze awhile but threw herself out of bed to get ready for work. In the bathroom she seemed to drop everything she picked up, swearing quietly as she did; she washed her hair in the shower and walked around afterward with a towel around her head. In the kitchen she broke a cereal bowl, shattering it into tiny pieces. By that time she was so far gone she didn't even speak, just swept up the pieces silently, her hands white-knuckled on the broom. Matt hoped her clients were feeling strong that morning. Over breakfast—grape nuts, wheat germ, raw oatmeal, and raisins for her, topped by two-percent and accompanied by a pot of Constant Comment; Matt had three sugar doughnuts and a cup of instant coffee (can this marriage be saved?)—she said, "I need to go out tonight. I'd *like* to go out tonight. If it's all right with you. It doesn't interfere with your plans."

"I don't have any plans." That was before even Wolf's first call.

"You don't have to go out?"

"Not that I know of."

"I wouldn't want to interfere with your work."

She made the statement pointedly, as if to ask if he had any work.

"We need to talk," Matt said.

"Oh?" Laurel looked up blandly.

"We're not connecting. We need to talk about things. What we're doing."

"I know." Laurel looked wearily into her tea.

"We're miles apart."

"I keep waiting for things to settle. Something to come to an end."

"Me too."

He meant for him to finally figure out who killed Hugh Bollinger. She meant for him to quit trying. She paused, as if waiting for him to say he would.

"Anyway," he said. "We've got to set up a time."

"But not tonight."

"Right. You're going out."

At least that had been established.

They had already had the conversation in the past (endlessly) about how their time was their own, they didn't have to account for every minute; Laurel had spent her life asking permission of men and didn't want to do it anymore. She didn't even want to sound as if she were doing it. Matt was in perfect agreement. Usually they told the other person where they were headed (as a matter of fact, when they didn't, it announced itself like a blare of trumpets; there was a gaping hole where the words should have been), but if they didn't it was out of bounds to ask. Each accorded to the other the freedom he asked for himself.

Still, Matt wished to hell he knew where Laurel was going that night.

Downstairs, he had left his guest nursing a beer. Matt knew that Chandler would have preferred something stronger, but he didn't keep much hard liquor in the house—vodka wasn't among the choices—and he wouldn't have presumed to fix him a drink anyway. Chandler was notoriously finicky about such things.

He wasn't wearing one of his really elaborate outfits that evening. He was as close, in fact, to being plainly dressed as Matt had ever seen him, in shorts, an open-necked sports shirt. The gold chain still hung from his neck, and his cologne was a little strong, and he was wearing high pale-blue socks to match his shirt, but those were the only concessions to his usual splendor.

He was smoking a cigarette when Matt came down. Matt couldn't remember ever seeing Chandler when he wasn't smoking a cigarette. Except in the movie.

"When do you expect your guests?" Chandler's face was drawn, and tight. His right knee kept hopping nervously.

"I expected them by now, to tell you the truth. They got an early start, and Wolf said it isn't that long a drive. They must have stopped for something to eat."

"Do they know I'm here?"

"No. I didn't even think of it until after I talked to Wolf." Matt liked that factor of surprise.

He walked over and sat in the chair in front of the fireplace, facing the couch where Chandler was sitting. He took a swallow from his own beer, which he was drinking mostly just to keep Chandler company.

"You were about to tell me how you met Todd Hunter," Matt said.

That was before Jonathan had thrown himself in the room and insisted Matt come and read to him.

"I actually first met him when I was doing that internship at the school," Mingins said. "Guidance, and other kinds of counseling. He had just been bounced out of another school for being caught with drugs, and was quite shattered by the experience."

"He told me about that." Though not about being shattered.

"It's hard to remember how much younger a boy is at fifteen than eighteen, but you'd have hardly recognized him. Thinner, and smaller, and smooth and pale and innocent. He was keeping up a brave front for everyone, rebellious troubled youth and all that, but in my presence he often went completely to pieces. He was from a prominent family, had what is called a strong father, which is what people call the kind of man who doesn't know the first thing about his child, and they all came down on him pretty hard. Sent him to Tabard, for one thing, which they considered second-rate. That was a very grievous punishment."

Matt could see where Hunter had gotten his opinion of the school.

"Mostly I did a lot of listening. But one thing I did tell him, right from the start, was that he was in a new environment now and should forget about the old, forget about the images his family held out to him and deal with the reality he found himself in. Any school could be a good school, if he made it one. He should start a new life there."

"Good advice."

"Which he largely followed, thanks to the help of some other people. Hugh Bollinger, for one. The lacrosse was very important. Helped Hunter take himself seriously."

"Were you"—Matt saw no way to put this discreetly—"involved with him then?"

Mingins turned a gaze on Matt, his nostrils flaring, eyes hard. "I am not, in the sense you mean, involved with any of my clients, ever. No counselor of any repute ever is. In another sense, of course, I was very much involved. Deeply sympathetic to his situation. Counselors wear a certain mask. Much of it is projected by the client, but a part is the way the counselor acts, the manner he must assume if he is to be any help. People have no idea what goes on behind that mask, or how difficult it can be to maintain. One speaks of transference in the client, but never the emotions of the therapist. I could have fallen in love with that boy if I'd let myself."

Mingins' face was stony, as if daring Matt to leer at the words.

"You left the school at the end of that year."

"I left."

"And you kept up with him."

"Not really. There's a fine line between therapy and friendship, and it's too easy to get them confused. I make my breaks as clean as possible. I did go to some of the lacrosse games, but stayed out of the way and left immediately afterwards."

"But you did keep up with Bollinger."

"Yes. And that was a way of keeping up with the boy. Hugh was one of the few educated, interesting, literate people at that school. At any school I've ever been to. And he was one of the few people available for a friendship, since he had no family or anything. He was also quite fascinated with me, with the life I led. Teachers have to be more discreet."

"You mean he was gay."

Matt wondered if he was finally going to get the definitive answer to that question, or if there was a definitive answer. You couldn't trust gay men in such matters. They think everybody's a fag.

"In his heart, his mind, his bones. In every important way. He just never acted on it. It wasn't an admissible thing for him. He lived in a male world, surrounded himself with attractive boys, talked with them all the time about sex, but I don't think he ever did a thing. He was effectively nothing, sexually. Except the man with the dirty pictures."

"But it was through him that you met Hunter again."

"Hugh noticed I asked about him. He often had students to his apartment anyway, Hunter more than anyone else. The boy was his prize. Captain of the team. I saw him at the apartment several times. We had a couple long conversations. Then we started to meet"—Mingins glanced out the window—"away from there."

Matt wasn't letting that slip by. "You did get involved."

"It hadn't gone on very long. I'm sure it wasn't all you imagine. Todd's changed a lot through the years. Bigger, tougher, more muscular. A beautiful young man. But I knew him back when . . . The little boy inside. And despite the knowing exterior, the man-of-the-world sophistication, I found him quite inexperienced sexually. He had to be brought along slowly."

"He looked like he knew his stuff to me."

"That's what I'm saying. He looked that way."

"I saw the movie, Chandler."

"Oh." Mingins' face sagged; he reddened. "Yes. Of course. I saw it too."

"He didn't exactly look like a bashful virgin."

"No. I guess he didn't. He wasn't."

Mingins had lost his stony exterior. In a way he looked more relaxed. He looked slack. Tired. Older.

"He picked things up rather quickly," Mingins said. "An eager pupil. People look at something like that, a relationship like that, and they see the older man at fault. He's the villain, he's the seducer. Takes an innocent young man and leads him down the road to degradation and ruin. But it isn't often that way. More often the other. The young seduce. They may not know exactly what to do, but they know they want to do it. They get the message across."

"I'm sure."

"And I was in love. That's another thing people find easy to overlook. It's an odd situation for a gay man. You love someone for his beauty, his innocence, his maleness. In a way you should go on loving from afar. Because as soon as you have him, he's no longer innocent, no longer quite as beautiful, no longer entirely male. He changes when you touch him. He gets to be more like you."

"It's the same with everyone. You know them and they're different."

"Seeing that movie was as much a shock for me as it may have been for you. You think everything's one way and it turns out to be quite another. I thought Todd Hunter cared for me. I thought his eagerness was genuine affection. But now I wonder. I wonder. The boy wanted sex. He wanted sex with me. I wonder why he wanted it."

"You think Bollinger put him up to it."

"Hugh never did anything himself. He lived through other people. He wanted to see the relationship, he didn't want to have it. Naturally he made it into a practical joke, out of embarrassment. But what I've been wondering ever since that night, ever since I saw the movie, is whether the whole thing with Todd, from the first meeting on, ever had any reality, whether it ever meant anything to him. Or whether it all just happened so Hugh Bollinger could get a few feet of film."

Matt nodded. "I can see how you'd wonder."

"The person who knows is coming tonight. That's why I'm here."

A little something for everyone.

"The other person who knew," Matt said, "is dead."

"Yes." Mingins reddened again. His mouth tightened.

"I imagine the police were interested in what you did after you saw that movie."

"They must have been interested that you had seen it at all. And in where you got it."

"Sure." At least they would have been.

"I left in the middle of the movie. Everyone saw."

"Whoever killed Bollinger might have come back."

"The man the police suspect apparently did come back."

"True."

Mingins was staring at Matt with what seemed remarkable composure, though he still wore a heightened color.

"I understand what you're suggesting. It makes me uncomfortable, frightened and guilty, as it would anyone. If I've ever been angry enough to kill anyone, I was angry enough that night to kill Hugh Bollinger. But whatever light it puts me in, and I've told this to the police, with no apparent effect, I don't believe Stanley Killian did it. I've known him for years. He's not the type."

"It's interesting to hear you say that."

"He might curl up and die himself, in a situation like that. But he wouldn't kill somebody else."

Matt nodded.

"I came here tonight," Mingins said, "to help you. Or not actually to help you, but my coming will have that effect. I've sat here and told you what I know. It only seems fair that you should do the same for me."

It did seem fair. Matt told Chandler a version of what had happened to him the night of Bollinger's party—there were so many versions by now he found it easy to pick and choose—and of what he had done and thought since. He was glad the man had come, and he did think Chandler would be a help to him, but he had no particular feeling Chandler would get the information he was after. Mingins might have been in love with Hunter—you could fall in love with anyone—but Matt still thought the kid a sneak and an opportunist, who didn't bother telling the truth about anything. There was no reason he should make an exception in Chandler's case.

Matt had gotten all the way to his visit with Dotty Droge—he was leaving plenty out—when he heard that familiar muffler coming around the corner, then the motor being shut off, the slamming car doors, the footsteps on the stairs. He had paused in his story; he and Mingins turned toward the door. The boy who stepped through probably wasn't the one either of them had been expecting. He looked older than before, if anything, hollow-eyed, weatherbeaten, the beginnings of a blond beard looking dirty and scruffy. His mouth within the beard wore a kind of sneer. At the same time, though, his eyes looked frightened, cringed at the light. His voice as he spoke was deep and rough, but also tentative, like a child stumbling out of bed at night and into the light where his parents sat, and the words he said—though he meant something else by them—were the words the child might have used.

"Could somebody get me a drink?" he said.

II

Laurel sat in the car out in the street. For seven or eight minutes she had sat there, as if to decide, though she knew she was going in. A light shone from the window of the second-floor apartment. High leafy trees overhung the street, shadowing the night sky. In a car down the block some kids sat drinking beer; from time to time the interior flared as one of them lit a cigarette. A breeze stirred, ruffling the trees; she shivered. Seventy-five degrees it must have been, near eighty—she could feel herself sweat—and she sat there shivering.

From the beginning of their marriage, from the very first day, it seemed, Matt had talked of wanting other women. Laurel had never understood. She thought he must be bringing up things he felt guilty about from the past, or that, in the sudden strangeness of a new marriage, he was reliving a former time, a more familiar one, when he had gotten together with boys and talked about girls they would like to feel up and fuck (in the presence of the girls, of course, they did no such thing; they couldn't even carry on a simple conversation). He would tell her—with that stupid guilty grin on his face—about the women he found attractive, what he found attractive about them, what he would like to do to them ("Does it bother you when I talk this way?" he'd say. "No," she would say dryly.

"Not at all"); he would ask her what men she found attractive, which ones she would like to sleep with. She had no idea what he was talking about. She had just gotten married, had just—after months of thinking about it—chosen the man who would father her children and with whom she would spend the rest of her life; of course she didn't want to sleep with anyone else. It was the last thing on her mind. Matt couldn't understand, he couldn't believe it, he thought she must be hiding things from him, out of guilt, or embarrassment, and he tried to get her to open up—after all, he had been perfectly honest with her—so finally, just to put an end to the conversation, she named a few men who, in theory, were attractive to her; in completely different circumstances she could imagine not being repulsed by them. Matt mulled over these choices. "Harold Wooldrich. Jesus. Would you really want to go to bed with him?" Of course she wouldn't, she wouldn't think of it, but if she had withdrawn his name she would have had to find somebody else. Yes, she said. She would. Harold Wooldrich.

Those conversations were one of the strange things about first being married, like cooking in what seemed such huge amounts and buying two kinds of soap and waking up always with this person in your bed. It was weird. She put up with it, as she put up with a lot of things, but she began to realize that marriage for Matt was different than it was for her, not that total absorption in another person, the abandoning of other choices for that one choice you had always known you would make. He took up residence with her, but there was plenty of old ghosts around.

At least she had thought they were ghosts. The woman in the film the other day had looked very much like flesh and blood.

She had never seen an act of sex on film before. Fake Hollywood fucking, to be sure, choreographed like a ballet, women with their slender backs arched and ecstasy painted on their faces and moans coming from their mouths like a melody, but she had never seen the actual act, poor Stanley Killian with his cock sticking straight out and his loose flesh jiggling as he humped; Chandler and that boy, in what looked more than anything else like an act of torture; the Droges in that parody of a sexual repertoire and their masquerade with the dog; finally Matt, who seemed more truly involved in what he was doing than anyone else in the film. Probably what hurt her most was the first glimpse of him, that tortured tormented gaze, the face of her marriage, it had seemed, for months, as if sex were some terrible punishment he was being forced to suffer. Then to see that woman appear in the room, throw off her garment as if it didn't mean a thing, with that really lovely body, no little bags of fat at the tops of her hips and the backs of her thighs and no soft floppy breasts that would never be the same as before she had nursed, but that exquisite slender torso and the grace of her movements and those goddam upturned nipples, hands that were so knowing and smooth. Matt had melted as soon as she touched him, the tension drifting from his face; he was at ease with her as he hadn't been for months with Laurel, beaming as he caressed her, thrilling and yearning as he kissed her breasts, his cock growing heavier and harder than it ever seemed to with her anymore; he positively leaped when he came. Matt could say what he wanted (though she didn't see how it was possible, in that grubby little room that didn't even look comfortable, with a woman who might as well have walked in off the street): he had the look of a man in love.

She would never understand. But she had decided finally that she didn't have to understand; it was one more kind of projection, or avoidance, to sit around wondering who Matt was and why he did what he did. What she had to decide was what she wanted to do, and as she had sat around pondering that, there was one person she knew she wanted to see. She could not have said exactly why; she just knew she wanted to. That was why she had made a phone call earlier in the afternoon, to make sure it was okay and to set up a time; that was why she now sat in the car, shivering in the heat, as if to make a decision, when she knew there was no decision to make. She was expected.

Finally she got out of the car, shut and locked the door, walked up the steps with a knot in her stomach and rang the doorbell. It was the kind of place where you were buzzed in, and there was a long wait. Laurel was about to ring again when she heard footsteps coming down the stairs.

The door opened. "Hi." Sandra's face was tense, hesitant, but she tried a smile, pulled a couple strands of hair out of her eyes. "I hope you weren't waiting long."

"No." Had she been watching at the window?

"I just heard the doorbell when I stepped out of the shower." Her skin looked fresh and ruddy. "Come in."

A light was on that illuminated the stairway. Laurel preceded her up. The wall was pockmarked and in need of paint;
scraps of paper and cobwebs of dust collected along the rubber
matting of the steps, as if it hadn't been swept for months.

Upstairs, though, the apartment was immaculate, unnaturally
tidy, as if everything had been picked up and stashed somewhere. Open the right closet and the accumulated junk of
three months would come piling out. Even the papers from
the dining-room table were gone, as if Sandra had been afraid
Laurel might walk in and torch them.

It was an idea.

"Would you like some coffee?" Sandra was standing at the
doorway to the kitchen. "I also have a bottle of white wine.
And about two inches of a bottle of rum. Left from the old
days."

"Coffee just jitters me up." That was all she needed. "I'll
take some wine."

"I will too."

Laurel sat uneasily on the couch, stared around the room.
It even seemed to have been dusted. She hated the feeling of
having been picked up for.

Sandra came out of the kitchen with a gallon jug of wine
and the kind of glass coffee mugs they use in advertisements
on television, so you can see the cream swirling in. She wore
cut-off jeans and a baggy T-shirt, as if to hide her figure, but
mostly she just looked young, her face bare of makeup and her
hair hanging straight, small spectacles halfway down her nose.
Laurel wore a peasant blouse and wraparound skirt, felt like a
dowdy old lady confronting her husband's teenage mistress
(this was ridiculous! Sandra had teenage children herself!). She
even had a sweater over her shoulders, and with all the
windows wide open felt a need to pull it around her. Why
was she so cold?

"I think you were planning to serve coffee," Laurel said, as
Sandra poured the wine.

"No. I always use these mugs. Wineglasses break."

Actually, that was the way Laurel served wine to friends too.
She had felt a real kinship with Sandra, in the few minutes the
other day when they had had a chance to talk; it was perhaps
for that reason that she had wanted to see her again, as if she
could forget the woman she had seen in the movie. And it had
seemed a different person, that woman from before the movie
began: she had had an apartment full of old furniture, books

and clothes scattered around, the dining-room table turned into a work desk, even her bicycles upstairs (where the hell had she put the bicycles? in the bathroom?). Laurel had felt at home here, the way you see an apartment and think, I should know this person. I would like this person.

Laurel, too, only cleaned up for guests she wasn't sure of.

"I'm worried that I spoiled the evening," Laurel said. "For you and the children."

"Not at all. They went to the movies with friends. They'll go to the friends' house when the movie is over. Call before they come home. They'll have a great time. They'd love it if you'd come every night."

"I'm keeping you from your work."

"The work will get done."

She seemed less sure when she said that.

Laurel took a swallow of the wine. Smooth, and grapy. She could have done with about a quart.

"I know you wonder why I'm here."

Now Sandra was drinking from her mug, staring at Laurel over the rim. "You must be terribly angry."

"I'm not. Really. I was. I admit that I was." As she spoke, she felt a wave of anger swell beneath all she said. "But I'm not anymore."

"I think I would be."

"I'm not sure why I wanted to come."

Sandra poured from the jug again. She filled the mugs slightly higher this time. It was shaping up as a big night for the wine.

"The way it looked was bad," Sandra said. "Even to me. I said this before, but not under the best circumstances. So I'll say it again. There was nothing between Matt and me."

"I know."

"When I walked into that room was the first time I'd ever seen him."

"Yes."

"I'd been with another man before. I was going to another man after."

Laurel suddenly felt that if they spent another moment at that, one more word discussing a scene she had been trying for two days to forget, she was going to cry.

"That's what I'd like to know," she said. The words surprised even her.

"What?"

"That's what I don't understand. I think that's why I came."

It was as if the words were saying themselves. They weren't, of course. She had known all along why she had really come. She just hadn't been willing to admit it.

She hadn't come to Sandra's to find out something about Matt. She had come to find out about herself.

"I don't know quite how to say this," she said.

Sandra's eyes had grown guarded. They stared at Laurel as she drank from her mug.

"I understand what you were doing with my husband. I don't need an explanation, in that sense. He was a customer. You were getting paid. But I don't see how you can do that. Any dirty man who comes in off the street. Taking your clothes off, letting him touch you. I don't know if I'm saying this right."

"You're saying it right."

"It's so far from anything I would ever do. Anything I'd ever think of."

"I'm sure."

Sandra stood from her chair, walked over beside the windows.

"I guess it's none of my business," Laurel said.

"It's a question I get all the time. 'How'd you get into this line of work, honey? Like were you raped by your father or what?' "

"I don't mean it that way."

"You don't say it that way. You mean it that way."

Sandra stared out the window as if she saw something, though as far as Laurel could tell it was all a blackness. She could see Sandra's face reflected, angry and intent.

"I don't want to hurt you," Laurel said. "Or maybe I do." Another possibility. "Maybe that's why I came. But I really would like to understand this. It's so far from my experience."

"Which is . . ." Sandra turned slightly from the window.

"What?"

"What is your experience? With men. Sex."

"Oh." Laurel reddened. "I don't know. Matt. A couple men before him. Only one I actually . . . slept with."

"How about when you were a girl? High school. Did you run around much?"

"I went to boarding school."

"Oh." The word spoke volumes.

"You didn't run around much there." Laurel smiled. The very idea was preposterous. "You couldn't leave campus, and boys couldn't much come on, and on the rare occasions when they could, social mixers and stuff, they almost seemed intruders. We resented them in a way. They spoiled things."

Laurel looked back with a certain fondness on those days, awful as they had sometimes been. The fierce competition in the classrooms, daily sports in different seasons, the extracurricular activities—newspaper, debate, drama—that were taken so seriously, the silly girlish life in the dorms. It had been a simple life in its way, plain in its values, and you had the feeling boys would be a complicating factor. You wanted to put them on hold.

Sandra was still turned slightly from the window, as if listening for something. "Did the girls ever fool around? I mean, with each other."

"No." Laurel spoke with disgust. "Jesus. That's like asking if you were raped by your father."

Sandra turned around, smiling with amusement. "Maybe we're even." She returned to her chair, sat down again and poured from the jug, filling the cups to the brim. Warily, she glanced up at Laurel. "None of the girls ever fooled around?"

Laurel gulped at her wine. "We had our suspicions about a couple."

"I *knew* it." Sandra sat back in her chair, put her feet up on the table. "Anyway. My experience was different. Not that I think it makes all the difference. But I didn't go to school just with girls."

All the worse for you, Laurel thought.

Sandra seemed more relaxed now, sitting back, her arms folded in front of her. She held her cup in one hand, sipped at it from time to time. She gazed toward the back of the room, off toward the ceiling.

"I grew up between here and Cleveland, a little town in Ohio. Not too far from either city, but we never got away much. You'd think we would have, but we didn't. High school was the major institution there. It was the biggest building in town, and one of the nicest, and everything went on there, social events, meetings, voting. The whole town turned out for games. Kids couldn't wait until they could go there, and adults talked all the time about when they'd been. You went to high school and it was like you'd grown up. Your parents hardly saw you again.

"You wouldn't have known me then. I was a skinny thing, thinner all over, especially in the face. Kind of pinched and mean-looking. A little of a tomboy type. But it was a real automobile culture, everything revolved around cars, and if you were a girl the first thing you did was try to get with the boys who had cars. If you did you were suddenly a part of everything. If you didn't, forget it. It was all kind of silly. Driving around with the muffler roaring, smoking cigarettes, drinking beer, listening to the radio turned way up. Everybody traveled in packs, rows of cars. One couple in the front, another in the back. At least one. All the girls smack up against the boys.

"People are so solemn now about the uses of sex. Sexual harassment on the job, and women using sex in their careers, and the way people use sex in marriage. But nobody thought about it then. The boys had the cars, and you wanted to ride in the cars, and you knew what you had to do. You tried to get a boy you liked, and you tried to get a boy who was good-looking, but mostly you tried to get a boy. Screwing was serious, at least for most of us. You only did that later, when you were in love. But anything else. Fooling around. Using your hands. It went with the ride.

"The thing of it was, I loved it. I loved it all. The cigarettes, the beer, the loud music, the cruising. The fooling around too. There were some boys I liked it with better than others, of course, and some I wouldn't even have touched. But I liked sitting close in the cars, and snuggling up at the movies, and dancing close, and hugging, and kissing. I loved to get felt up, and to feel the boys up too. I loved it all. It was so exciting. I love the memory of it. I'd go back there in a minute."

"It does kind of sound nice." Laurel smiled to say that. She would have thought Sandra was awful back in her boarding-school days.

"It has its disadvantages, of course. Running around like that, girls suddenly fall in love. Or think they do. A lot of early marriages in that town, and a lot of children with very young mothers. Like my children. With all that coming first, you get a late start on everything else. I'm still in school and have teenagers in the house. You're all set up, with just a little one."

"I wouldn't say I'm all set up." And Jonathan didn't seem that little.

"Anyway, when I got to a point in my life where I had to make some money, it seemed a good way." For a moment Laurel didn't remember what Sandra was talking about, she had been so roundabout getting to it. "There's lots of money to be made. The people who come aren't exactly the salt of the earth, and it isn't like high school. You don't have any choice. But you'd be surprised how many men come in three-piece suits and look like they just left a business meeting. You'd also be surprised at how many of them are the most obnoxious customers we have." Laurel didn't think she'd be surprised at that. "Being naked is the great equalizer anyway. Potbellies, and skinny little butts.

"It isn't really sex, like you think of sex. In a relationship, when it has meaning. The men who come in are looking for something. They've been away from their wives too long, or they've been together with their wives too much, or their wives don't do the things they like, or the man just wants to play. He never got a chance to play. There are men who think they're ugly, and men who really are ugly, and men who want to act out some bizarre scene, or who think they have a sexual problem. Some are just lonely. Some want to be cuddled, and mothered. You're not having sex with them, you're diagnosing them. It gets easy after a while. You can almost tell just to look. It's not like a relationship, where you are what you are. You become what he wants. You figure out what he needs, and give it to him."

Laurel stifled a terrific urge to find out—she was almost scared to hear—what Matt had needed.

"People wonder how a woman can work in a place like that. What kind of woman would work in a place like that. The way you wondered. All kinds of women work there, for all kinds of reasons. But I think I'm just somebody who thinks it's natural, these things men want. It's the way things are. It's not mature, like the entirely mature person you'd like to find and live with. Fully formed. But that's a dream world. You're not that way either. We're all part child, part adolescent. You make allowances. If more people understood that, if more people did make allowances"—Sandra sipped her wine, smiled —"I'd be out of a job."

III

Hunter sat hunched on the edge of the couch, forearms on his knees, a glass of beer on the table in front of him. Beside him, in effect behind him, Mingins sat in the far corner of the couch, looking severely disturbed, as if the boy had been brought in from a brutal beating. Wolf sat in a chair by the door, relaxed and imperturbable, as if waiting for somebody to deal the cards. He didn't even look wilted from his trip. All three of them smoked cigarettes. Matt sat in a chair toward the fireplace, facing them.

He couldn't make up his mind about Hunter. The kid looked terribly debauched, as if he'd been drinking for days and not sleeping at all. His hands shook like a son of a bitch. He looked as if he'd had a shock, but whether it was the shock of hearing of Bollinger's death or of suddenly being confronted at his hunting lodge Matt couldn't be sure. He could have been drinking because he had killed Bollinger and wanted to forget; he could have been drinking to forget something else from the night of the party; or he could have been drinking out of high spirits, because he and his friend had gotten away and were unobserved. He could have been hollow-eyed from worrying about his crime, or from staying up late and talking with his friend, or maybe the mosquitoes were just bad in the mountains. There was too much to think through at the moment. Matt didn't even try.

Now and then Hunter drank from his beer and made a face, as if it were medicine. For two or three minutes he had been talking at random, about the shock he'd had, all that had been going through his mind. He took care not to look at anyone. He did not speak Bollinger's name.

"He was like a father to me. In good ways and bad. He showed me a lot, and he was good to me, and he helped me when I was down, which I'll never forget. He took me for what I was, didn't try to make me something else. He didn't think everything I did was evil or stupid. He was a great coach. But he was also a father you got disappointed in. Who you saw in embarrassing situations. Drunk one time too many. Who could have been a decent teacher but wasn't, who you suddenly realized hadn't done much with his life, who was a drunken old bastard and half queer to boot."

Look who's talking.

He glanced in Mingins' direction. "Sorry."

Mingins nodded. He hadn't even flinched.

"It's hard for me to believe, when I think of the way he used to be. I know he must have been the same all along, it's got to be the way I thought of him that changed, but I swear to God he used to be different. He went downhill in the years I knew him. He was thinner when I met him, healthier, kind of brighter. He didn't look boozed up or hung over all the time. You wouldn't have said he looked great, but he was prosperous-looking, kind of classy, somebody you might look up to and admire. You'd want to know him. One day he stopped me in the hall and said, 'I hear you went to Greenfield.' He didn't say a thing about why I'd left. He said, 'I bet you played lacrosse there.' "

"I think you're right," Mingins said. "I don't think you've improved things in your mind. He was in better shape then."

It was remarkable the way Mingins was taking things. You might have thought he'd be openly hostile, but he watched Hunter with deep concern.

"He let me on the lacrosse team. I shouldn't say 'let me.' I wasn't great or anything then, but better than most of what he had. It gave me a place, made me feel useful. I was somebody, when I'd felt like nobody.

"That was the best time, that first year I knew him. I didn't know him well. But if I were to meet another kid now, somebody just starting out, I'd say if you really admire a teacher, if you like him and think he's great, don't try to know him too well. Leave it the way it is. It's better that way. Don't for God's sake start going to his apartment."

Matt couldn't help thinking of the way this had all started for him, that evening he had had dinner with Mingins and Killian and they had all joked about the parties Bollinger had with his students, at his apartment.

"Not that I didn't love it. I thought it was great. A teacher who let you come to his place. See how he lived. I don't know where the trouble starts. Maybe it's when he's getting a drink and asks if you drink, which is probably an unfair question and none of his business anyway. Maybe it's when you tell him you do, instead of lying like you would with any other teacher. Maybe it's the next time, when he says as long as you drink you might as well have one with him. He doesn't see anything all that wrong with it, and he hates to drink in front of you. I think that's it. It's one thing for a teacher to know you drink, and another to sit down and have one with him. You can feel the change. It's in the air. Kind of exciting. A cheap thrill. It's also somebody saying what you do is okay with him, it isn't wrong like everybody else says. While they're all drinking like fish. It's also a convenient place to go get mildly plastered. Anytime you like.

"Or maybe the trouble starts when he wants to talk to you about sex."

Mingins seemed distinctly to tighten behind him. They were entering a new field.

"Which reminds me." Hunter looked up at Matt. "That story about me and Farrell's cousin. That I rattled off to you the night of the party. The whole thing was a lie. Which shows about how far I'd come. I could make up something like that in the blink of an eye. Tell it to somebody I barely knew."

Matt was amazed. It was beginning to look as if there had been a whole elaborate network around Bollinger, supporting his dirty-story habit.

"If that story was about anybody"—Hunter glanced at Mingins—"the little innocent was me."

Mingins took it pretty well. He seemed to have steeled himself for a difficult time.

"It didn't start off as anything at all. Hugh and me talking" —it was the first time Hunter had used his name—"him asking about my girlfriends, which I didn't have any of, me getting real embarrassed and trying to pretend there were some. Like if I'd talked to the girl down the street that week I'd mention her. Then it went beyond that. If I'd just told him to fuck off one time I think the whole thing would have ended. But I didn't want to hurt his feelings. And there was such a pleading in his eyes. Like he meant, Say something. Say anything. Make it up. It was easy after a few drinks. Hugh would ask me these leading questions, like telling what he wanted me to say. The kind of conversation you look back on and it makes you sick. But it always seemed to make Hugh so happy."

He turned to Mingins. "It was on one of those days that I ran into you again."

"I remember," Mingins said.

"That was where it all started." Hunter turned back to his beer. "The beginning of the end for me."

Mingins was a deep red, his chin tucked against his chest. He had wanted to start this conversation, it concerned the things he wanted to find out, but he would obviously rather have had it under other circumstances. "I'm sorry to hear you say that."

"Things might have been all right if they'd stayed at the talking stage. But I was good and drunk that day. You sat there while I got slowly smashed. You were somebody I'd known before. Who I really respected. Wanted for a friend. You and Hugh sat on either side of me that whole afternoon. Then you took me home and seduced me."

"You can put it that way."

"You took me home when I was drunk and took advantage of me."

"I don't remember having much trouble."

"I didn't know what I was doing. I was smashed out of my mind."

"I'm not going to argue with how you say it happened. I wouldn't be surprised if that's the way you remember it. If you don't want to acknowledge the part of you that was involved. What I remember is a boy who carried out a rather elaborate seduction himself. Who sat beside me and laughed and smiled and talked very easily, about sex, in the most graphic detail. Who flirted like a girl and talked like a raunchy street kid. Who when he heard I was going home asked if I would give him a ride. Who suggested we stop at my place for one last drink."

"That's what I meant. A drink."

"Who smiled radiantly when I touched him."

"I'm not saying I didn't want to do it in a way."

"You were implying you didn't want to do it at all."

"I was ashamed."

"You wanted what you were ashamed of. I can't help you there."

"I didn't like myself when I'd done it. I wished the whole thing had never happened. I wanted to talk to someone."

"That's a perfectly natural reaction."

"I told it to Hugh."

Mingins closed his eyes. "Perfect choice."

"He said it was okay at my age. It didn't mean I was . . . that way. It was a stage a lot of young men go through. He'd gone through it himself."

"Bet on it."

"He said you were a kind intelligent man and I could learn a lot from you."

"I was doing what he wanted to do. What he'd always wanted to do and for some reason couldn't. I'm glad to hear at least that it wasn't planned beforehand by the two of you. But I wouldn't be surprised—we'll never know now—if he didn't have me over because he knew it would happen, he knew you were ripe for it and couldn't do it himself, he wanted it to happen so you'd tell him and the two of you would talk about it. Live it vicariously."

"He spoke well of you, Chandler."

"He also made a little movie of me."

Now it was Hunter's turn to redden and look away. "Yes. That's also true."

"The two of you got together and planned that."

"I knew about it." Hunter looked up, though not so far as to meet Mingins' eyes. "But I had less to do with those movies than I led people to believe. I did develop them. But Hugh made them. He had asked me to teach him to use the equipment. All it amounted to was pushing a button. He pushed the button, he sat behind the mirrors. It wasn't until he'd done a couple that he told me about it, this little joke he was playing on his friends. He wanted me to be a part of it. With you."

"And you thought that sounded lovely."

"It was another one of those long drunken afternoons. I was already pretty smashed when he brought it up. I didn't think about it a lot. You showed up, and we went downstairs, and he made some excuse about having to be someplace. And it happened."

"It hurt me terribly to see that movie. You should know that, Todd."

"I do know it now. I saw that at the party. But I swear I'd never realized before. I thought people would take it as a joke. Then I saw the way it really was. Killian just about dying. You walking out. I suddenly realized that what we were doing, what you and I were doing, was serious to you in a way it wasn't to me. It was kind of neat to me. It made me feel knowing. A man of the world. But for you . . ."

Mingins spoke bitterly. "I was in love."

"I almost went after you. But Hugh was acting pretty strange, laughing in that high-pitched giggle of his, very drunk. I could tell he was embarrassed and felt a little bad. I could also tell he kind of liked what had happened. He was glad in a way. But he really wanted me to stay. I said something about following you and he practically begged me not to. It was kind of pathetic.

"So we all wound up going downstairs. After Hugh had checked his little peephole and seen that you"—he looked at Matt—"were gone." Otherwise, apparently, they all would have watched. "I think the idea at that point was that I was going to fuck the girl they had down there. My first time ever. I was pretty nervous about it. But she was pissed off about something, took her money and left. Which left me with these three weird middle-aged people."

He closed his eyes, shook his head, as if incredulous at the thought.

"Hugh was acting stranger than ever at that point. Sympathetic, like he was trying to comfort me. But also making all these jokes about how it didn't matter. My friend Chandler might be gone, but he was still there."

"And he made a pass at you," Mingins said.

Hunter started to speak, then didn't, reddened and looked at the floor.

"He made a pass at you," Mingins said.

They were right on the verge of it, the moment of truth, and Matt might have thought he'd be intent on Hunter, but he found himself thinking instead of Hugh Bollinger, that lonely and oddly embarrassed man who had spent his life denying things, who seemed bold and brash in the way he talked but choked on what he really wanted, who in that story Hunter was telling was finally about to say what he was, ask for what he wanted. And be killed for it.

"I guess maybe he did," Hunter said. "Maybe that is what all those words were saying. But he had the most roundabout way of getting there. All this talk about how he was the one who was really my friend, he was the one who knew me, with his two friends standing there watching, the guy saying, "Let's play. Why don't we play?" and the woman actually stepping over and feeling me up. Right there in front of her husband. Hugh was getting redder and redder, making these dumb embarrassed jokes and giggling. But that woman touching me like that was the limit. I left."

226

"You left?" Matt spoke without thinking.

"I just wanted to get out of there. I went out to my car, and drove around for a while, and finally wound up going over to Farrell's, and telling him I wanted to get away. I suddenly did. From Hugh, from the city, from everything. Farrell had been talking for weeks about how we ought to go to this lodge his father had, out in the middle of nowhere. I went home and packed, and we left the next day."

Matt glanced at Wolf, who raised his eyebrows slightly, whatever that meant. The man had hardly spoken a word since he'd been there.

"I didn't think of Hugh that way," Hunter said. "I didn't see him that way. He was a friend to me. A father. And he was old, and bald, and fat, and drunk all the time. I wouldn't have wanted to disappoint him. But I certainly wouldn't have done anything with him. I knew the way that was. It ruined everything."

"It doesn't have to," Mingins said.

The phone rang. Wonderful. On the one hand, Matt didn't want to leave; he didn't know where the conversation might wander in his absence. On the other hand, the extension was ringing upstairs too, and the last thing he needed was for Jonathan to wake up and come downstairs to join the party. Everything had stopped at the sound; his guests all turned to him. He hurried out to the kitchen and answered on the third ring.

"Matt? Otto. Listen. I didn't know if I should call."

Matt could have answered that one for him. "I'm pretty busy, Otto."

"I might be all worked up over nothing." Otto's voice trembled as he spoke. "But Killian was here a while ago."

"Again?"

"He's still trying to get his hands on that movie. I never thought he'd come back here. But he's nuts. Asking all these questions. Repeating things over and over. It was all we could do to get him out. Dotty and me talked it over awhile. We thought we should maybe call the police."

"No. Don't do that."

"Then we thought we'd better call you. It's not like we said you have the movie."

"I don't have the movie."

"But it came out that you'd seen it. Dotty didn't mean to tell him."

"Listen, Otto. That girl. Bollinger's old friend. Angel. Do you know where she lives?"

"Not offhand. I guess you could look it up."

Under A in the phone book, Otto?

"You think Killian knows?"

"I can't see how he would."

"It's all right, then. There's nothing to worry about."

"I didn't think it was a problem."

"Listen, Otto. That night of Bollinger's party. Was there anyone there when you left?"

"What's this now?"

"The night Bollinger was killed. When you left the house. Was there anybody still there?"

"Hold it, Matt."

Through the muffled phone, Matt heard Otto yell at his wife. Did he have to ask her everything? Matt wondered if she had had to dial for him.

"Yeah, Matt. It was just that kid. Hunter."

"Nobody else."

"No."

"You're sure he didn't leave before you did."

"No, Matt. He was there. I saw him myself."

The infallible eyewitness strikes again.

Once Matt had hung up, he stood out in the kitchen and thought things over for a while. Since they'd been interrupted anyway, the best move at this point might be to talk to Wolf. Matt could say the phone call was business, ask him to step out of the living room for a minute. He really wished, anyway, that Wolf would give him some help out there. Maybe he'd been able to find out something on his long car ride with Hunter.

So when Matt walked back to the living room it was Wolf he first looked at, and Wolf seemed more relaxed and heavy-lidded than ever, like the skinny shortstop who looks like he's almost asleep before he darts behind the baserunner to take a pickoff throw. It was the way he always reacted to tough situations. "You've got company, Matt," he said.

Standing just inside the door—Matt hardly recognized him, it seemed so long since he'd seen him—was Stanley Killian, looking dirty, and weary, and desperate, and in his right hand, as if he were hardly aware of it—it hung loosely from his fingers, pointed at the floor—he held a gun.

IV

"I guess you see a lot of cocks."

"God. Do I ever."

Laurel and Sandra had paused in the midst of a fit of laughter, brought on by Sandra's anecdotes from work and—mostly—by the wine. Their faces were rosy and wore broad smiles; Laurel's eyes were moist. She sat in tailor-fashion with her shoes off, and Sandra had her legs gathered under her. For two women who had just had several mugs of wine, they were poised on the verge of the funniest topic of all.

Laurel had not drunk enough to think she might like to work in a massage parlor. She had drunk enough—she often felt this way even sober—to think she might like to see a lot of cocks.

"Every shape and size," Sandra said. "Some that are so long you can't believe they'd fit into the guy's clothes. He'd have to double it up, or tuck it into a pants leg. Others hardly seem there at all, especially when the guy's real nervous. Pardon me, you want to say, but I believe you forgot your cock."

The laughter had started again, Sandra's in convulsive bursts between phrases, Laurel's in long breathless gasps that were almost silent. They were starting to double her up.

"It's like the thing's retractable or something. You want to ask if there's a button to push. Some cocks are so fleshy. Fat. Other are long and thin like a stick. You go from one guy to another and can hardly believe it's the same thing. And the colors. Everything from fire-engine red to calves'-liver gray. It's like a tour of a meat market."

Laurel's laughter had come to resemble weeping. She was bent double in her seat, heaving as if with sobs, wiping at the tears in her eyes. "Oh," she kept saying quietly. "Oh."

She really had had too much of the wine.

"The orgasms. Lord. With some it just pours. Like you opened a hose. All in this great gush. Others fire off like a shotgun. Pump-action. Way up on their chest. Some guys just plop out. A little river on their bellies. It flows down into their navels."

"Please," Laurel managed a gasp. The laughter actually hurt now. She seemed in danger of cracking a rib.

"I understand there's also a wide variety in taste."

"Enough!"

Laurel had rolled on her back. Much better. It was the bending double that was causing a strain. Tears still poured from her eyes, and her torso was shaking, but it couldn't go on much longer. She had nothing left.

"It isn't just cocks that are strange," Sandra said.

"Oh please, Sandra. Please. No more." If they were moving on to balls she thought she might throw up.

"This isn't to be funny." Sandra had stopped laughing too, just smiled now. "It's something I think of a lot."

"No more cocks."

"I'm talking about bodies. The way whole bodies can be so different. Have a character of their own, apart from what a person says or does. They tell you something."

"Yes." Laurel was much relieved.

"You're walking down the street, and people look about the same. An occasional oddball maybe, but mostly the standard model. When their clothes are off you see certain things. Then you start working with your hands. A man might look a little soft, for instance, then you touch him and he's just like dough. Your fingers sink in a couple inches. It's positively embarrassing. Another guy has no flesh at all. Solid bone. One guy's so relaxed you could tie him into knots. Another's so tight you can't even penetrate. It's like plucking a guitar string."

Laurel had calmed down. She lay on her back, gazing over at Sandra. Above all she was relaxed. A fit of laughter like that was in itself a kind of massage.

"It's another kind of knowing, touching is," Sandra said. "I don't think you really know somebody until you touch him."

"You're talking about Matt," Laurel said.

"What?"

"The man who's all tense like that. You pluck him like a guitar string. You're talking about Matt."

Sandra was staring as if into the distance, over the couch. "I guess I am. I didn't mean to be."

"It's true. I go to bed with him after a hard day, when anybody else would be ready to drop, and he's still cranked up. I can feel it. Revving his engines. I don't know how he ever gets to sleep. In the morning it's the same. I move over to snuggle up and I'm lying against a dynamo. He's already going."

"He was always this way?"

"I don't think so. I seem to have a memory, from way back somewhere, that he was once more relaxed when we went to bed. Like a big warm bear, hibernating. I may just be making that up."

"I wonder what's going on."

Lord. Where to begin. Laurel started to talk—still lying on the couch, but with her head propped against the arm, padded by some pillows—and tell the story she had told many times, to Ned, and to other friends, and many times over to herself, of her slow ascent and Matt's decline. Usually it focused on her, but now she was speaking mostly of Matt, and it sounded sadder than ever. The boy who had been a hometown hero, led his little high school to the state finals in baseball—she hadn't known that boy, but had heard a lot about him from Matt's family—and who had become the young man she did know, so much an athlete on the field and so little one off it, because he didn't need to act that way, he knew who he was; the stupid little bike accident that had seemed nothing at the time and then his father's death, which had seemed very much something but which Matt had hardly talked about (she had felt it in him, though, a leaden sorrow); the endless last baseball season when he had looked just the same on the mound, seemed to throw the same way, but the batters hit him, and he had stood out there dark and frustrated and worried not just about what was happening in the game, but also about the career that he saw slipping away from him. It was as if things had started to go wrong when his father died, and he couldn't set them right. After that he had tried to pick up the pieces, but they never seemed to fit, not on those two stints as a cop when he had returned every day bone-weary and frustrated, closed off to her; not on the days when he had walked off in a sweatshirt to try to control the spoiled children of parents who were like nobody he had ever really known; certainly not now, when he walked off every day in a sport jacket to an office that had sleaze written all over it. And through the last few years— Laurel had told this too—he had watched while things rapidly improved in her career.

"If there was a change, a beginning to all this, I'd say it was back there in college. When he was pitching those games and never winning. It was as if he could only relax when he'd win, after he'd thrown the last pitch and retired the last batter, but he couldn't do that. There hasn't been any game, and there hasn't been any last batter, and he hasn't been able to win. For so long. So he can't relax."

"Yes."

The two women sat thinking for a moment, Laurel staring off at the ceiling. Sandra down at her hands.

"The day I saw him . . ." Sandra paused. "I don't want to say the wrong thing."

"That's all right."

"There's a certain kind of man," Sandra said. "That soft man. Relaxed. Who's an easy kind of massage. Your fingers sink into him, like kneading bread, and he lies there on the table like a lump, and he slowly gets very excited, like a mushroom growing, and when he comes he gives off this terrible groan. Like he's dying. He practically falls asleep right there. Then there's the other kind of guy. Who you touch and practically launch off the table. His motor's running, like you said. He's the kind of guy you have trouble with. Not that I had any trouble with Matt." She spoke slowly, chose her words carefully. "But he's the kind of guy who wants more than a massage. He's come in with something to prove. He wants to get in control. Be on top." She sipped her wine. "He wants to fuck."

Laurel looked over. The two women stared at each other.

"He didn't," Sandra said. "You saw the movie."

"I saw."

"But he's that kind of man. Always wanting to do the thing. Being massaged is a passive act. It doesn't work if you're trying to do something. You lie there and take it."

Laurel nodded.

"There's a kind of man who's not very good at taking. He's got to prove himself."

As a matter of fact, though, that was what Laurel most resented about the movie, the way Matt did seem to be taking, more than he ever did with her; he was positively basking in what Sandra did.

"There was this day he couldn't do it," Laurel said.

She looked down, as if ashamed. Sandra just watched from across the table.

"It was probably pretty stupid on my part. I should have been more sensitive. But it was one of those beautiful warm mornings last spring, sunlight pouring in the window, birds singing in the trees, and I was just exuberant those days, finally getting settled in my job. I must have had a dream or something, but I woke up terribly excited. Ready to go, right then. I imagine I was pretty overwhelming. It was right then that Matt was at a low point with his job, terribly tense, never sleeping well. He just couldn't get excited. I was in a crazy mood, very playful, taking it all rather lightly. I didn't know how much it meant. Finally he tried when he wasn't ready, and it was over before he really started. His body went hot, like a flash, and broke out in a sweat."

"Shame."

"What?"

"We flush like that when we're ashamed."

"Anyway. Things haven't been the same for us since. Sexually. I don't think the problem started there. I think that was the last in a long line of symptoms."

The two women were not looking at each other. They were both looking down, off in their own thoughts.

"Men put so much value on that," Sandra said. "It's who they are. When that goes wrong, there's nothing left."

"When I think of all the times it's gone wrong for me."

"But it's not the whole world for you."

"No."

"And it's not right there for the other to see."

The two women were silent for a moment. Laurel was thinking—something she hadn't thought before—of how much her whole affair with Ned was just an attempt to make sex fun again, a chance to make love without the memories of past failures crowding around.

"One thing I don't understand," Sandra said. "About all you've told me. I can see that Matt wanted to be an athlete, and it turned out he wasn't able to, and that happens all the time, to lots of people, but it's always sad. The loss of a dream. I can see your not liking that he'd be a cop. The way people feel about cops these days. And it didn't work out for him as a teacher. But I don't see what's wrong with what he's doing now."

"God. If you could see that office."

"He can move to another office."

"The guy he's got himself working for."

"He can work for another guy. But it all sounds kind of romantic to me. He's out seeing people, and he seems the kind of person who likes to see people. He's not wearing a uniform, not pushing people around. He's a free lance. He can do what he wants. Take up for the other guy. That day he was up here, talking to me, I had the feeling he enjoyed his work. He was excited by it. He'd be good at it."

Maybe he was just excited by her.

"I haven't had that feeling," Laurel said.

"You may not have wanted to."

Laurel frowned. "Meaning what."

"You've felt so guilty, for such a long time. Guilty, I'm sure, about leaving your child. I know that one. And guilty about liking it once you were gone. Guilty about how things were going for Matt."

"I'd love not to feel guilty about Matt."

"But it's habit-forming. Besides. It's a nicer kind of guilt. Not really anything you've done."

"It doesn't seem . . ." Laurel paused. "The work he's doing. It doesn't seem real to me."

"You haven't seen him do it."

"Even so."

"What does seem real? Playing baseball? Doing massage? There are lots of people who think psychological counseling has no reality whatsoever."

"That's for sure."

"Anything's real, when you do it. These things take time. You didn't become a counselor overnight."

It was strange for Laurel to hear someone speak well of what Matt did. She had spent her life apologizing for it.

"How much did the two of you talk?" Laurel said. "That day he was up here."

"Pretty much. I told him some things he didn't know. I thought then, though, I still think, that the answer is somewhere in that movie."

"I'm sure." Laurel's favorite subject.

"You'd think a couple intelligent people could look at that movie and figure things out."

"Nobody has yet."

"A psychologist and a masseuse. Experts in the field."

Laurel looked over. Sandra was wearing a mischievous smile.

"I've still got it," she said. "The movie, and the projector."

"My God. I said I'd return it the same day."

"I thought of calling you. But we hadn't parted on the best of terms."

"I forgot all about it. I never even gave it a thought. I wonder what they fine you for something like that."

"I don't have any idea. But we can't return it tonight. As long as we've got it, we might as well use it."

V

Killian looked in worse shape than anyone else in the room, and in the case of Todd Hunter that was saying something. Hunter had only proceeded slightly farther down the boozy road he was already on, but Killian was a changed man. Before, he had been soft and genial, all blond beard and broad smile, the kind of big guy who is always in the way in doorways and aisles, whose booming laughter shakes the room, who eats gooey food and two desserts and gets along with just about everyone. He was the kind of happy clergyman who longs to give the whole world a big sticky hug.

Now the smile was gone from the twinkling eyes, and from the middle of the big blond beard. The beard itself was scraggly around the edges, unshaven at the cheekbones, and seemed to hang in a frown, the mouth an empty hole at the middle. The eyes were terribly tired, not sad so much as washed-out and weary, as if they had seen an awful horror, known a great grief. The shoulders slumped, and the clothes were rumpled, and as Killian pulled up a stool from behind the door and sat down, he seemed utterly harmless, except for the gun resting in his hand. The casual and awkward way he held it made it seem all the more likely to go off. It was the gun that made all the difference.

Matt noticed he was no longer wearing his cross.

"I don't want you to be frightened," Killian had said, as he stood at the door and stared all around. "I'm a reasonable man."

Which was utterly ridiculous, of course. He was an emotional man. Reason had almost no part in him.

Wolf was nearest the stool—but still not all that close—in his chair by the door, looking ready to doze off. Over to the right, Mingins sat forward on the couch, as if he would reach out and touch Killian. Hunter sat very stiffly, suddenly sobered up.

Killian had rested his head in his free hand, closing his eyes. Now he pushed back his hair—it was lank, and greasy, hadn't been washed in days—and started to talk, as if in the middle of a conversation, or as if it were perfectly natural to start in on the first thing that popped into your mind. His listeners stared solemnly. No one would have stopped him.

"My friendship with Hugh Bollinger was the one big secret of my marriage," he said. "The one thing I lied about, made stories to cover up for. Helen was aware I knew him, of course. She'd even been to his house once or twice. But she didn't know I saw him often. She didn't know all the things I did with him. Helen *hated* Hugh Bollinger."

"They were different kinds of people." Mingins seemed to think he could engage this man in conversation.

Killian gazed over as if at some incomprehensible sound. "I'd met him through Chandler," he said. "We hit it off right away. 'Always like a member of the clergy around,' he'd say. Kind of a private joke between us. He was always wanting company. He liked to serve drinks, and serve food, and show off his stuff, movies and things, to people who liked them. I was a person who liked them."

He glanced around the room. "I guess some people might find that a little strange."

"Nobody here feels that way," Mingins said.

Wolf wasn't talking.

"The work I'm in," Killian said. "First as a minister, then a counselor. There's enormous pressure to project an image. Put on a collar, put on a cross. Be strong for the people who come in to see you. The thing about Hugh's place was, I never had to do that. I could be who I wanted. Be who I was. Watch what I wanted, think what I wanted. I get so little chance to do that."

"I know what you mean." Hunter did not really look at Killian, just darted a glance out of the corner of his eye. "I felt the same way there."

"I don't think I'd have enjoyed it so much if it hadn't been something I wasn't supposed to do."

He stared vaguely at the gun in his hand, as if wondering what it was.

"Anyway, my evenings with Hugh were the one thing I lied about to Helen, saying I had to do some work, or see a client. I honestly think she knew. There were a couple evenings she called at the center and I wasn't there, and once or twice she asked about the client I was supposed to be seeing, but after a while she just stopped. Calling or asking. She didn't want to know."

Without moving, without even turning toward Killian, Wolf said, "Where was she the night of the murder?"

Killian looked up as if he'd been slapped in the face. "Who's this?" he said.

"I'm an associate of Matt's," Wolf said. "We work out of the same office. But I was just wondering. I hadn't heard her mentioned before."

"She was at home the night of the murder."

"How do you know? You weren't there."

"I left her at home. We only have one car."

"There's buses. Cabs. A person can borrow a car."

Matt didn't like the looks of this. Killian was staring at Wolf with real anger, holding a gun. Wolf hadn't even glanced at him.

"I really don't think she's the type," Mingins said. "If you could just meet her."

"Lots of people aren't the type," Wolf said. "Nobody here's the type, in my opinion. But somebody did it."

"I'm *doing* this for her," Killian said. Doing exactly what, he didn't say. Apparently he meant running all over town with a gun, looking for that movie. "To keep it from her. She knows nothing about it."

What he said made no sense, of course. How did he know what she knew?

"Not that I ever thought there was anything wrong with what I'd done." Killian was back to the past. "It never hurt anybody, had nothing to do with my marriage." Where had Matt heard such words before? Oh yes, he had said them himself. "I went to Hugh's and watched some movies. He took me to his little club. Introduced me to that girl. Angel. But I was doing nobody any harm. Everything would have been fine if he hadn't made that movie."

"Stanley." Mingins leaned forward on the couch. "Nobody was bothered by that movie more than I was. I can see what it did to you at the time. But it was a one-shot thing. A practical joke for the party. Hugh never meant it for any more than that."

"If Helen saw that thing it would be the end of my marriage."

"I think she's more understanding than that."

"It could mean my job. My reputation. If the wrong people see it."

"There's no reason to think anyone ever will."

"It exists. Somebody has it." He looked at Matt. "Until I have it I won't be able to rest."

"A lot of people wonder what you might have done to get it," Wolf said.

Later, Matt would ask Wolf why he had acted the way he had, deliberately provoking the one person in the room who was dangerous. Had he picked up on something the man had said? Figured out something the rest of them hadn't? "He was only dangerous because he was sitting there with a gun," Wolf said. "I was trying to get a shot at it. Trying to get him off that stool."

At the time, though, Matt hadn't understood that. He had thought Wolf was out of his mind.

"I'm sure they do," Killian said, looking straight at Wolf.

"The police think you might have killed for it."

Matt could feel the whole room tighten. Everybody knew how things stood, but no one else had been accused to his face.

"I think I almost might have"—Killian looked down, shrugged—"the mood I was in. While I was still at the party, I couldn't react. I was stunned, and bewildered, and embarrassed, with other people around. I had to get out of there. At first I drove home, then I didn't stop, I couldn't have faced Helen at that point. I was in a state. I drove around for a while, thought about things. The more I thought about it, the angrier I got, that Hugh had just been using me, not seeing me as a friend. All of it, taking me downtown, introducing me to Angel, even asking about Helen, had all just been a cheap thrill for him. Most of all, I started worrying about that movie. Who might have it, what they might do. I decided I had to go back, however little I wanted to see those people again. I had to try to get it. But when I got back to the house, the place was deserted."

"Did you look for the movie?" Matt said.

"I looked all around upstairs. Went into rooms, banged things around. I was pretty wild at that point. Then I stormed downstairs to look, found Hugh on the waterbed, blood all over the place. That stopped me in my tracks. I was almost sick, I'd never seen a man dead like that. I was trying to figure out what might have happened, what I should do. I know it

238

sounds bad, the man lying there dead with me in the room, but that made me worry more than ever about the movie. Like someone had killed Hugh to get it, and now what were they going to do. I had about decided to call the police, just to let them know about the body, when I heard somebody upstairs. For all I knew it was the murderer. Or if it was somebody else, things looked bad for me. I went out the downstairs door, and sneaked around the side of the house, and left."

"Things looked pretty bad," Wolf said. "No question about it."

Matt said, "I believe you, Stanley."

Everyone in the room turned to him.

"I know what you're saying is true, because I'd been there before, and the movie was upstairs, in plain sight"—whoever had killed Bollinger had left the movie; that still seemed a strange fact to Matt—"and when I got downstairs I found the same thing you did." He turned to Wolf. "If he had killed Bollinger, he'd have taken the movie, and he wouldn't be here now. That's what he was there for."

"So you took it," Killian said.

"I took it."

"You have it here."

"I don't have it. But I know where it is. It's safe."

Killian stood from his chair. "We're going to get it."

Matt stared. Killian sitting down was one thing, his head drooping, the gun hanging in his hand, but now he was on his feet, wobbly, exhausted, a big oafish man who looked as if he might swing the gun on you to make a point, stumble over something and fire by mistake. His awkward presence filled half the room. Matt sure as hell didn't want to go anywhere with him.

"Let me make a call," Matt said.

"No calls." Killian took a step in Matt's direction. "We're going."

Matt looked at Wolf. He had sat slightly straighter, as if sensing Killian's presence near him.

From the stairway came a command. "Drop it, mister."

Everyone in the room turned. Killian turned just his head. In the middle of the stairway, holding Matt's gun in two hands, wearing an expression of stark determination, was Jonathan.

"This thing's loaded," he said, "and I know how to use it."

At first Matt just sat there. In all the confusion of the

evening, he couldn't think where Jonathan had gotten the gun. Then he remembered: after showing it to him that afternoon, Matt had left it in the closet of the spare bedroom, since they were hoping to go to the firing range the next day anyway. His first thought was that the gun wasn't loaded, and that seemed treacherous, a seven-year-old boy holding an unloaded gun on an armed lunatic. Then it occurred to him that the gun might be loaded—he had, after all, shown Jonathan how to put the bullets in—and that seemed even worse. Two loaded guns in the hands of people who knew nothing whatsoever about using them. There was no telling what might happen if those things started going off.

The moment seemed to last forever. He measured the distance between him and Killian, a good four strides, with him still sunk back in his chair and Killian nervous as a cat. Every other adult in the room was watching the boy on the stairs.

"Jonathan," Matt managed finally to say.

"Tell him I'm not playing," Killian said, going pale. "This isn't kid stuff."

"I'm not playing either," Jonathan said. "This thing is real."

"This is a child, Stanley," Mingins said. "You've got to remember, it's just a child."

"Put the gun down, Johnny," Wolf said. "Let's all just put down our guns."

"I'll put mine down if he puts his down," Jonathan said. "If he doesn't put his down I'll blow him away."

The gun in his hand was steady, hadn't moved from pointing at Killian.

Actually, when he moved a moment later, Killian was just turning his body toward Jonathan, probably just to speak to him, probably—if the truth be known—to plead for his life. But Matt was only watching Killian's hand, his eyes were riveted on the gun, and as Killian turned the gun moved, seemed to start up in Jonathan's direction. Matt threw himself out of his chair. Wolf was quicker, or maybe Wolf was just closer, leaping from his chair and making a quick pivot and lashing out with his foot, a little like a soccer-style kicker going for the extra point. His toe caught Killian in the tender spot just behind the knee. "Wah!" Killian shouted, and threw his hands in the air, as if to say, Yippee! Actually, that was just a reflex action on his way—hitting flat on his back, his skull cracking first—toward the floor. The gun sailed out of his hand, struck a corner of the ceiling, and crashed down onto the table beside Mingins, shattering an ashtray. In his lunge toward Killian, Matt was thinking only of disabling the man—he didn't have time to realize he was already out of commission—brought his fist down, pounding, into the place where he seemed most vulnerable (the tender source, as many a man will ruefully say, of all our problems). "Oof!" Killian shouted, and doubled up in pain. Wolf leaped toward the corner of the room where the gun had fallen. Jonathan let his gun fall from his hands, watched it tumble down the stairs. He sat down on a step and burst into tears.

The next few minutes passed in considerable confusion. Matt hurried to his son, who sat on the steps sobbing. "I didn't load it, Dad. I didn't have it loaded." Mingins stepped to help Killian, who lay rolling from side to side in a reddish-blond ball on the floor. "Put your knees down," he said. "Take deep breaths." Apparently he had had experience in such situations. Wolf, the practical man in the group, had picked up both guns. "Neither one was loaded," he said, after checking them. "Jesus Christ. The whole thing was a put-on." Matt sat down on the stairs, holding his son. Todd Hunter, perhaps in a sympathetic reaction to Killian's plight on the floor, walked out to the kitchen, bent over the dirty dishes in the sink, and threw up.

Eventually Mingins got Killian to stretch out on the floor, his pants loosened—careful there, Chandler—taking quick staccato deep breaths. He sounded like a child who has just recovered from a fit of sobbing. He sounded very much, in fact, like Jonathan, who had managed for the most part to quiet his sobs, but was still sitting in his father's lap, tears pouring from his eyes. From the kitchen came occasional sounds of gagging. Wolf sat slumped in the chair Matt had occupied, watching the proceedings, the guns in his lap.

"You know, Matt," he said finally. "Everybody's talking about this movie. What it meant to them. What it made them do. Here I am supposedly investigating this case, and I haven't even seen it. Why don't you go get the thing? Maybe pick up that projector you had the other day. Or we can locate one." He made it sound as if you might find one sitting in the street. "We got all night, after all. Nobody's going anywhere. We'll all sit down and have a look."

VI

The lights were mostly off—they had left on just one dim lamp—and the images flickered on the wall, Sandra in a straight chair beside the projector, Laurel lying on the floor, a pillow beneath her head. She hadn't wanted to object, but Laurel thought watching the movie was the next thing to useless. It wasn't in the actions on the screen, which were easy enough to remember anyway, but in the emotions of the people that she thought an answer was to be found. Stanley Killian, whom she knew to be a shy quiet man, despite his flirtatious attentions to women, who would have been deeply embarrassed by what the movie showed, who more than anyone else would have worried about people knowing what he had done; Chandler Mingins, who was more open sexually than Stanley but also much deeper emotionally, who would have been terribly hurt by what he saw on the screen; that boy, she couldn't even remember his name, who seemed so arrogant, with his blond hair and thick muscles and big cock, who seemed to have such an ambivalent attitude toward what he was doing, who might have felt remorse at humiliating Mingins or at being involved with him in the first place, who had many reasons for feeling a real rage at Bollinger; the Droges, who according to Matt made a big show of being sexually liberated and who had flaunted their behavior on the screen, but who—as Laurel knew from her clients—might well have been over-compensating for feelings of shame and guilt . . . What she thought was needed was not another look at the movie, but some hard thought, or maybe some conversation, about the people.

So she had been silent, watching the movie, and Sandra had been too, both of them off in their own thoughts, when a single image—it could have been anybody; it wasn't the people—caught her eye. She sat up on the floor.

"Stop it," she said.

"What?"

"Stop the movie. Show that again."

Sandra flipped the switch. "Show what again?"

"That part you just showed."

"The whole scene?" Sandra hadn't particularly noticed anything. "I'm not sure what you mean."

Laurel stood from the floor, walked over to the projector. "I'll work the switches. You watch the screen. Just the thing I show you." She reversed the movie, started, reversed it and started it again. "Now," she said. "Watch this."

VII

As Jonathan explained to his father, he had not actually been waked up in bed by the ringing telephone. He had been waked up by the telephone, but not in bed. A few minutes after Matt had put him in, Jonathan had gotten up quietly and walked down the three steps to the little first landing of the stairway, where he could listen to the living-room conversation without being seen. He could even stretch out, if he lay on the diagonal, and the carpet on the landing was thick and soft. The conversation proved so boring, however, that he soon fell asleep, and did not awaken until the telephone rang. It was while he was lying there rubbing the sleep out of his eyes—he could see just a part of the living room, through the slats of the banister—that a man walked through the front door holding a gun. Perhaps Jonathan was still half asleep, or thinking of the book his father had read him before bed. Anyway, he got up, walked to the closet of the spare bedroom, and got his father's gun. He had not even thought of loading it, or really shooting it (how could his father think he would be so stupid?). If the man had started to raise his gun, Jonathan was planning to jump back for the landing and head for the second floor. He hadn't really wanted to do anything. He had just wanted to be a decoy.

He had certainly been that.

After he got the whole story from his son—they had talked it over once Jonathan had calmed down, sitting together upstairs on the bed—Matt said, "I've got to go out for a few minutes now. To pick up that movie from the other day. You can get dressed and come if you want."

"I think I want to go to sleep."

"Wolf's downstairs. He looks like a pretty good baby-sitter."

"He's got a lot of babies to sit for."

Sometimes Matt wondered where Jonathan got the things he said.

When he got downstairs, Matt looked to Wolf. "Everything under control?"

Wolf nodded, smiled. "Everything's fine."

The men had all shifted positions in the room. Wolf was still sitting in the chair Matt had occupied, the guns on the floor at his side. Hunter was in the chair near the door, where Wolf had been, looking pale, weak, smoking a cigarette but no longer drinking. Mingins and Killian were talking quietly and intently on the couch. Killian looked better, was nursing a glass of wine. Wolf was drinking a can of beer.

"I won't be long," Matt said.

"Take your time," Wolf said.

Matt had decided not to call Sandra before he went; she might be busy and want him not to come, and then he'd have to go into a long explanation. It only took him a few minutes to drive to her house. He got out of the car and walked to the door, rang the bell. When she came down to answer she looked stunned to see him—"Matt. I don't be*lieve* it"—more surprised, he thought, than she should have been. She seemed embarrassed, wore a silly smile, and led him upstairs as if he were the butt of some private joke. When he got to the top of the stairs he saw the punch line.

"Laurel."

"Well." She raised her eyebrows. "You got more than you bargained for. Both your women."

"I thought you were . . . " Matt stopped himself. He had started to say he thought she was with Ned. That suddenly seemed an idiotic paranoid fantasy. "I didn't think you were here."

"Obviously you didn't. Or you wouldn't have come."

She was speaking coyly, not really accusing him; she wore the same embarrassed smirk that Sandra did, as if he had found them at something unutterably wicked. Matt glanced around the room. It looked surprisingly clean. The dining-room table had been moved, the way they had moved it the other day, and the two women had been watching the movie again. He hoped to God they hadn't been watching his performance. He noticed the clutter on the coffee table in front of the couch—there was even some wine spilled beside one of the cups—and suddenly realized the reason for the odd mood the women were in. They were both half crocked.

"I just came to get that movie," Matt said.

"Don't take the movie," Laurel said. "We were just starting to enjoy it."

"What do you want with the movie?" Sandra said.

"I've got some people back at the house. They want to try to figure this thing out."

The idea had come to appeal to him, watching the movie in the presence of the murderer. He could note everyone's reactions, hear what they said. He knew that was why Wolf had suggested it.

"We've already figured it out," Laurel said.

"Oh?" Matt said. Don't you think you could use a little coffee, sweetheart? Matt was staring at the projector, wondering if he could just unplug it and carry it out as it was. "We'll have to compare notes."

"We really have figured it out," Sandra said. Make that two coffees. "The answer's right there in the movie. People have just been watching it wrong. Only seeing themselves."

"There's more to that movie than meets the eye," Laurel said.

How could there be more to a silent movie than meets the eye?

"Such as," Matt said.

The two women looked at each other. They suddenly seemed to be sobering up.

"Why don't we all sit down," Sandra said.

Matt sat beside his wife on the couch. Sandra sat in the chair across from them. Sandra was looking at Laurel.

"There are lots of things in the movie," Laurel said. "Or about sex in general. That are embarrassing. Or people think they're shameful. But there's only one thing that's so humiliating . . . What's the one thing that's so humiliating that, if somebody else knew, it would make a man want to kill him?"

If Matt knew the answer to that, would he be sitting here with these two drunks?

"I think you know the answer," Sandra said.

"You know it," Laurel said.

Matt looked from one woman to the other. Aw, c'mon. Gimme a hint.

"Why don't we all watch the movie again?" Sandra said.

She got up and turned on the projector. Matt felt a little uncomfortable at the thought of the last time they had done this, but the women seemed used to the idea, and they all just sat there silently and watched. It was easier the second time, a lot less shocking once the surprise factor was gone. The scenes flickered by blurrily, seemed much less vivid; odd, brief, somehow amusing despite the circumstances—the crazy things people did trying to make themselves happy. What was surprising was the commotion they had caused since. Sandra tactfully snapped off the projector before the final scene.

"There," she said. "What did you see?"

Matt shrugged. "Same old stuff."

"You're still thinking about the people. You've got to watch what happens."

She ran the movie in reverse, then started it again, stopped it, reversed, started it again. The moment she was showing, as a matter of fact, was one Matt had taken no notice of whatsoever.

"You don't think a thing of it when it's somebody else," Sandra said. "You have to think of it as if it were you."

A prickly heat broke out on Matt's neck. He felt himself start to sweat.

"Lots of things in the movie are embarrassing," Sandra said. "But nothing else is quite like that."

She had turned off the projector, come back to her chair. They all sat there and talked for a while. Matt, for the most part, was thinking aloud, seeing if the women's suspicions fit in with the circumstances he knew. They did. In a way, they made all the nagging little puzzles disappear. The three of them took some time to sketch out what might have happened. There were any number of possibilities. But there weren't any fundamental problems that Matt could see.

Finally he called Wolf on the phone. "You can let those guys go. There's no need to look at this movie. I would appreciate you hanging around awhile. Just until Laurel gets home."

"Matt." Wolf sounded exasperated. "This is a perfect chance. Whoever did it is ready to crack. Besides. If these guys get away we don't know when we'll see them again."

"I know who did it."

"Great. Now you want to turn him loose on the streets."

"No, Wolf." Matt had to be patient. There was plenty of time. "It's like this . . . "

VIII

A killer was a killer, Matt thought, it shouldn't make any difference what he looked like, but he had never thought his first confrontation with a murderer would be anything like this. The man sat in front of him in old khaki shorts and dark socks, brown cordovans, a graying T-shirt with his belly squirting over his belt and his little woman's breasts straining their nipples against the cloth. His big dull dumb face stared; his hand kept reaching into a plastic bowl to feed his face with potato chips. Hold the chips! Matt should have shouted, when he first arrived and they started bustling around. Skip the Cokes! But he didn't have the heart. You had to let such people set out food for you so they themselves could eat. Otto's hands were slippery—at that point he could barely pick up his Coke—and his mouth was slick.

They had sat Matt off in a corner of the room, beneath a window. Dotty and Otto were together on the couch. Otto sat forward, in easy reach of the chips, while Dotty sat back with her legs gathered under her, fidgeting. She too wore shorts, and a plain white top, her feet bare. Her eyebrows came together in a hard little crease above her nose. She seemed all nerves. Otto was stolid and still.

All the same, he knew what was going on. There was a darkness to his eyes, a sternness, that seemed almost resigned. He listened to what Matt was saying, he didn't interrupt, but he seemed all the time to be waiting for the thing that Matt would say, and that would be the only part worth hearing.

For a while Matt did all the talking, sticking to the truth, about how Todd Hunter had skipped town and no one had been able to find him, the police hadn't even known where he was, though they hadn't worried about it much, thinking Killian was their man; Wolf had asked around for a whole afternoon and finally located him, brought him back to town; they had spent much of the evening questioning him.

Now he was starting to vary from the truth, make things up as he went, though he knew where he was going in general. He tried to sound casual, though he also wanted to keep his voice firm. He was staring at Otto.

"It's funny the way a kid that age can be," he said. "He looks like a man, and he acts like a sophisticate, but deep down inside there's a part of him that's still a scared uncertain child."

"That can be an act too," Dotty said, from the background.

"That's why I asked you that question on the phone," Matt said. "I wanted to see if you were sticking to your story."

"It's not a story," Dotty said. "It's not a matter of sticking to it."

Otto was staring back at Matt. He seemed not even to hear what his wife was saying.

"Todd Hunter left town because he was scared," Matt said. "Scared of something he had seen. Scared of what might happen if somebody found out."

"This is what *he* says," Dotty said. Her tone was growing progressively more strident.

"He hadn't left Bollinger's house when he said he was going to. When you two were still there, and you were all downstairs. He acted like he was leaving, and walked upstairs, but then he came back down by the other stairway, to Hugh's little perch behind the mirrors. Like a sneaky little kid. He saw everything that happened."

Otto stopped chewing for a moment. His hand stopped reaching for the bowl.

"Which was what, according to him?" Dotty said.

If she hadn't been around, Matt would have had him. Otto was staring, swallowing hard. His face had paled, and a pulse was throbbing in his neck.

"A kid can make up quite a story in a few days time," Dotty said.

"He was shitless," Matt said. "He didn't know what to do."

"This is ridiculous," Dotty said. "Bring the boy here."

"I'm afraid I can't do that. He's on his way to the police station with my associate. To tell his story." No telling what might pop out of your mouth once you got started.

"Maybe we should all just go down there," Dotty said.

Oh Jesus.

"Forget it, Dotty." Otto had finally opened his mouth for something other than a potato chip.

Dotty looked over as if a table had spoken. "Forget what? Some kid tells a crazy story."

"I'm not talking about the story. I'm talking about me."

Matt did not have the feeling he was in on the beginning

of some ordinary domestic squabble. Dotty looked outraged, incredulous, like a matron whose child has just uttered a vile obscenity.

"We can discuss you later," she said.

"I've got to talk."

Otto was staring down moodily at the floor. Dotty looked as if she would like to wipe him off the face of the earth.

"You don't have to say a word," she said. "He doesn't even have any right to be here."

"I don't mean that. I mean me. I can't stand it any longer."

"Just because some kid makes up a story."

"You don't have to live with it every minute. See it every time you turn around."

She reached out and touched his arm. "*Listen* to me."

"No." He actually hit her, smacked her in the shoulder with the back of his fist. It knocked her back against the couch. He didn't even look. "I've already decided anyway. And the kid saw it too. Tonight I talk."

Tears had sprung to Dotty's eyes, in anger, or at the pain. She slumped back and glared at her husband, rubbing the spot on her shoulder.

He turned his gaze on Matt, as if to say, Excuse my wife. I'll club her again if she gets noisy. Now that he had decided on a course of action he seemed sure of himself again.

"One thing you should understand from the start," he said. "Nobody intended it should turn out the way it did."

Matt nodded sympathetically, leaned forward in his chair. Take your time, old man. Have a couple hundred more potato chips.

"You figured one person might get mad. Take the whole thing as an insult and walk right out. But what we really hoped was everybody would think the movie was funny. It would break things down. We'd all start to enjoy ourselves, then get together and do something." Matt could see them plotting it out, Hugh and Dotty and Otto, each of them off in his own separate imaginings.

It was a real dream world they lived in. They'd get together and do something.

"Then everybody crapped out on us."

This man was all class.

Otto still sat forward. He took a long drink from his Coke. Idly he fingered the potato-chip bowl. He couldn't resist, took out a handful and started to munch.

"We were going to sneak down behind the mirrors first thing, after the movie was over. See what was going on." He spoke matter-of-factly, as if Matt shouldn't have minded at all. "But by the time Hugh got back there you were gone. I never could figure it, a beautiful chick like that. Why would you leave?"

"I got finished." No need to go into subtleties for Otto.

"You got finished pretty fast."

Matt shrugged. Don't get personal, fat boy.

"At that point Mingins had left. Which frankly didn't bother me any. A guy like that, who only goes one way, he can ruin a group scene. He's always in the way.

"Then Killian decided to go. That I never did get. All he'd done in the movie was a straight fuck. A pretty good job of it too. Nothing to be ashamed of. Hugh even told him, the girl was still downstairs. You were finished with her, hell. But Killian wanted to go. That still left us with five. Hugh was hot for Hunter. Hunter would've probably wanted a little of the other action. That still left two women mostly to me."

What was stunning to Matt, positively laughable, was the assumptions people made about everybody else. Projecting, as Laurel would have said. Nobody else's feelings were consulted. If there was one thing Matt was sure of, it was that Sandra would have never taken part in a scene like that. Otto had no idea what she was like. He didn't even know her name.

"I think you're wrong about Hugh Bollinger," Dotty said. She was still here? "I don't think he wanted people to have a good time." She seemed a few speeches behind. "His thing was humiliation. Degradation. He liked putting people in a position where they could be hurt."

Otto went on as if he hadn't even heard. "Hugh's big mistake was letting that girl go. He'd hired her for the night, that was the deal. He should never have let her out of it. Once she was gone Hunter would want to go too."

He had as much as admitted it now. Just him and Dotty left, and Hugh.

"Or not go, like you said."

Matt looked up, startled, at Otto's words.

"Go back behind the mirrors and peek. The little prick."

Oh, right. Matt had almost forgotten his own story.

Dotty listened quietly now, staring down at her hands.

"The thing of it is, Hugh and me were kind of alike. Or I wasn't bad off like him, but in that same direction. We were watchers. Like if it was a group scene, I was all right, or even just Dotty and me and another couple. If I could even hear something. But just doing the thing myself. Nothing else going on. That doesn't get it for me anymore."

From this point forward that would be known as the Hugh Bollinger syndrome. The fate of the perpetual adolescent. You started off peeking at something because you wanted to do it, got yourself excited imagining how great it would be, but when you finally got around to it you didn't want to do it anymore. All you wanted was to peek.

"You were tired," Dotty said. "You'd had a lot to drink."

"I hadn't had that much. There just wasn't enough going on."

"It's weird, anyway," she said. "Self-conscious. The two of you there, and a third person looking on."

"But you couldn't turn him down. He was so disappointed. That big party planned, and nobody left. The kid was gone. 'We'll have our own party,' he said. He was pretty well smashed. 'Make the greatest porn scene ever filmed.' He had the camera all ready, hoping to film everything. I knew it wouldn't work out. I know how I am. I should never even have tried.

"It was me and Dotty on the waterbed, and Hugh standing there with his camera."

Exactly. It was the moment Laurel had noticed in the movie, the same one she had shown first to Sandra and then to Matt. The source of murderous rage. Of course, Matt did not know precisely what had happened the night of the party, after Hugh had been left with the Droges. For all he knew they had just sat down and watched the movie again, or even just talked about it. He'd had no idea that they had, in effect, reenacted it. But it was the same moment he'd seen in the movie, the man on his back, the woman on top, both of them staring at that part of him that had to engage before anything else could happen. The woman touched it, tickled, pulled. The man just stared, more helpless even than she. They were the tribe of primitive people on a parched desert, praying to an unknown god to favor their soil with rain. It doesn't even cloud up.

Your penis did not seem a part of you at a moment like that; it lay off on your body as if at a place you couldn't even reach. It was as if something blocked the nerve impulses of your body, or as if somehow you were no longer whole; it was as if the penis were an other that could not be brought around to your point of view. It was the enemy. The tension that rose in your body at a moment like that was terrific. It should have been enough to raise a thousand penises.

It was certainly enough to clobber one drunken old man.

"It wouldn't have bothered me all that much," Otto said. "It had happened before. No big deal." Famous lies that men tell. "But then he laughed."

Jesus. Bollinger laughed.

"Him of all people," Dotty said.

He'd been standing at the side of the bed, then he came over and sat on the edge. 'I'm waiting,' he said. He kept focusing with his camera. Picking it up, putting it down. Then he started to laugh. That high-pitched fucking laugh of his. I got up from the bed. Kind of standing there, like to shut him up. He reached out and wiggled my dick. The faggot. 'Poor little thing. Doesn't want to play.' He started to laugh again. 'I should have invited one of the dogs. I forgot the most important guest. Here, Fido. Come here, boy. Where are you now, when we need you?'

"I just kind of went blank. It was like I wasn't seeing anything. I had the camera in my hand. I must've taken it off him in there somewhere. It was on a long leather strap, kind of dangling on my hand. He was still laughing, laughing. I leaned back"—Otto started to raise his fist—"like I could blot it out. I could make it not true. Christ. I swung." He brought his fist crashing down on the coffee table. His Coke jumped and spilled; the bowl of potato chips flipped over and onto the the floor; the glass top of the table cracked in a crazy zig-zag pattern. "He didn't even make a sound. Just went over like a ton of bricks. It was like I came to when the camera hit him. All of a sudden he was lying there in front of me. I kind of fell down on him when I saw him. Shouting at him. Talking to him. There was blood all over his head. It was oozing out in front of his ear, at this kind of caved-in place. I got some water and tried to wash him off, bring him to. I didn't know what the hell to do. I slapped him, shook him. I threw on my clothes and ran upstairs to call somebody. But while I was dialing Dotty came up and stopped me. She said it was no use. He was already dead."

The cool head that prevailed.

"It was an accident." Dotty was slumped on the couch beside him, staring at her hands. "Not anything Otto meant to do. And Hugh brought it on himself. The whole thing was his fault. He should never have had the party. He should never have made the movie. He should never have laughed."

That was for sure.

She sat there a moment, not looking at either man, then got up and walked out of the room.

"We didn't know what the hell to do," Otto said. "We tried to stay calm, and sit down and think, but you couldn't sit down there. We thought of cleaning up, making it look like we hadn't been there, then we thought what the hell. Everybody knew we had."

"What did you do with the camera?"

"Took it with us. We wanted to get rid of it, fast as we could, but every place we'd think of there was something wrong with. Finally we just threw it off the Highland Park bridge. All the crap there is in that river."

It had probably dissolved on contact anyway.

"But you left the movie."

"We just forgot about it at the time. Went out the door downstairs and never thought of it. When we got home and remembered we almost went back for it. But that looked too risky. Then after a while we figured it was just as good for somebody to find it. Everybody knows about us, the life we lead. If somebody brought it up we'd laugh it off like it didn't matter. Other people would be trying to hide it. That'd look worse for them. But then the police never found it. We actually had to tell them about it. When did you get it?"

"I went back and discovered the body. The movie was just sitting upstairs. I didn't even know what it was at the time. But it was the only thing in the apartment that looked . . . like it meant something. I picked it up."

Sounded very professional as he said it. He didn't mention how frightened and offhanded a gesture it really was.

"The one thing we did decide was to say we left before Hunter," Otto said. "Everybody knew Hugh had a thing for him. It would sound like he made a pass and got clobbered. Just Hunter's word against ours. Then all these other things worked out. Hunter disappeared, and Killian went kind of crazy, and Mingins didn't want to talk about what happened. Nobody was paying any attention to us. It all looked pretty good. Like I might get away with it."

"It still does look pretty good."

The voice came from the doorway to the kitchen. Matt and

Otto both turned. Dotty was there, and beside her, seated erect and alert, was a German shepherd, not the one from the movie, but its heavier companion. An enormous dog.

"What's Beauty doing in?" Otto said.

Must have been the name of the dog. He certainly wasn't referring to his wife.

Dotty was glaring at her husband. "You give up on everything," she said.

Otto looked bewildered. Hardly the man who had cuffed his wife a few minutes before. "What's this, now?"

"He comes in here with a cock-and-bull story about Hunter staying to watch and you swallow it whole. How do you know he's not just saying it? How do you know Hunter didn't just make it up? Even if he did stay, what's that going to prove? It's still his word against ours. A teenage kid against two adults."

Otto sat there dumbly, trying to spell out what she was saying.

"None of this occurs to you, of course. You'd rather lie down and let him walk all over you."

Matt was beginning to think Otto was wrong about the source of his problem. Any sensible penis would have laid low in the presence of this woman.

"It was better this way, Dotty," Matt said. "This was weighing on his mind."

"Better for you. Better for the rest of them. Not better for us." She glanced at her husband. "I'm involved in this too."

The presence of the dog was making Matt edgy. Dogs always made him nervous, a little hollow feeling down where he lived.

"Anyway," Matt said. "It's done now."

"Oh is it," Dotty said.

"Lots of people know I came here. Why I came."

"Lots of people know we keep a dog in the house while we're gone. We can't help what happens if somebody comes in. Different people have different stories about what happened the night of the crime. That's the way it was before. And you won't be around to tell about Otto's little confession. Maybe he can keep it to himself, now that he's told it once."

"Dotty," Otto said.

"Just get up. Get off the couch."

"Todd Hunter is at the police station right now," Matt said. Grasping at straws. "For all I know they're on their way over here."

"All the more reason for us to hurry."

"The whole thing doesn't make sense. Why would I snoop around here?"

"That's for them to worry about. At least you won't be around to talk. I said get up, Otto."

Otto slowly stood, a look of caution on his face, staring at Matt.

"Otto," Matt said. "Tell her this won't work."

"I don't know, Matt. I haven't had a chance to look at it. It just might."

Jesus Christ. What if you change your mind later?

"This just gets you in deeper," Matt said. "Don't you see?"

"I'm going to command this dog," Dotty said. "Get out of the way." She turned to the dog. "Beauty! Up!"

The dog leaped to attention, stood poised in a crouch. If it had been a puppy you might have thought it was about to chase a stick. But it was growling almost at a roar, baring its teeth. It was as if the dog had a motor, and Dotty had just pulled the cord.

"Otto," Matt said.

Otto had hurried over beside his wife, as if a bomb were about to go off. The dog growled louder.

"Listen," Matt said.

Dotty leaned down and shouted a word into the dog's ear.

Matt did not see the dog rush him. It must have happened terribly fast. He could imagine how it looked, the lightning strides across the floor, the sudden graceful leap, but what he was watching, as if with hope, was Otto's idiot face staring back at him. A white blur appeared in his line of vision. He had raised his arms instinctively. The dog hit him like a truck. He did not feel the jaws snap onto his arm. Later he would look at the deep gashes and marvel at the thought that he had not felt a sudden searing pain. His adrenaline must have been pumping like crazy. What he did feel, once he had been knocked back on the chair and the dog was on top of him, was the immense power of the animal, its primitive force. The jaws clamped on his arm like a vise, the muscles coiled in the body, the roaring growling all around: it was as if the dog would pick him up and shake him like a doll. He knew in that moment he could not keep it off him, his shoulders against the arm of the chair, nothing between those teeth and his neck but a mangled arm. The sheer presence of the animal was so overwhelming that he didn't even hear the glass of the window shattering above him, or recognize as gunshots the new sounds that roared. Suddenly the dog was jerking away, writhing in convulsions, then collapsed hard on top of him, dead weight, heavy, and hot, and furry, and—gradually—wet. The dead weight of the dog seemed enormous.

It was only then that he felt the pain in his arm, a searing throb, as if the teeth were still buried there.

He heard a motor start.

"They won't get far." Matt looked up as if at the voice of an angel. The face in the window, however, upside down, dead calm, was Wolf's. "Their back two tires don't have any air."

Chapter Nine

If anything, Tony looked worse that evening than usual. He actually seemed to have gained weight (can a three-hundred-pound man gain weight? an amount you can notice, that is), and he looked slightly pale, a few beads of sweat on his forehead. But he was a faithful maître d', and the large round table in the middle of the room was obviously his centerpiece that night, so, before the meal had progressed too far, he stopped by to check on it.

"Everything okay?" he said.

"Just fine." Matt spoke for the whole table.

"How's the pie?"

In the middle of the table were the remains of a large pepperoni pizza, which had arrived overbrimming its tray and was now two-thirds gone.

"Very good," Matt said. "But it's just an hors d'oeuvre tonight. We're feasting."

"That's the way to do."

Tony stood holding a few menus behind his back. He did not want to stare, but couldn't help noticing the thick gauze bandage and large white sling.

"What happened to your arm?"

"I had a little run-in with a dog."

"Jesus. Some dog."

"You said it."

Around the table sat a diverse group. Beside Matt, in a white sundress that stood in contrast to the deep olive of her skin, sat Laurel. Her hair was bright black, her face warm with color. Jonathan sat beside her, wearing a button on his shirt that said, Ban Handguns. Sandra was there, in a skirt and prim pink blouse that made her look like the academic she (sometimes) was. Her children were with her. Chandler

Mingins' dominant color that evening was a deep purple, shirt and socks; his suit was a cream white. Wolf sat beside him, and beside Wolf—"She might not want to come," he had said. "She doesn't like to go out much"—was his wife. She was a larger person than Wolf, especially below the waist. Her hair was dyed a dull red, and she wore it in curls. She smoked constantly, hardly spoke a word. For dinner she had ordered only french fries. "I ain't hungry tonight," she explained. Nevertheless, she had already had two slices of pizza, three breadsticks, two packs of crackers, and two cups of coffee with cream and sugar. She gazed off at the ceiling, smoking, as if no one else were there.

Todd Hunter had been invited and said he would come, but had never showed up. Stanley Killian had said that, frankly, he would like to spend his evenings at home for a while.

"How are *you* doing?" Matt said to Tony, who still hovered around the table.

Tony touched his midsection. "Little indigestion tonight." He *had* looked a little queasy at the sight of the pizza. He drifted away from the table. "Enjoy your meal."

Sandra's children were enthralled with the story of the case, especially Ken. This was the first chance they had had to talk to Wolf and Matt, and they had gotten the story bit by bit. Now they were going back for details.

"Did you know Wolf was following you to the Droges'?" Ken said to Matt.

"No. I told him he could go home."

"How did you know to follow him to the Droges'?" Ken said to Wolf.

"You don't like to leave a man on his own the first time he does something." Wolf spoke as if he had had countless assistants through the years.

"I don't think he was planning to go at first," Chandler said. "After Matt's call, he told us all we could leave. Then at the last minute he asked if I'd hang around. Until Laurel got back."

"It was just a hunch I had," Wolf said. "I figured, why take the chance?"

Wolf's wife was still staring at the ceiling, Laurel noticed, as if this were all very very boring.

Laurel herself felt rather differently about Wolf than she had before. He had not, as it turned out, really saved Jonathan, since Stanley Killian's gun had been empty, but he would have saved him if the danger had been real, and he really had saved Matt. That was the whole of her family in the space of a couple of hours. Rather generous of a man whose eyes she had tried to scratch out a few days before. That morning she had gone down to East Liberty to apologize, and to see if the building and the office were as bad as she had made them out to be. They were. But Wolf was quite gracious, invited her into the office and gave her a delicious cup of coffee from a pot he had perking on the floor. He talked about his job, showed her paperwork from a number of cases, told anecdotes he had accumulated through the years, told her of clients who still kept in touch with him. "Don't you think . . . " Laurel said. "Wouldn't it be better to switch to a nicer office?" "I like old things," Wolf said. "My car, for instance. Anyway, I'm not here all that much."

Though he had certainly seemed firmly ensconced, with no intention of leaving soon, that morning.

"I thought you didn't know how to shoot that gun," Jonathan said, at the table in Tony's.

"I don't, much," Wolf said. "But I'd loaded it that morning, knowing the kinds of things I was going to do. And I was right there, after all. A couple feet away. I stuck the gun right in the dog's hide. If that didn't work I could hit him over the head."

"It's a shame you had to shoot such a beautiful animal," Chandler said.

"Yeah." Wolf raised his eyebrows. "Well. It was either that or shoot Matt."

Ken turned to Matt. "When did you know it was Otto Droge who did it?"

The children had been told a somewhat selective version of the story. They had not, for instance, been told the key clue.

"I'd never even thought of him, to tell you the truth. He was the last person I would have suspected. But when Todd Hunter was telling his story, and he said he'd left before the Droges . . . Just the way he said it. Like he had nothing to hide. Something went click."

Laurel smiled at Sandra. Sandra was smiling back. Matt saw the smiles of the two women.

"Actually," he said to Ken, "I think it was your mother who got the idea first."

"No," Sandra said. She turned to Jonathan. "It was your mother."

"Maybe she should be a detective," Jonathan said.

"And I could go down to the counseling center," Matt said.

"You'd probably do about as well," Laurel said.

"Anyway," Wolf said. "Tomorrow it's back to the old grind. To tell you the truth, I'll be glad of it."

"You know what jerks my chain." It was startling to hear that voice. It had not uttered a sound since placing an order for french fries. Dolores Harpe finally looked away from the ceiling, stared at Laurel. "He didn't have to be doing all this crap. He could've had a job writing insurance."

"What?" Wolf blushed at the embarrassing interruption. "And miss all that excitement?"

"Not one cent did you make from all that excitement." She still looked to Laurel. "He could've had a job writing insurance with my sister's husband."

"That was years ago." Wolf turned to Laurel, raised his hands. "This was *years* ago."

"He'd take you right now," Dolores said. "He'd take you tomorrow."

"I don't want to work with your sister's husband," Wolf said. "I don't like your sister's husband. I don't like your sister." I don't like you, he seemed to want to say.

"I don't like my sister either," Dolores said. "But they make good money."

"I make good money," Wolf said.

"You make diddly shit," Dolores said.

"I help people. I do a lot of good for people."

"You did a lot of good for this Otto Droge. I'll say that."

"I'm my own boss. I take orders from nobody."

"You take orders from me."

"I take the cases I want. I get around and see the city. I have my own office."

"Christ. You call that an office?"

"He doesn't spend much time there," Laurel said.

"I'd like to know where he does spend his time, then. He's never at home."

Wolf gazed around the table. Can anyone blame me? he seemed to be saying.

"I think people should do the work they want to do," Chandler said. "That's what I tell all my clients. It's the best way in the long run."

"Do they pay you, these clients?" Dolores said. "Or don't they have any money?"

Chandler ignored this dissenting voice. "The last time I was here I proposed a toast. I don't think anyone took me seriously then. Tonight I'd like to propose it again. To new beginnings." He raised his glass. "New careers."

Around the table were raised glasses of wine, Cokes, a ginger ale, glasses of beer.

Matt remembered that other toast. It had embarrassed him then, sounded false. Now he raised his glass with a little more assurance. Probably you never felt quite right in a career, never felt fully capable. Wolf, hell, even Wolf was still learning new things. That was what the toast said. It didn't drink to things accomplished. It drank to new beginnings.

Laurel was beside him. He felt her presence there. They both knew now, more than ever, how volatile their life together was, not, perhaps, the way they had once thought it would be. It wasn't that your marriage was stable, but that you stayed with it, through all the changes. You tried to trust the other and let it happen. There was something interesting about that, seeing a new person emerge where the other had been. There was also a love that accompanied it, that seemed to grow as changes accumulated. A love that had to do with surviving them together.

These things had not been stated between them. To state them would have been redundant. Some feelings do not need words. Some feelings are diminished by words. Now, at the table, he turned to her, a big man somewhat the worse for wear, his shoulders slumped, arm in a sling, his face flushed, tired little wrinkles at the corners of his eyes. She had already turned his way, not what you would call a young woman, exactly, but a vivacious woman, voluptuous, who looked as if she had been around and still had plenty of places to go. The rest of the table had turned to them. They both held frothy glasses of beer. Their faces smiled. Their eyes were bright. Their glances met. Lightly, their glasses clicked.

F